LAVENDER LAKE

SADDLES & SPURS BOOK 2

EMMA SLATE

Tabula Rasa Publishing

For the girlies with big chaotic emotions . . .

And the men who love them.

CHAPTER ONE

"Hadley," I wheezed. "Now isn't a good time!"

"You're running to your gate, aren't you?" my twin demanded.

"Yes," I admitted. "But it's not my fault I'm about to miss my plane."

"Then whose fault is it?"

"Take your pick. My plane out of New York was late taking off. There was a rogue spring snowstorm that grounded all the planes when I landed in Denver. The airport shuttle arrived late to the hotel this morning. Then there was traffic to the airport."

"And you don't think you might've brought this on yourself? A little self-sabotage, maybe?"

"You can lecture me when you pick me up."

"Promise?"

"Promise." I smiled despite the verbal lashing I was

getting from my sister. "I'll be held hostage in your car. Nowhere to run."

She chuckled. "Oh, I forgot to tell you—"

"Later, gator." I hung up on Hadley just as I made it to the gate. The sour-faced attendant shot me a maternal look of disappointment.

"I know," I huffed. "I'm sorry. Am I too late? Did I miss the flight?"

"No." She shook her head, sending her curtain of silver hair swooshing over her shoulders. "You made it just in time."

I put my phone under the code reader. It beeped and turned green. Favoring my weak ankle, I made it down the flyway. A blonde flight attendant pursed her lacquered red lips as I approached the aircraft door.

"Sorry," I said, wrestling my monogrammed suitcase onto the plane. I made it to my row and collapsed the handle of my luggage so I could stow it above me. I was getting ready to lift it above my head when a deep, masculine voice said, "Let me help you with that."

Prickles of awareness and familiarity raced down my spine as I looked over my shoulder at the man I'd spent the previous night with.

My eyes and mouth widened in shock.

"I'll take that as a 'thank you.'" He grinned.

He took my bag in his large hands and hoisted it effortlessly into the overhead compartment.

I was standing there like a gaping moron when the flight attendant came toward us.

"Please take your seats," she said, her left eye twitching as she stared at me. But then she looked at the man whose name I still didn't know, and yet who I was intimately familiar with. She beamed. "Can I get you anything, Mr. Bowman?"

"No, thanks," he said, a slight smile curving his generous, talented lips.

"Ma'am? Your seat," the flight attendant said pointedly.

3A.

I scuttled into the row and hastily dropped into my window seat. I quickly turned off my phone and shoved my shoulder bag underneath the seat in front of me before buckling myself in.

Mr. Bowman took the aisle seat next to me. He settled his large frame into the oversized first-class seat, but he still looked like he was sitting in a sardine can.

"She knows your name," I said as the flight attendant began walking through the cabin away from us.

"She does," he agreed, looking at me. His steely gray eyes raked over me from head to toe, but then he paused and examined my neck. "Didn't do a good enough job hiding that."

His finger reached out to graze the hickey he'd left on my skin.

I batted his hand away but couldn't stop the shiver of want his touch elicited.

Glaring at him, I tightened the seat belt around my waist. "What are you doing here?" I hissed.

He raised his brows. "Same thing you are, I'm guessing."

I rubbed my third eye.

"You snuck out of my bed this morning," he said, pitching his voice low. "While I was still sleeping."

I swallowed, my mouth dry; my memories blazing with heat at the forefront of my mind.

"Look," I began. "The flight to Spokane isn't long. Let's just be quiet and pretend not to know each other."

He fell silent and I thought for sure that was the end of it.

But then he said, "No."

I'd been looking out the window at the tarmac. His simple

one-word reply had me whipping my head around to stare at him. "No?"

"No," he repeated.

"Fine. I won't talk to you."

I was being childish. But I had never expected to see him again. He was a one-night stand, and yet, here he was sitting in the seat next to me wearing a pair of faded jeans, cowboy boots, and a red and black flannel shirt.

"You're talking to me now," he pointed out. "You can at least tell me your name."

"Speaking of names, how does the flight attendant know yours?" I asked.

His lips twitched. "Jealous?"

"No," I stated flatly.

"Tell me your name, and then I'll tell you why she knows mine."

"I know why she knows your name."

"Oh yeah? Why's that?"

I gestured to him. "You're a country music star, aren't you?"

That had him laughing. A deep, booming chuckle that softened the angles of his face.

His laugh made my insides quiver, and I hated myself for it.

"No. I'm not a country music star. Nice guess though."

"Then what are you?"

A voice came over the intercom, effectively ending our conversation. I listened with one ear as they took us through the safety precautions.

When the intercom fell silent, my new companion said, "You're really not going to tell me your name?"

The man had seen me naked.

My legs had been wrapped around him while still wearing my heels.

What was a name?

"Salem," I said.

"Salem," he repeated, his brows furrowing. "As in Salem Powell?"

My eyes widened. "How did—"

"You're Hadley's sister, aren't you?"

I turned my body and my back hit the side of the plane as I tried in vain to put distance between us. "What is this? Are you *stalking* me?"

"Stalking? What the hell kind of a question is that?" He glared. "No, I'm not stalking you, but you're Hadley's sister. Hadley is marrying Declan. I'm Bowman."

"Yeah, so the flight attendant said."

"Bowman," he repeated. "Cas Bowman. I'm Declan's best man."

My mouth dropped open in horror as the plane began rolling down the runway.

I closed my eyes and held in a groan.

I'd had sex with Declan's best man.

Declan's best man had seen me naked.

My throat was sore because Declan's best man had made me scream into a pillow all last night.

"Hadley's going to kill me," I stated, flipping my eyes open. "She's going to kill me dead and then make Poet her maid of honor. She should've done that anyway. Poet never would've done this. Poet never would've done anything like this."

I rubbed my temple.

Bowman took my hand.

"You're panicking."

"*No shit.*" I glared at him and tried to tug my hand from his, but he linked his fingers through mine to stop me. "The wedding isn't for three weeks. Why are you flying up there now?"

"I had some time off from the circuit. I haven't met Hadley yet and I wanted to get to know her a bit before the wedding."

"The circuit." My expression slackened. "Oh. *Oh, no . . .*"

"What?"

My eyes swept down his body and I finally wrenched my hand from his. "You're a—"

"Bull rider."

I groaned. "You're an adrenaline junkie that likes danger."

"I also like temperamental beasts." He cocked his head to the side and grinned. "No wonder I like you."

I snorted. "You don't know me."

He leaned closer. "After last night, I think I have a pretty good idea of who you are."

I swallowed but forced myself to hold his steely gaze. "Oh yeah? Go ahead then. Tell me who I am."

"Bold. Bratty." He grinned and tugged on a strand of my red hair. "And beautiful. And you're not afraid to go to bed with a stranger."

"No, I'm not."

"*But . . .*" He let go of my hair and his eyes raked over me from head to toe again. "You're clearly scared to wake up with one."

Cold terror enveloped every part of my body. It rushed through my veins, turning my blood to ice.

He continued, "I wasn't done with you. But lucky for me, I get another chance to get you into bed."

I raised my brows. "Fat chance."

His grin was slow.

I didn't like that grin.

It was arrogant. Assured. As if *I* was a forgone conclusion.

Sure, I'd gone to bed with him last night and it had been incredible. Unlike any other experience of my life . . .

But that didn't mean it was going to happen again.

"Even if I wanted a repeat performance, which I don't—"

"You do."

"I *don't*."

"You *do*," he insisted. "You're still trembling, aren't you?"

"*Shut. Up.* There are other people on this plane."

"They're all wearing headphones. No one is paying any attention to us."

The man across the aisle glanced at me before quickly turning his face forward again.

I pointed to him. "That guy, right there, is listening to our conversation."

"I'm not," the man lied. "I swear I'm not."

"I'll buy you a drink if you put in noise cancelling headphones," Bowman said to him.

"I think I'd rather listen to this conversation," he said. "I work in television. I'm a writer, and this is *really* good stuff."

I cursed.

"Fine." The man sighed. "Out of respect for the lady."

Bowman waited until the man put his headphones on before he looked at me and winked. "You were hardly a lady last night."

"I'm really starting to hate you."

His gaze dropped to my mouth. "Yeah? How much? So much you want to take it out on me?"

"Never. Going. To. Happen."

"We'll see." He shrugged.

CHAPTER TWO

After the flight attendant brought us beverages, I decided to rip off the Band-Aid.

"So, what do we do?" I asked.

"About what?" He took a sip of his coffee and made a face. "God, this is awful."

"It's airplane coffee. What did you expect?"

"Something better than this," he muttered.

"Back to what I was saying—what do we do? About us, I mean?"

He raised his brows. "There's an *us?*"

"Bowman," I drawled.

"Powell," he said in the same tone.

"I mean, how are we going to deal with"—I gestured between us—"this. I feel like we should be adults and tell Declan and Hadley that we slept together."

"No."

"No? Really? That seems juvenile."

"It's not juvenile. It's self-preservation. Declan is my best friend. But he's marrying your sister. And he's going to be protective of you. And if he finds out that I slept with you, we're looking at black eyes for the wedding. And I'm pretty sure Hadley doesn't want that in her wedding photos."

"I don't like the idea of lying to Hadley." I chewed my lower lip, which drew his attention. "Though I do see your point. And it doesn't make sense to spill the beans over a one-night stand. A one-night stand that'll never happen again."

"Keep telling yourself that," he quipped.

I glared at him. "You just said you don't want a black eye." I raised my fist in a mock gesture.

"Easy there, Powell." He curled his huge hand over my fist and gently pushed it down.

"So, if we're not telling them the truth, we need to come up with some sort of plausible story."

"How about we met on the plane and found out who the other one was," he suggested.

"I guess that could work. Still . . ."

"What?"

"Maybe we shouldn't be so . . . *familiar*. With one another."

"Familiar how?"

"You know."

"I don't, actually."

"I don't know. We just—you talk like—"

"Like I've seen you naked?"

I bared my teeth at him.

"You're cute when you're feral."

"Drink your coffee," I muttered.

"How are you going to explain that," he asked, pointing to my neck.

"I'll tell Hadley I'm anemic."

"It's clearly a hickey."

"I should've told you not to mark me." I glared at him.

"You weren't thinking coherently. What with your eyes rolling into the back of your head."

I flushed. "You've got a mouth on you."

"Want me to put it to better use?"

"Look, I don't go around having regular one-night stands, okay?" I took a deep breath and attempted to reign in my infamous Irish temper. "But last night, I needed something to take my mind off things. You were there. You did a good job, okay? But the ego you have . . . it's going to get you into trouble."

"God, I hope so." He cracked a grin, but when I didn't smile back, it slipped. "What things?"

"Hmm?"

"What things did I take your mind off of?"

I blinked. "Declan knows you're coming, right?"

"Not exactly."

"What?"

"I was going to surprise him. I was just going to show up."

"So, then you don't know," I murmured.

"Know what?"

I looked him in the eyes. "My dad, Bowman. My dad is in the hospital. That's why I came home three weeks before the wedding."

"Shit. The hospital? What happened?"

I swallowed. "Kicked in the head by a horse. Hadley called me two nights ago and I got on the first plane out of New York, but then the weather in Denver . . . He had brain surgery yesterday—to relieve the pressure. He was stable as of this morning."

But that could change. At any moment. Just like life. I

hoped we were still going to have a wedding in a few weeks, not a funeral.

"Surprise," I said with a strained smile. "Not all happy and joyful, you know?"

"Guess not."

"It's not too late to turn back. Get off the plane and get on another and head back to where you came from. Most people would do that."

He didn't reply for a long moment, and then he shrugged. "I'm not most people."

Yeah, no kidding.

"How are you doing? I mean really. Are you hanging in there?"

I lifted my Bloody Mary in the plastic cup and took a sip. "This helps."

"Hmm. And here I thought it was me causing you to drink. Glad to know it's not."

"80 percent my dad, 20 percent you."

"20 percent, huh? That's high. You close with your dad?"

"Yeah, no. We're not doing this. You and me and the deep talks. No way."

"That would be a no, then." He raised his brows.

"We spent one night together, Bowman. Let's not make this into something it isn't."

He let out a laugh.

"What?" I demanded.

"You're okay going to bed with a complete stranger." He leaned closer and lowered his voice. "But you don't want to talk about your dad?"

"Spare me the therapy session," I said, my tone cold. "Now if you don't mind, I'd like some quiet time."

Bowman did me a favor and fell silent, but he didn't stop watching me out of the corner of his eye.

Last night, Bowman had been exactly what I needed.

This morning, the fantasy was dead and in the light of day, reality set in.

The man saw more than I wanted him to.

"Who's Poet?" he asked.

His words dragged me from my own thoughts. "What?"

"Poet. You mentioned Hadley making Poet her maid of honor."

"Oh." I remembered my rant. "Poet is our best friend and my roommate. So is Wyn. You'll meet them at the wedding."

If there's still a wedding...

"It'll happen," he said.

"What?"

"The wedding."

I frowned. "Did I say something out loud?"

He poked my furrowed brow. "You don't need to speak out loud. You say it all right here. You must suck at poker."

"I'm great at poker," I snapped. "Because I cheat."

His lips quivered. "Better sober up, Powell. Wouldn't want the booze to loosen your lips. Might fuck up and say something you regret."

"Too late."

"Aw, tater tot, I'm hurt."

"None of that."

"None of what?"

"Nicknames," I stated.

"If you were to call me a nickname, what would it be?"

"Annoying."

He grinned. "So, you like poker."

"Yes." I cocked my head to the side, thrown by the change in conversation.

"You consider yourself a betting woman?"

"Occasionally."

"Okay, then how about we make a bet?"

"A bet? About what?" I asked, my natural competitive streak coming out to play.

"I bet you can't keep your hands off me."

"I'll lose that bet in five minutes," I said with a smirk.

"Oh yeah?"

"Don't get excited." My eyes dropped to his lap, but then I reached my hand out and gripped the back of his neck. "I meant you're five minutes away from me strangling you."

His eyes darkened. "You're the one who likes breath play."

I dropped my hand like I'd touched a hot coal stove.

"Scared you're going to lose the bet?" he taunted. "The real bet, I mean?"

"Hardly." I scoffed.

"Care to make it more interesting?"

"I'm listening."

"The first one to make a move loses."

"Obviously. What are we betting?"

"Whoever wins gets an entire night of fantasies fulfilled."

A smarter person would demand boundaries.

A smarter person would ask a few clarifying questions.

A smarter person would walk away.

I wasn't smart, and I saw the challenge in his eyes.

"Deal." I held out my hand. "Let's shake on it."

He took my hand in his and gave it a slow squeeze before tickling my palm.

My mouth turned up in a grin. "Amateur."

"We'll see."

"Yeah. We will." I leaned forward, close enough that if I wanted to lose the bet right then and there, all I had to do was dart my tongue out and graze his bottom lip.

"Bowman?"

"Yeah, Powell?"

"I play to win."

He pulled back just enough to stare into my eyes. "So do I."

Air whooshed from my lungs and my focus narrowed on him.

Something told me we weren't talking about the bet anymore.

CHAPTER THREE

"Oh my God! Can I get your autograph?"

The young boy, who couldn't be more than thirteen, was decked out in a pair of cowboy boots and cowboy hat. He stared up at Bowman with hero worship in his eyes.

Bowman looked at him and smiled, his gray eyes crinkling at the corners.

Ugh. The eye crinkles.

Stupid girl, no, stop it.

So hot . . .

"Sure thing," Bowman said easily. "You got a pen?"

The boy's face fell and he shook his head. He glanced over his shoulder at his frazzled parents who looked like they wanted to be anywhere except the passenger pick up area of the Spokane International Airport.

"I've got a pen." I let go of the wheely suitcase and began riffling through my bag. I found a pen at the bottom and handed it to Bowman.

"Any paper?" the boy asked hopefully. "I wasn't expecting to see a legend or I would've brought my own."

I couldn't help the grin that spread across my face. "Legend, huh?"

"Oh yeah." The boy nodded. "He's the best bull rider in the world!"

"Thanks," Bowman said. "That means a lot."

His tone was sincere and I paused in my paper search to look at him. He was staring at the boy and there wasn't a trace of arrogance.

"Did you always want to be a bull rider?" the boy asked.

"Yeah," Bowman said. "You want to be a bull rider when you grow up?"

"Yes!"

"Let me give you one tip."

"What?" the boy asked.

"Make sure you stay on the bull." Bowman winked at the boy who grinned.

"Brock!" his mother yelled.

"Almost finished," Brock called back.

"I've got a dry-cleaning receipt or pharmacy prescription bag." I looked at Brock. "Your choice."

"Oh. Dry cleaning, I guess," Brock said.

I handed the receipt to Bowman who took it to the bench. He set it down and quickly scribbled his name. He then gave it to Brock who held it like a priceless artifact.

"How about a picture," Bowman offered.

Brock gasped. "Really?"

"Really."

Brock whipped out his phone and opened it. "Will you take our picture?"

"Sure thing. I'll take a few. Okay, smile." The camera app shuttered rapidly. "Okay, now do silly."

Brock stuck out his tongue and Bowman screwed up his face in a comical expression of cross-eyes and puffy cheeks.

"Perfection." I handed Brock his phone.

"Can I get a photo with you?" Brock asked me.

I blinked. "Me? But I'm not a legendary bull rider."

"No." Brock angled his head and shot me a cocky grin. "But you're really pretty. And I want to show my friends."

"Hmm. You might just be a legendary charmer, you know?" I quipped, and then gestured to him. "Let's get this picture quickly before your mom blows a gasket."

Brock stood next to me and I placed my hand on his shoulder.

"Do you have a boyfriend?" Brock asked.

Bowman held the camera steady, but his eyes were on me, as if he, too, was waiting for my answer.

"No," I said. "I don't have a boyfriend."

"Good," Brock said. "Then I have a chance."

I laughed. "Maybe in a few years."

"Here you go," Bowman said, lowering the camera and handing it back to Brock.

"Thanks!" Brock grinned up at him. "This made my day!"

"Meeting me?" Bowman quipped. "Or her?"

"Her. Definitely her." Brock blew me a kiss, and then ran back to his parents.

"That kid isn't lacking in the charm department," I said, looking at Bowman. "When he's older, women everywhere won't stand a chance."

"Pretty sure that's what he's counting on," Bowman said. "Pharmacy bag?"

"Hmm?"

"You've got a pharmacy bag. Like for a prescription?"

"Yes. I had a mild sinus infection. Anything else you want to know?" I crossed my arms over my chest.

"Why don't you have a boyfriend?"

That wasn't the question I thought he was going to ask.

Thankfully, I was spared from answering because a black SUV with Idaho plates pulled up to the curb and my sister waved excitedly from the passenger side.

The car had barely parked when her door opened and she all but fell out onto the sidewalk. "Easy there, tiger," I said with a laugh, happiness bubbling inside of me at seeing my twin.

A grin spread across her face, and then she lunged at me.

I caught her in my arms. I was older by four minutes and five inches taller, but Hadley had always been the one to take care of me.

"Sorry we're late," she said, pulling back to stare at me. Her blue eyes drifted to my neck and I forced myself not to squirm under her gaze. "My fault."

"Stomach or bladder?" I asked.

Her cheeks heated. "Both."

I let out a laugh.

"Uh, Salem?"

"Yeah?"

"Who's the guy standing behind you?" Hadley asked in confusion.

"Oh, funny story. That's Bowman."

"Bowman?" Hadley frowned. "As in Declan's best friend from the circuit, Bowman?"

"The one and only," Bowman said, taking a step toward us.

The driver's side door opened, and my sister's tall, dark-haired fiancé stepped out of the car. He came around the front of the vehicle and his jaw dropped open.

"What the hell are you doing here?" Declan demanded, a wide smile spreading across his face.

"Surprising you," Bowman said easily.

"We met on the plane," I blurted out.

"Did you," Hadley murmured, her gaze bouncing between me and Bowman.

"Damn glad to see you, brother," Declan said.

The two of them clasped hands in a shake, but then Bowman pulled Declan close for a quick man-hug. Declan had a couple inches on Bowman and was leaner.

They separated and Bowman looked at Hadley.

"So, you're Hadley," Bowman drawled.

"Yep." Hadley smiled.

"You sure you want to marry this fucker?" Bowman asked, gesturing to his best friend.

She placed a hand on her belly that had just started to show. "Not really. But he kind of wore me down."

Declan pulled Hadley to him, wrapped his arm around her shoulder and pressed a kiss to her forehead. "That's not what you said last night."

She elbowed him in the ribs, causing him to grunt, and then laugh. To me, she said, "Let's get your luggage into the car."

"That's not a car, that's an AT-AT," Bowman said.

"A what?" I asked in confusion as Declan took my bag and opened the hatch of the SUV.

"An AT-AT," Bowman said again. "You know, those machines from *The Empire Strikes Back*? They're on Hoth and attack the rebel base?"

The three of us stared at Bowman in silence.

"You're a Star Wars fan?" I asked slowly.

"Geek," Declan said. "The word you're looking for is *geek*."

"Oh, shut up, you Trekkie," Bowman fired back.

Hadley whipped her head around to stare at her fiancé. "You like Star Trek?"

Declan snapped his spine straight and pinned her with a stare. "Yes. I like Star Trek. So what?"

Hadley attempted to swallow her lips to keep from laughing. She looked at me and mouthed, *"Hot nerds."*

"You should've told Brock about your love of Star Wars," I said to Bowman. "Pretty sure he would've kissed the ground you walked on."

"Brock? Who's Brock?" Hadley asked as she opened the back door. "Bowman, you take the front."

"No," Bowman said. "I'll sit in back."

"But your legs," she said.

"Yes, I have them." Bowman smiled. "Your car, you sit in the front."

"Good man," she said.

"While we were waiting for you, a boy recognized Bowman and wanted an autograph," I said. "Because he's sooooo famous."

Declan laughed as he shut the hatch.

"But then he wanted a photo with your sister because she's sooooo pretty," Bowman teased.

"Very pretty," Hadley agreed, her gaze once again bouncing between me and Bowman. She climbed into the passenger side and Bowman closed the door.

Once the four of us were in the car, Declan pulled away from the curb and drove toward the highway.

"So, you guys met on the plane," Declan said, looking in the rearview mirror. Our eyes met.

"Yep," I lied.

"And you . . . talked?" Hadley asked.

"Clearly," I said. "Because we both figured out who the other one was."

"And does he know . . ." Hadley prompted.

"Yes," I said, my throat tight. "I told him about Dad."

Hadley turned in her seat and addressed Bowman. "Sorry your surprise is kind of . . . overshadowed."

"Hey, I'm just glad I'm here," Bowman said, his tone sincere. "Whatever you guys need. You let me know."

"Thanks." Hadley's smile wobbled. "We're going straight to the hospital."

It wasn't up for a debate: it was a statement.

My phone chimed with a text.

I pulled out my cell and looked at the screen. Our group chat had a new message.

WYN

you at the hospital yet?

My fingers flew across the screen.

ME

Hadley and Declan just picked me up.

Hadley's phone buzzed in the front seat.

"I'm texting Wyn and Poet," I explained.

"Ah," Hadley said.

"Poet," Bowman said. "She mentioned Poet should've been maid of honor?"

I glared at him.

He grinned.

"You guys really got to talk, huh?" Hadley asked. "If you already know who Poet is."

"Not that much," I lied again.

"I love Poet," Hadley said. "But Salem's my twin. No one else was ever going to be my maid of honor."

More like Maid of Dishonor.

I'd slept with the best man.

To be fair, I hadn't known he was the best man when I went to bed with him.

But if I admitted it to myself, I still would've found a way to go to bed with him even if I'd known.

And damn if he didn't look at me like he knew what I was thinking.

CHAPTER FOUR

The Hospital

"Oh, sugar." Muddy wrapped her arms around me and held me tight.

I closed my eyes and sank into my grandmother's embrace. Despite being nearly seventy, the woman was strong—physically, emotionally—and at the moment, I desperately needed a shot of her fortitude. Her long silver braid fell over one shoulder, and she smelled like baked apples.

"Any change?" I asked when I pulled back.

Muddy shook her head. "You want to go in and see him?"

No.

"Yes," I lied.

The hospital smelled like nothing. Sterile.

"Who are you?" Muddy asked, dropping her arms and looking over my shoulder at Bowman.

"Cas Bowman, ma'am," he said.

Muddy frowned. "Cas Bowman."

"My best man," Declan supplied. "He flew in early as a surprise before the wedding."

"Salem and Bowman were on the same flight," Hadley said. "Oddly enough."

"Oddly," Muddy murmured. She moved away from me and embraced him before stepping back. "Hadley? You want to come too?"

Hadley nodded and left Declan's side. He watched her go and a pang of envy shot through my heart.

She had someone to lean on. Someone to care for her.

My eyes went to Bowman. He was staring at me with a blank expression across his face.

I quickly turned away and followed my sister and grandmother. "You have to gown and glove up just for the first few days," the nurse said, handing me a gown. "He's at a high risk of infection."

The three of us donned the medical gear and then went into my father's ICU room.

I stared at him.

The man had always been larger than life. A cowboy. A stubborn, steady presence. A bear of a man.

And now he just looked . . . *human. Fallible.*

I hated seeing him like this. Broken. A shell of who he truly was.

A horse had kicked him in the head. Would that rob me of my father like the ovarian cancer had robbed me of my mother?

"He looks better today," Muddy said. "He's not as pale."

"You're right," Hadley agreed.

I bit my tongue.

Hadley reached out and touched Dad's hand despite having a glove on. "We love you, Dad. Get better."

I wasn't doing this. I wasn't saying goodbye. I would not mourn at his bedside.

"We should go," I said quietly. "Let him rest."

Hadley looked at me. Seeing without needing words. We were twins. We didn't need words.

The three of us stepped out of the hospital room and began to take off the gown and gloves.

"When was the last time you slept?" I asked Muddy.

"I don't need sleep." She lifted her chin, presenting a stubborn angle that I recognized from years of looking in the mirror. "I'm staying in the waiting room. They let me see him for a few minutes every couple of hours, and I want to be here in case something changes."

"I'll stay with you," Hadley offered.

"You don't have to, sugar," Muddy said.

"I know. But I want to."

I couldn't sit in the waiting room with nothing to do except let my mind hold me hostage.

Muddy handed me her keys.

"What are these for?" I asked.

"I know you want to be anywhere but here," Muddy said softly. "So take my truck and go for food or something. Take Bowman with you. He shouldn't have to sit here with the rest of us."

I swallowed. "You sure?"

"Yep." She cradled my cheek in her hand. "There will be plenty of time to catch up later."

I let out a breath. "Call me if something changes?"

"Will do." She nodded.

We headed back to the waiting room to Bowman and Declan. They stood when they saw us.

"How is he?" Bowman asked me.

"He's . . . I don't know." I rubbed my third eye.

"He has more color in his cheeks," Hadley said. "But he's in a medically induced coma. They'll wake him up in a few days if everything goes well."

Try to wake him up. She forgot the word 'try.'

"We have a ride," I said to Bowman as I dangled the keys in my hand. "You want to get out of here?"

"Sure," he said.

"Take him to the Ridge," Muddy suggested. "Show him around. Get him settled. He can stay in Hadley's room."

Bowman . . . in my twin sister's bedroom . . . right next door to me?

DEFCON 1 for my loins.

"Wouldn't he be more comfortable at The Regal Beagle?" I blurted out.

Muddy frowned. "No. He's Declan's best friend, which makes him family. He stays with us."

"First of all, I'm right here. Also, what's The Regal Beagle?" Bowman asked with a cheeky smile at me.

"The only bed and breakfast in town," I replied, ignoring the teasing glint in his eye, as if he knew what was going on in my brain.

"It used to be a brothel," Hadley said with a smile. "It's seen the error of its ways though, and now it's a respectable Victorian bed and breakfast."

"They serve tea and crumpets," I said. "They used to anyway."

"Still do," Hadley said. "In fact, I'd be okay having my bachelorette party there when the girls are in town."

"You wild thing," I quipped.

She pointed to her belly. "My wild days are over."

"We could still have a male stripper," I joked.

"Absolutely not," Declan said. "And for the record, I'm not having a stripper either."

"What *are* we doing for your bachelor party?" Bowman asked.

"You tell me. You're the one who's going to plan it," Declan stated.

"Oh, right." Bowman winked at Hadley. "No strippers jumping out of cakes, I promise."

"You're a good man, Bowman," Hadley said.

"No, he's not," Declan said.

"And yet he's your best friend," Hadley pointed out.

"History at this point," Declan stated. "It would take too long to find another one."

Bowman shoved Declan's shoulder, causing him to laugh.

Despite the fact that my father was in a hospital bed in a coma, my spirits lifted. Being around Hadley always had that effect. But it was something more now. Declan, Muddy, Bowman . . .

I'm home.

A stunning brunette with high cheekbones came into the waiting room while Declan and Bowman continued to verbally rib each other.

I frowned in confusion as she strode over to us. Her expression was wreathed with concern.

"Muddy," she greeted, placing her hand on my grandmother's arm.

"Jane." Muddy embraced her. "So glad you're here."

"Of course," the woman asked. "You hanging in there, Hadley?"

"Barely," Hadley stated. Her gaze shot from me to the woman. "Jane. This is my sister, Salem."

"Salem," Jane greeted. "It's nice to meet you."

"You too," I said in perfunctory politeness.

"Let me take you to see him," Muddy said, grasping Jane's elbow and pulling her away. Over her shoulder, she said, "Hadley?"

Hadley sighed. "Yeah, I'll tell her."

"Tell me what?" I demanded.

Hadley waited until Muddy and Jane disappeared before saying, "That's Jane. Dad's girlfriend."

CHAPTER FIVE

"*Girlfriend?*" I shrieked.

Hadley winced. "Can you keep your voice down? This is a hospital."

"I don't care where we are! *Girlfriend?*" I snapped. "Why didn't you tell me?"

My twin glared at me. "Oh, I don't know. Maybe I was worried you'd *overreact.*"

"This is un-fucking-believable!" I whirled and stomped out of the waiting room.

Blind rage colored my vision. Emotion blistered my throat, and I was ready to spew it at anyone who came near me.

My sister, my own twin, hadn't told me about our father's girlfriend.

"Powell," Bowman called after me.

I didn't stop when I heard his voice. Instead, I continued

to stalk toward the elevator. I pushed the button several times in rapid fire as if that would make it arrive faster.

"Where are you going?" Bowman asked, coming to my side.

"Anywhere but here."

"You can't drive," he said. "Not in the state you're in."

I turned and glared at him.

He was there and had instantly become the target of my rage.

"You're not the boss of me!"

"Someone needs to be the boss of you." His tone was mild, but his jaw clenched. "Give me the keys."

"No!"

"Powell, I'm warning you . . ."

"Oh, you're *warning me?*" I placed my hands at my hips and glared up at him. "You sure you want to get in my way?"

He sighed.

And without a word, he bent down, grasped me by my legs and hauled me over his shoulder.

"Bowman!" I screeched. "Put me down!"

"No."

I smacked his butt.

He swatted mine in return.

"You're making a scene!" I hissed.

"You started it. Now stop it."

"You're horrible."

"And you're a brat."

"People are going to stare," I whined.

"Should've thought of that before you freaked out."

The elevator doors opened, and he walked into the carriage. I almost groaned when I realized we weren't alone. Two doctors in scrubs were standing next to each other.

"Lobby, please," Bowman said politely, pretending he didn't have a hysterical woman dangling over his shoulder.

"Oh," the female doctor said. "Sure." She pushed the button and the doors closed.

"Nice weather we're having," Bowman said in a conversational tone.

"Yeah." The male doctor bobbed his head. "It was a rainy spring. Seems to have cleared up though."

"I love the smell of the rain in the forest," Bowman remarked.

"Absolutely." The female doctor flashed a smile.

The carriage came to a stop and the doors opened.

"Well, this is us. Have a good one," the male doctor said.

"You too," Bowman replied.

When it was just the two of us again, I intoned, "Please let me down."

"You promise to behave?"

"No."

"Behave or I'm carting your ass out of the lobby this way. So far only a few nurses and two doctors have seen you like this. Your choice if you want to draw a crowd."

I grumbled. "Fine. I'll be good."

"Doubtful." He lowered me to the ground.

I stepped away from him and raised my fist.

His jaw ticked. "Don't even think about it."

I lowered my hand.

"Keys." He held his palm flat. "I'm driving you. I'll take you wherever you want to go, but you're not getting behind the wheel."

I handed over the keys.

The doors to the elevator opened. Bowman gestured for me to go out first, and then he followed, keeping close.

We stepped out of the hospital, and the warm, late Idaho spring air bathed my cheeks. It did nothing to soothe my temper.

"Probably should've asked your grandmother where she parked," Bowman said.

"Look for a rust bucket with no modern safety features. Ah, there it is." I pointed and immediately began my trek toward the old farm truck.

"That's not a rust bucket, that's a liability."

"Dad bought her a new truck with all the bells and whistles and she hates it. She prefers a truck that doesn't try to think for her," I quipped. "Can you handle a stick?"

"If I ask for lessons, will you teach me?" he teased.

"You and I are talking about two different sticks entirely."

"Yeah, babe, I can handle a stick without a problem. Even the one you have up your ass."

I glared at him and picked up the pace.

When we got to the truck, Bowman went to the passenger side.

"What are you doing?" I demanded.

"Opening the door for you."

"Why?"

"Because even though you're in a mood, I still have manners."

With a grumble, I climbed into the passenger seat. He shut the door and I buckled myself in.

He started the truck and backed out of the lot. We didn't speak for a few minutes, and then I asked, "I'll give you directions to the family ranch."

"We're not going to Elk Ridge yet," he said.

I crossed my arms over my chest and stared out the window. "You said you'd drive me wherever I wanted to go."

"I lied."

"Then where are you taking me?"

"To get something to eat. Your blood sugar is low. And after you get something into your system, we'll talk."

"I don't want to talk."

"You're right, you want to yell." He looked at me. "You're not the least bit embarrassed, are you?"

"Why should I be?" I demanded. "Because the normal thing to do is mash down your feelings and slap a smile on your face and pretend like everything's okay?"

"Your sister didn't deserve your anger. But you can't be angry at the person you really want to be angry at because he's lying in a hospital bed in a coma."

I swallowed. "Bowman?"

"Yeah?"

"Shut. Up."

"Struck a nerve, huh?"

"Let's play the quiet game. Whoever talks first loses."

Silence finally reigned in the truck.

"I lose. Let's play another game."

I groaned. "No."

"Why do you hate the idea of your dad having a girlfriend?"

"I don't."

"Could've fooled me."

I whipped my head around to look at him. "Muddy and Hadley—neither of them bothered to mention her."

"So you're telling me that if you'd known about her, you wouldn't have reacted the way you did?"

When I paused, he shot me a wry grin. "Thought so."

"Arrogance makes you look three inches shorter."

"Going for the height? Really? I must actually be pissing you off," he joked. "Now tell me where you want to go for comfort food and I'll take you there."

"The Diner," I said. "Best poutine in the world."

"Just direct me."

I smirked. "A man asking for directions. How original."

"You deserve a good spanking, Powell."

"You already gave me one, remember? When you carried me over your shoulder like a lumberjack carries a log."

"I remember," he said. "That was hardly a spanking. Doubt your ass is red like it needs to be."

"Should we pull over? And you can give me the spanking you think I deserve?"

"You'd lose the bet. You do remember the bet, don't you?"

"No, I wouldn't," I said as I shook my head. "You would. You'd be the one to put your hands on me on purpose."

"Yet, you're the one asking for it."

"Guess we're at a stalemate then."

Twenty minutes later, Bowman and I drove into Huckleberry Hill. The main drag was Silver Street, with cute little retail shops, a bakery, and of course, The Diner.

"There's no way you grew up here," he stated.

"Uh yeah, I did."

"It looks like a movie set. It's the epitome of small, charming mountain town."

"Why do you think I left?" I said, a pang flitting through my chest. "There was nothing to do here. There's *still* nothing to do here."

I'd left for other reasons too . . .

He maneuvered the truck into a parking spot.

"There has to be stuff to do here," Bowman said after we got out of the truck and shut the doors.

"If you're not old enough to drink at the Copper Mule—the only bar in town—then you either eat at The Diner or grab a pastry from Sweet Teeth. Not into food? There's the bank with one teller who loves to gab, or if you need to go shopping, you hit up General Mercantile, which has everything from tractor parts to raw milk. Lots to do in this town, I'm telling you."

"What about festivals? Towns like these always have festivals and seasonal activities."

"Oh, right. We do have those," I agreed. "Spring there's the Mushroom Festival. In summertime, it's the Huckleberry Festival. Autumn is the barn dance and belly basket auction. Winter we have the Snow Queen pageant, sledding on Maple Mountain, ice skating on Lavender Lake, and fondue at Sweet Teeth."

"What's a belly basket auction?"

"You've heard of the time-honored tradition of women making baskets full of food and having men bid on them?"

"In this century?"

I arched a brow. "Well, we do it differently here. Instead, men make baskets and women bid on them."

Bowman opened the door to The Diner and held it for me. I went inside. The smell of fried food hit me and my stomach growled in adoration.

"Salem Powell!"

A smile greeted my lips. "Mr. Bixby."

His face was ruddy from the heat of the back kitchen and his balding head had a sheen of sweat. He wiped his hands on his apron as he came around the counter and enveloped me in a bear hug.

"Good to see you, honey. How's your dad?"

He pulled back and stared at me with solemn brown eyes.

"We just came from the hospital," I said, my throat tight. "He had brain surgery. Now we're just waiting a few days, and then they'll try to wake him up."

He nodded. "Lucy told me about the surgery."

"How did—Muddy?"

Mr. Bixby nodded. "I'm making up a care package for you before you leave. You take it home, yeah? And if you need anything, you call."

"Thank you," I said, sincerity permeating my tone.

Mr. Bixby dropped his hands from my shoulders and looked at Bowman. "Who's your friend?"

"I don't know about friend, but this is Cas Bowman," I muttered.

Bowman shot me an amused look before turning his attention to Mr. Bixby and holding out his hand. "Cas Bowman. I'm Declan's best man."

"Oh, so you're the famous bull rider, eh? He told me about you!" Mr. Bixby clasped Bowman's hand and gave it a hearty shake. "Welcome to Huckleberry Hill. Meals are on the house today. You're lucky you came in when you did. You just missed the noon rush." He ushered us to a vacant table.

"Usual for you?" Mr. Bixby asked me.

I nodded.

"Cas?"

"Call me Bowman. And I'll have a burger with everything on it, and a cherry coke."

"You got it."

After Mr. Bixby got us our drinks, he went to the back, leaving me and Bowman alone.

"Why do you go by Bowman?"

He shrugged. "I've always been called that. Even when I was in school."

"Were you on the football team?"

"Yes."

"Oh. That tracks, then."

"But even my teachers and other students called me Bowman."

"What's Cas short for?"

"Guess."

"Casper."

"No."

"Cassian."

He frowned. "That's not a name."

"It's a name," I said.

"Of someone real?"

"No one I know," I admitted with a wry smile. "Caspian?"

"Nope."

"I'm so calling you Caspian," I quipped. "Until you tell me what Cas actually stands for."

He ignored my pronouncement when he said, "You never answered my question."

His change in conversation gave me whiplash. "What question would that be? About my father's girlfriend? I thought we weren't going to talk about that until after I'd been sedated with poutine."

"Not that. You never answered why *you* don't have a boyfriend."

I raised my brows. "When did you ask me that?"

"We were at the airport and Brock asked you. You never said why."

"And you're still thinking about it?"

"Clearly."

"Why don't you have a girlfriend?" I fired back.

"Who says I don't?"

"Because if you did, you'd be the lowest form of life on this planet for cheating on her."

He cracked a grin. "No argument there. Cheating is a character flaw I do not have."

"How reassuring," I drawled.

"It *should* be reassuring," he insisted. "If someone is a cheater, what's to stop them from cheating at business? Or being a shit friend?"

"Valid," I admitted. "So, no girlfriend?"

"No. Now answer my question."

"Say the magic word."

"Spank."

A huff of a laugh escaped my lips. "I don't have a boyfriend because I don't want a boyfriend. Happy?"

"Hmm. What's your type?"

"I don't have a type."

"Everyone has a type."

I reached for my soda. "I'm twenty-three. Everyone is my type."

"Twenty-three. God damn, that's young."

I wrinkled my nose. "How old are you?"

"Thirty-four."

"Not old enough to be an antique, but definitely vintage," I quipped.

"Some of the shine has definitely rubbed off," he joked.

"Thirty-four . . . and you're still bull riding."

"Borrowed time," he stated. "Hate to say it, but I'm one major injury away from retirement. It's why I took a brand deal."

"What kind of brand deal?" I asked. "Cigarettes? Liquor? Clothing?"

"Coffee, actually. Have you ever heard of Cowboy Coffee?"

My brow wrinkled. "Sounds familiar."

"They wanted Declan too," he said. "But he passed."

"Ah, I remember now. Hadley mentioned something . . ."

"The coffee company is looking to push various roasts into every smokehouse and BBQ joint in the country. It's not as simple as a photo shoot and a paycheck. They want the publicity that goes with a rodeo tour. So, when I get back on the circuit, my beans are spoken for."

Mr. Bixby came out of the kitchen carrying our plates. He set them down in front of us. "Can I get you anything else?"

We shook our heads and Mr. Bixby went into the back again.

I picked up a tater tot and swirled it around in the gravy before placing it in my mouth. I let out a groan that was borderline pornographic.

Bowman raised his brows and smirked, no doubt thinking the exact same thing.

"I thought poutine was with fries," he said.

"Yep. But I like mine with tater tots." I shrugged. "Just one of my many quirks."

My phone chimed. While I was distracted by attempting to find my cell phone at the bottom of my bag, Bowman took his fork and stabbed a gravy drenched tater tot and brought it to his lips.

"Hey, that's mine."

The tater tot disappeared into his mouth and he chewed and swallowed. "Damn. That's good. Better than my burger."

He reached for my bowl.

I smacked his hand. "Are you trying to lose a finger?"

He grinned. "What if I say please?"

"No."

"What if I beg?" His gray eyes swirled with heat.

With a sigh, I reluctantly pushed the bowl toward him.

I grabbed my cell and looked at the screen.

HADLEY

You still mad at me?

She'd purposefully left out a very important detail about our father's life.

Damn right I was mad at her.

I didn't know what to say, so I shoved my phone back into my bag.

Bowman pushed the bowl of poutine back toward me. "You need this more than I do."

CHAPTER SIX

The Diner

"You feeling any better?" Bowman asked.

"I'm full. That's something." I pushed my empty bowl away.

"What about your dad?"

"I still don't want to talk about that."

"Something tells me you have a turbulent relationship with your father."

"A girl with daddy issues, now there's a stereotype."

He peered at me for a long moment, and then he said, "I think you're a woman with mommy issues."

I froze. "What do you know about my mother?"

"Nothing," he said. "Nothing at all, actually. But the way you reacted to finding out your dad has a girlfriend leads me to believe it's more about your mother than it is about your father."

"Just when I thought you were turning out to be okay,

you have to go and say something like that." I rose from the table. "Mr. Bixby!"

"Coming!" he called back. A moment later, he stepped out of the kitchen holding several brown bags. "Just packing up some food for you."

"You're a gem," I said, kissing his cheek.

"Keep us posted about your dad, yeah?"

I nodded.

"Don't worry, honey. He's a fighter. He'll pull through." Mr. Bixby looked at Bowman. "Good to meet you, Bowman. Enjoy your time here."

Bowman looked at me. "Oh, I will."

He took the bags of food from Mr. Bixby and we left The Diner just as a group of people came in. I held the door for them and then followed Bowman outside.

As we passed Sweet Teeth, the door opened and Gracie stepped out onto the sidewalk. She carried several boxes of pastries and said, "You didn't think you were going to sneak off without saying hello, did you?"

I grinned and gave her a side hug. "No. I didn't think that."

"Liar." She chuckled. "Mr. Bixby called me and said you were having lunch, so I had time to bake you some fresh pastries."

"You didn't have to do that," I said, taking the boxes from her.

"Like hell I didn't. Fair warning, I called Lucy, so she'll probably stop you too." Gracie looked at Bowman. "Hi, I don't know you."

"This is Cas Bowman," I said. "Declan's rodeo BFF. Bowman, this is Gracie. Hadley and I have known her since third grade."

"Second, actually. Ms. Milford's class." Gracie made a quick perusal of Bowman. "You're going to cause quite a stir."

"I hope so," Bowman quipped.

Gracie looked at me, her expression sobering. "Your dad is strong and stubborn. He'll get through this."

"Yeah," I said faintly. "I hope so."

"I know so," Gracie said. She squeezed my wrist.

"Did you know he was dating someone?" I asked bluntly.

She blinked bright blue eyes. "Oh, shoot, I need to get back to—ah, Hell. I need to be anywhere but here."

Gracie skuttled back into the bakery.

"Did everyone know about my dad's girlfriend but me?" I snapped at Bowman.

"You really want me to answer that?" Bowman asked.

I sighed. "Let's go before we're hounded by someone—"

"Salem!"

The dimpling woman with wrinkles at the corners of her eyes popped out of General Merc before I could make a run for it.

I slapped a smile on my face. "Hi, Lucy."

"Oh, *this* is Lucy," Bowman remarked softly as the woman approached us.

"Gosh, your hair is shiny," Lucy said as she stroked a long red strand of my hair. "What are you doing to it?"

"Hair mask."

"Huh."

Lucy embraced me for a moment and then pulled back to stare me directly in the eyes. "If you need *anything*, you let me know. We're here for you, Salem. Whatever we can do to help. Your grandmother won't ask. But don't let that stop you."

My heart melted in my chest. For all the annoyances of a small town and everyone knowing your business, sometimes it was nice not having to explain the intimate details of your family idiosyncrasies.

Lucy's hands dropped from my shoulders and her attention turned to Bowman. She raised her brows. "You Salem's beau?"

I nearly choked on my own tongue, but Bowman smiled and held out his hand to her. "I'm Declan Brewer's best friend. Please, call me Bowman."

"Oh." Lucy beamed and clasped his hand. "I'm a fan of Declan. Welcome to Huckleberry Hill, Bowman."

"Thank you," Bowman said.

Lucy looked at me. "Remember what I said, honey. About asking for help."

"I'll remember," I promised. "So, I met Jane . . ."

"Jane," Lucy repeated.

"My father's girlfriend," I supplied.

Lucy looked at her wrist, which was currently devoid of a watch. "See ya later, honey, I gotta go."

"Go where?" I pressed.

"I have inventory to order." She shot Bowman a smile. "Take care."

She whirled and hustled back toward the store.

I looked at Bowman who clearly was about to say something.

"Don't," I commanded. "Don't say anything."

"I'm not saying a word." He started to laugh as we walked to the truck. "You're like the town's modern-day outlaw. You're a gunslinger with a temper, aren't ya?"

I groaned. "Bowman, stop."

That only made him laugh harder. "If I walk around, will I see your picture on signs in the windows? Is there a reward for turning you in?"

"You're rotten."

"And you're infamous." He shook his head and then winked at me. "I have a thing for the wicked."

CHAPTER SEVEN

The Ranch

"So, what did you do?" Bowman asked as we drove out of town toward my family's ranch.

"Do?" I peered at him as I kept hold of the pastry boxes on my lap.

"Gracie, Lucy . . . they seemed to know you're a hair trigger. Clearly, you've got a track record. Or a rap sheet."

I glared at him.

"Come on, tell me a story," he begged. "I'll tell you one of mine if you tell me one of yours."

He glanced at me but didn't take his hands off the wheel.

For a moment, I was mesmerized by the size of them. They were huge, and I instantly remembered the way they had coasted over my skin and spread my thighs . . .

"Salem?"

"Yeah." I dragged my eyes up to his.

He arched a brow. "I'll trade you story for story."

"You have youthful transgressions?" I asked.

"Several. Come on, tit for tat."

"I'm not showing you my tat."

"I've seen your *tat*." He grinned. "And I've seen your ink, too."

"A youthful transgression." I wanted to get far away from the conversation about my ink.

"Yep. You gotta go first, though."

"Why?"

"Because."

"That's not a reason."

"Humor me."

"Fine." I sighed, knowing he wasn't going to let it go. "There was a really mean girl named Amber in high school who made Hadley cry. So, one day I put hair removal cream in her face cleanser bottle. After soccer practice while she was showering and washing her face, she got a nice little surprise—her eyebrows mysteriously fell out. Oh, and her hairline got pushed back about a half an inch since she got some up on her forehead."

"Vicious. What did she say to Hadley that made her cry?"

"I don't remember," I lied.

He looked at me but said nothing.

"Now you. Tell me one of your youthful transgressions."

"There was a stray cat in our neighborhood," he began. "It only had three legs. But it was a scrappy little fucker. These two idiots—just big, dumb, mean motherfuckers—managed to trap it."

Dread coiled through my stomach.

"You can tell when a kid is off, you know? They were fourteen. And they definitely knew better. Anyway, they trapped the cat and were tying firecrackers to its tail."

"*No . . .*" I whispered.

"Yeah. But I stopped them in time before they could set

them off." His fingers clenched the wheel and his knuckles began to turn white.

When Bowman fell silent, his eyes still on the road, I prodded, "That's not the end of the story, is it?"

Bowman looked at me and cracked a grin. "No, that's not the end of the story. I got expelled for what I did next, but it was worth it. My foster mother was not happy."

"You grew up in the system?" I asked in surprise.

"Another story for another day," he said, clamping his mouth shut.

Hmm. Guess he has things he didn't want to talk about either.

I was now curious about him. More than just the man that he was, but the boy he'd been. And how he'd become a bull rider.

I did not like having curiosity where he was concerned, so I shoved it aside and slapped armor around my heart.

"Hate to break it to you, *Caspian*, but that isn't a youthful transgression."

"No?"

I shook my head. "No. Whatever got you expelled was vigilante justice."

A smile flitted across his sultry mouth. "Same goes for you. What you did was for your sister."

"I guess so," I agreed.

"Ah, so we have something in common." He looked at me. "We protect the innocent."

I felt my armor crack. Just a bit.

"Yeah," I said softly. "I guess we do."

My phone rang, startling me out of the moment. I dug around for it in my bag and saw Hadley's name flashing across the screen.

I debated silencing it, but if it was about Dad, then I didn't want to miss the news.

"Hey. Is everything okay with Dad?" I asked as soon as I picked up.

Hadley paused, and then she said, "Dad's okay. I mean, okay as can be."

I closed my eyes. "So, this isn't about Dad?"

"No. You didn't text me back."

"Can I call you back in a few minutes?" I asked, glancing at Bowman, who was clearly pretending not to be listening. "We're almost home."

"You're not home yet?"

"We got food at The Diner," I replied. "And then Gracie stopped me and added pastries. And then Lucy. . ."

"Oh, I see."

There was a lot going on that was clearly not being said between us, but it wasn't a conversation I wanted to have over the phone.

"When are you going to be back at the Ridge?" I asked.

"I don't know. We get to see him for a few minutes at a time, but only every few hours. Muddy's trying to browbeat a nurse into putting a cot in Dad's room so she can stay the night."

"If browbeating doesn't work, we can always make a sizable donation."

Hadley paused. "I should've thought of that."

"Money opens doors."

That was one thing the Powell family had a lot of. Plus, the Powell family was a staple in the community. Everyone knew who we were.

It was one of the reasons I'd left.

"I feel bad for the nurse that tries to stand between Muddy and her son," I said dryly. "The woman doesn't take *no* for an answer."

"If all she's going to do is sit and crochet or sleep, I don't understand why they won't let her," Hadley remarked.

"Protocol, I guess."

"Hmm. Yeah." She sighed. "Anyway, I'll talk to you later."

I hung up with my sister and then stared out the window.

"What's the word?" Bowman asked.

I glanced at him and smiled. "You want me to recount an entire conversation I know you already heard?"

He grinned. "Nah. Just trying to be polite."

"Hmm. I don't know if I like you polite."

"But you like me, huh?"

"I wouldn't go *that* far."

"Oh yeah, you definitely like me."

"Only when you're naked," I quipped, trying to lighten the intensity of the conversation I'd just had with my sister. "And when your mouth is otherwise occupied instead of talking. Talking ruins everything."

"We talked. That night."

Despite my saucy barbs, my cheeks flamed with heat. "That wasn't *talking*. That was . . . something else."

"Something you desperately want to do again."

"Turn," I commanded, pointing to a fork in the road. "Go up that way."

"I'm right, right?" he demanded. "You liked when I whispered dirty depraved things in your ear. Things I wanted to do."

I couldn't stop the memories or the shivers that pattered up my spine and settled at the base of my neck. If he was trying to get me to concede the bet—he would have try harder. A lot harder.

"Not going to happen, Caspian," I said, my tone raspy.

"We'll see, Powell. We shall see."

CHAPTER EIGHT

THE RANCH

Bowman parked the truck outside the front of my childhood home—a home that hadn't felt like much of one since my mother had died several years earlier.

It had been so long since I'd been here.

I always made an excuse, so I didn't have to come home and relive the best and worst times of my life. So I didn't have to replay the fights I'd had with my father over and over.

I swallowed down bitter thoughts and shadows of times when I'd once been happy. Sometimes I wondered if my mother had lived, would I have learned the art of temperance? Would I have learned to think before acting? Or was I wired to lead with emotions first and always?

Bowman climbed out of the truck, while I sat there in the passenger seat. "You coming?"

"Yes."

I made no move to get out.

Bowman came around to the passenger side and opened the door and waited. He didn't ask what was wrong. He already knew.

"Some homecoming," I murmured before I could stop myself.

"Won't get easier staying in the truck."

"I know," I admitted. "I have to go to the bathroom."

"That wasn't what I meant."

I inclined my head and handed him the pastry boxes that rested on my lap. He took them, and then I hopped down. I gathered the brown bags Mr. Bixby had given us and then shut the truck door.

The sound of it echoed in the quiet afternoon.

With heavy footsteps and an even heavier heart, I marched toward the porch. Muddy boots and shoes rested on the mat just to the side of the door.

I set the bags of food onto the porch. "Boots off," I said, removing my shoes.

Bowman didn't complain as he set the pastry boxes down and then took off his boots. He set them next to mine.

It was inadvertent and it meant nothing, but something about them lined up next to each other made it look like they belonged together.

With exasperation, I shook the thought aside.

This place.

It was this place making me think things like our boots looked good together.

Four Border Collie Australian Shepherd mixes dashed up the front porch steps, their nails clacking across the wooden planks.

"You have dogs," Bowman said with a smile.

"Ranch dogs," I said. "Herding dogs."

Their noses nudged the pastry boxes and brown bags in excitement, but their tails went crazy when Bowman bent down to give them some affection.

"What are their names?" Bowman asked.

"Peter, Susan, Edmund and Lucy," I said. "After the characters in *The Lion, the Witch, and the Wardrobe.*"

Because they were working dogs, they quickly lost interest in us and bounded off the porch in search of more amusing companions.

I reached for the handle and turned the knob without bothering with a key.

"They don't lock the front door?" Bowman asked in surprise.

"No," I said. "Not usually."

There was nothing to steal. Pictures, gingham curtains, cast iron.

There were only memories here.

The house smelled like bacon grease and familiarity. Half-drunk cups of coffee were in the sink. Dishes with forgotten food were on the table.

It was as though our whole family had gotten up from the table one night and left; just moved on to a new place and time.

But the house itself was a time capsule.

"You grew up here?" Bowman asked. The awe in his tone had me looking over my shoulder at him.

"Yeah."

"God damn, you were lucky." His eyes feasted, gorging themselves on every nook and cranny. He walked into the den, pastry boxes still in hand. He saw my grandmother's patchwork chair and the fireplace.

"What was it like where you grew up?" I asked, taking the pastry boxes from him and walking toward the refrigerator.

"Not like this. *Nothing* like this. I was lucky to get clean sheets." He shook his head. "Wow, Powell. This isn't what I was expecting."

"What were you expecting?" I asked in confusion.

"I don't know. You hear cattle ranch and you start thinking of haciendas and huge windows. This is . . . this is . . ."

"Homey," I finished for him. "It's homey."

"Yeah, and not at all showy." He looked at me. "I was wrong about you."

"Wrong about me? How?"

"The night we met. The clothes you wore. I knew you came from money. So I was expecting . . . not this."

I wasn't sure what to say to that, so I said nothing and began cleaning up the kitchen. Bowman helped, bringing me plates and wiping down the table. But he didn't move the papers that were haphazardly strewn about.

"I'll show you where you're staying," I said. "Oh, our luggage is still in Hadley's car."

"They'll be back with it at some point."

"Right," I said, suddenly realizing we were alone. "Well, let me show you the upstairs."

The second step from the bottom of the staircase squeaked.

"God, you even have a squeaky stair," Bowman said with a chuckle. "This is great."

I couldn't help the smile that blossomed across my face. His enthusiasm for something I'd always taken for granted made my heart happy, though I couldn't say why.

When we got to the second floor, I went to the linen closet and grabbed two sets of sheets. I opened the door to Hadley's bedroom.

I set down the sheets with the tiny rosebud pattern,

deriving joy from the visual of the big, masculine bull rider sleeping on something so dainty and feminine.

Bowman looked around, taking it all in.

"There's the bathroom," I said, pointing to another door. "We share it, so just make sure you knock before you enter."

"Can I see your room?" he asked.

"My room? Why?"

"Curiosity." He shrugged. "I promise I won't throw you down on the bed and ravish you. Unless you want me to."

"Behave," I warned.

He grinned. "So, can I? See it?"

"Sure," I said, my heart beating in trepidation.

We walked through Hadley's room into the bathroom. The counter was devoid of personal products. No make up, no lotion.

She didn't live here. She lived with Declan in our family's guest cabin. And she was expecting a baby. Our lives were so different now.

"Penny for your thoughts," Bowman said as I just stood there, looking in the mirror.

"Just a penny?"

"Twenty-five cents—adjusted for inflation."

My mouth quirked. "They're maudlin. Not worth talking about."

"You're sad. Aren't you?" He cocked his head to the side. "I mean on a deep, deep level."

I turned to him and gently placed my hand on his chest.

His eyes widened in surprise at my voluntary touch. "What are you—"

"Tour's over," I grumbled, shoving him back toward Hadley's room. When he was clear of the doorway, I closed the connecting door and locked it.

He knocked on the door. "Hey, I have to use the bathroom!"

"There's one in the hallway and another downstairs," I called back. "And there are a few trees out back. Take your pick."

I went into my bedroom and made up the bed, wishing I was anywhere but here.

CHAPTER NINE

The Ranch

An hour later, I came out of my bedroom and listened for sounds of movement.

But when I didn't hear anything, I called out, "Bowman?"

Nothing.

I called his name again, but the house was silent.

"Great," I muttered.

Now I was alone in my childhood home with no one to talk to, which meant I had nothing but my own mind to occupy myself.

I went downstairs and into the kitchen. I pulled out mixing bowls and muffin tins, and then I set the temperature on the oven.

An array of aprons hung on the cast iron hooks by the pantry door. Muddy's was well-worn and splattered with tomato sauce, grease, and other ingredients I couldn't decipher.

Hadley had an apron, too, but I didn't reach for hers, or for Muddy's.

Instead, I took the blue and white striped apron from its resting place and held it in my hands. I brought it to my nose, but the scent of my mother was long gone.

Swallowing a bout of tears I'd never let myself shed, I thrust the apron over my head and tied it behind my back.

As I set the timer, the doorbell rang. I opened the front door and my eyes widened at the tall, blond man wearing a cowboy hat. "You."

"Me," Gideon agreed with a rueful smile. He held up a pie. "My mom wanted me to bring this over."

I stepped back and waved him inside.

Gideon came in and I closed the door.

He turned to look at me. Without a word, he touched my cheek. "Flour."

"Baking." I hastily scrubbed my cheek, wishing I'd thought to look in a mirror.

"You look good, Salem," Gideon said as he followed me into the kitchen.

"Do I?"

"You know you do." Gideon laughed as he set the pie down onto the counter. "Wasn't sure anyone was home. Probably should've called to find out, but . . ."

"We're just a hop, skip and a jump over, huh?"

"Something like that." He cocked his head to the side. "I'm surprised you're here."

I raised my brows. "You didn't think I'd come home, even with Dad in the hospital?"

"Nah, you're not that callous, but still. You'd rather be anywhere else, wouldn't you?"

"You know me well," I quipped.

"I did. Once." His smile slipped and the corners of his eyes turned down ever so slightly. "How's he doing?"

I blew out a breath of air, prepared to give a perfunctory answer, when the front door opened and a moment later, Bowman came inside.

He looked at Gideon and his amiable expression shuttered.

"Hey," I greeted.

"Hi," Bowman said, his eyes still on Gideon.

"Bowman, this is Gideon. His family owns Dark Timber Ranch on the other side of the valley," I explained. "Gideon, this is Cas Bowman. He's Hadley's fiancé's best friend."

Bowman held out his hand to Gideon.

Gideon stared at it for a moment and then took it. The two of them shook hands, but it was clear the both of them were attempting to out squeeze the other one.

"I didn't catch what it is you do," Gideon said, refusing to release Bowman's hand.

"I'm a professional bull rider," Bowman replied.

"No kidding," Gideon murmured. "So, you only last eight seconds."

Bowman's smile was feral. "I can last a hell of a lot longer than eight seconds."

"Ooookay," I interrupted, pressing my body to where their hands were clasped, forcing them to drop their grip on one another.

I grabbed Gideon's elbow and tried to drag him toward the front door, but he was six feet tall and he had no intention of moving.

Gideon and Bowman continued to stare each other down.

"Tell your mother thank you for the pie." I peered up at Gideon and batted my lashes. "And tell your siblings hi for me."

He looked down at me and smiled. "You should come over for dinner one night. She'd love to catch up."

"Right, will do." I tugged on his arm again, but this time he let me lead him. He stepped out onto the porch, and I waved at him before closing the door.

The oven timer dinged and I rushed back to the kitchen, but Bowman was already opening the oven door and pulling out the muffin tins with a pair of singed red oven mitts.

He set them on the stove to cool and then closed the oven door.

"What the hell was that?" I demanded. "I thought I'd have to get the water hose and turn it on the both of you."

"What the hell was *that*?" His gray eyes glittered like gunmetal. "I come in and find him eye-fucking you in the kitchen."

"So what?" I snapped. "If he wants to eye-fuck me, he can eye-fuck me."

A muscle in his jaw clenched. "Do not play games with me, Powell."

"I'll play whatever games I want to play with you, *Caspian*. And for the record, I wasn't playing any fucking games."

"You guys have history."

I crossed my arms over my chest but said nothing.

"Don't you?" he pressed.

"Where were you?" I asked instead.

He shook his head. "Answer me."

"No."

"No?"

"No. I don't owe you an explanation."

"So, you're going to go to dinner and *catch up*?"

I grinned, but it was an evil, femme fatale, I've-got-you-clocked, kind of smile. "Jealous?"

"I thought it was fairly obvious. And don't smile at me like that."

"Like what?"

"Like if I gave you a knife, you'd gladly carve out my heart and serve it on a platter."

"Ah, you're afraid of me. I love this," I boasted.

His gaze narrowed. "Are. You. Going. To. Dinner?"

"None. Of. Your. Business."

He stalked toward me and my pulse drummed in the side of my neck. Bowman gripped my upper arms. "You make me crazy."

"I make you feel alive," I countered.

His grip tightened and his head bent toward mine . . .

And then the front door opened.

Bowman dropped his hands like he'd touched hot metal.

"Salem?" Hadley called.

"In here," I croaked out.

Hadley, Muddy, and Declan came into the kitchen. Bowman was still standing close to me, but it no longer looked like he was about to whisk the papers off the table and have his way with me.

Sadly.

Hadley frowned, her gaze pinging from me to Bowman and back to me. "You okay? You're flushed."

"Muffins," I said, pointing to the oven.

Muddy arched a brow and then looked at me. "Do you have my keys?"

I shook my head and gestured to Bowman.

"You've got my keys?" she asked him.

"Yes." Bowman nodded.

"Well, can I have them back, please?" she asked, a slow smile curving her lips.

"Oh, right." Bowman dug into his pocket and fished out her keys. He placed them in her outstretched palm.

Declan looked at the pie. "Did you bake that, too?"

I cleared my throat. "Gideon brought it over."

"Gideon," Hadley repeated, her eyes once again bouncing between me and Bowman.

"Nice boy, Gideon," Muddy murmured. "Always thought he and Salem made a cute couple."

I inwardly groaned.

Yep. Bowman's jaw was back to looking like he could chew granite.

"Well, I'm grabbing a bag, and then I'm heading back to the hospital," Muddy said.

"They're letting you stay in Dad's room?" I asked. "Did you play the donation card?"

"Tried that," Muddy said. "But it didn't work. I'm staying in one of the on-call rooms. It's the best they can do. But I'll be right there in case anything . . . changes."

Muddy turned and went upstairs.

"Let me show you around Elk Ridge," Declan said to Bowman.

"I've already had a look around," Bowman replied.

"Fine. Then let's go have a chat. And then we can bring in the luggage."

"Oh, yay," Bowman drawled. "A chat."

Declan brushed a kiss to Hadley's forehead, and then he and Bowman left. Bowman didn't even look at me.

Hadley went to the cabinet and grabbed a plate. Then she began fishing the warm muffins from the tin and putting them on the plate.

"Let's go," she stated.

"Where?"

"We're going outside and we're having a talk."

"Goody," I said in the same dry tone Bowman had used.

Her gaze sharpened. "We'll be talking about Bowman, too."

I untied the apron and placed it back on the hook. Muddy came down the stairs, an overnight bag in hand.

"That was fast," I said.

"I always have a bag packed and ready to go."

"You have a phone charger?" Hadley asked.

"Yep." Muddy nodded. She quickly hugged Hadley, and then me. "Hold down the fort. I'll call later tonight."

She swept out the door in a flurry of energy. Most women half her age didn't possess it.

"I want to be her when I grow up," I murmured.

"Join the club," Hadley remarked.

We took the muffins to the back porch and Hadley settled into a chair with a deep seat. "In a few months, I'll need help being pulled out of this thing."

It was just another reminder that her life had taken a turn. A turn away from me. I was happy for her, but Hadley was my twin. My best friend.

But even I knew that when you chose someone and built a life with them, that bond was strong, too. Stronger, even. She'd chosen Declan to be her family. She'd been stuck with me.

"I used the last of the huckleberries," I said. "Hope Muddy doesn't mind."

"Not if we go out and pick a few gallons more," Hadley said, taking bite. She moaned. "Dear God, what have you done?"

I sniggered. "Lemon and huckleberry. Made with olive oil instead of butter."

"This just became my new pregnancy craving."

It was afternoon and the sun was high in the sky. But it was the perfect temperature, and the air was clear. Notably absent were the smells of Manhattan. No aroma of urine or hotdogs. No scent of BO while shoved into someone's armpit on the subway.

"You didn't call me back," she said.

I blinked. "I completely forgot."

"Understandable. But we have a lot to talk about." She reached for another muffin. "Let's start with Dad's girlfriend."

"Let's start with how the whole town knows about her and apparently all agreed not to tell me," I snarked.

"Whole town? Hardly the whole town," Hadley said.

"Gracie knew. And she couldn't get away from me fast enough when I asked her about it. Same with Lucy. So don't deny it."

"Fine. We all knew how you'd react. Declan was rooting for you, though. Now he owes me five bucks."

"Five bucks? That was all he bet?"

"He wanted to bet more, but I told him you were my twin and I know you." She quirked a grin, but then it slipped. "I'm sorry I didn't tell you when I found out a few months ago."

When I didn't say anything, she went on, "Now you."

"Now me what?"

"Now you apologize for your reaction."

"I will not," I scoffed. "I was blindsided. And already uneasy about coming home. You know how hard it is for me to be here. I was ambushed, Hadley."

She blanched and her skin drained of color. "Salem—"

"No, listen. I get it. Mount St. Salem, right? I blow up. I have big emotions. And they make people uncomfortable."

"Your emotions don't make people uncomfortable. How you choose to express yourself does."

"You still should've told me," I reiterated.

"When?"

"Any time between you finding out and Dad's accident."

Hadley stared at me, and then her expression softened. "Fair."

"You kept it from me. Deliberately. Admit it."

"I admit it. I'm sorry, Salem. Truly."

And just like that, my anger washed away like a stick in a river.

I nodded in tacit forgiveness.

"She's kind of great," Hadley said. "Jane."

"I don't want to hear about her."

"Okay." She paused. "But she's going to be around. She's going to be here to help Dad recover when he gets out of the hospital. And she's coming to the wedding. So you'd better get used to it."

I appreciated that Hadley spoke with such assurance that Dad would get well and come home. I was the glass-half-empty type. Still, I wouldn't say what I was thinking.

"Now onto other things. What's going on with you and Bowman?" she asked.

"Nothing."

"Liar."

"Nothing," I insisted.

"You two looked like you were in the middle of a fight when we came in."

"Gideon . . . took him by surprise."

"Yeah, that's another thing," Hadley said. "You've been home five seconds and he found out you were here."

"He brought a pie from his mom," I explained. "That's it."

"You remember back in high school when we did *Footloose* and Gideon punched Adam and he went through the set piece?"

"Vaguely."

"Gideon never got over you," she said. "And now that Bowman is in the picture, I'm worried we're going to have another incident."

"Bowman isn't in the picture, so there won't be another incident," I assured her. "Now, I can't guarantee there won't be another *Unsinkable Molly Brown* situation . . ."

"I can't believe they let you do the musical the next year after all the drama you caused."

"Honey, do you really think the musical was the reason they sold out of tickets?" I grinned.

"I'm glad you're home, Salem. This town can use some spice."

CHAPTER TEN

THE RANCH

Hadley looked at her cell phone. "It's past seven in New York. We should call Wyn and Poet and give them an update."

Nodding, I scooched my chair closer to hers. She fiddled with her cell and found Poet's name first.

She held up the phone to our faces as we waited for our best friend to answer.

Poet appeared after two rings. Her glasses were smudged, and her brown hair was in a haphazard, lopsided ponytail.

"Hey," she greeted.

"Hey," Hadley replied. "Are you okay?"

Poet's fairy-esque face morphed into a frown of confusion. "Yeah. Why?"

"You look a little . . ." I trailed off.

"Oh. I was napping."

"Napping? At seven at night?" I pressed.

Poet clamped her mouth shut.

"Let me get Wyn on the line," Hadley announced. "And

then we can talk about the fact that going to bed at seven at night is not a nap—that's depression."

"It's only depression if you make it a habit," she grumbled.

"How many times this week?" I asked.

"I'd rather not say. Besides, we've got more important things to talk about," Poet replied.

A few moments later, our other best friend joined the call. Her blonde hair was down around her shoulders, and the dim lighting of her surroundings sculpted her cheekbones, carving them into a work of art.

"Hey," Wyn greeted.

"Where are you?" I asked.

"The Carrington's Park Avenue apartment," she replied. "They're at some fundraiser, so I'll be spending the night."

"Show me Mildred," Hadley demanded.

The covers rustled, and then a long-haired miniature dachshund appeared, looking completely put out that she'd been awakened from a sound sleep.

"God, she's cute," Hadley said.

"Super cute," I agreed.

"Think she'd get along with Tempest?" Wyn asked.

"My baby goat thinks she's a dog," Hadley said with a laugh. "So yes. I'm pretty sure Mildred would get along with Tempest."

"So, what's going on?" Poet asked, directing the conversation away from adorable animals. "How's your dad?"

"Muddy's staying the night at the hospital," Hadley explained. "She coerced the nurses into letting her sleep in an on-call room that the staff normally uses. So far, there's no real change. I mean, Dad came through surgery and the pressure on his brain has been relieved. But we won't know more for a few days—until they try to wake him up."

"Say the word," Poet said. "And we're on the first flight out of here."

My heart panged. I opened my mouth to tell them to come, but Hadley jumped in first.

"You guys are the best. Really," Hadley said. "But there's no reason for you to be here right now. It's chaos and we're just trying to figure out a way through it."

I looked at her and frowned.

"I think Salem disagrees," Wyn murmured. "Don't you, Salem?"

I blew out a breath of air. "Yeah, I disagree. I want you guys out here. But Hadley's right about it being chaos."

"Well, if anything changes, you say the word and we're on our way," Poet said.

"Even though we'll be there in a few weeks for the wedding . . . these are extenuating circumstances," Wyn said.

"You think the Carringtons can spare you not being with them for a month?" Hadley asked. "Who would raise their child? And tuck him into bed?"

"And change his sheets after a nightmare," I added.

"Yeah, you're right. God forbid they parent their own child." Wyn shook her head. "They're talking about having another one."

"Dear God," I murmured.

"I know, right?" Wyn snorted.

"I wouldn't mind coming out early," Poet said.

"It's getting worse, isn't it?" I asked. "Your job."

"There's no joy anymore," she admitted. "I'm starting to wonder why I ever wanted to work in a traditional publishing house."

"Because bookworm," Wyn said with a rueful smile.

"I'm not cutthroat enough for this environment," she said. "Maybe I'll take a sick day tomorrow and go visit my grandfather in Bay Ridge."

"Oh, can I come? It's my day off tomorrow," Wyn said.

"There's that bakery right by your grandfather's house that makes me salivate just thinking about it."

"Yeah." Poet brightened. "I'd love that."

Another pang went through my heart. They would have one of those perfect New York days. Riding the subway, adventuring to a different neighborhood that might as well be a different country. A whole world of experiences just waiting to happen because it was a city of eight million people.

"Keep us posted on your dad, okay?" Wyn said.

"We will," Hadley replied.

"He's got a girlfriend," I blurted out.

"No way," Wyn said.

I nodded. "Way."

"When did this happen?" Poet asked.

"Ask Hadley, I only just found out about it," I stated.

"Oh no," Wyn murmured.

"Oh yes." Hadley nodded, frowning at me like a teacher disappointed in one of her students. "They've been together for a few months."

"Months?" Poet asked. "And you didn't tell Salem?"

"Thank you," I said, crossing my arms over my chest. "She's on my side."

"I'm on no one's side," Poet protested.

"Of course she wouldn't tell you," Wyn said with a smug look. "How did you find out? Where did you find out? And what did you break?"

Poet giggled.

My cheeks heated. "Hey. I'm not *that* predictable."

"Only in the sense that you probably went nutty," Wyn said. "Didn't she, Hadley?"

"Only a little," Hadley said.

"I was blindsided. It wasn't fair," I said. "And after seeing

Dad, I find out he has a girlfriend—a *hot* girlfriend by the way, who doesn't look that much older than us . . ."

"Shut up," Poet said, her eyes widening.

"Oh yeah." I nodded.

"She's pretty," Wyn said. "And young?"

"Yep." I popped the *p*.

"Well, of course she is," Wyn said with a nod. "Your dad is hot, so two hot people getting together? Makes sense."

"Ew," Hadley and I said together at the same time.

"Ew, ew, ew," I repeated.

"Yeah, I'm with Wyn on this one." Poet nodded. "Your dad is attractive. Not sorry."

"Ugh, you guys . . ." I mumbled.

"What's her name?" Wyn asked.

Hadley sighed. "Jane."

"Nothing fucking plain about her, either," I said, my tone snarky.

"She's a vet, too," Hadley supplied.

"Like your mom was?" Poet asked, her eyes drifting to me. "Oh. I see."

"We gotta go," I announced.

"Right." Wyn nodded. "Too many feelings for Salem."

"Wait, I want to hear what happened after you found out about Jane," Poet said.

"Yeah, I'm curious too," Wyn agreed.

"Later," I said.

Wyn pouted. "Tease."

"Say hi to Declan," Poet added. "And Muddy."

The two of them waved, and then their faces disappeared from the screen. Hadley ended the call and set her cell phone down.

She reached for my hand and gave it a squeeze. "You look downright miserable."

"I'm jealous of them," I admitted. "They get to be there. And I have to be . . . *here*."

"Dad'll be fine. You'll be back in New York in no time."

Hadley shifted her position and her shirt pulled across her gently swelling belly. She wasn't showing too much yet, but by the wedding, she would definitely have a baby bump.

"Yeah. I'll be back in New York before I know it."

And for some reason, that thought depressed me too.

I was setting the dinner table when the front door opened. Declan and Bowman stalked into the kitchen and I pretended Bowman's gaze hadn't locked directly onto me.

"Something smells good," Declan announced.

"Peppercorn steak, mashed potatoes, and green beans." I looked at Bowman. "And pie for dessert."

His jaw ticked, but he said nothing.

"Where have you guys been?" I asked.

"Thought we'd give you and your sister some twin-time. So I took Bowman for a trail ride," Declan said.

"Gorgeous property," Bowman said, his eyes resting on me. "Must've been a nice place to grow up."

"It didn't suck," Hadley said as she came into the dining room, carrying a platter of steaming steaks. She set the platter down as Declan came to her. He cradled her cheeks in his hands and planted a kiss on her lips.

I turned away, wishing it didn't feel so intrusive to watch them.

But then my eyes found Bowman's and something stirred between us.

The spell broke when Declan dropped his hands and stepped back. "Let's eat."

We took our chairs, and without Muddy and Dad, it felt empty. I glanced at the chair that had been Mom's.

Did Jane sit there when she came over for dinner?

It was on the tip of my tongue to ask, but I decided not to start a fight.

"You get settled in okay?" Hadley asked Bowman as she handed him the bowl of mashed potatoes.

"Yeah, fine," Bowman said. "Clean sheets and everything."

"Good. Make yourself at home," Hadley said.

"She means it, too," Declan said. "People say that all the time, but they don't really mean it. But Hadley does."

He took her hand and gave it a squeeze.

"There's something wrong with the bathroom lock, though," Bowman said, glancing between me and Hadley.

"Which door?" Hadley inquired.

"The one in your bedroom leading to the bathroom," Bowman explained.

"Probably just accidentally locked," Hadley said with a shrug. "Salem can take a look at it."

"I'd appreciate that." Bowman smiled and then cut into his steak. "Ah, perfect."

"Not too rare?" Hadley asked.

"Just rare enough," Bowman stated.

"I miss rare steak." Hadley sighed. "I have to eat mine well done for a while."

"Criminal," I said, slicing into my perfect pink steak.

"Seriously." Hadley sighed. "Better get creative with dinner choices or it's going to be a long seven months."

"We can do chicken," Declan said.

Hadley looked at me. "Chicken."

I nodded. "Chicken."

"Tomorrow morning, I'd like to go to the hospital," Hadley announced. "Bring Muddy breakfast."

"How early?" Declan asked. "I've got to be here to meet the crew."

"Crew?" I asked. "What crew?"

"We're starting construction on the house," Declan announced. "We found a family from Sandpoint, actually. Dad's the builder, and the four sons do everything else from engineering to general contracting."

"Oh, right," I murmured. "I'd love to see where you decided to build."

Declan nodded. "We'll ride out there."

Hadley cleared her throat.

"Or take the side-by-side," Declan said. "Pass the beans, please."

Bowman picked up the bowl and handed it to him. But to me he asked, "You don't ride horses?"

"No."

"But you grew up on a ranch."

"Yep." I shoveled a heap of mashed potatoes onto my fork and ate it so I wouldn't have to answer.

"Scared?" Bowman taunted.

My eyes narrowed. I swallowed and replied, "I'm afraid of nothing."

"Then why don't you ride?" he pressed.

"Because I don't *like* it. I love horses. But I don't like being atop them."

"What about motorcycles?" Bowman asked. "Do you like motorcycles?"

"Love them," I stated.

"You've never been on a motorcycle," Hadley interjected.

"I've been on a motorized scooter," I stated. "How different can they be?"

"Very different," Bowman and Declan replied at the same time.

"When were you on a motorized scooter?" Bowman asked in curiosity.

My brow furrowed in thought. "Few years ago. When I was in Paris."

"Paris?" Declan asked.

I nodded and went back to eating.

Hadley sniggered.

"What?" Declan demanded. "What do you know that we don't?"

"You tell them," Hadley said to me.

"We were out one night, the four of us—Wyn, Poet, Hadley, and me. And we met these guys that were having their last night in New York. They were flying back to Paris the next day. Well, it was one of those crazy New York experiences and by the time the sun was coming up, the four of us had an offer to go to Paris with them."

"I think I know where this is going," Declan muttered.

"Hardly," Hadley laughed. "I was in a relationship, Poet was too afraid to go, but Wyn was between nanny gigs, and Salem was jobless. She'd just gotten fired from the coffee shop."

I shook my head. "Dog walking."

"Oh, right. The dog walking stint." Hadley nodded.

"Anyway. Wyn and I went with them. We stayed a week. Lived to tell the tale," I said with a smile. "Saw Paris on the back of a scooter. Ate like a local. And to this day, I still don't speak French."

"Neither does Wyn," Hadley said, causing us both to laugh.

The two men at the table did not look amused.

"You went to a foreign country with strangers?" Declan asked me. "That's dangerous."

I raised my brows. "It was a once in a lifetime experience.

And you used to rope calves for a living. You really want to lecture me on dangerous activities?"

Bowman laughed. "She's got you there."

I looked at him. "No lecture from you?"

"Nope. I'm all about the experiences."

"They didn't even pay for their own plane tickets," Hadley said with a smirk. "Salem has the kind of charisma that makes grown men start wars."

"Stop it," I said with a laugh.

"It's true. And you know it." Hadley shook her head. "That night was unreal."

So was that entire week, but by the way Declan and Bowman were looking at me, I decided not to expound.

"Does your dad know what you did?" Declan asked.

"Yes. I told him after the fact."

And the moment he'd started scolding, I'd put the phone on silent and let him talk until he realized I wasn't listening. And then after he hung up, we didn't speak for six months.

"I'm sure he loved that," Declan replied.

"Lecture, lecture, lecture." I snorted. "But then when I finally got a chance to defend myself, I called him a hypocrite."

"Why did you call him that?" Bowman asked.

I shrugged. "Because he is one."

The table fell silent and suddenly, our previously good-natured conversation turned and the meal-time began to sour.

I was no longer hungry.

"Dinner was good," I mumbled, taking my plate and rising from the table. I set it on the counter, and then fled out the back door, wondering why I was always trying to escape.

CHAPTER ELEVEN

The Ranch

The night sky was clear and stars were everywhere. I picked out my favorite constellations as I lit a fire in the stone circle.

I wondered who would find me. Hadley or Bowman.

The heavy clomp of boots told me Bowman had come first.

He took a seat in the camp chair next to me. He didn't say anything as he craned his neck and peered up at the sky.

The back door opened, and Hadley called out, "I've got a headache, so I'm going to bed."

"And I'm going with her," Declan added. "See you both in the morning."

"Put the food away, yeah?" Hadley asked.

"Sure thing," I called back. "Good night."

"Night," Bowman added.

A moment later, the screen door shut, leaving me and Bowman alone.

"Why's your dad a hypocrite?" he asked finally.

"Been waiting to ask that question, huh?"

"I have several questions I want to ask. I'm just trying to figure out which ones I think you'll answer."

"Where were you? This afternoon, I mean. When Gideon came over," I asked him.

He shifted his legs and stretched them out. "After you locked me out of the bathroom, I went to the barn. And then I walked around the pens for a bit."

"And you had a good ride with Declan?" I asked.

"Yes. Why is your dad a hypocrite?"

"Dog with a bone," I muttered.

"You started it by mentioning it."

I sighed. "I'm a lot like my mother. She had a nomadic spirit, and it was one of the things my dad loved most about her. But as I grew older and began to show a similar inclination—it shocked him. Or angered him. Both, I guess."

"Dads are put on this earth to protect their children," he said quietly. "That's their job."

"He doesn't let me breathe," I blurted out. "I—he—this place. It stifles me. It cages me in and he just doesn't get it. He never did."

"And New York lets you, what? Fly?"

"It lets me be whoever I want to be. No one knows me there. I can be anything, anyone. I don't have to constantly be running from my reputation or preconceived ideas about who I am." I rubbed my head.

Talking about this was like swallowing glass. Brutal, painful, destructive.

"So you ran away?" he asked. "The moment you could leave, you ran."

"I didn't *run*," I denied. "I just wanted a chance to be something else."

"And are you? Did you become everything you wanted to be?"

I snorted. "Still a menace. Still the same old Salem, I guess. I come back here and fall into all my old patterns."

"Old patterns. Like letting your emotions explode uncontrollably? You're telling me you're not that way in New York?"

"It took me a long time to find something I love to do. I've left or gotten fired from every job I've ever had. But the one I've got now . . . I don't want to lose it. So, I'm doing everything I can not to be . . . me."

"What is it you do now?"

"I work at a marketing company. I was just given the title of creative director for a client that wants to expand into an equestrian and western line of clothing." I let out a laugh. "It's funny, actually . . ."

"What is?"

"I said I was trying not to be me so I could keep my job, but that's exactly why Rudolph Lancaster wanted me. I sat in on a meeting with them and told them point blank that their creative direction lacked authenticity. I was me for a moment, and I just blurted it out. And you know what? They liked that."

"People appreciate truth. Now more than ever, I think."

"Yeah." I peered up at the sky again. "It's weird, you know? I wouldn't be able to speak with such authority if I hadn't grown up on a ranch in Idaho. And yet I don't want to be here."

"Why not?"

"What do you mean why not?"

"I mean, why don't you want to be here? Because your dad is in the hospital? Because your mom died here? Because you haven't gotten over her death?"

"*Gotten over*," I screeched. "You've never lost a parent, have you? It's not something you get over. It's something you learn how to manage."

"From where I'm sitting, you haven't learned how to manage it. And no. I haven't lost a parent because I never even knew mine. I was left at a fire station when I was six days old."

His words were a bucket of cold water that doused my anger.

He waited a moment and then continued. "We've all got wounds that slice deep. It's your choice if you cauterize them and move on after you heal or pick at them the rest of your life."

Bowman got up out of the chair and walked away from the fire.

Away from me.

As I sat there alone, his words hung in the spring night, heavy with truth.

○

The longer I sat by the fire, the worse I felt.

Bowman's words haunted me. For several reasons.

He saw beneath the surface of who I was, cut right to the heart of the matter, and called me on my shit.

My father tried to fit me into a box he understood.

Hadley was my biggest cheerleader but being the recovering people-pleaser that she was, she backed off when I blew up.

If I wanted the down and dirty, raw truth, I'd talk to Muddy; which was why I'd been avoiding her phone calls for months.

But at the moment, Muddy had more important things on her mind than watching over the train wreck that I was.

There was only one other person who I trusted to give it to me straight.

I opened my phone and shot out a text.

ME

You awake?

It took a moment, but Wyn finally replied.

WYN

Yeah. I had a feeling you'd need to talk.

With a deep sigh, I pressed the call button and put the phone to my ear.

She answered immediately.

"Let's get right into it," Wyn said. "The parents should be home soon."

"If I tell you something, you can't tell anyone."

"Mystery. Intrigue."

"Wyn, I'm serious. Not even Hadley knows about this . . ." She paused for a moment. "It's serious."

"It's . . . complicated."

"I'm listening."

I rubbed my third eye. "I kind of slept with Bowman."

"Bowman? Declan's best friend? Declan's man of honor? That Bowman?"

"Yeah."

"Jesus, Salem. You've been there less than a day and you already slept with him?"

"Wait, no. Let me rewind," I said. "The night my flight was delayed in Denver, I was staying at a hotel near the airport. So was Bowman and we met in the hotel bar. We didn't exchange names, and I slept with him. I was never supposed to see him again, but guess who sat down next to me on the airplane? Yeah, Bowman. It took about five minutes for us to realize who the other one was."

"That's a wild coincidence."

"Right?"

"So, how was it?" she asked.

"Incredible," I admitted. "Unlike anything I've ever—but that's not why I told you."

"Why did you tell me?"

"Because there's more to it. To him, I mean. You asked how I reacted to finding out about my dad's girlfriend?"

"Yeah."

"Bowman, he—" I shook my head. "I was having a meltdown and he sorta, I don't know, swept me up, threw me over his shoulder and carted me out of the hospital."

"And then you guys had sex in the truck?"

"Will you be serious?" I demanded.

"No. I will not." She snorted. "So, you didn't have sex in the truck and work out all your frustration on him then?"

"No, I didn't," I agreed. "We sort of have this bet . . ."

I then explained the parameters.

"Sounds like a win-win to me," she said. "I mean, if you lose, you win in the end. A night of pure, unadulterated, no-holds-barred, do-whatever-he-wants-to-do-to-you sex? Sign me the fuck up! I'd lose that bet on purpose. Then again, I don't have your competitive nature."

"No." I smiled into the flames. "But here's the thing. He—I think he gets me, Wyn."

"Oh," she said softly.

"Yeah."

"Gets you like, you've told him about your mom and stuff?"

"Not really. But we've had these moments, where things spill out of me. And I don't mean them to, but I don't feel like I have to guard what I say around him."

"You never guard what you feel, but you definitely guard what you say. As a general rule, I mean."

"Yeah. Well, it's easier to be a destructive volcano," I said.

"Look over there and not over here. I get you."

"I know. That's why I called you. So, what do I do?"

"What do you *want* to do?" she asked.

"I'm not sure. Being here makes everything so murky."

"It doesn't have to be that way."

We were silent for a moment, and then I said, "Hadley's happy."

"Yeah."

"*Really* happy."

"And you're not," she stated.

"I'm . . . I don't know what I am. Happy for her, definitely. But sad for myself. I feel like I'm losing her."

"Well, you kind of are. We all are. It's not the four of us anymore."

"No." I swallowed the lump in my throat. "Declan and Hadley are a family now. A unit. And I'm over here, just falling into old dynamics."

"Programming runs deep," she agreed. "But we're also adults in our own right."

"Are we?" I joked. "I don't feel like an adult. I feel out of whack."

"How's that different from any other time?" she teased.

"I lean into the chaos, usually."

"And you also create it."

"Hey!"

"You're such a drama llama. I think it fuels you," she said.

"It's exhausting, isn't it?"

"Truth?"

"And when have I ever wanted that." I sighed. "Yeah, give it to me."

"It's exhausting sometimes, for sure. But it's who you are."

"Why am I chaos and my mom was just—it was different for her. It's hard to explain. I'm so similar to her, but so different. She had the energy, but none of the negativity."

"We are who we are, Salem."

"What if I want to be something else? Someone else?"

"Who do you want to be?"

"Someone reliable. Someone stable."

"So, you want to be Hadley? You know why the four of us work? Because Poet and Hadley are the calm to our storms. You can't be anyone other than who you are. But maybe we can have more awareness about the messes we leave for others to clean up. Maybe as adults, it's time we all start cleaning up our own messes."

"Something to think about," I murmured.

"Is that all?"

"No."

"So, there's more? Do tell."

"Gideon came by today. With a pie from his mom."

"Your high school boyfriend? Well, that's interesting. What was it like seeing him?"

"It was fine. Until Bowman saw us together, and then he got all weird and jealous."

"You're going to use that against him, aren't you?"

"Damn right I will." I laughed, feeling lighter than before I talked to her. "I told you, I'm competitive. And I'm playing to win."

"Hmm."

"What's that mean?"

"It means, I'm not sure you two are playing the same game," she said. Before I could reply, she went on. "Oh, gotta go. The parents are home. Keep me posted."

Wyn hung up and my screen went dark.

Light from my bedroom window suddenly sprung to life.

Frowning, I made sure the fire was out, and then I went upstairs to investigate.

CHAPTER TWELVE

THE RANCH

"What are you doing in here?" I demanded, trying desperately not to enjoy the sight of Bowman in a pair of flannel sleep pants and a T-shirt that strained over his biceps.

"You locked the bathroom door," he reminded me. "I came into your room to unlock it. I was going to leave, but then I saw some pictures on your wall and I got curious."

I crossed my arms over my chest, unsure if I liked him in my space. He invaded it, but also, it felt like he belonged there too.

My head was going to drive me insane.

My body, however, knew instantly that it wanted him. Tousled hair, no doubt minty breath, warm skin.

Fuck. Me.

Bowman walked over to the wall and pointed to a picture of Hadley, me and our parents.

"What's going on here?"

I stepped closer to the photo and couldn't stop the laughter as the memory assaulted me.

"Have you heard of the Hiawatha Trail?"

He shook his head.

"It's a 15-mile bike trail on the Idaho and Montana border. It used to be a railway line, so you ride through old train tunnels and there are these incredible trestles with these awesome views. As you can see from this photo, I loved it. But Hadley didn't."

I was smiling in elation at the camera, while Hadley's face was streaked with tears.

"Why is she crying?" Bowman asked.

"I hate riding horses and Hadley hates riding bikes. Only we didn't discover that until this adventure."

"Oh no," Bowman said with a slight chuckle, his eyes devouring the framed photograph. "How old were you?"

"Ten."

"Let me guess, you were in the front, far ahead and your parents had to call you to stay close."

"Nah. Mom rode with me. Dad rode with Hadley."

I reached out and touched my mother's face.

"You look like her," he said quietly.

"Yeah," I agreed. "Pretty sure that's why my dad can't look me straight on."

He was silent for a moment, and then he said, "I wanted to apologize."

"For entering my room without invitation?" I joked.

"No. For the stuff I said by the fire."

"Why?" I asked, finally looking at him.

We were only a few inches apart. If either of us moved ever so slightly, we could brush our lips against one another.

"Because I spoke to you like I know you. Like I had the right to be so honest. It's how I'd want someone to speak to me, but . . ."

"So, you're not apologizing for *what* you said, just *how* you said it?"

"Something like that."

I shrugged. "It's okay. It probably needed to be said."

"Oh, it definitely needed to be said," he said with a slight smile.

When my eyes slid from his, he reached out and gently grasped my chin and turned my gaze back to his. "But I'm not soft or tender."

I shivered. "I remember."

He released my chin, but then his thumb skimmed along the apple of my cheek. "I don't think you need soft or tender. I think you need someone who can withstand the onslaught."

The night we spent together flashed through my brain. And I knew he was thinking about it to. Desire reflected in his eyes.

"I'm here. Any time you need to work it out. You get me?"

I took a step back, forcing his hand to drop from my skin. I missed the connection immediately.

"And our bet?"

He peered at me for a long moment. "If you come to me and ask, the bet is a draw. Neither one of us would lose. In fact, I think we'd both win."

But if I came to him and asked, I would be losing so much more than a bet. It would be proof that I needed him. Needed him in a way that I'd never needed anyone before.

His eyes searched mine for a moment, and then he inclined his head. "Good night, Powell."

He strode into the bathroom, and then the connecting door to Hadley's room closed.

I got ready for bed, my thoughts a whirling mess. They weren't any clearer when I climbed into bed. I stared into the dark, wondering if I was brave enough to cross the divide.

The time change from New York, along with sunlight at 4:30 a.m. peeking in through the curtain I'd forgotten to close, roused me from bed.

Sleep, when it finally came, had been fitful. When we were younger and lived at home, if I had trouble sleeping, I'd crawl into bed with Hadley and make her tell me stories until I fell asleep.

But she wasn't asleep in the room next to mine.

With a sigh of exhaustion, I flung off the covers and traipsed toward the bathroom. I opened the door and came to a halt.

Bowman was leaning over Hadley's sink, toothbrush stuck in his mouth.

His blond hair was tousled and his shirt was off.

And I finally had a good look at the ink that spanned his chest and arms.

"Sorry. I didn't expect you to be up," I blurted out, rubbing the corner of my eye and stifling a yawn.

"New bed. New place," he explained.

"Right."

He gestured to the other sink. "Plenty of room."

Nodding, I stepped fully into the bathroom and grabbed my toothbrush.

"Why are you awake so early?" he asked.

"Time change. And the sun."

I stuck the toothbrush underneath the running water and then doused the bristles with toothpaste.

"Declan texted me last night and asked me to feed the chickens," Bowman said. "He wants Hadley to sleep in."

"Pregnancy. The get-out-of-ranch-chores card," I quipped.

He smiled, his steely gaze raking down over me. I was

wearing a tight black tank and a pair of faded plaid boxers that hung low on my hips.

"Gideon's?" he asked, jaw clenching. "Or one of the Parisians?"

I grinned around my toothbrush. "I know jealousy is supposed to be a red flag, but I gotta tell you, I'm totally here for it."

He growled and then rinsed his toothbrush. He eyed me again and his brows raised.

Bowman's finger touched the ink peeking out the top of my boxers. Before I could say anything, he lowered the elastic waist and saw the tattoo in all its glory.

"Jean Luc," he read, his eyes darting up to mine.

I batted his hand away. "You saw my ink the other night."

"I did, but I was kind of busy with other things," he drawled. "I didn't have time to ask about it. You have another tattoo, right?"

I mumbled confirmation around the toothbrush in my mouth.

"Show me."

I spit in the sink. "No."

"Guess I'll have to discover it on my own." He glowered. "What?"

"How many men's names do you have on your body?"

"Just the one."

"So not Gideon's?"

"Not Gideon's," I assured him.

He let out a slow, long breath as if he was trying to stop himself from ripping out the sink counter with his bare hands.

"Jean Luc I can deal with. Gideon I cannot."

"Why?" I frowned, rinsing my toothbrush. "Jean Luc's name doesn't bother you?"

"I don't know Jean Luc. I've met Gideon. The idea of his

name inked permanently on your skin . . . it pisses me off to no end."

"I didn't know you cared so much, Caspian." I fluttered my eyelashes at him and then let out another laugh when his jaw clenched.

But my laughter faded when Bowman stalked toward me. He had me backed against the sink counter before I knew what was happening. He caged me in with his strong arms.

"Careful, Powell." His voice was a whisper against my skin as he pressed his thigh against my cleft. "Don't toy with me."

"Who's toying?" I purred, my fingers clasping the counter as I thrust my breasts forward.

My nipples grazed his chest.

One of his hands left the counter to come up and touch a tender spot on my flesh. "I plan on giving you many more hickeys. In places easily covered. Just say the word."

"Word," I taunted.

With another growl, he pushed away and put space between us.

"I'm making coffee," he grumbled and turned.

I watched him walk away, giddy with the thrill of the chase.

Oh, what would I do when he caught me?

Bowman wasn't in the kitchen by the time I made my way downstairs. I poured myself a cup of coffee, splashed cream into it, and then headed to the chicken coop.

He was just closing the gate when I approached.

Without a word, he took my coffee and sipped it.

"That's mine," I said with a laugh.

"Was. Now it's mine." He shrugged.

"I'm running on a few hours of sleep and extreme emotion. You sure you want to do that?" I placed my hands on my hips and stared at him. "It's like waving a flag at an angry bull."

"Me without coffee and I will be an angry bull rider," he quipped.

"You forgot to collect the eggs," I said, picking up the basket that hung on the gate and handed it to him.

"I thought you were coming out here to do that."

I shook my head and turned toward the stump that was about twenty feet away. I walked to it and picked up the hatchet and gripped it in my hand.

"I have something else to do this morning."

His hands immediately went to the fly of his jeans.

I laughed.

"It's about to get messy," I said, raising the hatchet.

"I can handle messy."

We both knew he wasn't talking about chickens.

"You're really going to do this?" he asked.

"Hadley wants chicken for dinner." I shrugged. "And she's never been able to do this kind of thing. But I'm home now, so I can do it for her."

I looked at the other coop—the coop where the hens that were no longer laying were corralled. They were enjoying bugs and feed.

"You might see me differently after you watch me do this," I warned him.

When he didn't reply, I looked at him.

His gaze was intense as he murmured, "Too late."

CHAPTER THIRTEEN

THE RANCH

"You look how I feel," Hadley grumbled as she came into the kitchen and poured herself a cup of coffee.

Declan cleared his throat.

She looked at him over her shoulder. "One cup, Declan. I'm allowed to have one cup."

"You already had a cup," he said.

"No. I had a sip before it sent me running for the bathroom." She glared at him. "You really want to fight me right now?"

"What about a hot chocolate?" he urged. "I'll run to Sweet Teeth and get it for you."

"I don't *want* hot chocolate," she snapped. "I want a cup of coffee with mondo doses of caffeine. And I want it sugary and creamy and delicious."

He sighed but nodded.

"And here I thought I'd take the cake for orneriness," I quipped.

"I'm not ornery. I'm pregnant."

"If it quacks like a duck . . ." I smiled. "Look in the fridge."

She went to the fridge and opened it and squealed in delight. "You didn't."

"I did," I said with a wry smile.

"What?" Declan asked. "What did she do?"

"She slaughtered a chicken," Bowman said as he came down the stairs and into the kitchen. "And then she gutted it and plucked the feathers from it and everything."

"Boy, you can take the girl out of Idaho, but you can't take the Idaho out of the girl." Hadley grinned. "Did you wear your fancy pants and silk blouse to do it?"

"No." My smile deepened. "I wore one of your old shirts."

Hadley laughed. "Well, thanks, I guess."

Declan blinked. "Oh, I get it now."

"Get what?" I asked.

"Last night at dinner. Hadley said chicken. You guys had a complete conversation in one word."

"Yep." Hadley nodded. "Twin thing."

"Spooky," Declan said.

"Is anyone hungry?" I asked. "I can make breakfast."

"I think we should get to the hospital," Hadley said. "I need a to-go cup."

Declan made a noise that sounded like a rumble coming from this throat.

"Our child will not have a third eye because Mommy couldn't live without caffeine," Hadley told him. "And if you know what's good for you, you'll sit quietly by and let me have this one."

Declan sighed. "Yes, dear."

"Ah, and so it begins," Bowman quipped.

"Maybe we should stop by Sweet Teeth anyway," I said. "Pick up some pastries for the nurses that let Muddy stay the night."

"Oh, good idea." Hadley nodded. "You guys want to handle that? We need to be back here before nine. And I want to visit Dad."

"Sure," I said, my eyes sliding to Bowman. "You good with that?"

"Yeah. Which car are we driving?" he asked.

"Take Dad's," Hadley said.

"Keys?" I asked.

"Hook."

"Right." I nodded.

"There they go again," Bowman said.

Hadley's phone buzzed in her pocket and she reached for it.

"Muddy?" I asked.

"Jane." She looked up from her screen to me. "She's going to be at the hospital when we get there. Are you going to behave?"

"Do I have a choice?" I asked, my mood beginning to sour.

"Yes," she said. "It's going to upset me if you're upset, and stress isn't good for the baby. So . . ."

"Oh, playing the baby card, are we?" I teased.

"I tried to play the baby card," Declan remarked. "And you ignored me."

"Hush, you," Hadley quipped to her fiancé.

Declan rose from his seat. "That's my cue."

Bowman looked at me. "I'll wait out front, yeah?"

I nodded.

The two of them left, leaving me alone with my sister. I went to the cabinet and pulled out a thermos.

"Okay, have at me," Hadley said.

"Have at you, what?"

"We only touched on the Jane stuff yesterday. But we didn't actually discuss her in detail because you didn't want to talk about her."

"Now? You want to do this *now?* Right when we're supposed to leave?" I filched her coffee cup and went to the sink. I poured the hot liquid into the thermos, careful not to burn myself.

"Salem," she said quietly.

"Does he love her?" I blurted out.

"Yes."

"Are they—are they going to get married?"

"I don't know." Hadley went to the fridge and pulled out a carton of cream. "Even if they do, it doesn't take away what he had with Mom. Nothing can ever take that away."

"I know," I mumbled.

"He's not trying to replace her, Salem. Don't you want him to find someone? Don't you want him to be happy again?"

"She's closer to our age than his," I pointed out.

"Yeah, she is." She opened the carton and I handed her the cup.

I swallowed. "Does she want kids?"

"I haven't asked her."

"Hadley," I warned.

"What?"

"Stop tip-toeing around it. I walked into a minefield. Now at least give me the courtesy of being honest about it."

"I haven't asked her if she wants kids. But she makes him happy. They make each other happy. Isn't that all we can ask for?"

When I refused to reply, Hadley clenched her jaw. She looked at her phone. "You'd better get going. You don't want to hit Sweet Teeth during the morning rush."

◡

"Damn," I murmured as Bowman passed Sweet Teeth. "There's already a line out the door."

"That's good news. The pastries will be fresh. Probably right out of the oven," he said, sliding the truck into a vacant parking spot on Silver Street.

"You're a glass-is-half-full kind of guy, aren't you?" I teased, reaching for my door.

"What are you doing?"

I frowned. "Getting out of the truck."

"Wait."

He climbed out and shut the door before coming over to my side. Bowman opened the door and held his hand out to me. I took it and hopped down, but my boot missed the step and I wobbled.

Bowman pulled me into the hard wall of his body and slid his hand to my waist to steady me. I peered up at him and I couldn't stop myself from looking at his mouth.

"You good?" he rasped.

I nodded.

Bowman's hand tightened and his head dipped.

"Salem!"

My head whipped around in the direction of the voice and I smiled at the dark-haired, muscular man sauntering toward us.

"Hey!" I greeted, putting my hand on Bowman's chest and gently pushing against it in an attempt to put space between us.

But Bowman wasn't having it, because he yanked me even closer and refused to drop his arm.

"How are you, Wade?" I asked.

Wade's gaze drifted from me to Bowman and back to me. "I'm good. Really good." He held out his hand to Bowman. "Hey, man."

Bowman stared at Wade's hand, and then he looked at me. "Another ex of yours?"

I hid my laugh behind my hand and shook my head.

"No. I dated Hadley," Wade said with a rueful smile, his hand still outstretched.

Bowman's countenance cracked. "Ah." He clasped Wade's hand, but this time it didn't look at all like a macho show of strength.

"Wade's family owns the Copper Mule," I explained, attempting to step away from Bowman again.

Bowman shot me a look that said *I'm not letting you go, so stay put*.

"We've got the best local beer in town," Wade said. "Of course, that might be because we're the *only* bar in town."

"That's true, but also your dad has a gift for brewing."

"You guys should come by sometime this week," Wade invited.

"Yeah, maybe we will," I said, not wanting to promise anything.

"Any news on your dad?" Wade asked.

I shook my head. "We're headed to Sweet Teeth, and then to the hospital."

Nodding, it was clear Wade didn't know what to say. He cleared his throat. "Give Muddy my best, will you?"

"I will."

With a smile and wave, Wade headed toward the Copper Mule.

"This *me Tarzan, you Jane* thing has got to stop," I said.

"Why?" he asked.

"Seriously?" I pushed against his chest, but this time he let me go. "You can't be jealous of every man I talk to."

"Not every man. Just familiar ones."

I rolled my eyes. "How would you feel if I behaved the same way toward you and any woman who flirted with you?"

"Are you kidding? I'd be overjoyed."

"Oh, you would not." I laughed despite myself and began walking toward the Sweet Teeth line.

"Sure, I would. You don't think men like knowing women want them?"

"Never going to happen, bull rider. I don't get jealous."

We stepped in line behind a couple I didn't recognize. I wondered if they were new to Huckleberry Hill, or if they were from Silver Springs, the nearest town over.

Things changed, even in small towns. New faces, new places.

"So that was Hadley's ex?" Bowman fished.

"Yeah. They dated all through high school."

"What happened?"

"What do you mean?"

"I mean why did they break up?"

"Aside from only being eighteen?" I quipped. "Well, I wanted to go to New York the moment we graduated and Hadley wasn't going to let me go alone. She was afraid I'd get myself into trouble."

"And did you? Get yourself into trouble."

"So much trouble." I looked at him and winked. "What about you?"

"You're going to have to be more specific."

I bit my lip. Bowman had sprinkled just enough information about his past that I was curious. But I didn't want to seem too eager to know more.

"When did you join the circuit?" I clarified.

"I was seventeen," he said. "I didn't bother graduating high school. I didn't see the point."

"Ready to see the world, huh?"

"Ready to leave where I was."

"And where was that?" I asked. "Did you and Declan grow up in Bonner's Ferry together?"

He shook his head. "No. I'm from Spearfish, South Dakota."

"No kidding," I murmured. "So how *did* you meet Declan?"

"We were both drinking in the same bar, pissed off at the world. A couple of guys picked a fight with him. Thought two versus one was going to be easy. I decided to lend him a hand and even the score. We've been buds ever since."

I smiled. "For some reason, I find that whole story completely endearing."

"Yeah?" His eyes peered at me. "How endearing?"

"Not *that* endearing."

The line moved inside. Gracie was behind the register, two young women were at the bakery display, and there was another on the espresso bar making coffee drinks.

"You think Hadley will drink a hot chocolate if we bring her one?" Bowman asked.

"Loyal to your friend. I like that."

"To the bitter end," he stated. "To the bitter end."

"We have that in common."

"We do," he agreed.

We were more alike than I realized. On the outside, we clashed. We both liked being in control, we both liked calling the shots. But something told me Bowman and I were cut from the same cloth.

"What does your grandmother drink?"

"Vanilla latte," I said.

Bowman reached into his back pocket and pulled out his wallet.

"He opens doors and he pays," I said with a smile. "Such a gentleman."

"Guess I gave you the wrong impression of me," he said with a laugh.

We stepped up to the register and Gracie smiled in greeting. Her cheeks were flushed pink.

"Hi!" she chirped. "What can I get you guys?"

I listed off an impressive order that had the girls flying behind the counter.

"Taking it to the hospital?" she asked.

I nodded. "Muddy stayed there last night. We want to bring a gift to the nurses for making it happen."

Gracie grabbed a few drink trays and started setting the to-go cups in their holders. "I'm adding a few extras in there. Some new stuff we're trying out."

"Thanks, girl," I said.

Bowman tapped his credit card against the machine. It beeped, and then he slid it back into his wallet. And then he dropped a ten-dollar bill in the cash jar.

"Thank you," Gracie said.

One of the girls handed me the paper bag with the pastry box. I took one drink tray and Bowman took the other.

"Wade invited us to the Copper Mule sometime this week," I said to Gracie. "Think you guys can get a sitter and come out with us?"

"Definitely," she said.

With a chin nod, we left the bakery.

"Is that weird?" I asked Bowman on our way to the truck.

"Is what weird?"

"That I'm planning something so normal while my dad is in the hospital?"

"What are you supposed to do? Sit around and wait for bad news?"

"If I did that, I'd go crazy." I sighed. "Let's get to the hospital. How do you feel about speeding? I don't want the drinks to get cold."

His lips twitched. "You *are* trouble."

"Fine, no speeding. But five over won't kill you."

CHAPTER FOURTEEN

THE HOSPITAL

"He looks better," Hadley said. "I'm convinced of it."

"You're right," I agreed.

Dad's pallor had a bit more pink to it beneath the sprouting of a beard. I reached out and grasped his hand. I couldn't feel his skin because my hand was encased in a glove.

"Hey, old man," I murmured. "I came home. Aren't you going to wake up and yell at me?"

"Starting a fight in the ICU. That's so like you," Hadley said, smiling behind her mask. Her eyes crinkled at the corners. "Oh, I need to get out of here."

She rushed from the room, no doubt to find a nearby trashcan.

"Just you and me," I said to my father as I took a seat next to the bed. "I don't have a long time. The nurse could be back any minute to kick me out."

I found it easier to talk to him today than yesterday. It

was still a shock—seeing a tube in his throat. The monitors beeped with stats I didn't understand.

"So, you've got a girlfriend," I stated. "Muddy's with her in the cafeteria. She said something about resource guarding, but I have no idea what she means by that."

The door to his room opened and a nurse stepped inside. "I'm sorry, Salem. Time's up."

Nodding, I squeezed his hand one last time before letting go.

It was pure imagination that he squeezed it back, but I held onto the feeling anyway.

Hadley wasn't in the waiting room when I returned, but Muddy was and she was talking to Declan and Bowman.

Declan nodded and Bowman was listening intently.

"Hey, sugar," Muddy greeted as I came toward her. She wrapped her arm around my waist and pulled me into a side hug. Then she took a drink of her vanilla latte we'd brought her. "You okay?"

I nodded. "Where's Jane?"

"Hiding from you," Muddy stated.

Bowman rubbed his mouth but couldn't stop the smile from appearing.

I decided to ignore her statement. "What are you guys talking about?"

"Ridge stuff. Nothing that would interest you."

It was another reminder that I'd purposefully chosen to separate myself and I tried not to feel the hurt, but it permeated every bit of my chest.

"Hadley wants to stay here for a bit," Declan said. "But I've got to get back."

"Salem will go with you," Muddy said. "Hadley'll keep me company."

"I can stay," I said, my voice weak.

"And drive us all insane." She released me and then

cradled my cheek. "Too much energy in there. Go. With my blessing."

"If you're sure," I murmured.

"Positive," Muddy said.

Declan reached into his pocket and handed Muddy his keys. "In case Hadley wants to leave separately from you. Are you staying the night again?"

"I'm not leaving this place until my son does," Muddy said, a glint of determination in her hazel eyes. "Cafeteria food might send me over the edge, though. It's vile."

"We should've brought the food from Mr. Bixby," I said. "We'll bring some when we come back."

"Don't make an extra trip, but yeah, I'd love some of his mac and cheese. And after the pastries, I'm sure the nurses won't mind sharing space in the fridge in the nurses' lounge."

Hadley returned to the waiting room and joined us, looking a bit wan.

"Can we bring you anything else?" Bowman asked. "Anything to make you more comfortable?"

Muddy smiled at him. "You're a sweet boy. I need more yarn from my crochet basket."

"Consider it done, ma'am," Bowman said.

"Muddy," she said.

"Excuse me?" Bowman asked.

"Call me Muddy, everyone else does." She patted his cheek, and then linked her arm with Hadley and the two of them moved toward the corner of the room.

Bowman looked shell-shocked at my grandmother's declaration, but that was Muddy.

Declan went to Hadley and bent down to kiss her head. He said something to her and she nodded.

"Ready?" Declan asked as he returned to me and Bowman.

"Yeah, let's go," I said.

Before I run into Jane and make another scene.

The shock of the news of my father's girlfriend was slowly fading, but I still wasn't happy about it. And even more so, I had no desire to get to know her.

She would be around for his recovery, but would I be? After Hadley's wedding, wasn't I going back to New York?

The idea of staying hurt me, in more ways than one. But my family needed me. Especially when Dad got out of the hospital.

"Fuck," I muttered.

"You okay?" Bowman asked, glancing at me as we got into the elevator.

"Fine," I lied.

His gaze pinned me with a stare, as if he knew I was lying.

And that was something else that was bothering me.

It seemed Bowman and I were constantly being thrown together. And I wasn't sure how to feel about that either.

I sat in the back of the truck and gave Bowman the front since he had longer legs. Declan and Bowman carried on a conversation while I stared out the window, lost in my own thoughts. My phone buzzed with a text from my boss.

JACK

Just checking in and seeing how you're doing.

ME

thanks. I'm doing okay. I'll call later.

"Salem?" Declan asked.

"Hmm?"

"I've got to meet the crew out at the build site. You want to go with me?"

"Sure," I said.

When we got back to the Ridge, Declan parked the truck in front of the house and we climbed out.

"You good for a bit?" Declan asked Bowman.

"He's not coming with us?" I asked in surprise.

"He saw the site yesterday," Declan explained. "On our ride."

"Oh. Right." I nodded.

"Check on Tempest for me, yeah?" Declan asked his friend.

"She in the barn?" Bowman asked.

"Probably."

Bowman looked at me for a second, and then he trekked in the direction of the barn and my sister's pet goat.

"It was a mistake, letting a goat sleep in your bed," I said with a laugh.

"Don't I know it." Declan grinned as we headed toward the side-by-side. "But I can't say no to Hadley."

"I love that for her," I said. "I like how you treat her."

"Thanks," he said.

We got into the vehicle. He started the engine and it roared to life. It was loud and rendered conversation difficult.

It was a five-minute drive to the building site, and there was already a double wide and several RVs parked in an area nearby.

"When did those get here?" I asked in surprise.

"A few days before you came," he explained. "It's a family crew that will oversee everything, and crews of workers will rotate in and out."

"You mean they're going to live here for the next few months while they build?" I asked.

"Yeah."

"Wow," I said. I looked around. "I don't see any people."

"We're early," he said.

He cut the side-by-side engine and my ears hummed from the noise.

"I wanted to talk to you. Out here and away from everyone else," he said.

"What about?" I asked, turning to face him.

His expression was stoic. "Hadley is the most important thing to me. You know that, right?"

"I do."

"Then, what I'm about to say—it's coming from that place, okay?"

I frowned and nodded.

"I want her to be happy. And in order for her to be happy, she has to have an easy pregnancy and a healthy baby. I won't have her needlessly worried or stressed in any way." He pinned me with a stare. "It's hard enough with Connor in the hospital. Do you get what I'm saying, Salem?"

"Me," I said flatly. "You mean *I* shouldn't worry her, or stress her out."

"You're her twin. She loves you so much. But I'm asking—no, I'm fucking *begging* you—please don't be something else she has to worry about."

I swallowed and nodded.

"One more thing," he said.

"What?" I croaked.

"Stay away from Bowman."

CHAPTER FIFTEEN

THE RANCH

"Stay away from Bowman," I repeated.

He sighed and raked a hand through his hair. "Look, he's my best friend, my best man, and basically my brother. But he's not . . . he's had a hard go of it. A hard life, I mean."

"You mean the foster kid thing and the abandoned at birth thing?" I queried.

Declan paused. "He told you?"

I nodded.

"I wasn't expecting that." He leaned back in his seat and went on, "He's not a family man. I just don't want you to have any illusions about him."

"No illusions," I assured him. "But this talk is kind of unnecessary, don't you think? He's here to get to know Hadley. I'm here to—for my dad. There will be a wedding. And then I'll go back to New York and he'll go back to the circuit."

He looked at me for a long moment, like he was

pondering saying something else, but then a caravan of trucks drove up behind us. One by one they parked in front of the double wide and climbed out. After a while, an older woman stepped out of one of the vehicles.

"Who's that?" I asked in confusion.

"Stella," Declan said. "Come on, let me introduce you to the Monroes."

We got out of the side-by-side and headed toward the group of people standing outside the double wide.

"Declan!" the older man greeted, holding out his hand. His smile warmed his weathered face.

"Hey, John." Declan clasped his hand and then dropped it so he could hug the woman. "Good to see you, Stella." He stepped back and gestured to me. "Everyone, I'd like you to meet Salem, Hadley's twin."

"Nice to meet you," John said. "Let me introduce the family."

"Maybe we should make name tags," one of the younger men said, winking at me.

"That's Harlan," John said. "And it's best if you ignore everything he says."

I laughed.

"Grady, Killian, and Chase." John pointed to the other three. "And my wife, Stella. She keeps us all in line."

"You're heathens," Stella said with a smile, and then looked at me. "It's a full-time job."

"Looks like it," I said, enjoying their easy familiarity. "Declan says you're from Sandpoint?"

John nodded. "We're not that far from home, but—" He gestured to the RVs. "This will make our extended stay a lot more comfortable and cut down on unnecessary travel time."

"How long are *you* staying?" Harlan asked, running a hand through his dark hair.

"Just for the wedding," I said, looking at Declan. "And then I'll go back to New York."

"New York?" Grady repeated as he scratched his scruffy jaw.

"Yeah." I clamped my mouth shut, not wanting to have to tell a group of strangers about my father in the hospital.

John took the social cue well. He cleared his throat and addressed Declan, "I'd like to talk to you about some things."

Declan nodded. "Of course. Salem? You mind driving back alone? Someone'll give me a ride when I'm finished."

I let out a breath of relief. "Sure thing. It was nice meeting you all."

"I hope we see more of you," Harlan voiced a bit too enthusiastically.

Stella smacked his arm. "Professionalism, Harlan."

"What's your role in the family business?" I asked Harlan.

He grinned. "I'm the one in charge of blowing things up."

"In more ways than one, I'll bet."

With a chuckle, I walked back to the side-by-side and climbed in. I'd learned to drive a side-by-side long before a truck, so I was very familiar with it.

I was thankful for the noise blasting from the vehicle, but my conversation with Declan was at the forefront of my mind. I had to keep my shit together—for Hadley's sake. How I felt about Jane, among other things, didn't matter.

Only Hadley's well-being mattered.

I was instantly ashamed. I had to do better. I had to *be* better.

Bowman was nowhere to be found when I got back to the house and parked. I was just about to go inside and call my boss when I heard, "Son of a bitch!"

I turned and looked for the source of the yell but couldn't see anyone. I walked around the side of the house and saw two human legs sticking out from underneath the back porch and a pair of boots digging into the ground.

"Bowman?" I asked.

A heavy thunk followed by another curse had me wincing.

"This goat is going to be the death of me!"

"Tempest?" I asked.

"The damn idiot thinks she's a dog. She saw something scurry under the porch, and she went in after it. And then I went in after her. Only she's refusing to come out and I can't go any farther."

"Did you think of trying to lure her out with a carrot or something?" I asked, trying not to laugh at the bull rider attempting to corral a baby goat.

"Fuck!" he roared.

It took a moment, but then I smelled it; the scent of rotten eggs, sulfur and decaying onions. It instantly made my eyes water and my stomach revolt.

Tempest bleated, clearly in protest.

Bowman backed out from under the porch and the stench became instantly worse.

I pinched my nose and ran away.

"Powell!" Bowman shouted.

"You're on your own!" I yelled with a laugh.

Even as I was saying it, I pulled out my cell phone and called Muddy.

"Hey, sugar."

"Hi," I said, trying to stifle a giggle and failing.

"What's going on?"

"I need your skunk spray remedy."

Muddy laughed. "You?"

"Nope. Bowman. And Tempest."

"I'll text it to you," she said. "So we've got a loitering skunk?"

"Seems that way, yeah," I said.

"Hey!" Bowman barked, causing me to twirl, phone still to my ear.

"I'm getting a skunk stank removal recipe," I said to him. "You might as well go back under the porch and get Tempest. She'll need a dunking, too."

Bowman muttered another curse, but he headed back to the porch.

"Talk to Josiah," Muddy said. "He'll set a trap for the skunk. And send pictures."

"Of the skunk?"

"No. Of Bowman having a meltdown."

"Judging by his reaction, I'm thinking this is his first skunk spraying."

Muddy sniggered. "Keep me posted, sugar. Thanks for the laugh."

I hung up with Muddy and a few moments later my cell buzzed, no doubt with her recipe instructions.

Bowman crawled out from under the porch, Tempest bleating against his chest.

"What do I do now?" he demanded.

"You wait right there, don't move, don't let go of that goat. I'm going to go make Muddy's skunk spray destroyer recipe, and then I'll be back."

"You might want to change your clothes," he stated.

"Why would I need to change *my* clothes?" I demanded.

"You're washing the goat."

"Like hell I am."

"Either you wash her or I turn her into goat kababs."

"Goat curry would be better," I joked.

He looked down and glared at the baby goat who peered up at him and then licked his cheek.

"Son of a bitch," Bowman muttered again.

"Nothing cuter than a man holding a baby goat," I said as I skipped my way to the house.

"What about a man holding a baby?" he tossed out.

Declan's words came roaring back about Bowman not being a family man.

I didn't reply, and instead just kept on walking.

"My, my, my, how things change," I said, raising the bottle of beer to my lips.

Bowman ran a hand down Tempest's back—Tempest who was currently curled up in a towel on Bowman's lap.

"Not a word," Bowman said.

"You're a goat convert," I quipped, completely ignoring him. "Something happened when you bathed the skunk stink from her fur. You bonded. You're connected. You're going to goat-nap her from Hadley, thus inciting a fight between you and Declan. Fists will fly over a baby dwarf pygmy goat."

"I'll pay you to stop talking." He grabbed his bottle of beer that rested on the stump next to his camp chair.

We were outside, enjoying the afternoon sun and a beer, but the scent of skunk still hung in the air. It would take days to clear out.

The sound of a truck rumbled up the driveway on the other side of the house, but the noise didn't disturb Tempest who was perfectly content in Bowman's beefy arms.

I want him to hold me with those arms.

A groan escaped my lips.

"You okay?" Bowman asked.

"Peachy," I grumbled.

A truck door slammed shut.

"Declan," Bowman said.

I nodded.

A few minutes later, the back door of the house opened and Declan came outside.

"What's going on?" he asked. "And what the fuck is that God awful smell?"

"I guess you haven't talked to your fiancé," I said with a laugh. I got up from my seat and headed to the porch. "Bowman can give you a rundown."

"Where are you going?" Declan asked.

"I need to make a call," I said.

"I'm gonna head back to the hospital," he said.

"Don't forget the yarn," I reminded him. "And some of the food in the fridge."

"Thanks for the reminder."

I headed up the stairs to my bedroom and closed the door. And then I pulled out my phone to call my boss.

"Salem," he greeted. "How are you?"

"I'm hanging in there," I said honestly. "Dad made it through surgery, but we won't know more for a few days. If all goes well, they'll try to wake him up."

"What do you need?" he asked.

Jack was ten years older than my father, with salt and pepper hair, and he'd taken me under his wing when I'd started working at Beckett & Bastion.

We had an honest relationship that most people didn't have with their bosses. I liked and respected him, so I had no qualms about being forthcoming.

"I don't know how this is going to go," I admitted. "I mean, when they wake him up. There might be . . . mental deficiencies."

It was the first time I'd said it out loud. Neither Muddy nor Hadley had even talked about it. Maybe they couldn't, but we had to be realistic. There was a chance he wouldn't even wake up, but that was too much, even for me to consider.

"There might be," Jack said slowly. "But he's healthy. There's a good chance that he wakes up without any issues."

I sighed. "Either way, I don't—I can't say what the future is going to look like."

"You don't have to know. Take as much time as you need, Salem."

"Thanks. You don't know what that means. But . . . Rudolph Lancaster. They're not going to wait forever. Not after their botched marketing campaign. They're chomping at the bit and I don't think they're going to want to wait on me."

Things moved fast in New York. If you didn't jump on opportunity, there were ten people behind you ready to take your spot, and all ten of them were fighting to be the best in their field.

That had been me. Ready to prove myself. Determined to succeed and clawing my way to the top.

But now . . . none of it seemed to matter. Not with Dad in the hospital.

"I'll talk to them," Jack offered.

"I'd appreciate that. I don't have the bandwidth to be diplomatic or placate anyone right now."

"Understandable, considering the situation." He paused. "I was going to tell them you had a family emergency and you're unavailable for the time being. Is that okay?"

"Tell them the whole story," I said. "They seem to appreciate authenticity."

"It's your family business. You sure you want that out there?"

I shrugged even though he couldn't see me. "It is what it is, Jack. I'd rather they know everything, and then they can decide what to do."

"Your call. I'll be in touch."

"Thanks, Jack."

I hung up the phone, and then sat down on the bed, staring at my dark screen.

The life I'd been building for myself felt like it was slipping away, and I was doing nothing to hold onto it.

CHAPTER SIXTEEN

The Hospital

"Salem," Muddy whispered.

I snapped my head up and my eyes flipped open. The hospital waiting room took a moment to come into focus.

Hadley was asleep on my shoulder, and I gently nudged her.

"What's going on?" She rubbed her mouth.

"He's awake." Muddy smiled, her hazel eyes shiny with unshed tears.

"He's awake?" Hadley repeated.

Muddy nodded.

Hadley jumped up. "I want to see him."

I put my hand to my neck and rubbed it. Falling asleep sitting up in a hospital waiting room didn't lend itself to comfort.

"He's groggy," Muddy explained. "And he keeps falling asleep. The nurse said that's the sedation wearing off."

We arrived at Dad's room and Muddy pushed the door open. I stilled.

Jane was sitting by his bedside, holding his hand.

Hadley looked at me in tacit warning.

It had been four days since Declan had spoken plainly to me. And I was determined not to be the cause of any stress.

Dad was currently awake and a smile bloomed across his face.

Hadley immediately burst into tears, went to Dad's bedside, and crouched down. She grasped his hand and brought it to her lips.

"I'm okay," Dad rasped.

She blubbered but couldn't form words.

Jane let go of my father's other hand and stood. She leaned over and pressed a gentle kiss to his forehead and then whispered something into his ear. She stood up straight and walked around the bed. Jane looked at me but didn't say anything. When she got to Muddy, she reached out and gave her hand a squeeze before leaving the room.

Dad's gaze met mine. "Salem."

"Well, aren't you a dramatic one," I said, forcing the emotion down my throat. "You'll do anything to get me to come home."

My dad cracked a grin and he made a motion to lift his arm, but it was too much of a struggle. He curled his finger and I immediately went to the side Jane had vacated and hooked my finger with his.

"Muddy hasn't left the hospital in five days," I said to him, shooting my grandmother a look. I then turned my attention back to my dad. "I've had to cook meals. Unforgivable sin. You're looking good with scruff, Dad."

Dad's eyes fluttered, and then they closed.

"I'm glad you warned us this would happen," Hadley remarked. "It's kind of unnerving."

We stayed for another hour. Dad kept waking up briefly and then falling asleep a few minutes later. He didn't contribute much to the conversation, but his eyes tracked whoever spoke and his grip grew firmer as time passed.

"Go home," Dad said to Muddy. "Sleep in your own bed."

She jutted her chin, clearly ready to fight.

Dad's gaze slid to mine, pleading.

"He's right," I said to her. "You should get a good night's sleep. We can come back early tomorrow morning."

"They're going to be doing neurological tests every few hours," Hadley said. "No use in both of you not sleeping."

I took a step closer to Muddy and lowered my voice. "You won't help Dad get well if you burn the candle at both ends."

That got through to her and she nodded. "All right. But I'm coming back early tomorrow morning." She went to Dad's bedside and brushed her lips across his forehead.

Hadley kissed his cheek and then stepped back.

Dad looked at me, and even though he was still groggy from the sedative, I could read the words in his eyes.

I nodded and leaned over to whisper, "I'll hold down the fort. I promise."

Hadley's phone buzzed as we left Dad's room. "Declan."

She put the phone to her ear and talked to her fiancé. Muddy linked her arm through mine and said, "We need to have a talk."

"We do?" I asked. "Oh joy."

"Smart ass," she said lightly. "What I meant was, I need to speak to you, Hadley and Declan."

"When? After dinner?"

She shook her head. "Tomorrow after we see your father. Tonight, you should go out."

"Go out?" I asked in confusion.

"Out." She nodded. "The four of you need to go out and celebrate."

"Isn't it too soon to celebrate?" I asked, my brow furrowing.

Muddy turned me to face her and then cradled my cheeks in her hands. Hazel eyes that mirrored my own peered at me. "It's never too early to celebrate. Life is filled with tragedy, Salem. So celebrate when you can and to hell with the rest."

CHAPTER SEVENTEEN

The Ranch

The house was quiet when we got home. Declan and Bowman weren't around. I'd barely seen Bowman the last several days; just at breakfast and dinner. During the day, he was with Declan, lending a hand wherever he was needed. I spent time around the house, doing laundry and baking. I made sure there were clean towels in the bathroom and the sheets were washed.

I remembered Bowman's reaction when he'd first come into the house. It reminded me of his upbringing and the fact that clean sheets hadn't always been a given. Now they were.

At night, my sleep was restless, knowing he was only steps away.

Still, I couldn't bring myself to cross the divide.

"I'm going for a ride," Muddy said.

"Now?" I asked.

"I need it," she said. "It'll clear out the cobwebs."

"I'll ride with you," Hadley said.

"You sure that's a good idea?" Muddy asked. "Declan will give you hell."

"My OB said it was fine since I'm an experienced rider. Goldie would never throw me," Hadley said. "And I'll handle Declan."

"You want to go with us?" Muddy asked me.

I shook my head.

Muddy hugged me. "Thought so, but I wanted to extend the invitation anyway."

The two of them went to the stables and I was left in solitude with my thoughts. I couldn't decide if I wanted the leftover poutine in the fridge or a shower.

Shower.

I ran up the stairs into the shared bathroom between Hadley's room and my own. I turned on the shower and then stripped out of my clothes.

The water was scalding, and it turned my skin pink. I closed my eyes and let the heat envelop me. My breaths became short, rapid, and a lump of pain in my chest swelled. It shot up my throat and exploded from my mouth in a gruesome, horrifying noise I didn't recognize.

It was violent and loud; an entity threatening to choke me.

It poured from my eyes.

It leapt from my heart.

Anguish, hurt, grief—*years of it*—came out now.

And there was nothing I could do to stop it.

It wasn't quiet.

It wasn't convenient.

But my body had had enough, holding onto pain and remorse that no longer served to protect me, but had instead been slowly killing me. And yet I'd been too obstinate to notice.

I was lost in a sea of memories; assaulted by them. Like

bullets ripping through my flesh and exploding to cause even more pain inside me.

My hand clawed at my chest as if I could rip my heart from my skin and toss it away so it could no longer hurt me.

The door to the bathroom opened, but I paid it no mind, too lost in my own misery.

"Salem?"

A noise escaped my throat, like a dying animal writhing in pain, determined to live despite its life draining away.

The shower curtain pulled back and revealed Bowman. He tossed his cowboy hat onto the counter, and then without a moment's hesitation, he climbed into the shower with me even though he was still fully clothed.

He closed the curtain and then pulled me into his arms. My wet, naked, unadorned body pressed against the fabric of his shirt and jeans.

I balled my fists and began to beat against him, my red hair lashing my cheeks and neck as I made the most unhinged noises.

His arms tightened around me, but he didn't shy away. He let me lose myself against him, like a flash flood battering its way through rocks.

Eventually, my anguish turned to whimpers.

He placed his hand on my head and pressed me deeper into the wall of his chest.

Awareness returned and my mind began to clear.

Embarrassment was the first emotion I registered. Horror that Bowman had witnessed my meltdown had me pushing against him in an attempt to flee.

He let me go.

But now I no longer had the protection of his body against mine. I hastily covered my breasts by crossing my arms.

"Are you okay?" he asked, his steely gray eyes searching mine.

I nodded.

He didn't say anything else; he just kept looking at me. And then he pulled back the shower curtain and got out. A moment later, the door to the bathroom opened and closed again behind him.

I slid down into the tub and didn't move for a long time.

◡

"We talked about this," Declan said.

"No, *you* talked, and I listened," Hadley fired back.

Grimacing, I paused my descent on the staircase, but I forgot the second stair from the bottom squeaked. And apparently, it was loud enough to make Hadley and Declan stop arguing.

"Salem?" Hadley called.

I sighed and then came down the stairs and into the den. "Sorry, I didn't mean to interrupt."

"Please interrupt," Hadley said.

Declan raked a hand through his hair and then looked at me. "Maybe you can talk to her. She's not hearing me."

He stalked from the den and Hadley called after him, "I love you!"

"I love you too!"

The door shut, leaving me alone with my twin.

She sighed.

"Was that about you riding horses?" I asked.

"No, actually, it wasn't." She bit her lip.

"What was it about then?"

"Can we talk while we make dinner?" she asked. "I promised Muddy we'd take care of it."

"Where *is* Muddy?"

"With Lucy, drinking in the back of General Merc, if I had to guess."

"She earned it," I said. "Have you seen Bowman?"

She shook her head. "Why?"

"Just curious," I lied. "I don't want to get interrupted while we're talking."

More like I didn't want to face him after he'd seen me stripped down to my marrow.

"You snap the peas," she said. "I'll take care of the trout. Thankfully, Wade already gutted them for me."

"Your ex-boyfriend is bringing you fish?" I asked. "Is that like an Idaho mating ritual or something?"

"Oh, please. He and his dad limit out every time they go. They went fishing today and did it again, so they were giving them away this time. And you haven't met Wade's girlfriend yet, have you?" She opened the butcher paper and revealed several trout, still with their heads on.

"No."

"She's nice. They seem happy."

"Well, good." I got a colander and the peas and went to the sink. "Start talking."

"I asked Declan to push back the wedding."

"What? Seriously? But Dad's awake. And if all goes well, he'll be a couple weeks into recovery by the time the wedding happens."

"Yeah. But he won't be able to walk me down the aisle. Or do the father-daughter dance," she said, looking at me. "You think I'm stupid."

"Did I say anything?"

"You didn't have to."

"Hey." I turned off the faucet and dried my hands on a dish towel. "It's not wrong to want to have the wedding of your dreams, but . . ."

"But what?"

I gestured to her belly. "You kind of put the cart before the horse anyway. Did you think your wedding was going to be completely traditional?"

Hadley grinned. "No. I guess not."

"Hads?"

"Yeah?"

"You don't know how long Dad's recovery is going to take. You want to wait six months? A year? For what? He's going to be at the wedding. That's the miracle. That's the blessing."

Her eyes filled with tears.

"Damn it," I muttered, dragging my sister into an embrace. "I didn't mean to make you cry."

"Well, you did, you idiot."

I laughed but then sobered and pulled back so I could look at her. "Mom isn't here to see you in your dress or watch you eat cake and dance with your husband. But Dad is. There's no promise of tomorrow, and he wouldn't want you to postpone."

She sniffed. "Of course he wouldn't."

I patted her arm. "Go tell Declan I talked sense into you."

"He would've done it, you know? Postponed it because I asked."

"I know." I nodded. "He's a good man."

"The best," she agreed. "I hope you find one too."

I picked up a trout and held it close to my face and made a kissing noise. "I found a perfect one right here."

CHAPTER EIGHTEEN

The Ranch

After a quiet dinner, Hadley and Declan went to our family's guest cabin that was within walking distance of the main house. They currently lived there while their house was being built.

Muddy had texted that she wouldn't be home until late because she was drinking bourbon with Lucy. The woman had been living in the hospital the past many days and clearly needed to blow off steam.

I sat in the middle of my bed with a wooden jewelry box in front of me. The paint was peeling and the hinges needed to be oiled so they didn't squeak, but when I opened the lid, a smile bloomed across my face.

The jewelry box housed my most sentimental trinkets that I couldn't bear to part with. I refused to bring them to New York out of fear that I'd lose or misplace them.

There was a knock on my door.

"Come in," I called.

Bowman appeared in the doorway. He was still in a pair of jeans and a button-down shirt, but his cowboy hat was nowhere to be found, and his blond hair was effortlessly mussed.

"Hey," he said.

"Hey." I eyed him warily, unsure of his mood. During dinner, he'd been relatively quiet, but his eyes had sought mine often. "You gonna stand there holding up the doorway or come all the way in?"

He stepped across the threshold and gestured to the jewelry box I hadn't closed. "What's that?"

"Just some things of mine," I evaded.

"What kind of things?"

"Bowman."

"Powell."

"Ah, so I'm back to being Powell, hmm?" I shut the lid and set the jewelry box on my nightstand.

He paused. "I wasn't sure you remembered."

Remembered that he'd called me Salem or that his voice had grounded me in a way I couldn't have anticipated.

"I remember," I murmured, my eyes meeting his. I patted my bed. "Sit. I'm getting a crick in my neck from looking up at you."

He walked over to the bed and sat at the end of it.

"Are you okay?" he asked.

"I'm fine. It was . . . it's been a lot. Being here."

He rubbed his scruffy jaw. "Yeah. I can imagine."

"And Dad waking up, it just . . ."

Opened something up inside me. Split me right down the middle and all of the anguish I'd been carting around poured out of me.

"That wasn't just about your dad," he said. "Was it?"

I swallowed, a lump forming in my throat. I shook my head.

"Did you tell Hadley?"

"Tell Hadley I had an epic meltdown and that you climbed into the shower while I was naked in order to comfort me?"

His eyes burned with intensity. "Yes. That."

"No."

"No? Why not?" he demanded. "Oh. I get it. You don't have to mention me at all if you don't tell her."

"It's not that," I said quickly. "It's Declan."

"What about him?"

"It's about what he said." I chewed on my lip.

Bowman reached out and pulled at my lip to stop me from biting it. "What did he say?"

My skin zinged from his touch.

He dropped his hand and waited for my reply.

"He asked that I not stress out Hadley. That she's got enough to worry about. And with the baby . . ."

"I see," he said. "You call your friends? Have you told them?"

"About the meltdown? No. About my dad waking up? Yes. Hadley and I did a video chat with them when we were making dinner."

We continued to stare at one another, like both of us wanted to say more but neither one of us wanted to cross the chasm.

"Have I thanked you?" I blurted out. "For the—ah—comforting?"

He flashed a smile. "No."

"Thank you, Bowman." My tone was sincere.

"You're welcome, Powell."

And just like that, the walls of my fortress were once again erected between us.

The front door opened. "Salem?" Muddy called out.

"I'm here!" I called back.

Bowman rose from my bed and quietly moved toward the bathroom.

I got up and went downstairs. Muddy's head was in the fridge when I made it into the kitchen.

"What did you all have for dinner?" she asked.

"That plate is for you," I said with a smile. "Trout, snap peas, and rice."

She wrinkled her nose. "Fish?"

"Hadley's choice. Variety is the spice of life, you know? Not all of us want game meat and beef."

We looked at each other, and then both cracked up. She pulled the plate out of the fridge and took it to the microwave.

"How many drinks did you have with Lucy?"

"Just one," she said. "I nursed it while I told her about Connor. By tomorrow morning, the whole town will know everything, so I don't have to keep rehashing it."

"Lucy is Huckleberry Hill's town crier."

"Thank God, too." Muddy put the plate in the microwave and placed the silicone cover over it before pressing the start button. "Sit with me?"

I nodded. "Another drink?"

"Yes." She nodded. "Now that I'm home, I have no place to go but upstairs. Is Bowman around?"

"His room, I believe," I said.

The microwave beeped. She pulled out her plate.

"Kitchen table?" I asked. "I'll get you another drink."

"Den," she clarified. "And we'll close the sliding doors."

"Uh oh. You mean business."

We went into the den and I closed the doors while she got settled in her patchwork chair and set her plate on her lap.

"We haven't gotten much of a chance to talk since you've been home," she said.

"No," I agreed. "We haven't. But there have been some other more pressing issues."

"Hmm." She picked up her fork. "How are you doing, sugar?"

"Me? I'm okay. Better now that he's awake. How are *you* doing?"

"I'm holding it together."

"Because that's what you do?"

"Yes. That's my job. I'm the matriarch of this family. If I crumble, the whole house of cards collapses."

I rubbed my temple. "Are you prepared?"

"For?"

"When he gets out of the hospital? His recovery? We don't know how long it will take."

She didn't reply but instead took a bite of fish. After she swallowed, she looked at me studiously. "I don't expect it to be easy. Or short, for that matter. Despite him being active and in good health, I don't expect him to just spring back. I don't know what this will look like, but it'll be harder on him than the rest of us."

I clamped my mouth shut.

"It's not the same," she said quietly. "What happened with your mother."

I swallowed a painful lump in my throat. "No. It's not the same. Her suffering came to an end."

"And yours continued."

I nodded.

"I'm worried about you, Salem."

Normally, I'd push it away. I'd make a joke. I'd divert the conversation. But after the shower, something inside of me wasn't so ashamed of being vulnerable. Not around the people who loved me most in this world.

"I know," I said softly. "And I know I haven't made it easy."

"Who is easy?"

"Hadley. Hadley's easy."

"She's challenging in her own way. We all are."

I chuckled, but it wasn't in humor. "Hadley came home and stayed. And she has no interest in anything other than this life, this land, and being with family. I envy her sometimes."

"You, my dear, are a true pioneer." She smiled, her eyes crinkling in the corners, the brackets around her mouth disappearing into her cheeks. "Pioneers adventure. They ask questions like *what's over there, what lays beyond those mountains?*"

"Pioneers also died of dysentery and snake bites," I quipped.

"What's life without a little risk?" She winked and went back to eating her food for a moment. "You talk to your boss?"

I nodded. "He's great. Very understanding. But there's only so much time I can be away from my job before they replace me with someone more dedicated, more focused."

"You are dedicated and focused. It was a relief, actually, to see you thrive in something you loved to do. Hadley told us how well you're doing."

I got up and went to the bar cart to pour myself a drink. "What do I do, Muddy? I can't go back to New York while Dad is recovering. But if I stay, my entire life in New York might not be waiting for me when I finally get back."

"You know, life is a funny thing." Her fork clanked against an old, chipped plate. "The things we think we want . . . sometimes when we get them, they end up not mattering at all."

"Like what? You've always wanted to be here. Same with Hadley. You two are made for this life. I'm not."

"You know what else is funny about life?"

"What?"

"When you look back, you'll realize there were things that you took way too seriously that ended up working out in the end anyway."

"So why worry?"

"Pretty much. You're not the worrier of the family, Salem. Leave that to Hadley."

I snorted. "So, what is it you wanted to talk to us about? Will you give me a clue?"

"Tomorrow," she said. "It'll keep until tomorrow. Why didn't you go out tonight?"

"None of us felt like it," I admitted. "Running on fumes. We're all exhausted. And now that Dad is—well, not necessarily in the clear—but on the mend, it's like we can all take a collective breath. I expect I'll finally sleep well tonight."

"You're not sleeping well?" Her eyes twinkled. "Maybe you need to be getting more exercise."

"Yeah, maybe I'll go for a run or something."

"I didn't mean *that* kind of exercise."

"What kind did you—*Muddy!*"

She cackled. "Gideon still has the hots for you."

"I'm not interested."

"No? What about Bowman? He's handsome. And right next door. I have a pair of ear plugs. The really good kind that expand in your ears."

I stood up from my seat and grabbed my drink. "Good night, Muddy."

"Good night, sugar."

CHAPTER NINETEEN

The Hospital

"Oh, and the dogs have been sleeping with us in the cabin," Hadley blabbed on. "Because Tempest whines when they're not all together. And they keep trying to get on the bed because you and Jane have spoiled them."

Dad smiled at Hadley's exuberance, but his eyes found mine for a moment before focusing back on Hadley.

"And I have my final dress fitting in a few days, and I think that's all," Hadley finished.

"That sounds good," Dad said. His voice wasn't loud or strong, but it came easily. I worried that he had to reach for words, but in the short time we'd been there for a morning visit, I was already hopeful about his mental state.

Declan placed his hands on Hadley's shoulders and gave them a comforting squeeze. "Some fences on the east side of the property needed fixing, so I took Bowman with me to help and we knocked it out in a few hours."

Dad frowned. "Bowman?"

"Declan's best friend," Hadley said. "Remember, Dad?"

Dad gently shook his head.

"He came to town early as a surprise," Declan said. "I don't know if we told you."

"Oh, *Bowman.*" His brow smoothed out.

"Yeah. And he's been helping out around the ranch," Declan went on. "It's been nice having him here."

The door to Dad's hospital room opened and Muddy and Jane entered. Jane only had eyes for my father and immediately went to his side and placed a kiss on his lips.

"We're going to leave you in good hands," Muddy said. "I need to take care of some things, but I'll be back later."

"I'll see to him," Jane said, smiling at my father who smiled back.

My internal hackles raised. I thought I was doing a good job of keeping my thoughts to myself until Hadley elbowed me in the ribs.

"Resting Salem face," she whispered.

We said goodbye to Dad and left him with Jane. It was midmorning, and it had already been a full day. Feeding the chickens and collecting the eggs, mucking out stalls with Hadley, and relocating the skunk family from underneath our porch.

Declan had driven all of us, so we piled into his oversized SUV. I wondered how many car seats they'd end up having. Knowing Hadley, she'd want a handful of kids. And Declan, whose sole mission was to make her happy, would oblige.

The ride back to the ranch was quiet and when we were about ten minutes out, Muddy said to Declan, "Text Bowman to meet us at the house, would you?"

Hadley sat next to me in the back seat. Declan handed his phone to her and said, "Do it for me, yeah?"

"Why do you need Bowman to meet us at the house?" I asked.

"Because what I want to talk about involves him."

Hadley and I exchanged a confused look, but she unlocked Declan's phone and shot off a text to Bowman. He was waiting for us on the porch when we drove up a few minutes later.

"I've been summoned," Bowman said, clapping his hand to Declan's. "How's Connor?"

"Better." Declan looked at Muddy who nodded in agreement.

"He was more lucid," she said. "Still tires easily and didn't speak a ton, *but* he wasn't grasping for words."

"I noticed that too," I said.

"He'll be back threatening you with a shotgun before you know it," Hadley teased Declan.

Bowman looked at me in confusion and I shrugged.

"Let's all go to the den, yeah?" Muddy said, walking inside, not even bothering to see if we were going to follow.

But of course, we followed. She called the shots in our family.

"Everyone, take a seat," she commanded.

Declan sat at one end of the couch and Hadley cuddled up next to him, leaving another spot on the couch which I took. Bowman sat on the ledge in front of the unlit fireplace and Muddy took her chair.

"So, I'm just going to get right to it," she said. "Connor's recovery is going to take some time, which means we need someone to fill his position to oversee the running of the ranch. The most obvious person would be Declan."

Declan frowned. "Me? Not Josiah or Henry? Or one of the others who's been here a long time."

"They're good men," Muddy said. "But they're not family. You are. Besides, you've been acting foreman for a while now. So, it makes the most sense for you to step up."

"Whatever you need," Declan said.

Muddy nodded. "Good. But we're still going to need more help."

My eyes swept over to Bowman who was leaning over, his arms resting on his thighs. His gaze was trained on Muddy.

"I know you're only here for a short while," Muddy said, addressing Bowman. "But until we can hire more men, would you be willing to—"

"Yes," Bowman said immediately, his eyes flitting to mine quickly before returning to Muddy.

Muddy smiled. "I knew I could count on you."

"You've been working the ranch with me anyway the last few days," Declan pointed out with a laugh. "Might as well get paid for it."

"Absolutely," Muddy said with a nod.

"How many men are you looking to hire?" Bowman asked.

"Two," Muddy remarked. "To replace you when you go back to the circuit, and to replace Declan who will be acting foreman. But the job isn't for everyone."

"I know some guys," Bowman said. "Brothers. One's a farrier and blacksmith. The other is a horse groomer. They might be interested."

Muddy nodded. "If you have contact information, I'd love to speak to them."

"They're from the circuit?" Hadley asked.

"Yeah," Bowman said.

"Why would they want to leave?" she inquired. "I mean, they'd make far less working for us than on the circuit."

"It's not always about money." His tone was clipped and he clamped his mouth shut.

Tension filled the room.

"Get me their contact information and I'll give them a call," Muddy reiterated.

"Do I know them?" Declan asked Bowman.

"Archer and Brooks Keel," Bowman said.

"They sound familiar," Declan said. "But I've never met them."

"They're from Spearfish, South Dakota," Bowman said. "They used to belong to a motorcycle club before they joined the circuit."

"No kidding," Declan murmured.

Bowman nodded. "Speaking of which, my Harley is on a hot shot truck as we speak."

"You ride a motorcycle?" I asked in shock.

Bowman looked at me and grinned. "I like to live dangerously. I'll give you a riding lesson, if you want."

"Just what we need. Salem, the adrenaline junkie, finding a new hobby that takes ten years off my life." Hadley stood. "I'm making lunch."

"I'll help," Muddy said as her gaze bounced between me and Bowman.

"Do not get Salem on the back of your bike," Declan commanded as he pointed to his best friend before following Hadley to the kitchen.

Bowman stood up and came toward me and lowered his voice, "I won't tell if you won't."

I grinned. "Deal."

CHAPTER TWENTY

Town

Declan opened the door to the Copper Mule. The sounds of bluegrass and the smell of barbecue hit me and I took a deep breath.

"Oh, this is going to be so fun," Hadley squealed, linking her arm through mine and marching us both inside. Declan and Bowman followed.

Wade was behind the dimly lit bar, along with a blonde I didn't recognize. "Who's that?" I asked, gesturing with my chin.

"That's Chelsea," Hadley explained. "Wade's new girlfriend."

She twirled a bottle of liquor and then poured a few shots. Wade took the bottle from her and then pressed a kiss to her cheek. She beamed at him and then laughed at something a customer said.

"I hear wedding bells," I quipped.

Hadley looked over her shoulder at her fiancé. "I'm taking Salem to the bar. What can I get you?"

"Whatever microbrew is on draft," Declan said.

Hadley looked at Bowman who said, "I'll have the same."

He looked at me, his eyes dragging down my body. I was in a pair of old jeans that hugged me tight and boots that added another two inches. Bowman looked like bull riding perfection in a clean flannel, jeans, and his cowboy hat.

If I looked at him for too long, I'd definitely lose myself in him.

Hadley dragged me toward the bar, maneuvering through a group of people. It was busy and the tip jar was already half full.

"Where's Gracie and Cole?" I asked.

"They'll be here in a bit," Hadley said. "This is fun. It feels good to be out and about."

"Sorry you have to drink cranberry juice."

She grinned. "I don't mind. Besides, Declan will dance with me and that's all I care about anyway."

"You guys are so gross," I teased. "But I'm happy for you."

"I'm happy for me too."

We got to the bar and Wade smiled. He reached over to give Hadley a one-armed hug, and then did the same to me.

"You guys came!" Wade said. "It's good to see you! Lucy told me the news about Connor. I'm so glad to hear it."

"Yeah, we're celebrating," Hadley said.

Wade's girlfriend sidled up next to him and shot Hadley a smile. "Hey!"

"Hi, Chelsea." Hadley gestured to me. "My twin, Salem."

"Nice to meet you," Chelsea said before she was called away by a customer.

"Jeez, you guys are busy," Hadley remarked.

"You know when that video went viral for Sweet Teeth?" Wade asked.

Hadley nodded.

"Well, it kind of spilled over onto us. There are people here I've never seen before."

"Rats, I hope people haven't discovered our town," Hadley said. "Small and quaint towns never stay that way after they get discovered."

"Yeah, but who doesn't love making money?" Wade remarked. "We can finally think about a new roof instead of having to patch this one again."

"Blessing and a curse, I guess," Hadley said.

The bluegrass song came to an end, and a moment later a classic country song started. Everyone in the bar cheered and clapped.

I looked at Hadley and grinned. "It's nice to have things you can count on."

"Right?" Hadley smiled.

"What are you guys drinking?" Wade asked. "Whatever it is, it's on me tonight."

"But then how will you afford a new roof for this place?" I teased.

"You plan on drinking that much?" Wade quipped.

"Hmm. We *are* celebrating," I reminded him.

"Two microbrews on draft, whatever fun mocktail you feel inclined to make for me, and for Salem?"

"A Manhattan," I said. "On the rocks."

"Missing the city, are we?" Wade asked as he grabbed two pint glasses.

"Something like that," I said.

Wade was quick and before I knew it, we had our drinks, along with a round of shots on a tray. Declan and Bowman had managed to score a table and I carried the tray toward them.

I passed around the drinks and then took a seat by

Bowman in the booth. Hadley slid in next to Declan and he immediately wrapped an arm around her.

Declan grabbed his pint and raised it. "To Connor."

"To Dad," Hadley said.

We clinked our glasses together, and then each took a sip.

"Cinnamon whiskey shots?" I asked, passing one to Bowman, and then Declan.

"Not for me," Declan said. "I'm driving."

"Salem," Hadley warned.

"Just this round," I said. I turned to Bowman. "It's just you and me."

He raised his glass, stared into my eyes, and then downed the shot.

I did the same.

Gracie and Cole showed up and after they got a round of drinks, they joined us at the table. Gracie and Hadley began chatting about all things baby related, and Declan and Cole were discussing Cole's job as a smokejumper.

Bowman leaned his head close to mine and asked, "Are you interested in what they're talking about?"

"No."

"Dance with me," he commanded.

I grinned at him. "You dance?"

"I do." He winked.

"Well, this, I have to see." I slid out of the booth and Bowman followed. Hadley momentarily looked at us before returning her attention to Gracie.

Bowman headed for the vintage jukebox which still took coins. He pulled out a quarter from his pocket and fed it into the machine, and then he pressed a few buttons. A moment later, the sound of a fiddle blasted through the speakers.

I let out a laugh and took Bowman's offered hand. He led me toward the center of the room and several people who congregated in the area backed up when they saw us take the floor.

I wasn't sure if it was the bourbon or the way Bowman smiled at me while we line danced, but my head was light and happiness bubbled inside me. Others joined and soon we had a herd of customers on the floor with us.

When the song ended, I attempted to catch my breath. Bowman grabbed my hand and dragged me to the bar.

"Shots?" I asked.

"Why not?" he said.

"Don't tell Hadley. She thinks I can't hold my liquor."

"No?"

"Wine yes, liquor no."

"I won't tell her."

"Good man."

Bowman signaled to Chelsea who poured us two shots of rye whiskey.

We downed them quickly.

"Another round of shots?" Chelsea asked.

"No way," I said, touching my heated cheeks. "But maybe another Manhattan?"

"And I'll take another beer," Bowman said, reaching for his wallet.

"Put that away," I said to him. "We're drinking on Wade's tab tonight."

Once we had our drinks, neither of us seemed inclined to hurry back to the table. Bowman's eyes held mine as he took a drink of his beer.

"You're a good dancer," I said.

"I'm better at slow dances."

His voice was deep and raspy, and it made me shiver.

I loved the idea of him pulling me close and holding onto me. I was taller than the average woman, but Bowman towered over me and it made me feel protected. Cared for.

He took a step toward me and brought his hand to my hip.

I didn't push him away.

I moved ever so slightly closer.

"Powell."

"Bowman."

A customer bumped into me from behind, sending me face first into Bowman's chest. "Oof," I muttered, as my Manhattan sloshed onto his shirt. I placed a hand on his pec to steady myself.

He took my drink and set it on the bar before grabbing a stack of bar napkins.

"Sorry!" the man said behind me. "Are you okay?"

"I'm okay," I said. "Don't worry about it."

I took the napkins from Bowman and blotted the spot on his shirt.

"Did I get you wet?" the man asked in contrition. "Can I buy you a drink to make up for it?"

"No, I'm fine, but you did get my friend wet."

"Sorry, man," the guy said.

Bowman raised his eyebrows. "What, no drink for me?"

"I'm not trying to sleep with you," the guy announced with a drunken smile.

Bowman's muscles bunched beneath my hand. I curled my fingertips into his shirt. "Hey, let it be."

I looked over my shoulder at the guy who'd bumped into me. His cheeks were ruddy and his eyes were glassy. "Did you drive here?" I purred.

His gaze widened and he nodded.

I dropped the soiled napkins on the bar and turned toward the man to give him my full attention. "Can I have your keys?" I asked, holding out my hand.

He fumbled in his pants pocket and extracted a key ring and plopped the set of keys into my palm.

"You gonna drive us, sweetheart?" he asked.

I flashed him a grin. "Wade!"

A moment later, Wade appeared behind the bar. "What's up?"

I handed him the keys and pointed to the drunk man. "He's not allowed to drive home."

"Hey!" the drunk man whined.

Bowman sidled up next to me and draped an arm across my shoulder. "Be thankful she's taking care of the problem and I'm not."

The man's Adam's apple bobbed as his gaze darted from Bowman back to me. "So, you're not going home with me?"

"Nope," I said.

"Take my number."

Bowman's arm tightened around me.

"No," I said. "But thanks for the offer. Wade?"

"I'll take care of it."

I turned in Bowman's embrace. "Come on. I need some air."

Bowman and I trailed our way through the throng of people until we got to the door. We went outside and I breathed in the warm night.

"The fucking audacity," Bowman grumbled.

"What?"

"That guy. Trying to get you to go home with him right in front of me."

"Hmm. They don't call it liquid courage for nothing."

"True. I'm impressed, actually."

"With what?"

"With how you handled that."

"Handled what exactly?"

"You got him to give you his keys without a fuss. And you shut him down without causing a scene. A lot of men get shitty when a woman tells them no."

"I've had a lot of practice."

He glowered.

"Don't look at me like that," I said, my brow furrowing. "I live in Manhattan. I go out a lot. It happens, okay?"

"You take any of them up on their offers?"

"Getting personal, are we?"

"More personal than we've already been?"

I cocked my head to the side, rye humming through my veins.

There was something about Bowman. Even though he'd seen me vulnerable, he didn't lord it over me. He didn't use it to manipulate me.

I felt safe with him, I realized.

He'd never use my feelings against me.

"Bowman?"

"Yeah, Powell?"

"Are you going to kiss me or what?"

"Kiss you? Out here? Where anyone could see?"

"Is that what you're worried about?" I took his hand and led him around the side of the bar to the back of the building.

I leaned against the brick wall and waited.

He stared down at me. "You're not drunk."

"No," I agreed. "I've had a few, but I'm in my right mind. And I can even do this . . ."

I held out my hands and alternated touching my nose with a finger on each hand.

He stepped forward, grasped both my hands, and lifted my arms, pinning them, and me, in place. His body was warm, solid. And I wanted to feel it moving against me.

In me.

I thrust my breasts forward.

"No regrets tomorrow," he warned.

"None," I agreed.

His head dipped and his mouth grazed mine, ever so slightly.

"Bowman," I growled. "Stop teasing me."

His tongue plunged into my mouth and I opened to him. Lust exploded between us. I strained forward, but he still held my hands captive.

Bowman moved, sliding his thigh between my legs and gently pressing against me.

Desire pulsed in my core and I was greedy, desperate for more of him.

But Bowman would not give, proving that he was in control and would dole out pleasure at his own leisure.

While his tongue ravaged my mouth, he kept moving his thigh, easing back only to press forward once again. He edged me closer, stopping when I was on the verge of coming.

"Beg me for it," he growled as he stared down at me.

His face was contorted with desire and moonlight.

"Beg me for it," he rasped again. "And I'll make you come."

"Please, Bowman."

He shook his head slowly.

I frowned in confusion, but then understanding dawned.

"Please, Cas. Make me come."

He pressed his thigh and began to move it between my legs. The friction of my jeans, combined with expert pressure had me tumbling over a cliff.

I shuddered against him and clenched my thighs around him. I rode out my pleasure, wave after wave.

A long shaky breath exhaled between my lips, stirring the hair at his temples.

He turned his head and placed a gentle kiss below my ear. "Good girl."

I trembled with aftermath and closed my eyes.

He let go of my arms and they flopped to my sides like noodles. They prickled as feeling returned to them.

His fingers clasped my chin.

"Open your eyes and look at me."

My eyes flipped open and I peered at him. His gaze was glittery, dark.

Searching.

He leaned forward and kissed my lips. Brief. Chaste. A footnote on the chapter that had just closed.

Because he was no longer Bowman.

Bowman was a veneer, a facade. A persona he showed the world.

But with me, he was Cas.

And I was Salem.

CHAPTER TWENTY-ONE

The Bar

"We should go back inside," I murmured, peering up at him.

"In a second," he said. He pulled me away from the wall and into his arms.

I pressed my cheek to his shirt and then reared back. "You're still wet."

"I am. Are you?" he quipped.

My gaze met his and I grinned. "Why don't you find out for yourself."

He kissed my forehead, my nose, my lips. "If I start doing that, I won't be able to stop. And I'm not fucking you against the wall of a bar. At least not right now. Maybe another time."

"Another time?" I skimmed my lips across his scruffy jaw, marveling at the fact that touching him now came so easily. "You promise?"

He chuckled. "Yeah. I promise."

"So, is now a good time to talk?" I asked.

"About what?"

I smirked. "You lost the bet."

He raised his eyebrows. "I think you've got it wrong, tater tot. *You* lost the bet."

"How do you figure? *You* kissed *me*."

"Because you begged me to kiss you," he pointed out.

"Hmm." I tapped my chin with my finger. "You did say one night not that long ago that if I came to you and asked, the bet was null and void. Or am I having selective amnesia?"

"No, you're remembering that correctly," he agreed. "But I have another idea."

"What's that?"

"Seeing as that you're highly competitive—"

"Pot meet kettle—"

"Then the only way to truly settle this, once and for all, is to say that we both lost."

"Meaning?"

"We both lost." He dipped his head and bit my earlobe. "Which means we each get a night of fantasy fulfillment."

I shivered in his arms. "That would be okay with me."

"Good." He leaned back and stared at my face.

"We should probably get back inside."

His fingers played with the fly of my jeans. "What a good idea . . ."

I batted his hand away. "I thought you didn't want to do it against a wall."

"Then let's get out of here," he said.

"Declan drove," I reminded him.

"Fuck."

I flicked the brim of his cowboy hat. "Patience bull rider. You will ride me soon enough and all will be well."

With a laugh, he released me.

My expression sobered.

"What?" he asked.

"I don't want them to know." I gestured with my chin to the bar.

"You mean, you don't want them to know that you just rode my leg like a bronco?"

"I think keeping this just between us is for the best," I said.

He rubbed his jaw, and then eventually nodded. "Yeah."

My heart dropped into my stomach like a stone. Part of me had hoped he'd demand we walk in there holding hands.

But rationality won. It would get too complicated if we took whatever this was public.

"It's just easier, you know?" I asked. "It's not because I'm ashamed of you."

"Ashamed of me? Good to know." He flashed a grin. "Don't worry about it. I'll be your dirty little secret. It wouldn't be the first time."

"Other women have—"

"High school. I was good enough to sneak out windows, not good enough to be introduced to the parents."

Though his tone was light, his words saddened me. But now was not the time to talk about it.

The bar crowd had thinned ever so slightly, and we made it back to the table.

"Where have you guys been?" Declan demanded.

"Relax," I stated. "I had to get some air. He came with me."

"You guys were tearing up the dance floor," Gracie said.

Cas slid into the booth and I took the spot next to him. "Yeah. I can't believe I remembered all the steps."

"It's like useless trivia," Cole said. "Some things just stick."

"You missed Amber's entrance," Hadley said, reaching for her mocktail.

"She say anything to you?" I asked.

"*Congratulations*," Hadley said.

"That bitch," I muttered.

"What am I missing?" Cas asked. "Isn't congratulations nice?"

"Amber Winston, resident mean girl of our class," Gracie explained. "It was snide. It's hard to explain. She just has the perfect tone of snark and censure."

"Amber," Cas repeated. "Why does that name sound familiar?"

I shrugged, hoping he'd drop it.

"Wait," Cas said, looking at me. "She's the one, right?"

"The one what?" Declan asked.

"The one who made Hadley cry, so Salem put hair removal cream in her face wash," Cas said, looking at me again.

The table fell silent.

"You're the reason?" Gracie said with surprise. "You're the reason Amber didn't have eyebrows in her yearbook photo?"

"I plead the fifth," I muttered, glaring at Cas.

"What?" he demanded.

"I didn't know," Hadley voiced. "No one knew who did it. Or why."

Embarrassment heated the back of my neck. "She made you cry. So, I got even."

"She made Hadley cry?" Declan demanded.

"It was a long time ago," Hadley said, patting his arm.

"What did she say?" Gracie asked.

"It was about the Huckleberry Pageant," I said.

"The *what?*" Bowman asked.

"The Huckleberry Pageant. It's a mother-daughter thing. And the year that Amber entered with her mom, she said—"

"She said we'd never be able to enter, let alone win, because we didn't have a mom anymore," Hadley said, her face stricken.

She looked just like she'd looked years ago when Amber had said the worst thing in the world.

"God, she really is the nastiest human being." Gracie shook her head.

"I had no idea you were behind that prank," Hadley said to me.

I shrugged. "I didn't want you to know."

"I'm surprised you didn't punch her in the eye," Cole said. "That seems more your style."

I grinned at him. "Poison is a woman's weapon."

Cole raised his eyebrows. "Duly noted."

"So not only is there a yearbook photo of Amber with penciled in eyebrows and a few missing eyelashes, but the bitch lost the pageant, too," I said with a smirk.

"How did you know about the story?" Declan asked Cas.

"We exchanged war stories," Cas said.

"Times of vigilante justice," I clarified.

"Let's raise a glass to Salem," Declan said. "Our hair-trigger defender."

"I don't have a drink," Cas said.

"Me neither," I remarked, sliding out of the booth. "I'll get us another round, and then we can cheers to me."

"We need another round, too," Cole said, lifting his beer that only had one more sip. He quickly downed it.

"I'll help you," Cas said to me.

We headed toward the bar. "I need to use the restroom real fast. You order the drinks, and then I'll help you bring them back," I said.

"Sounds good."

I wove my way through the crowd toward the bathroom at the back of the bar, but the unmistakable, grating voice of Amber Winston filtered through the noise to hit my ears.

"I mean, seriously," she intoned. "Can you believe she got pregnant? Like, oh my God, keep your knees closed. So it's no wonder they're having a shotgun wedding."

"She looks happy," one of Amber's friends said.

"Yeah, *happy*. I'm surprised he put a ring on it. He already got the milk for free. It's not like he has to buy the cow." Amber sniggered. "And in a few months, she's going to look like a cow!"

Rage swept through my veins, obliterating everything—including my frontal lobe's ability to regulate my emotions.

I marched up to the table where Amber and two of her friends were sitting. One of them widened their eyes when she saw me. The other let out a squeak.

I stood behind Amber's chair and crossed my arms.

Her blonde friend gestured with her chin toward me.

Amber's spine snapped straight and she slowly twisted her body and faced me. She peered up at me with cornflower blue eyes. Her hair was raven-wing black. She would've been gorgeous if her heart wasn't so ugly.

She flashed a fake grin. "Hey, Salem. Long time no see."

"Not long enough," I remarked. "I heard what you said about Hadley."

"I wasn't talking about Hadley," she lied. "I was talking about someone else."

"Who?"

"Who?"

"You sound like an owl. Yes. Who? If you weren't talking shit about Hadley, who *were* you talking shit about?"

"A girl from Silver Springs," she said, tossing her long hair over her shoulder.

"Uh huh." I leaned forward and pressed a finger to her eyebrow. "Your eyebrows never did grow back fully, did they?"

Anger mottled her face, turning her skin a blotchy red.

"You bitch!" she yelled, standing up so fast her chair crashed to the floor.

I grinned. "How does it feel to have peaked in high school?"

The woman lunged for me. Her nails raked down my arm, leaving long trails of red on my skin.

There was a reason it was called a bitch fight. Screaming, clawing, and hair pulling ensued.

Rage was all I saw.

I got in one good face punch, but then I felt arms wrap around me and pull me close. I breathed in, recognizing Cas's scent. I took deep, gulping breaths.

"Easy," Cas whispered.

Another man had Amber caged in his embrace. She glared daggers at me. "Let me go," she commanded.

The man paused and then released her.

"You gonna behave, tater tot?"

"Nope," I said, shooting Amber another feral smile.

She lunged again, but Cas turned and gave her his back.

"Hey, that's enough!" Wade yelled as he hopped over the counter. "This is a respectable establishment and if you're going to fight, then you at least need to give us time to place our bets."

"My bet is on the red head!" someone yelled.

"Mine too!"

I looked up at Cas. "Want to make some money tonight?"

With a sigh, he let me go and then scooped me up over his shoulder. "You're in time-out."

As he carted me toward the door, I lifted myself up and looked at Amber. And while she was still spitting mad, I blew her a kiss.

CHAPTER TWENTY-TWO

"You're insane," Hadley said, pushing the front door open.

"Yep," I said as I hobbled up the porch steps after her. My ankle had twisted sometime during the bar brawl. "You guys go. Check on Tempest. Get some sleep."

"You sure?" Hadley asked, biting her lip.

I nodded. "If I need any help doctoring, I'll wake Muddy."

"Okay, if you're sure," Hadley said.

"I'm sure."

She reached out and gently hugged me. I winced but kept quiet. "You'll tell me later. What she said to make you fly off the handle."

"Nope." I pulled back and smiled at her. "It's not worth repeating."

Declan looked at me as he wrapped a protective arm around Hadley. "Must've been bad."

"Amber Winston was a nasty teenager. Now she's a nasty adult." I shrugged.

Hadley giggled. "If anyone asks, I don't condone this kind of behavior. But in private, I'm Team Salem."

The two of them left and headed toward the guest cabin. I hobbled toward the bench and sat down. Without a word, Cas kneeled in front of me and gently removed my boots.

"Thank you," I murmured.

"You twisted your ankle the night we met in the hotel bar," he said, stroking the outside of my foot, up my calf.

"I remember," I smiled slightly. "You seem to have a habit of checking to make sure I'm okay."

Adrenaline was still buzzing in my blood, along with the last vestige of rye.

I leaned over and cradled his cheek.

"Let's get some ice on that ankle," he said.

He helped me up from the bench, quickly took off his boots, and then aided me inside. The house was quiet—my grandmother was likely asleep.

"What do you need first?" Cas asked. "Ice for the ankle? Aspirin?"

"My neck stings," I remarked. "I think she used her claws."

"Oh, yeah, she did."

"There's witch hazel in the cabinet," I said. "And cotton balls."

Cas went to the cabinet, and then said, "If I ask you something, will you answer truthfully?"

"Depends."

"What did you say to Amber that made her lunge for you?"

"What makes you think I said anything?" I asked, feigning innocence.

He set the bag of cotton balls on the table and then opened the bottle of witch hazel. "You're not as feral as you let people think. I think you *want* them to believe that, so they don't know the truth."

"Which is?"

"You're protective of those you love. Everything you do, you do for them."

I nibbled my lip. "Yeah, I do."

"This isn't the first time you've been protective of Hadley."

"No. Definitely not."

"So, what happened?"

He dabbed my neck and I hissed at the sting. He blew air across my skin, soothing it instantly.

"She said unkind things about Hadley getting pregnant . . . and a shotgun wedding. And I might've touched her eyebrow and said it never did grow back all the way. Then she went crazy."

"I see. What else have you done in the name of protecting those you love?"

"Hmm. Let me see . . . the list is long."

He laughed and began to clean up.

"Oh, here's a good one. Wyn was dating a guy and she found out he was cheating on her. But instead of confronting him, she cooked him a nice dinner at his place . . ."

"Weird sort of punishment." He dumped the cotton balls into the garbage and put the witch hazel back into the cabinet.

"I wasn't finished. I had this idea to put laxatives in his wine. And it was also my idea for her to put a can of sardines deep in an air vent where he couldn't get to them. And while he was fighting for his life in the bathroom, she found the girl's social media on his computer and left it open so he would know why he was suffering."

"I bow at the feet of the master," Cas quipped.

"You did that earlier," I reminded him.

"You want to ice your ankle down here or upstairs?"

"Depends."

"On."

"Are you going to help me get ready for bed?"

"How sure are you that your grandmother is asleep?"

I smiled. "I'm pretty sure. Besides, she wears ear plugs."

"Does she?"

"Yep." I grinned. "And the walls are thick. This house was built to last."

"I'll sleep next to you tonight, but I'm not putting my hands on you. Even I have some sense of decorum."

I snorted. "Well, I don't. You're really not going to touch me?"

"I'm really not going to touch you."

I grinned.

"What?"

"We'll see."

"If you don't behave, I'll sleep in my own bed."

"Fine, I'll keep my hands to myself."

"Good."

"And I'll even wear pajamas."

"Salem," he warned.

My smile widened.

"What?" he demanded.

"You called me Salem."

"I did."

"You're not going to be able to resist me."

He took my elbow and led me toward the stairs. "That, I already know."

☙

"Salem," he growled.

"What?"

He placed a hand on my hip. "Settle."

I sighed and rolled over onto my back and stared up at the ceiling. It was dark in the middle of the night, and I should've been asleep.

But I couldn't sleep because there was a big, brawny bull rider in bed next to me. And even though I was wearing pajamas, he had stripped down to his boxers, so every time I moved, I grazed warm bare skin.

"Tell me a bedtime story," I commanded. "Something boring that will put me to sleep."

"I could explain how a combustion engine works," he said.

"Yeah, tell me. That's boring as fuck."

Cas started talking, but unfortunately it had the opposite effect from what I had intended. He was speaking technical jargon, but I was busy visualizing him working on said engine with a wrench in his hand and grease on his arm.

Shirtless.

Fantasy Salem brought him a bottle of beer, wearing a pair of cut-off shorts that showed a little cheek, and a threadbare tank top without a bra.

And suddenly Fantasy Salem was bent over the hood, getting railed from behind.

Cas fell silent, and then whispered, "You asleep?"

"No." I placed my hand on his chest and began tracing a pattern on his skin.

He grabbed my fingers to stop me. "No? You were actually interested in what I was talking about?"

"I had a nice visual of you working on a truck engine. And then my imagination got away from me. You want to hear my fantasy?" I asked.

"I'm begging you not to tell me." He groaned and released my hand.

My fingers inched lower. "What if I told you I still have

bloodlust from my fight? And that I need to work out my aggression."

I slid my hand into his boxers and grasped him. He was hard and ready and my fingertip grazed the head of him.

"Fuck it," he muttered. "I'm only human."

I released him, and then slithered out of my pajamas, and then pulled back the covers. He took off his boxers and reached for me.

I slid my leg over him and grasped him again, guiding him inside me. I sank down on top of him, loving the feel of him stretching me, filling me.

His hands went to my waist, clenching my hips and urging me to ride him.

I leaned over and pressed my breasts to his chest and our lips met. His tongue plunged into my mouth as his hands skated up my ribs and toward my head. His fingers plowed through my hair as he angled his mouth.

He stole my oxygen but gave me pleasure.

"Salem," he whispered, tearing his lips from mine and bathing my cheeks in kisses. "My pull-out game isn't strong."

"It doesn't have to be." I placed my hands on his chest and pushed up, forcing his hands to drop from my hair. I arched my back. "I'm on birth control."

His hands cradled my breasts, his thumbs grazing my nipples. "I need to taste these."

"Later. I'm close, Cas."

"Then use me," he commanded. "Use me all you want."

I picked up speed, undulating and grinding against him. Clenching and gasping, desire shivered up and down my spine, prickling the back of my neck.

I bit my lip to stifle my scream as one of the best orgasms of my life ripped me apart. And while I was still convulsing, Cas grabbed my hips and rolled me over so I was on my back and he loomed over me.

He lifted my leg, wrapped it around his waist, and then he drilled into me. Mindless, determined.

His lips met mine again as he slid his hands beneath my ass, angling me just the way he wanted me. I was overwhelmed, overstimulated. He assaulted my senses, but he knew what my body needed.

"Cas," I gasped.

He covered my mouth with his hand to silence me, and then somehow, he continued at a breakneck pace. He didn't stop. Not even when I clenched around him again, not even when I felt him spill inside me.

Cas wrung every last bit of pleasure from me, finally stilling. We were still connected when he bit my shoulder, causing another wave of pleasure to shoot through my core.

"How's the bloodlust?" he whispered in my ear.

"Manageable," I said with a grin.

He pulled out of me, slowly.

"We made a fucking mess," he said. He reached over the side of the bed for a shirt and handed it to me. I shoved it between my legs and then hobbled my way to the bathroom.

I cleaned up as best I could and then headed back to my room.

"Your turn," I said.

He shook his head and grabbed my arm, pulling me back into bed. "Roll over," he commanded.

"Cas—"

"Roll over, Salem."

His commanding tone had me shivering.

I gave him my back.

He scooted closer and I felt his erection pressing against me.

"How are you—"

I gasped when he slid back inside me.

"Go to sleep, Salem."

"But you're—"

"You'll take what I give you. I want to be deep inside you, and when you're half asleep, I'll make you come again."

He brushed his lips across the shell of my ear.

"You need to be fucked deep and often," he whispered. "And I'm man enough for the job. Go to sleep."

CHAPTER TWENTY-THREE

THE RANCH

Half asleep and delirious, I felt my body being rolled over until my face was pushed into a pillow. Cas was inside me from behind, fucking me slow and deep.

I felt everything at this angle and soon I was screaming into a pillow.

He collapsed on top of me, covering me with his heated body. Cas slid out of me and kissed the small of my back.

"What time is it?" I asked when I'd regained my breath and my eyes were no longer crossed.

"A little before six."

"Rise and shine, huh?"

"Let's shower."

"We can't shower together."

"Why not? We slept together. Twice. And I locked our bedroom doors so there's no chance of someone walking in on us."

"Someone, meaning my grandmother."

"Yeah."

"Maybe we shouldn't tempt fate then. Both of us coming downstairs at the same time, both of us with wet hair . . ."

He sighed. "You want to shower first or should I?"

"You," I said, snuggling deeper into bed.

I fell back asleep and didn't awaken again until Cas kissed my shoulder. "Shower's all yours."

"Thanks," I murmured. "I'd kill for a cup of coffee."

"And if we were in a relationship, I'd bring you one. But if your grandmother's in the kitchen and she sees me bringing you a cup of coffee, we'd be in trouble. Right?"

I opened one eye and glared at him.

His smile was cheeky. "The sooner you shower, the sooner you get caffeine."

It wasn't until I was halfway through my shower that I dissected Cas's words and wondered if they meant something more.

He'd mentioned a relationship.

Did he *want* to be in a relationship?

Did *I* want to be in a relationship?

I held onto the idea for a moment, waiting to see what emotions would pop up and scare me. But there was nothing. Nothing except a blooming warmth at the idea of Cas Bowman, famous bull rider, wanting to exclusively ride me.

But reality intruded: he traveled the rodeo circuit, and I lived in New York. Long distance relationships never worked out. I'd tried to date someone in a different borough of the city once, and even that had failed. If I couldn't make something work with someone three subway trains away, how could I possibly expect to make it work with a nomadic bull rider?

The thought saddened me.

But Cas was going to be here for a little while. All I could do now was enjoy the brief time we had together.

I turned off the water and got out. I towel dried my hair and decided to let it air dry the rest of the way. The bottom drawer of my dresser had the faded, worn jeans I hadn't taken with me to New York and I pulled them out. I slid them on but frowned when they didn't button easily.

I usually worked long hours at my job and often skipped lunch. But I was home and I blamed Sweet Teeth and Hadley —she put butter in everything.

The scent of coffee dragged me from my room, along with the aroma of bacon grease. My mouth watered and all my self-restraint went out the window when I saw Muddy at the stove, apron around her waist, flipping pancakes.

"I've died and gone to heaven," I said, coming to her side and kissing her cheek. "What do I have to do to get the first batch?"

"Pour me another cup of coffee," she said with a grin.

"Your first batch is always the best," I said, taking her coffee cup and refilling it.

"Text Hadley, would you? Let her know they'll be ready soon."

"Is she awake?"

"Oh, yeah, she's awake," Muddy said. "She wakes up when Declan does, and then the morning sickness hits. If you really loved her, you'd let her have the first stack."

"There's love, and then there's your pancakes," I quipped as I pulled out my phone and shot off a text to her.

"You have a good night last night?" she asked.

I looked up from my screen. "Yes. Why?"

"Just making conversation." She slid the spatula underneath the first pancake and put it on a plate. "Hey, will you bring me the paper? It's on the kitchen table."

"Sure." I went to the kitchen table and looked at the newspaper. "*Oh. My. God.*"

"You're so photogenic," she said. "Even when you're bitch-slapping Amber Winston."

"*Oh my God!*" I screeched this time as I picked up the paper and brought it closer to my face. "I'm on the front page of the Huckleberry Hill Crier!"

"The story is continued on page three," Muddy said.

I groaned and slapped my face with the paper.

"So, you want to tell me about last night?" Muddy asked as she brought me a plate of pancakes.

"You already know! Just like the rest of town, apparently."

"I have the Crier's point of view, but we all know journalistic integrity doesn't exist anymore and they're just trying to sell papers."

"All five of them?" I said, my tone snarky.

She took the paper from me. "Eat. And talk."

"Okay, but you can't tell Hadley," I said.

"It was about Hadley, wasn't it? Why you slapped that little tart?"

"I didn't slap her."

"No, you're right. You punched her in the eye. I texted Lucy to let me know when she sees her. I want to know how bad it is."

"Amber's vain. She won't go out until the black eye disappears."

The front door opened, and a moment later, Hadley, Declan and Cas walked in.

Declan grinned at me. "Hi ya."

I pointed at him. "You know."

"Of course I know. Wade texted me."

"Us. Texted us," Hadley said.

I groaned.

"Know what?" Cas asked.

Muddy handed him the paper. He opened it, glanced at it,

looked at me, and then he said, "God, you're so damn photogenic."

◡

"He made a statement," I snapped at Hadley. "Wade made a fucking statement!"

"You know what calms me down when I'm mad?" Hadley asked.

"*What?*" I demanded.

She picked up the baby goat sitting on her lap and set it on mine. Tempest didn't seem to care that her resting spot had changed. She snuggled down and stuck her head beneath my arm and tried to burrow.

My gaze softened.

"Told ya. Nothing like holding a baby goat to make you happy," Hadley said.

I sighed. "Yeah, you're right." My lukewarm cup of coffee was on the end table next to the couch and I reached for it, trying not to disturb the new occupant who'd made me her newest nap spot.

"He was willing to bet on you, though," she said with a wry smile. "So you might want to cut him a little slack."

"Heartwarming."

"Anyone that saw you play field hockey in high school knows to bet on you." She nibbled on her lip. "So are you really not going to tell me what she said?"

"Why does it matter?" I asked. "It was rude and it was about you and I took care of it. And if anyone asks, you can tell them the altitude got to me. I'm not used to the thinner air. I wasn't thinking clearly because I was oxygen deprived."

"No, don't do that," Hadley said. "You've been protecting me since we were kids. You don't have to do that now."

"Yes, I do," I said. "That's what we do. You followed me to

New York to make sure I always had someone to bail me out of jai—my problems—and I protect you from people who are mean to you. It's our way. Trust me, Hadley. You're not missing anything by not knowing what Amber said. Okay?"

"Okay. But you have to promise me one thing if you're not gonna tell me . . ."

"What's that?"

She took my hand in hers and linked her fingers through mine. "I want my child to always know they can call you. They won't always want to call me or Declan, but if they're in trouble and they're afraid, I want them to know they can count on you."

Emotion thickened my throat. "Are you sure you want me to be their emergency call? You trust me with the safety of your child?"

"Salem, you're my twin sister. You're my favorite person on this planet. Aside from Declan." She smiled. "Of course I trust you."

"Even though I'm a hair trigger?"

"Even though you're a hair trigger."

"I'm not an adult, Hadley. I can barely take care of myself."

"You don't give yourself enough credit."

"I don't give myself *any* credit," I mumbled. "Starting bar fights—"

"Hey, as far as I'm concerned, Amber started the fight and you finished it. And that's a good life lesson to teach a kid."

I stroked a hand down Tempest's back and got lost in my own thoughts for a moment.

"What are you thinking about?" she asked.

"A lot of things," I admitted. "Dad coming home. Your wedding. Poet and Wyn coming out here. Me going back to New York. My job."

Cas.

"That's a lot."

I nodded. "Yeah."

"Okay, what's going on with you?" she demanded.

"What do you mean?" I frowned. "I just told you all the things in my head."

"No, there's something else. Something you're not telling me."

"You're my twin. What do you think I'm keeping from you?" I asked, desperately trying to bury the knowledge that Cas had spent the night in my bed—*inside me*.

"I don't know." Hadley pondered, peering at me like she could see below the surface of my face. "Something."

"I'm not keeping anything from you," I lied.

"Okay. Whatever you say."

CHAPTER TWENTY-FOUR

THE RANCH

"I love fucking you," Cas growled as he thrust between my legs.

I clawed his back, scoring his skin with my nails.

"Cas," I moaned.

"Come for me again," he commanded.

"I can't."

"You can. You will."

He shifted the angle of his pelvis, grinding against the perfect spot that was already primed and sensitive.

Cas knew my body better than I did and I clenched around him, gripping his tight ass in my hands.

With a few more thrusts, Cas came, holding me close and whispering words of approval in my ear.

The scent of us was in the air, along with hay and horses. We were on a pallet in the loft of the barn—where we'd spent every spare moment together that we could find. The last week, we'd been insatiable, desperate for one another.

Insane for each other.

We hadn't slept in the house since our first night together, deciding we could be freer and louder in the loft of the barn. We always crept inside an hour before my grandmother woke up to tend to the chickens. So far, we hadn't been caught.

Cas slid out of me and I gushed.

"God, I'm never going to get tired of seeing that." He grabbed his shirt and cleaned me up as best he could.

He laid down next to me and propped himself up on an elbow to stare down at me. There was a battery-operated camping lantern that cast a soft amber glow, giving us just enough light to see shadows and smiles.

"I like this," he said, grazing my nipple and pinching it between his fingers.

"My breast? Yes, I'm aware."

He laughed. "Not just your breast. Or breasts. But *this*. Just you and me. Up here. Not a care in the world."

Up here, without a care in the world, each brick of my fortress was slowly being dismantled.

"So," he began.

"So." I stretched out my legs and sighed.

He traced the ink on my rib cage. "Okay. Time to explain this."

"It's been driving you crazy, huh?"

"Just as crazy as seeing another man's name on you," he grumbled.

"It happened because of a drunken girls' night," I explained. "I wanted the four of us—Hadley, Wyn, Poet and me—to solidify our friendship. They all thought it was a great idea, too. So the next day, after a greasy diner breakfast, we all went to a tattoo parlor in the East Village."

"Hmm. Do all the tattoos match?"

"No." I grasped his finger to stop him from tracing my rib cage because it made my skin buzz, and not in a good way.

"*Do it scared.* I don't need much of an explanation. It's pretty self-explanatory."

I looked at the barn ceiling when I replied, "About a week before the tattoos, I found a card my mother had written me. She always signed her notes with *do it scared*. It was her mantra. And so I got it inked on me in her handwriting."

"It's your mantra too, yeah?"

I nodded, my eyes filling with tears. "When she—when she died, I didn't feel much of anything. I did some things that I really shouldn't have done just so I could hope to feel something. But then . . ."

Cas reached for my hand. I let him take it even though it felt uncomfortable, even though it felt cumbersome at that moment.

"Then something really terrifying happened. One day, I wasn't numb anymore. I felt *everything*. It's why I ran off to New York. It's why I refused to come home often. The numbness I could understand. The numbness got me through life. But feeling? There were times I couldn't breathe it hurt so bad."

"The shower," he murmured. "You couldn't hold it in any longer."

"Nope."

We were silent for a moment, and then I said, "You don't talk about your childhood."

"No. I don't."

"Was it bad?"

He inclined his head. "Not terrible, I guess. But it's wild, you know? From the first moment I can remember, I knew I wasn't wanted. Abandoned six days after I was born? No mother. No father. No one coming back years later trying to claim me. I bounced from foster home to foster home until I was old enough to leave."

"You chose a nomadic life, too," I said softly. "Mine was because of nature. Yours was from nurture."

"Or lack thereof, but yeah." He frowned. "We have a lot in common. Maybe not when you first take a look, but deeper shit."

"Is this . . . are we trauma bonding?" I quipped.

"Don't."

"Don't what."

"Don't make a joke and turn the focus away from the reality of how heavy this is." He skimmed his thumb across my knuckles. "What is it you want, Salem? What do you want from life?"

"Adventure," I said automatically.

"Adventure," he repeated. "Like travel?"

"Adventure comes in many forms. But yeah, travel is good. I want new experiences. I want memories that are so poignant I can taste them, smell them . . . remember them when I'm old. I don't want to roll into the grave thinking about a life unlived."

"You're not living just for yourself, are you?" he asked quietly. "You're living for her, too."

I both hated and loved that he seemed to understand me so easily. But the thing was, I understood him too. I understood everything he did in his life stemmed from that one pivotal moment of being left at six days old. Babies that young needed skin to skin contact, to hear their mother's heartbeat. They needed love and security. And he'd never had that.

"There will be a time in my life that I'll be the age she was when she died. But I'll still be alive. I'll still be breathing. So yeah, I'm living for both of us." I turned my head to stare at him. "You think I'm crazy."

"Yes."

I frowned.

"Not in the way you think," he explained. His face screwed up into a pensive expression as if he was searching for the words. "I've never known anyone like you, Salem. So determined, so fearless to live. But so . . ."

"So what?"

"Scared to love."

"I'm not scared to love."

"No?"

"No, of course not. I have people in my life who I love deeply."

"Sure. Your family. Your friends, who you consider your family. But have you ever been *in* love?"

"That's a different question." I tugged my hand free.

"You've never had your heart broken, have you? The death of a parent . . . that's a different type of grief. I'm talking about a lover. A partner."

"Don't need to jump off a building to know you'll splat on the pavement," I remarked.

"Entirely my point," he said. "Why have you never been in love, Salem?"

"Why haven't you?" I fired back.

"Who says I haven't?"

"You've loved?" I asked quietly.

"Yes. I've been loved. And I've loved. It never lasted. That's not the point. The point is, I've experienced it. I know the agony of true heartbreak."

I shoved out of his arms. "Where's my shirt?" I muttered.

He gently clasped my arm, forcing me to stop. "Oh, I get it."

"Get what?" I forced myself to look at him.

"You think the next heartbreak will destroy you. For

good. Your explosive emotions are just a way to keep people at bay. Am I right?"

I'd felt fear before. Fear when my mother's diagnosis was announced. Fear when it became obvious that her prognosis was undeniable. Fear of those first few nights in a home that was no longer a home because she was in the ground.

But this . . . this was something else entirely.

This was all-consuming terror that flew through my body. I reached for the numbness that was never far out of reach. Only, this time, it wasn't there. My one true coping mechanism had somehow disappeared. And I knew where it was. Down the shower drain, along with my tears.

So I did the only thing left that I knew how to do.

I draped my leg over Cas's and wiggled my body close to his. I pressed the heat of me against him, tacitly begging him to take my body so I could leave my thoughts behind.

He plowed his fingers through my snarled hair and brought my face closer to his.

"Kiss me, Salem. And I'll make you forget."

CHAPTER TWENTY-FIVE

Town

"You look happy," Gracie said as she handed me my coffee.

"I am happy. Dad's coming home from the hospital today," I said.

"I knew that. But that's not what I meant. There's something else."

"Something else?"

She leaned closer and lowered her voice. "You look like you've been getting some. On the regular."

"You're crazy. Who would I possibly be having sex with in this town?" I demanded.

The few customers who'd been sitting at tables nearby suddenly went silent.

"I asked that at full volume, didn't I?" I drawled.

"Hmm. Indeed. And to answer *your* question, I can think of two people."

"And they would be?"

"The high school love who never got over you and the handsome bull rider that can never take his eyes off you."

"Neither," I lied.

"Okay, I'm just saying, I know you. And you're never this happy to be home. You've got color in your cheeks and you've started dressing different."

"Different? Different how?"

"Different like, you don't care to style your hair or put on a full face of makeup because you're not going to an office. Plus, you're rocking the jeans and boots. Very Idaho style."

"Seems kind of dumb to dress for Manhattan when you're on a ranch," I quipped. "As for the jeans, they're Mom's. My old jeans don't button as easily."

"Been there," Gracie said. "I live for the day I can get back into my old jeans. Though I think that's a pipe dream, what with having a baby and all."

"That'll do it," I said with a laugh. "And on that note, you might as well give me one of those cinnamon rolls. The one in the back with twice the amount of frosting."

"You got it."

The door to Sweet Teeth opened and Amber strode inside with Gideon right behind her. She batted her eyelashes at him and thanked him for holding the door for her. Gideon smiled down at her and laughed at something she said.

I turned away in disgust. Not because I was jealous, but because Amber made my stomach queasy. I hadn't seen her since the night we'd gotten into it.

"I'm not Wade," Gracie warned me. "I won't take bets and I will kick you both out of here."

"I'll behave, I swear. I haven't had any bourbon today, so the town is safe."

"Glad to hear it." She picked up the tongs and grabbed a cinnamon roll and stuck it into a bag. "Hi, Gideon. Hi, Amber. Be right with you two."

"Take your time," Gideon said, his eyes finding mine. "Hey Salem."

"Hey," I greeted.

I looked at Amber and the evil part of me was glad to see that the corner of her eye was still a faint yellowish green from the black eye I'd given her.

Hell hath no fury like a protective sister.

I ignored her and she ignored me.

"Anything else for you?" Gracie asked.

"A few of your chocolate chip cookies, please. Thanks." I took out my card.

Amber's expression was clearly judgmental and snarky, but she wisely kept her thoughts to herself.

I tapped my credit card on the screen. It beeped and I shoved my credit card in my pocket. "See you guys later."

I took my coffee and bag of pastries outside and lowered my sunglasses that rested on my head to the bridge of my nose.

The door to Sweet Teeth opened behind me. "Salem," Gideon called out.

I stopped and turned.

"I didn't think you could do it," Gideon said.

"Do what?" I asked.

He grinned. "Ignore Amber."

"A feat, believe me," I muttered and took a sip of my coffee. "I guess neither of us has changed that much since high school."

"I think you've changed more than you think you have."

I nibbled my lip. "I'm sorry, Gideon. I don't think I've ever said that to you before."

"No. You haven't," he said quietly. "It's okay, Salem. I knew it wasn't about me."

"I'm embarrassed, you know? We graduated and I just left. Without a word to you. That was the wrong way to handle our relationship. I know the apology is long overdue, but I really hope you know I mean it."

"I do know you mean it. That's the thing about you, Salem. You're always very honest with your feelings. People know where they stand with you."

His words should've made me feel better, instead they made me feel worse because they only reinforced the fact that I was sneaking around with Cas behind everyone's back.

A motorcycle rumbled in the near distance, and then a moment later, I saw Cas drive down Silver Street. Our eyes locked and his jaw clenched when his attention focused on Gideon.

For some reason, I felt extremely guilty. Like I'd been caught doing something I shouldn't have been. But that was crazy. It wasn't like I was kissing Gideon and Cas had caught me. Then again, we weren't technically exclusive. The word exclusive had never been mentioned.

Cas parked his motorcycle and got off just as the door to Sweet Teeth opened and Amber strolled outside, coffee and pastry bag in hand.

"Oh, look, a party," Amber said with a wide grin. "Bowman, I meant to thank you for rescuing me the other night."

Cas shoved his motorcycle keys into his jeans pocket. "Glad to be of service."

"I don't know what I would've done if you hadn't come along when you did." She beamed at him and tossed long, glossy hair over her shoulder.

"Hey, man," Gideon said, holding out his hand to Cas. "Nice bike."

"Thanks." Cas shook his hand but glanced at me. "Didn't know you were here."

"Yep." I popped the p and tried to keep the heat from my cheeks. "What are you doing in town?"

"Muddy, Declan and Hadley went to the hospital to pick

up your dad. I thought I'd bring them some lunch so no one has to cook."

"And where would you put it?" I asked.

He gestured to the plastic case on the rear of his motorcycle.

"You're so thoughtful," Amber simpered. "I meant to ask— did I leave my sunglasses in your truck? I can't find them."

"I haven't seen them," Cas said, gritting out a smile.

"Okay, well, if you do, call me!" She waved and then sashayed down the street.

"Well, I'd better get going," Gideon said. "Salem, give your dad my best."

"I will."

Gideon nodded at Cas and then left us alone.

"You gave Amber a ride?" I asked, trying to appear nonchalant and clearly failing as Cas began to grin.

"How's that jealousy feel on the other end?"

"I'm not jealous."

"Yeah, right."

He began walking toward The Diner, forcing me to either stand on the sidewalk or follow him.

"Don't walk away from me!" I yelled.

He looked at me over his shoulder. "We don't have a lot of time for this, Salem. Your dad will be home soon and I need to pick up the order. You can yell at me later, if you want."

"Oh, I'll yell at you later," I huffed.

He stalked toward me and said quietly, "Preferably while my tongue is buried inside you."

My cheeks flamed. "Cas!"

"This fight will keep, right?"

"When did you give Amber a ride home?" I demanded.

He didn't reply. Instead, he opened the front door of The Diner and held it for me. I went in and took a deep breath of grease and gravy.

Eloise and Lucy were sitting at the counter while Mr. Bixby was putting to-go containers into bags.

"Hey, Bowman," Eloise chirped.

"Ma'am," he greeted with a dip of his hat.

I couldn't stop my eye roll.

"You okay, honey?" Lucy asked me.

I forced a smile. "Fine, thanks."

Cas handed cash over to Mr. Bixby who tried to refuse, but Cas insisted.

"You let us know what we can do to help," Lucy said.

"You already did so much," I said. "You cooked and froze meals for us. And put them in the freezer when we were out of the house."

"You never lock the door," Eloise said with a smile. "You make it easy."

"Seriously. I can't tell you how much we appreciate it. Especially the poutine."

Lucy frowned. "We didn't make poutine."

"You didn't?" I asked. "Then where did it . . ."

My eyes darted to Cas who took the bags.

He looked at me. "Ready?"

Nodding, I waved to Lucy and Eloise and then got the door for Cas.

"You ordered all that?" I asked once we were on the sidewalk.

"No, I ordered about half this much. Mr. Bixby added extra. Good thing you drove the truck."

He followed me to my father's truck and set the bags down on the passenger floor.

"So it was you," I said. "You're responsible for the poutine in the fridge."

"Yeah."

"Why didn't you tell me?" I demanded.

"The same reason you didn't tell me you've been washing my sheets," he said, looking at me.

We stared at one another, emotion bubbling between us. It was an emotion I didn't want to feel in the middle of town.

"You're really not going to tell me about Amber?" I asked in exasperation.

He peered at me, and then he grinned. "I think I'll make you sweat a bit."

CHAPTER TWENTY-SIX

The Ranch

"It's good to be home," Dad said, leaning his head back against the pillows.

He was tired and every now and again he winced, but he didn't complain. Tempest was curled up next to him in bed and his hand was on her back.

Jane hovered over him while the rest of us filled the empty space of his bedroom.

"There's a bell on your nightstand," Muddy said. "You ring it if you need anything."

"That's ridiculous," Dad said. "I'm not gonna ring a bell."

"You'll ring the bell," Muddy insisted. "You don't need to exert energy yelling for anything, you understand?"

"Okay, Mom," he said with a rueful smile. "If you say so."

"How Downton Abbey is this right now?" Hadley asked.

"Right?" I laughed.

"You sure you want me to . . ." Jane asked.

Dad's eyes flitted to mine quickly before darting back to Jane. "Yes. I want you to stay."

It felt like a knife to the ribs.

"I love having a full house," Muddy said with a smile.

Jane leaned over and pressed a gentle kiss to Dad's forehead. "I'll go home and pack a bag right now."

"Bring the cat," he said.

"You sure?" she asked.

"I'm sure," Dad replied.

His eyes began to droop, and it was the sign we needed to leave the room. We trailed out and Muddy closed the door behind her.

"You want to stay for dinner, Jane?" Muddy asked. "Bowman brought food from The Diner."

"No thanks. I'm going to get home and pack," Jane said as she jogged down the stairs. A moment later the front door opened and closed.

Hadley's lips quivered.

"You're about to cry," I said with a frown. "Why?"

"Because," Hadley blubbered. "Dad's home."

Declan wrapped an arm around her, brought her to his chest, and placed a kiss on her head. "You're okay."

"Hormones," Hadley sniffed.

"Well, I'm hungry," Muddy said as she shot Hadley a sympathetic smile. "What about you, Salem?"

I shook my head. "I think I need to go for a drive."

Jane was moving in.

And I didn't expect her to move out.

I went down the stairs and into the kitchen. Cas was getting plates out of the cabinet and setting them on the counter.

"How's he doing?" Cas asked.

"Sleepy."

My sister and her fiancé came into the kitchen behind me, along with Muddy.

"See ya later," I said.

I took my father's truck keys and headed out.

My feet dangled in the cool water of the lake. Unfortunately, it was doing nothing to cool my anger.

I'd been off-kilter since Cas and I had talked in the barn loft the other night. I felt rearranged, like parts of me no longer fit where they should.

The sound of footsteps along the path had me frowning. I wanted to be alone, and I'd purposefully walked halfway around the public lake to a secluded spot so I wouldn't be disturbed.

But now a stranger out for a late afternoon stroll would intrude on my serenity.

I turned to see who approached and my mouth gaped. "What are you doing here?"

Cas came to stand next to me. "Mind if I sit?"

I shrugged.

"What a warm welcome," he joked as he settled himself beside me on the bank. "Though I hardly blame you for your attitude. I knew you wanted to be alone."

"I did. I do." I picked up a pebble and tossed it into the lake. The water rippled, but a few moments later it smoothed out. Once again, the surface was placid.

We sat in silence, but Cas didn't try to get me to talk. I hated that I found his presence a comfort.

"Why is it called Lavender Lake?" he asked. "I don't see any lavender."

"The sunset," I said. "The sky turns lavender during the summer evenings, and the light reflects off the water."

"Are we going to sit here until sunset?"

"No. It won't be dark for hours."

"I know. But if you wanted to sit here for hours, I'd sit with you."

I swallowed hard and tears threatened to burst from me. "How did you know I was here?"

"Muddy."

"Muddy? Really? How did she—"

"Because she knows *you*. She knows where you go when you need time to think."

"Why would she tell you?"

"Really, Salem?"

I looked at him and waited.

"She knows about us."

"Us? There's an *us*?"

"Of course there's an *us*," Cas said quietly, peering into my eyes.

"Cas," I began.

"I love when you say my name. I love when you scream it. And I love when you say it when I'm deep inside you."

I shivered.

"What do you think the other night meant? The night in the barn?"

"We've had several nights in the barn."

"You're being purposely evasive. Too many feelings all at once, huh?"

I glared at him.

"Let's start with the reason you're pissed."

"At you?" I clarified. "You know why."

"Amber."

I didn't reply.

"She had a flat tire. And because she didn't have a spare, I offered her a ride."

"There wasn't a tow truck available?" I grumbled.

He set his hand on my leg. "Look at me."

"No."

"Salem, look at me."

With an annoyed sigh, I looked at him.

"Nothing happened with Amber."

"I know."

He raised his brows. "Do you?"

"Yes. I know when she's trying to get my goat."

"Well, she might've gotten your goat, but she didn't get me. So you don't have to be mad at me for that."

"This isn't all about you, you know!" I snapped.

"I know." His tone didn't change and he kept his eyes on me. "It's about your dad and Jane, and the fact that no one asked you if you wanted to share space with your father's girlfriend."

"It's stupid. And I'm being selfish," I lashed out. "I get all that. And yet, I can't—I can't believe she's going to be sleeping in my father's bedroom—the bedroom he shared with my mother—and I'm going to have to see her in the mornings and I just—God, I hate myself for being such a brat, but I can't help it!"

"Salem?"

"Yes?"

"Take off your pants."

My eyes widened. "What?"

"Take off your pants. The only way to deal with you when you're like this is to lick you or fuck you. Now take off your pants. I want my tongue inside you." He began to unbutton his flannel shirt.

"What are you doing?"

"Giving you something to lay down on." He stripped off his shirt and revealed his sculpted, gorgeous chest.

His words short-circuited my brain and before I knew

what I was doing, I was unbuttoning my jeans and laying back on his shirt.

Cas knelt on his haunches and positioned himself between my thighs. He slid his hands beneath my ass to raise me toward him.

"You're in your head too much, so I'm going to force you to think of nothing but my tongue between your legs." He nosed my underwear and breathed in. "God, your scent . . ."

He tongued me through the lace, causing me to quiver. It was both too much and not enough, the teasing, the licking of his tongue as he pleasured me through the fabric.

I wanted more and I wanted it all.

"Cas," I whispered.

He sucked the lace into his mouth and sparks of pleasure erupted between my legs.

"You promised," I moaned.

"What did I promise?"

"Your tongue. Inside me."

"You're not in control here. I am. And you're being a menace."

"Only you can make it sound like a compliment."

"It *is* a compliment. Because now we both win."

He dove back into his task with enthusiasm and verve. My inner thighs were wet with my desire and I knew he could see it.

And still he wouldn't take off my underwear.

I was going to punish him. I was going to punish him like he was punishing me.

He played my body, slowly, as if he didn't care that we were outside in public. And even though we were off the beaten path and there was hardly any foot traffic, the thrill of being caught heightened my awareness, heightened my pleasure.

Finally, *finally,* he slid my panties off and tossed them

aside. And then he began to feast. He pressed his tongue flat against me, sliding between my lips to find my clit. He sucked it into his mouth which made me buck against him.

"Fuck, Salem," he whispered.

My fingers plowed through his hair, gripping his head, keeping his mouth against me while I came with a gush.

He ate me. Greedy. Licked me clean. And left me a quivering mess.

I loosened my hold on him, and he lifted his head. His mouth was wet from me, his brow furrowed.

"Now who's in their head," I rasped, tracing his forehead with my finger.

"You taste different," he announced.

"Different? Different how?"

"Tangier. Not bad. Just different."

It was my turn to frown.

He would know, too. One of his favorite hobbies was making me come just using his mouth.

Cas's fingers drifted over my hip bone, and then toward the apex of my thighs. My deliciously languid body hummed with pleasure. Somehow wanting more.

"Don't," I warned.

"Don't what?" He slid two fingers inside me.

I quivered. "Fuck."

"Yes, exactly."

He gently thrust his fingers, gliding them against my flesh and grazing that elusive spot that was so difficult to find on my own. My second release was soft and not nearly as powerful; my body already wrung out from pleasure.

"Taste," he said, removing his fingers and bringing them to my lips.

My mouth enclosed his fingers and I licked them clean.

"Better?" he asked.

I nodded and then sat up.

He sighed and raked a hand through his hair. "I'm tired of sneaking around. I'm tired of lying."

I winced as I shoved my legs back into my jeans. "You make it sound sordid."

"It *is* sordid," he said. "And I don't want it to be. Don't you get it? I want to take you to Hadley and Declan's wedding. As my date."

"Why are you doing this?" I demanded, rising and pulling up my pants the rest of the way and buttoning them. "Everything was going great, and then you had to ruin everything!"

"How am I ruining everything?"

"I'm going back to New York. And you're going back to the circuit. This can never be anything more." I picked up his shirt and shoved it at him. "This is all I can give you. This is all I'm capable of giving."

"*Bullshit*," he snapped. "You're afraid. You've been afraid of me since the first night we met."

"I don't do afraid," I yelled.

"You wouldn't wake up with me," he pointed out. "You snuck out of my hotel room like a—a thief!"

"I was supposed to wake up with a complete stranger?" I demanded. "You're out of your mind!"

"You make me insane!" he snapped. "So God damn insane, I can't even see straight!"

"Then why the hell would you want to be around me anyway?" My cheeks flashed with heat and my blood boiled with emotion.

"God damn it, she was right," he muttered, rubbing the back of his neck.

"Who was right?"

"Hadley." He shook his head. "She told me to stay away from you. She told me you would chew me up and spit me out. And you wouldn't even do it on purpose. That it's just the way you are."

I swallowed. "Hadley told you that?"

"Yes. So I have no one to blame but myself. I just never expected . . ."

"What?"

"To fall so fucking hard and fast for you."

"You can't. You don't feel that way," I insisted.

"I don't?" He smiled slightly. "God, this sucks. You don't feel the same. Do you?"

I didn't reply.

He shoved his arms into his shirt and stalked away. "See ya around, Powell."

CHAPTER TWENTY-SEVEN

I'd skipped dinner and stayed out past bedtime, only returning when the house was quiet and bedded down for the night.

Hadley had texted before she'd gone to sleep, but I hadn't replied.

All of Cas's personal belongings had been removed from the bathroom.

I was staring at my bedroom ceiling, my mind a whirl.

My chest was a hollowed-out cave.

In New York, my heart had been a blackened, charred mess. But being here, being with Cas, our honest conversations, him seeing me at my worst . . . something had begun to grow from the ashes of my pain.

I'd been momentarily stunned by Cas's declaration. But after the shock had worn off, terror had been the next feeling.

Not because what he said frightened me.

Not because I wasn't sure about what a future with him looked like.

But because I felt it too.

The magnetism between us. The easy laughter, the camaraderie; the pure joy that came with finding someone who completely understood you.

All of you.

Every crevice. Every shadow.

Did I know what Cas was short for?

No.

Did he know my favorite color?

No.

But we *knew* each other, the way two people are supposed to know each other.

The way my parents had known one another.

The way Hadley and Declan knew one another.

And I'd ruined it because my first instinct was to fight.

With a labored sigh, I threw off the covers and climbed out of bed. My bare feet touched the cool floorboards as I padded my way to the door.

I opened it slowly, hoping the hinges didn't squeak. I went out into the hallway and listened for a moment at my father's door, not sure what I was expecting to hear, but there was nothing. Not even the gentle sounds of his snoring.

The kitchen was dark and I moved toward the stove, careful not to bash my toe on the heavy wooden kitchen table leg. I turned on the burner and opened the spout of the tea kettle so it wouldn't whistle and wake everyone up.

Just as the sound of frantic bubbles ricocheted through the copper tea kettle, the kitchen light flicked on.

I whirled.

Muddy stood with her arms crossed, the worn blue bathrobe tied around her waist, her silver hair braided down her back.

"Did I wake you?" I whispered.

She shook her head as she walked to the cabinet. She opened it and pulled out two mugs, and then she reached for the looseleaf tea in the mason jar by the stove.

I riffled through a drawer and extracted two tea strainers and handed them to her. While she filled the strainers, I put local crystalized honey into our mugs and poured in hot water.

Muddy opened the drawer and grabbed two teaspoons and then handed me one. I stirred the water, watching the honey melt. She submerged a tea strainer into each of our mugs and then waved me toward the den.

I sat down on the couch and held the hot steeping tea on my lap, wrapping my cold fingers around the mug.

Muddy closed the double doors and then took a seat on the couch next to me. She set her tea on the end table.

"It's time you and I had a talk," she said. "I've bided my time. I've waited, but some things can't wait anymore."

I winced. "This is going to hurt, isn't it?"

"I know about you and Bowman."

I paused and then nodded slowly. "Yes. He told me that. At the lake."

"What the hell did you say to him?" she demanded, her brows slashing together.

"Is that really any of your business?" I fired back.

"Whatever you said made him take off on his motorcycle. So yeah, it is my business. This ranch is my business. *You* are my business."

I kept hold of the mug with one hand and with the other, I rubbed my third eye.

"Salem," she said, her tone softening. "Who do you think has been pushing you two together?"

My head snapped up and I stared at her. "What?"

She smiled and let out a low chuckle. "I'll give it to you

both. You did well trying to hide what was going on beneath everyone's noses. But you never fooled me."

"When did you know?" I asked, still in shock.

"The moment he introduced himself at the hospital," she said. "I knew what was going on between Declan and Hadley before they did. And I knew what was going on between you and Bowman before you did."

"He and I—we'd already met, Muddy," I said. "The night of my layover in Denver."

"Oh?"

"It was pure coincidence that we wound up on the same airplane and figured out who the other one was. We'd already—we'd—" I sighed. "We spent the night together."

"Well, of course you did." She reached for her mug. "The first time I saw you two together, he was looking at you like he couldn't wait to get you naked again."

"Muddy!"

"What? I'm not a prude. And knowing the blush in your cheeks and spring in your step the last two weeks, I'd guess you're not a prude either."

I groaned.

She patted my knee. "So tell me what happened at the lake and I'll help you fix it."

"I don't know if it can be fixed," I said softly.

"Love fixes everything."

"You don't really believe that, do you?"

"Of course I do. Love brought you home, Salem. Love is going to fix your relationship with your father. Love will heal you. If you let it."

My throat tightened.

"You never get over the death of someone you love," she said. "You just learn how to live around it. But it's always there. Like a knot in a tree."

"Cas never said he loved me," I admitted. Just that he fell hard and fast. Still, that wasn't him declaring *I love you.*

"Not with words, maybe." Muddy brought the mug to her lips. She took a tiny sip and lowered it.

I thought back to the moment when he'd gotten into the shower with me, clothes and all. He'd held me while I sobbed and hadn't asked what it was about. Because he knew. He always seemed to know.

"Did he tell you when he was coming back?" I asked.

"Before the wedding, I'd imagine. But he didn't say." She cocked her head to the side. "You call him Cas."

"That's his name."

She shook her head. "To everyone else, he's Bowman. With you, he's Cas."

"I hurt him," I said, my lips wobbling. "I didn't mean to. I just—that's what I do to people."

"That's not what you do."

"No?" I got up and set my tea mug on the fireplace mantle. Then I began to pace. "I hurt Dad."

"He hurt you too."

"I hurt Gideon," I added. "I hurt everyone around me."

"Hadley doesn't feel that way. Poet, Wyn. I'm guessing they don't either. Your problem isn't that you don't love people, Salem. You *do* love them. And when you do, you love them deeply. You love them on a level that's hard for other people to understand. That's what I told Bowman."

I came to a halt. "You told him that?"

"Yes."

"Hadley told him that I'd break his heart and that he should stay away from me."

"She probably thought she was doing the right thing."

"Declan told me Cas isn't a family man."

"And what do you think?"

"I think I drove away the only man who truly understands me. And doesn't hold my flaws against me." I sighed. "I didn't mean for any of this to happen."

"I'm guessing he didn't either." She smirked.

"He's going to leave," I pointed out. "He's on the rodeo circuit."

"Yes."

"And I live in New York."

"Uh huh."

"How would that even work?"

"No idea."

"*Muddy*," I snapped. "You're supposed to be full of wisdom and knowing."

"I am," she said. "But you're *you*. And *you* have to figure things out for yourself. All I can do is guide."

"And matchmake," I drawled.

"And matchmake," she agreed.

I bit my lip as I pondered where we were supposed to go from here.

"You haven't told Hadley, have you?" Muddy asked.

I shook my head. "I wasn't sure what to tell her. And I don't want . . ."

"What?"

"I don't want to steal her thunder, you know? I have big moments, big emotions. But she's getting married. It needs to be all about her. I don't want to cause any drama."

"Huh," she picked up her mug again. "Way to have some self-awareness, sugar. I call that character growth."

CHAPTER TWENTY-EIGHT

THE RANCH

"Oh!" Jane exclaimed as she stood in the doorway of Hadley's and my bathroom. "Sorry! I didn't know you were in here. I didn't want to wake Connor, so I thought I'd use this bathroom. And with Bowman gone . . ."

I had a toothbrush shoved in the side of my mouth. My eyes were bleary from my middle of the night chat with Muddy and overall lack of sleep.

"S'okay." I spat in the sink and rinsed my mouth out. "I'm finished." I turned to leave the bathroom.

"Salem, wait," Jane said. "Can we talk?"

"Don't you have to . . ." I gestured to the toilet.

She smiled, making her even more attractive. I understood why my father was smitten.

"Yeah. I do. But can we find a time to—to talk?"

"Talk," I repeated.

"Yeah. We didn't get a chance to talk yesterday about"—she paused—"me staying here."

"You're not going away. Are you?"

It wasn't an accusation, but a question that came from a deep-seated place of childhood trauma after losing my mother.

But it wasn't just about me. My father had lost his wife.

And now he was in bed, recovering from brain surgery, and the last thing I wanted for him was a fair-weathered woman that would run when things got hard.

Her smile slid off her face. "No, Salem. I'm not going away."

We stared at one another for a long moment. Something passed between us. Some sort of understanding.

"Do you want to get lunch?" I asked.

Her smile appeared again, like sunshine after the rain. "Love to. You mind if we go somewhere that's not in town?"

"There's a decent bistro in Silver Springs. Does that work?"

"That's perfect."

Nodding, I turned and left the bathroom, closing the door behind me. I changed into jeans and a loose shirt and then poked my head into my dad's room. He was asleep with Jane's cat curled up on the bed next to him.

I had no desire to wake him, so I quietly closed the door. I had a few hours to kill before lunch with Jane so I went to Hadley and Declan's cabin, but Hadley wasn't there. I texted her, but when she didn't reply right away, I got into the side-by-side and drove out to the build site.

The crew was walking around a level lot with freshly packed dirt and wooden stakes with brightly colored rope outlining what would soon be a home. John and two of his sons were in a conversation when I pulled up and parked.

"Hey, Salem!" Harlan called out, jogging over to me the moment I got out of the side-by-side.

"Hi, Harlan."

"You remembered my name. I'm flattered," he teased.

Not even his bright smile or willingness to flirt made my heart lift, but I forced a smile that I hoped didn't show how defeated I really was.

"How are things?" I asked.

"Good. Moving along. We staked the house out and now we're finalizing orientation and checking for water drainage issues before we go further. If everything checks out, tomorrow we'll begin digging the foundation, and in a few days, we'll begin setting rebar and pouring concrete."

"Exciting," I murmured.

"Yeah. So hey, I was wondering—you know the town . . ."

"Uh huh."

"Would you want to show me around?"

"Oh. Harlan, look—"

"Say no more." He grinned. "Just thought I'd ask."

"Have you seen my sister?"

"Yeah." He nodded. "She's having tea with my mom in the doublewide."

The door to the doublewide opened and Tempest hopped down the steps as Hadley stood in the doorway.

"What are you doing out here?" Hadley asked.

"Looking for you," I said. "Morning, Stella."

"Hi, Salem," Harlan's mother greeted. "Can I get you a cup of tea?"

"No thanks, I'm good." I looked at Hadley. "Can we talk?"

"Sure, you want to drive me back?"

"Tea with Stella . . . are you two friends?" I asked after I parked in front of the cabin.

She opened the side-by-side door and Tempest immediately jumped down. "Her daughter lives in Waco and she misses her. Plus, she's surrounded by testosterone day in and day out."

"Ah." I nodded and climbed out.

She peered at me as we walked toward the porch. "You disappeared yesterday."

I nodded.

"And then Bowman left."

I took a deep breath. "Yeah, I heard. Any idea where he went?"

"He told Declan he was going for a motorcycle ride and would be back in a bit. No idea how long *a bit* is. He told Declan he just needed to clear his head."

"I see."

We both sat down on the porch steps next to one another.

"Are you okay?" Hadley asked.

"I'm fine."

"You don't look fine," she said.

"How do I look?" I asked in exasperation.

"Tired."

"Thanks," I muttered.

"Just being honest."

"I didn't sleep well last night," I admitted. "I'm having lunch with Jane today."

"No way."

"Way."

Her brows rose. "Are you going to be nice?"

"Yes, I'm going to be nice. *I* asked *her* to lunch."

"And what are you two going to talk about?"

"I don't know. I suppose I'm gonna try to get to know her."

"And maybe apologize?"

"For . . ."

"Salem!"

I smiled. "You're so easy to rile. I'm making amends. You think she'll stick around?"

"Yes. She loves Dad."

"Yeah." I rubbed the back of my neck. "I got that message loud and clear."

"You could've texted me this. You didn't have to track me down to tell me you were having lunch with Jane."

"I know." I sighed. "But I couldn't sit still and I just needed to . . ."

Hadley touched my arm and smiled. "I understand."

My shoulders softened. "Of course you do. You always understand. Thanks, Hads."

I sat across the cafe table and peered at Jane who was currently sipping on her iced tea, looking anywhere but at me.

The restaurant was quiet and we were tucked into a corner table with some measure of privacy. We'd already given our order so there was no chance of interruption.

"What are your intentions with my father?" I asked.

She blinked and set her iced tea down. "Getting right to the meat of it, huh?"

"Yep. No point in beating around the bush."

"Fair," she said. Her gaze dropped to her lap and she fiddled with her napkin before looking at me again. "You know, they warned me about you."

"Muddy and Hadley?"

"And your father," she said.

"What did he say?"

"That you'd have a problem with him dating."

"That makes me sound like a child."

"You're acting like one," she said slowly.

I blew out a huff of air. "Yeah. I know. And I explode all over everyone and everything. It's why they call me Mount St. Salem."

She nodded. "I know what it's like to have someone come into your world and shake everything up."

"You do?"

"Yes. My dad passed away when I was seven. My mom remarried when I was eleven. Boy, I did *not* make it easy on my stepfather." She smiled. "But he stuck it out and I'm so glad I have him in my life."

"Eleven and twenty-three are not the same," I said.

"No, they're not." She leaned forward. "I'm trying to let you off the hook, Salem. This is a lot to process—and I know being home is . . . challenging for you."

I sighed. "He told you."

"Of course he told me. We're in love, Salem."

Guilt swamped me.

Sitting with Jane across the table made me realize that I'd been judging my father because he was my father. But he was a person with real feelings and a life to live, and it was his first time living, too.

"He and I butt heads a lot," I admitted.

"You're both stubborn."

"Hey!"

"It's true." She grinned. "You asked what my intentions are with your dad. Well, I know it won't be a quick recovery. And I don't expect it to happen overnight, but . . . I'm here, Salem. For the long haul."

The tension in my chest eased.

"Marriage? Kids?" I pressed.

She blinked. "No one's ever asked me that before."

"No?"

"No."

"I'm stubborn—and blunt," I said. "And even though it's early in your relationship, I bet you already know, don't you?"

She leaned back in her chair and studied me. "I'm thirty

years old. I've been married once already. We're still good friends despite being a rotten romantic match. But something happens when you find the person you can't live without. And that thing happened with your father."

"I see."

"I love him, Salem," she said. "And I hope, in time, you and I can be . . . friends."

"Friends."

"I'm not looking to replace anyone."

But if she married my father and they had children, I'd have half-siblings. And my dad would have a whole new family.

Nothing stayed the same.

And the fact was, I didn't want it to stay the same. I didn't want to be Salem the Stubborn, Salem the Grudge Holder.

I wanted to move on. I wanted to be happy. I wanted my dad to be happy.

"You've been understanding," I said. "And far too gracious. If I'd been in your shoes, I would've slugged me a long time ago."

She laughed lightly and grasped her iced tea. "Apology accepted."

CHAPTER TWENTY-NINE

THE RANCH

"Salem," Dad mumbled as his eyes opened.

I clam-shelled my laptop and set it aside. "Hey. Good nap?"

"Not bad." He propped himself up against the pillows. "Can I get some water?"

I rose from the plush, comfortable chair and walked to his nightstand to pick up the half-drunk glass of water that had a straw stuck in it.

"It's room temperature," I said.

"That's fine."

I went to his bedside, angled the straw, and held it out to him.

"I'll take the glass," he said.

I hesitated.

"I'm not an invalid. Don't treat me like one."

Smiling, I gave him the glass. "Now I know you're going to be okay."

Dad finished off the water and I took the glass from him and set it aside.

"How long have you been here?"

"About an hour," I said. "After I got back from lunch with Jane, I relieved Muddy of her *watching you sleep* duties."

"It's going to be a long recovery if there's always someone by my bedside," he quipped. "Lunch with Jane?"

"I want you to be happy, Dad," I said.

"You do?"

I nodded.

"I want you to be happy too. Are you happy?"

"Right this minute?" I smiled, but it trembled. "Yeah. We're talking without yelling. Of course I'm happy."

"Salem."

"Don't worry about me, Dad. Just get well. And rest up. You've got to be able to watch Hadley walk down the aisle without falling asleep."

"You think she'll ever forgive me? For not being able to walk her down the aisle?"

"She wanted to postpone the wedding."

"She did?"

I nodded. "I talked her out of it, though."

"Good." He messed with the covers and finally tugged them off.

"What are you doing?"

"Going to the bathroom." He took a moment, and then he slowly moved his legs to the edge of the bed. He was wearing a pair of sweatpants and a T-shirt.

I hung back. My father's masculine pride was at stake. Still, I didn't want him to fall. He eventually made it to the bathroom on his own, but by the time he got back into bed, he was exhausted.

"Soup?" I asked.

"No thanks," he said as his lids began to close. "Maybe later."

I grabbed my computer and crept from the room. The house was quiet. Muddy had gone for a ride to get some air, so I had the place to myself.

I walked into the den and looked at the family photos on the mantle. My grandmother's half-crocheted project. The ashes in the fireplace.

This house was a home. It offered more than shelter. It offered comfort.

Hadley's baby would crawl around on these floors.

Christmas morning would be filled with presents and matching pajamas, Muddy's chocolate chip pancakes, and hot chocolate with a little spice added to it.

Tempest would curl up next to the fire and fall asleep.

Dad and Jane would . . .

Well, they'd get married. And have at least one kid.

And where would I be?

Back in New York. Working in a high-rise building with glass windows and empty take-out boxes. Smushing myself into a subway car during early morning rush hour. Getting my heels caught in sidewalk grates. Going home to an apartment that still had my friends, but not my sister.

There was a fork in the road. A clear fork.

I could go back to New York. I could get on the hamster wheel and pray that I'd be able to carve out some time for Thanksgiving or Christmas to come home . . . but not both, because there would never be enough time off for both if I chose that life.

And there would be men. Gorgeous, suit-clad men, who didn't understand me or how I'd grown up. I'd be forever hungry in New York. Hungry for the one true human connection I'd ever made that I'd run away from because it had been too powerful.

I'd always gone after what I wanted. Even if I hadn't known what that was, I knew if I dove headfirst in a direction, I'd eventually find my way. I always did.

But at this moment, my way seemed to be leading me back to my roots. Back to something I never thought I'd want again.

A Family.

A home.

Love.

Living with regret was something I'd never do.

So, I opened my phone and stared at the screen for a moment. Then I scrolled to his name and pressed it.

His phone rang.

And rang.

And rang.

Until it switched over to voicemail.

It beeped.

"Please," I said. "Please come back."

And then I hung up and hoped like hell I hadn't fucked it all up.

"I can't believe I get to hug your faces in a week!" Wyn said, a huge smile spreading across her lips.

"I'm literally ex-ing off days on the calendar," Poet added as she held up a black marker.

I got up from the couch in the cabin and went to refill my glass of lemonade. Declan had gone into town with Harlan to hang out with Wade, leaving me and Hadley to have sister time in their cabin.

"One more week, and then we get to show you the town, the ranch, and maybe chain you to the porch so you can never leave," Hadley said.

"Chain? Please, throw away the key," Poet said.

I came back and took a seat next to Hadley. "Work still dragging you hard?"

"It's the worst," Poet grumbled.

"She comes home and cries every day," Wyn said.

Poet frowned. "You weren't supposed to tell them that."

The phone shook and Wyn quickly righted it. "How long are you going to stick out the misery for?"

"I don't know," Poet said. "It's gotta give, right? I'm working toward something. It would be a shame to throw it all away because it sucks in the interim. A vacation in Huckleberry Hill will give me the break I need to go back there and kick ass."

"Or at least kick Alma's ass," Wyn quipped.

Tempest jumped up onto my lap and then flopped down onto it.

"It's only a matter of time before Salem gets a matching goat," Poet said.

"Nah, I'm not into farm animals," I said, even as I stroked Tempest's head.

"Could've fooled me," Wyn said.

"I'm ranch fluff," I explained. "I'm here for the vibes, not the poop."

"So how did the final dress fitting go?" Poet asked.

"Good," Hadley said. "You can't even tell I'm pregnant when I put it on."

"Why are you frowning, Salem?" Poet wondered.

"Oh, because even though Hadley looks gorgeous, my dress doesn't fit," I said. "That was a fun little surprise."

"What do you mean it doesn't fit?" Wyn demanded. "Did they get your measurements wrong?"

"Maybe? I dunno, I'm bloated," I said. "It might be the poutine every morning and the butter Hadley puts in everything."

"Hmm, butter," Wyn said in understanding.

"What's with the face," Hadley said to Poet.

"Hmm? Oh, just—well, yeah. I don't want to say it."

"Say it," I said.

The door to the cabin opened, effectively ending whatever Poet was going to say. Tempest jumped off my lap in order to greet Declan.

"Oh, damn," he said. "I came back too early, didn't I?"

"I thought you were going to stay out with Harlan all night. And by all night, I mean at least until ten," Hadley said with a grin.

"I left him to it. He and Wade are fast buds," Declan explained.

"Hey Declan!" Wyn called out.

Hadley turned the phone toward Declan who grinned. "Ladies." He came over to Hadley and kissed her forehead. "Missed you."

"Awwww." Poet giggled. "We're still here, you know."

"On that note," Hadley said. "Talk to you guys later."

"Good night!" Wyn called out.

Hadley hung up with them and I rose. "That's my cue."

I closed the door to the cabin and went down the porch steps. It was still light out, and the sun wouldn't set for at least another hour, so it was easy to see the path to the house.

As I got closer, I saw a motorcycle out front.

My heart tripped with emotion.

The house was quiet as I went inside—Dad's door was closed, and he was probably asleep. I peeked into Hadley's room, but Cas wasn't there. With a sigh of frustration, I traipsed downstairs and opened the sliding glass door.

Cas stood on the deck, his back facing me, acting as though he hadn't heard my approach.

I paused, unsure of what to do.

Finally, he turned.

It had only been a few days since I'd seen him, but it had felt like a lifetime.

We stared at each other, drinking each other in.

"You came back," I croaked.

"You called."

I wasn't sure who reached for who first, but suddenly I was in his embrace, and his lips were on mine.

He placed his hands underneath my thighs and lifted me into his arms. I wrapped my legs around him, fusing our mouths together.

I tore my lips from his. "Wait."

"You're right, let's go to the barn loft."

"No."

It was like I'd dumped a bucket of ice water over his head. "No?"

"No," I repeated, cradling his cheeks. "This isn't the part we have a problem with, Cas."

"This can solve most of our problems, Salem."

I smiled. "You're not getting into my pants tonight."

"Let me try."

Laughing, I pressed my forehead to his. "I'm glad you're back. Where did you go?"

"Montana. You know they have swarms of mosquitos the size of bats."

"Yes. I'm aware."

I lowered my legs and dangled in his arms until he finally set me down.

"You told Declan you had some things to sort out?" I asked tentatively.

"Yeah."

"So, did you? Sort them out?"

"Think so. What about you?"

"Some stuff," I admitted. "Other stuff is still hazy."

He nodded in understanding.
"I want—can I show you something?" I asked.
"Now?"
I nodded. "It's important."
He held out his hand to me and I took it.

CHAPTER THIRTY

The Ranch

I parked the side-by-side at the base of a hill and cut the engine. We climbed out and Cas came around the hood of the vehicle to grasp my hand. There was no path where I was taking him. But he was quiet as I led him up the hill. The fading sun kissed green earth, turning everything a whimsical gold.

"Gorgeous, isn't it?" I asked, taking in the surroundings and breathing it in deep.

"Gorgeous," he agreed.

I looked at him. He wasn't staring at the view.

"Come on." My throat thickened as I turned in the direction of my favorite place on earth.

The red cedar tree came into view, its trunk thick with age and deep roots. It leaned to the side and I couldn't believe it hadn't fallen over yet.

"Mom found this tree one day on a ride," I explained. "She loved riding. Exploring. It's funny. I love exploring too, and you'd think I'd enjoy horseback riding, but it never stuck. Hadley, though. She loves it."

I took a step closer to the tree and placed my hand on the trunk. "The tree's actually dead. It was dead when she found it, but because it's so old, it can stand for years. We're technically not on our land, which is why she never had anyone come tend to it and cut it down. This is national forest."

Cas came closer to the tree and I watched his eyes scan the bark. I knew he saw it when he stilled and then placed his palm on the tree.

My mother's initials and mine were carved inside of a heart.

"She never would've carved it on a live tree. She wasn't about destruction." I laughed softly. "She wasn't, yet I am."

"What have you destroyed, Salem?" His hand dropped from the tree and he placed his hands on my shoulders to turn me to him. "Nature's a funny thing, you know? Some things can't grow until other things die."

He pulled me into his arms, and I buried my head against his chest.

"Some trees don't release their seeds until they burn in a fire," he said, his lips brushing my head.

Emotions ricocheted through me. My insides rearranged; they burst open and began to make space for something new and beautiful.

My heart had been closed like a metal chest, and yet it suddenly sprang open.

"That day . . . in the shower," I murmured. "You didn't make me talk about it. Why?"

"Because if you needed to talk about it, you would have. That wasn't about me. It was about you. And what you needed."

"It wasn't just about my father in the hospital."

"I know."

I pulled back, just enough so that I could stare up at him. "I didn't need to say anything because you just understood."

"I understand you, Salem."

"Yeah. You do."

He leaned down and pressed a kiss to my forehead. "I think a lot of people try to change each other instead of loving the person as they are."

I buried my face against his chest again. "I wish you'd known her."

"You'll tell me about her. You'll show me photos. You'll tell me stories. And I'll listen."

"Death is so weird, Cas. It's so very personal and yet universal. My world changed when she died. And I looked around at everyone else and I just wanted to scream because they were smiling and happy and they had no idea that someone so wonderful was gone. I was angry—on their behalf—because they'd never gotten to know what a wonderful, amazing woman she was."

Tears I couldn't contain finally spilled from my eyes. They blotted his shirt, but they wouldn't stain. When his shirt dried, there would be no evidence that they'd ever been. Only a memory.

She was a memory.

And one day, I wouldn't be here to remember her anymore either.

"Why do we do this?" I wailed. "Why do we live? What's the point of it all if all we do is lose the ones we love?"

He cradled my cheeks and forced me to look at him. "We live to love, Salem. That *is* the reason. It's the only reason that makes it worth it."

My heart fissured even more. It cracked all the way open, and pain and remorse and loss and love and everything that had to do with hope sprang forth like a geyser that spewed from the broken earth.

But I wasn't broken.

I'd never been broken. I just hadn't healed fully.

Not until now.

Cas held me long after the tears had run their course, long after the emotions had passed, long after the sun had finally set.

I pulled back and scrubbed my face. "Take me home, Cas."

We walked down the hill, his arm wrapped around me, the dead tree that would one day be gone from this world behind us.

○

Cas took me back to the house. He undressed me, put me in his clothes, and then tucked me into my childhood bed, sliding in next to me. He left the bedside lamp on its lowest setting.

We didn't speak for a long time.

I was exhausted. There was nothing like the storm of an emotional break that left you empty, but lighter in a way too.

"I'm jealous of Hadley and Declan," he murmured. "They have the cabin—their own space."

"Not much space. Not with a baby goat and four crazy working dogs."

"Privacy, Salem. They have privacy."

"Yeah, privacy would be nice," I murmured against his chest. "I love that cabin. We used to have movie nights in there."

"Yeah?"

I nodded. "It was our place to go and hang out with our friends."

"What kind of movies did you guys watch?" he asked.

"When it was just Hadley and me, we watched old musicals. Mom's favorites. When we had friends over, we usually let them decide. Never horror movies, though."

"No?"

"Definitely not. We were in a cabin near the woods. I know how those movies end."

He chuckled, brushed my hair away from my face, and pressed a kiss to my brow.

"Thank you for showing me the tree."

"No one else has seen it," I said.

"No one?"

"No."

"Not even Hadley?"

"Not even Hadley. It was a me and Mom thing. Hadley has things that are just between her and Mom too, I'm sure of it. It's nice, actually. We're twins, you know? And people call us *the twins* and sometimes it feels like we don't have a separate identity. Mom always made sure we felt like individuals."

His hand stroked up and down my arm. "So, you never showed Gideon the tree either?"

"No. Gideon's never seen the tree."

I placed my hand on his heart, loving the steady pulse of it. Reminding me that he was alive. We both were. And that I was no longer scared of the future or what it looked like.

"He sent letters," I said quietly. "One a week from the moment I left and went to New York. I returned them all to him. Unopened. He stopped writing after a year."

"Why?"

"Because he finally understood that I wasn't coming home."

"No, not why did he stop writing. I meant, why didn't you open them?"

"Hadley was the only person, the only connection I could stand from home. Everything and everyone else . . . it was too painful. Too much of a reminder. Gideon was everything I was trying to forget. I hurt him, deeply. When I left and when I didn't answer him."

"Self-protection."

"Something like that. I didn't want to hurt him. But I was hurting too much to even be able to think of anyone else's pain."

"You were young."

"And I'm not young anymore? Old at the ripe age of twenty-three?"

"You're not even close to old. Not like me."

"Right. You're thirty-four. What was it like during the Civil War?"

"Brat."

I giggled. And then Cas rolled me over so I was on my back, and then he attacked me with tickles until I was gasping for breath.

"Surrender!"

"Never!" I fired back.

He clasped my wrists, held them above my head, and pinned my lower body with his.

Cas peered into my eyes. "You're a fighter. I love that about you. And I love you, Salem."

I swallowed. "You love me?"

"Yes."

No flowery words. No poetic delivery.

Just blunt truth.

Because that was Cas.

"The name inked on my hip," I said. "It doesn't mean anything."

"I know it doesn't mean anything."

"No, you don't understand. It doesn't mean anything because there is no Jean Luc. It was just a name I had tattooed on me because I knew it would drive other men crazy."

"Jean Luc doesn't exist?"

"Nope."

"There was never a Jean Luc?"

"There was never a Jean Luc."

He let out a laugh and pressed his forehead to mine. "You were put on this earth to drive me insane. I'm convinced of it."

I wiggled underneath him.

He moved just enough so I could free my legs. And then I wrapped them around him.

"You're welcome to drive me insane." I lifted myself up and brushed my lips against his. "In fact, I insist that you do."

CHAPTER THIRTY-ONE

THE RANCH

I kicked Cas out of my bed in the middle of the night. He didn't want to go, but we were tempting fate.

After he'd made me beg, he wouldn't let me come for an hour. I wasn't complaining. When he finally slid inside me, I came immediately and it had been one of the most powerful orgasms of my life. I'd bitten his shoulder to keep from screaming.

I was tired, wrung out and ready to fall into deep sleep.

My phone was on silent, but it lit up with a text.

I fell into a light doze and just as I was drifting off to sleep, the conversation I had with the girls floated through my head. Poet had been about to say something when Declan had interrupted.

Suddenly, I was wide awake. I opened my calendar app and scrolled from the previous month to the current one.

My period was late.

Very late.

I was on birth control so why was my—

I'd spent the night with Cas in the hotel, and we'd used condoms. Every single time.

Had one of them failed?

Was stress the reason my period was late?

It had been a hell of a homecoming.

But the bloating and my pants no longer fitting comfortably . . .

I had no other symptoms that I might be pregnant.

Still . . .

A niggle of worry took root. There was no way I would be able to go to sleep. Not now.

But what the hell was I supposed to do? Sneak out of my house and pray the hot bull rider in the room next to me didn't wake up?

It was 3:04 a.m. when I pulled into a drug store in Coeur d'Alene. It was 3:10 a.m. when I bought a pregnancy test. It was 3:14 a.m. when I peed on said pregnancy test in the drug store bathroom. It was 3:19 am when a big, fat, pink plus sign showed up on the pregnancy test.

A knock sounded on the door.

"Be out in a second!" I called back.

I hastily shoved the pregnancy test back into the box and into my purse. I quickly washed my hands, and then I opened the door and came face to face with the middle-aged store clerk in her blue vest and a look of worry on her face.

"It's all yours," I said, gesturing to the door.

"Oh, I don't need the restroom. I just wanted to check on you."

I promptly burst into tears.

"Aww, yeah, I thought that might be the case," she said.

And even though she was a complete stranger, she pulled me into a maternal embrace and patted my back.

"It'll be okay," she crooned.

I stepped back and wiped the tears from my eyes. "You're really nice."

She smiled. "Do you want a cookie? I've got some up front."

Nodding, I followed her toward the register.

"How did you know I was—that I'm . . ."

I couldn't even finish the sentence because my brain still hadn't wrapped around the truth.

"We don't get a lot of foot traffic this time of night. And a young woman coming in looking a bit frazzled, wearing two different shoes"—she pointed to my feet—"asking for a pregnancy test—it was an easy bet."

I looked down at my feet. One clog and one of Muddy's loafers. "Would you look at that."

"Sit," she said, gesturing to the chair behind the counter. "I need to stretch my legs a bit."

"So, a cookie?" I asked hopefully.

She smiled. "There's a bag next to the register."

I found the plastic bag of cookies and took one.

"Pumpkin chocolate chip," she explained. "Secret family recipe."

I bit into it and immediately felt better. "This is so good."

"Goes better with milk. Hang on."

She walked to the mini fridge of drinks and pulled out a plastic bottle of milk. She unscrewed the lid and handed it to me. "On the house."

"Thank you. God, you're nice." I took the milk from her

and drank half of it in one go. "Yeah, you're right. That was perfect."

"So, I'm guessing this wasn't a planned thing?"

I shook my head.

"Some of the best things in life aren't planned," she murmured. "You have family?"

I nodded.

"Are they supportive?"

I nodded again.

"The father . . ."

I winced and shrugged.

How the hell is Cas going to take this news?

I'd been warned that he wasn't a family man. Did I really expect him to stick around?

I finished off the cookie and rubbed the crumbs on my sweats. "Thank you for this. It was—I don't even know your name."

She looked down at her vest. "Oh, shoot. I forgot my name tag." She reached over to the register and ran her hand underneath the drawer. "There it is!"

She held up her name tag and pinned it to her vest. "I'm Kathleen."

"Kathleen," I whispered, my eyes filling with tears again. "It was really nice to meet you."

"The pleasure was all mine, sweetie. The pleasure was all mine."

♘

"You're avoiding me," Cas said three days later.

"What? No," I lied as I unlatched the chicken coop gate. "I've been with my dad. Talking to him. Keeping his spirits up, you know?"

"Your dad falls asleep after like, ten minutes of conversation," he said. "You're telling me you sit by his bedside for hours while he sleeps?"

I frowned. "How do you know he falls asleep that fast?"

"Because it happened the other day when I spoke to him."

"Why did you speak to him?" I demanded.

"I wanted to introduce myself," he said. "And stop trying to change the subject."

"Is that why you're cornering me at five a.m. at the chicken coop?" I asked.

"You're not an early riser by nature," Cas said. "So why are you at the chicken coop this early?"

"I'm pitching in." I found a brown egg and put it in the basket.

"You're quiet at family dinners, and then you escape up to your room. You don't invite me to your bed. You're avoiding me because of what I said."

I frowned. "What did you say?"

"I told you I loved you, and then you ghosted me."

"I didn't *ghost* you," I mumbled.

"I told you I loved you, and you never said it back, and now you're absolutely ghosting me. I want to know why."

"I did too—tell you I loved you," I fired back, feeling my cheeks heat with anger.

"Uh, *no* you didn't."

"Did too."

"Did not."

"I took you to the tree," I clarified. "And then I told you the truth about my tattoo." I raised my eyebrows. "That means I love you."

"In what language?" he snapped. "Because I speak English."

"I thought you spoke Salem."

"You expected me to realize those two things meant you loved me?"

"Yes."

"And you don't see the problem with that?"

"What? Do you want roses and chocolates or something?" I glared. "You and I are both people of action. Not words."

"And yet, I still said the words. And if you do love me, then that doesn't change the fact that you've been avoiding me and I want to know why."

I clamped my mouth shut.

"Ah, so I get to guess why you ghosted me. Lucky me." He pushed the brim of his hat back. "Okay, let's see. Your emotions scare you."

When I didn't give an inclination that he was right or wrong, he continued.

"You slept with someone else and don't want to tell me. But, I gotta say, if you did that—"

"I didn't sleep with anyone else, you idiot," I retorted. "And screw you for even suggesting that could be an option. I wouldn't hurt you that way."

"I don't think you'd hurt me that way either," he protested. "But God damn it, Salem. You give me so little. Some reassurance would be nice, you know?"

"Oh my God, do you want it on a billboard? Salem loves Cas Bowman and is pregnant with his baby!"

Cas went still. "Say that again."

"I'd rather not," I grumbled, feeling my cheeks heat.

"Salem!" he barked.

I sighed. "Salem loves Cas Bowman."

"Not that part. I already knew that part. I'm talking about the pregnant with my baby part."

I swallowed. "The first night we were together . . . we had a failure of some sort."

"Not operator error," he said, his voice sounding very far away.

"No, not operator error," I agreed. "We were regular Boy Scouts. But one of the condoms was clearly defective."

"You said you were on birth control."

"I was. Am." I sighed. "It was a perfect storm, Cas. A perfect storm that resulted in a positive pregnancy test."

He gripped a fence post that surrounded the chicken coop. "You found out three days ago, didn't you?"

I nodded.

"Salem, look at me."

With a sigh, I turned to face him and waited.

"Now we *have* to tell people."

"No. We don't. Not until after the wedding," I stated. "I won't do it, Cas. I won't steal the limelight from my sister. This is her time. If I announce this, it's just going to cause drama. I want her to be happy. She deserves her day. Surely we can keep this between us for a little while."

"You're having a baby. Our baby."

I nodded.

"This changes everything."

"I know."

"Salem?"

"Yeah."

"Put down the basket."

"Why?"

"Just do it."

With a sigh, I set it down. Cas came toward me and wrapped me in his arms. "I've got you."

I buried my face in his shirt and breathed him in.

"I've got you both. I'm not going anywhere."

♘

"Did you and Bowman make up from your fight?" Muddy asked.

I closed the back door and set the basket of eggs onto the counter. "What are you talking about?"

"Rule number one: I know all. I see all." She lifted a cup of coffee to her lips and waited.

"Still not following," I lied.

"I saw you two hugging in the chicken coop, but not before you both were gesturing wildly at each other. No doubt your voices were raised?"

"Were you standing in the kitchen and spying on us?" I demanded.

"Of course not. I stood on the back porch and spied on you." She grinned. "Couldn't hear anything, though. Not even when the wind changed."

"You need a hobby," I muttered.

"I have one. Several actually."

"Meddling in your granddaughters' lives is not a hobby."

"Sit," she commanded.

I sat at the kitchen table.

"Are you going to tell me why you snuck out of here a few nights ago?"

I stilled.

"No use lying, sugar. I woke up and heard the truck engine rumble out of here."

"I thought you slept with ear plugs."

"Not right now. Not if your father needs something. I have to be able to hear him."

Did that mean she'd heard us the other night? My cheeks heated at the thought.

"Funny things, secrets. They always have a way of coming out." She smirked. "Like you and Bowman sharing a bed."

I groaned. "You know everything."

"Sugar, you have to at least *pretend* to be quiet."

I looked at her in horror. "Oh God—"

"Relax. I'm kidding. Though I'm glad to see my suspicions

were correct. You were the reason Bowman went on a motorcycle ride, but you're also the reason he came back. Right?"

"Yes."

"And you're together now?"

"Yes."

Please don't ask, please don't ask, please don't ask.

"Are you excited to see Wyn and Poet in a couple of days?"

The change in conversation threw me. "Yes. Very excited."

"I'm glad they're coming a few days before the wedding. I'm looking forward to getting to know them better."

"Yeah. You'll love them."

"I know I will." She nodded. "So how are they going to feel?"

"Feel? About what?"

She cocked her head to the side. "About sharing their apartment with a baby."

CHAPTER THIRTY-TWO

"I'm going to be sick!" I shoved away from the kitchen table, made it to the back door, and puked all over my grandmother's tulips.

I hastily wiped my mouth and stood up.

"Was that morning sickness or emotional sickness?" Muddy asked.

I glared at her over my shoulder before another wave of nausea hit me and I bent over the porch railing again.

"There can only be one dramatic person in this family," I said after I recovered. "And I've long claimed that title. So next time, don't drop a bomb so casually. Speaking of casual, how did you know? And why aren't you shocked?"

"I had a hunch," she said. "But I didn't know for certain. Now I do. As for shocked, nothing shocks me. Someone has to be level-headed in this family. God knows you're not. Neither is your father."

"My father," I groaned. "I'm going to have to tell him I'm pregnant."

"Yep."

"Not before the wedding," I said. "No one can know."

"You don't think the morning sickness is going to give it away?"

"Muddy, please," I begged. "I can't do this to Hadley."

"Do what to Hadley?"

"I can't announce this before her wedding. I won't. I won't steal her day. Because you know the minute this gets out, it won't be about her anymore, it'll be about me."

She patted my cheek. "You're a good egg, Salem."

"I'm cracked."

Muddy grinned. "This stays between us. I swear."

I hugged her tightly.

"One more question and I'll let it drop," she said.

"What's that?"

"Does this mean you're staying?"

I pulled back to peer at her.

"Cas and I haven't talked about anything like that yet."

"Okay." She gave me a squeeze and then let me go. "Whatever you need though, you come to me, yeah?"

I nodded.

"I lied. I have one more question to ask."

I couldn't stop the smile. "Shoot."

"Are you scared?"

My smile softened. "No. I'm not scared. I was in shock. But that wore off pretty quickly. And in its place . . ."

"Yeah?"

"Love."

"Love. It's almost like that's the entire point, huh?"

I laughed. "Yeah. The entire point."

♘

"It's not my birthday," Dad said, looking at the cupcake in front of him. "Why is there a candle in my cupcake?"

"It's a celebration," Hadley said. "You just had your first meal at the kitchen table since you've been home."

Jane touched his cheek. "It's your delayed welcome home party."

Dad turned his head and kissed her palm. "Still doesn't explain a candle."

It was so natural and sweet, and it stupidly brought tears to my eyes. I wasn't sure if it was the hormones or the fact that I'd opened the floodgates so my emotions were constantly at the surface now.

"If you don't want the cupcake, I'll take it," Declan quipped.

"Get your own." Dad blew out his candle. He went to grab it, but his arm dropped suddenly.

Exhaustion appeared to be kicking in, but no one said anything. Jane picked up the cupcake and peeled the wrapper from it and held it up to him.

"I'm fine, thanks. Actually, I'm a little tired." Dad struggled to stand, but he did so without any assistance. "Dinner was great, Mom."

"I didn't cook," Muddy said. "Hadley and Salem did."

"Which means the boys get to do the dishes," Hadley said to Declan.

"On it," he said, rising.

Cas was sitting next to me, but not too close. He rose, and then the guys began clearing dishes from the table while my dad headed for the stairs. Jane followed behind him, clearly ready to lend a hand if needed.

Dad wouldn't ask, though.

Muddy got up and put the untouched cupcake on a plate. "I'll run this up to him in a bit. I know he wants it. It's his favorite."

"Red velvet with cream cheese frosting." Hadley made a face. "Ew. Give me one of the chocolate ones."

"Better do it," I warned. "She's looking a little piqued."

"Then I'd better take two chocolate cupcakes." Hadley grinned. "Wouldn't want to go feral on anyone."

"Feral Hadley? Yeah, right," I teased.

"Am I allowed to say anything?" Declan asked.

"No," Hadley and I said at the same time, and then both dissolved into giggles.

Muddy took the cupcake upstairs to Dad as the boys finished cleaning the kitchen. After the dishwasher was loaded and running, Declan asked, "Fire circle?"

Hadley shook her head. "I'm beat. Can we go home?"

"Sure, bear snack. Whatever you want." Declan leaned over and kissed her forehead.

"That's both the cutest and grossest nickname I've ever heard," I said.

"Agreed," Cas said.

"How are you doing, Bowman? The full house must be driving you crazy," Hadley said as she moved toward the front door. The rest of us followed.

"It's fine," Cas said. "But Salem's a bathroom hog."

"I am not," I muttered.

"You are," Hadley said with a grin.

Cas and I stood on the front porch and I waved to Hadley and Declan as they headed to the cabin.

"Alone at last," I said, turning to Cas.

"Your room?" he asked.

I nodded and the two of us went back inside and headed up the stairs. Once I had the door to my bedroom closed, I turned to him.

"Muddy knows I'm pregnant," I said without preamble.

"How?"

"She suspected, and then I confirmed it by puking on her

tulips. She understands why I want to keep this between us until after the wedding."

"But after the wedding, we tell people."

"We have to." I took a seat on my bed and propped a pillow against the headboard and laid down. Cas sat at the foot of the bed and patted his lap.

I stretched out fully and placed my feet on his thigh.

We sat in silence for a moment. It felt like contentment, but also as though each of us was waiting for the other person to talk.

Finally, I broke the silence. "Look, Cas. This baby threw us both for a loop. And I don't want you to think that you have to be involved—"

"Stop right there," he commanded.

I fell silent.

"It takes two to make a baby. I love you. I'm not going anywhere. You hear me?"

I nodded.

"Say it. I need you to say it."

"I hear you," I murmured.

"You thought I was going to bail."

"I thought this wasn't something we planned," I said slowly. "And so I'd never ask you to—"

"I'm trying not to get upset. Because if I get upset, that'll get you fired up and you need to be calm. Especially now that you're pregnant. So, I'm not going to yell. But you're going to listen to me now, okay?"

"Okay," I whispered.

"I'm here. I'm in this. We're doing this. Together. Yeah?"

"Yeah."

"Good." He nodded. "Glad we got that settled."

"But nothing else is settled. We have a bit of a geography problem."

"Yeah, we do," he agreed.

"I'd planned on going back to New York, but not until Dad was stable. More stable, I mean."

"Yeah?"

I nodded. "I haven't told my boss yet, but now . . ."

"Go on."

"I definitely don't want to raise a baby in New York," I said simply.

"Hallelujah."

"I want to be here," I admitted. "Close to family. I can't believe I'm even saying that. God, I can't believe I'm pregnant. And Hadley's pregnant. They'll be cousins so close in age. I kind of like that."

"Can I say something?"

"Always."

"You don't seem at all fazed by this turn of events."

"What in my life has ever gone according to plan?" I asked with a wry chuckle. "This is just par for the course. Plus, I crave adventure. Clearly."

"But it's a baby."

"Yes."

"That's a pretty big curveball."

I peered at him. "You're having doubts."

"What? Not at all."

"No?" I pulled my legs away from him and sat up. "I'm not expecting you to change your entire life because of this. I know you're not a family man. You can be as involved as you want. You can come and go as you please. When you're on a break from the circuit you can come back and—"

"Woman, are you fucking delusional?" he snapped.

"Delusional is in the eye of the beholder."

"Don't be cute and quippy, Salem. Not right now."

I smiled. "You called me cute."

He scooted closer and grasped my upper arms gently and

stared into my eyes. "What do you mean *I'm not a family man?*"

"Well, Declan said that. I don't want to try to change who you are."

"You're telling me that you expect me to go about my life as if nothing's changed? Christ, woman, we made a baby together. You and I. You think I'm not going to be there every step of the way? You don't think I'm going to love you and care for you and rub your feet and catch everything you throw at my head when you're in a hormonal rage? You don't think I'm going to watch your body change and go to doctor appointments? You don't think I'm going to plan a life with you and our child? Jesus, woman, do you know me at all?"

I blinked, tears coating my eyes. "Do I know you at all? Yes, I know you, Cas. But I also don't, not really. Because we haven't been together long at all. You're at the height of your career. Kids ask for your autograph at airports. You're talking like you're willing to give all that up."

"Of course I'd give all that up! It's not even a question."

"But—"

"*Salem,*" he said, his tone harsh. "I'm going to tell you how this is going to be. We're going to build a house like Hadley and Declan. We're going to raise our baby in the mountains of Idaho and he or she will grow up with family and friends and want for nothing. And if this life isn't enough for you, then you can start your own marketing firm and travel wherever you need to for clients. You don't need New York. And when you're ready, we'll have another baby. Or if you just want one, we can do that too. Not a family man . . . Tater tot, you just made me one."

"Cas," I whispered.

He leaned forward and pressed his lips to mine and mumbled close to my mouth. "I'll give you whatever you want in this life. I'll give you everything you've ever dreamed of."

My hands slid to the back of his neck and into the blond hair at his nape. "Is it that simple?"

"It's that fucking simple."

"You'll have regrets."

"No, I won't."

"What if you do, though?"

"I won't," he said. "I promise you, I won't. We should probably talk about when we're getting married."

"Uh, what?" I asked.

"Marriage. A wedding. Fall, maybe?"

"Veto."

"Fine, winter, but I gotta warn you, it's going to be a bitch for guests to trudge through snow."

"No, I meant veto on the wedding," I clarified.

"Ah, elopement then? Hadley will never forgive you—"

"Cas," I began, dropping my hands from his neck. "I meant, no to the marriage."

He smiled.

"What?" I demanded.

"Didn't I tell you how it was going to be?"

"Well, yes, you did, but this—"

"You're going to be my wife, Salem. You're the mother of my child, and if I have it my way, you'll be the mother of my children."

My lips quivered with the need to smile, but I held it in.

"I don't want to get married just because we're having a baby," I protested. "That's not a reason to get married."

"Is *that* why you think we're getting married?"

"Well, uh, yeah?"

"Hmm. That's my fault. I told you I wasn't one for flowery words."

"No, you're not," I agreed.

"Okay, I take it back."

"Take what back?"

"The marriage proposal."

"*That* was your idea of a marriage proposal?" I snapped.

"It was. No wonder you said no."

"Actually, I'm saying *hell no*."

"All right." He nodded, not looking at all upset by getting his wants denied. Cas stood up. "You want something to drink? Water?"

"*Get back here,*" I commanded as he walked toward the bathroom door.

"I can hear you fine from here. You can keep talking if you want."

"*Cas Bowman.*" I rose and placed my hands on my hips. "You do not tell a woman you're marrying her—at least not without some romance."

"You're right. Which is why I took back my marriage proposal and formerly request a do-over."

"A do-over?"

"Yep. A do-over. It'll be a surprise. And next time, you'll say yes."

"Oh, will I?"

He grinned. "You will. Because you love me and that little temper tantrum you're throwing is bluster."

"Bluster? Bluster this!"

After I fired off a crude gesture, I marched to him and pushed him into the bathroom.

"Enjoy your hand tonight, buddy!" I closed the door in his face.

He lightly rapped on it.

With a glare, I opened it. "What?"

He leaned forward and brushed his lips against mine. "Christ, you're quite a woman. And you're mine."

CHAPTER THIRTY-THREE

Town

"Is time moving backwards?" Hadley asked as I opened the door to Sweet Teeth.

"Uh, no?"

The bakery was nearly empty since it was just after the lunch hour, but the scent of butter and sugar made my mouth water.

"The wedding is in a week," Hadley said. "And I'm so damn excited I swear the earth is rotating backwards just to punish me."

"I love that you're excited," I said. "Seriously, that's everything."

She beamed.

Her excitement only reinforced that I'd made the correct decision to keep the pregnancy between me and Cas.

And Muddy.

I worried that Hadley would lose a bit of her sparkle when I told her I was pregnant too.

"Morning, kids," Gracie greeted as she popped out from the back kitchen with a tray of fresh baked goods.

"What do you have?" I asked, gesturing to the tray.

"Lemon curd tartlets," she said. "Topped with meringue and huckleberries."

"Yum." Hadley licked her lips. "I'll take five."

Gracie raised her brows. "Five?"

"Oh, you're right, they're small. Better make it six." Hadley looked at me. "Don't leave me out here all alone."

"I'll take three," I said.

"You're no fun." Hadley stuck her tongue out at me.

"We've got to leave some for other customers," I said. "We ordered three quarters of the tray between us."

"I'm eating for two," Hadley said.

"Yeah, that excuse only lasts so long," Gracie said as she plated our tartlets. "What are you drinking?"

"Nothing too sweet," Hadley said. "So how about a hot chocolate with extra whipped cream and caramel drizzle?"

"And I just became a diabetic," I said. "I'll have an herbal tea. Hibiscus if you've got it."

"I've got it," Gracie said.

"No coffee for you?" Hadley asked in surprise.

"I'm coffee'd out," I lied.

"You guys take a seat and I'll bring you the drinks," Gracie said.

"And we'll take the rest of those tartlets," Hadley said. "To go. For Dad and Jane."

"Uh huh." Gracie grinned.

"Five bucks says they're gone before we get home," I quipped.

"Why would I bet against you?" Gracie asked.

Hadley and I took our tartlets to the corner table and sat down.

"This is nice," she said. "Just you and me, out and about. We hardly get to do that anymore."

"That's because you're too busy sucking face with your fiancé to want to do anything else," I teased.

"Hmm. He's just so delicious, I can't help it."

"Can I change the subject?" I asked.

"Sure." She picked up a tartlet and bit into it. And then she moaned.

"I'm telling Declan you cheated on him with a lemon curd tartlet," I said with a laugh at her reaction.

"After he has one, he'll understand. You want to talk about something?"

I nodded.

Gracie came over to the table and dropped off our drinks. "I meant to tell you I met the Monroe brothers the other night at the Copper Mule. The whole fleet of them."

"Oh yeah?" Hadley took her hot chocolate and licked off the top of the whipped cream peak.

"Yeah." Gracie looked at me. "Harlan has a thing for you."

"No, he doesn't," I protested.

"Then why did he ask me questions about you all night?" she asked. "When he found out we were friends from school, he held me hostage and asked all about you."

"Harlan would be perfect for you!" Hadley said to me. "At least while you're home. No muss, no fuss."

"I'm not interested," I said.

"Why not? He's cute," Gracie said.

"He is cute," I agreed. "I'm just not interested."

"So unlike you," Hadley said. She looked at Gracie. "I invited him and his family to the wedding."

"Yeah, he said that. You should bring him as your date," Gracie said to me.

"Why are you guys trying to foist him on me?" I asked.

"Because I think you need a little . . . *foistage*." Hadley picked up another tartlet. "And by foistage, I mean—"

"I know what you mean," I said. "We all know what you mean."

The door to the bakery opened, momentarily stealing our attention.

"Hey, welcome to Sweet Teeth," Gracie said, addressing the two women who'd just walked in.

Hadley and I both jumped up from our chairs, sending them crashing to the floor.

"Oh my God!" Hadley gasped. "What are you guys doing here? You're not supposed to be here for another two days!"

Wyn grinned and looked at Poet. "Told you her reaction would be worth the surprise."

"You were right," Poet agreed. "We came early. God, this bakery is even cuter in person."

The four of us hugged and laughed and my heart lifted in my chest at seeing my two best friends in my hometown.

"Gracie," I said, turning with my arm around Poet's shoulders. "This pint-sized fairy is Poet. And the Viking over there is Wyn."

"You have one shield maiden who pillaged towns in your family history and suddenly no one will let you live it down," Wyn quipped. Her sunglasses were perched on top of her blonde hair as a makeshift headband.

"Oh, I'm so glad to finally meet the both of you," Gracie said. "You two sit, and I'll bring you a variety plate."

"Thank God, I'm starving," Wyn said. "We've been up since three a.m."

We grabbed two more chairs and the four of us crowded around the small table, our knees bumping together underneath it.

"Okay, so, you decided to surprise us," I said. "Best surprise *ever*."

"How did you manage to swing it?" Hadley asked. "Or has this been the plan all along?"

"It just worked out," Wyn said. "I miss Mildred, though."

"Who's Mildred?" Gracie called from behind the counter.

"I nanny for a family. It's their dog," Wyn said. "Though I'm the only one who takes care of her."

"She's usually at our apartment," Poet added. "On the nights that Wyn actually gets to sleep in her own bed, that is. Mildred is right next to her."

"What kind of dog?" Gracie asked.

"Miniature long-haired dachshund. Cream colored. She looks like a mini golden retriever in a way," Wyn said.

Gracie brought over another plate of baked goods. "I forgot to ask what you're drinking."

"That," Wyn said, pointing to Hadley's hot chocolate. "I need the sugar."

"Same for me," Poet said as she pushed up her tortoise-shell frames.

"And you?" I asked Poet. "How did you skip out of town early?"

"Candace took Alma to a conference," Poet explained. "So, I bounced."

"Wait, how did you guys get here?" Hadley asked. "We were going to pick you up from the airport."

"We rented a car," Wyn said.

"No, *you* rented a car. I don't drive," Poet said. "It's okay we came early, right?"

"Oh my God, of course it is!" Hadley said with a huge smile. "But we do need to talk about some lodging logistics. The house is currently full since Bowman is staying in my childhood bedroom."

"We can book you some rooms at The Regal Beagle," I said.

"The what?" Wyn asked, her lips twitching.

"The Regal Beagle," Hadley repeated. "It's a bed and breakfast that used to be a brothel."

"There's a lot of chintz and rosebud wallpaper," I warned. "But they have a good breakfast. Not as good as Muddy's, but it'll do. Plus you'll be able to sleep in and not have to deal with ranch hours."

"Hey, we're easy," Poet said.

"Spread that around, would you?" Wyn asked. "I'm looking for a hot cowboy to have a fling with while I'm here."

Gracie brought the drinks over. "We've got plenty of those in this town."

"Thank God," Wyn said. "Manhattan is a veritable cesspool of men."

"They're not that bad," Poet remarked.

"The last one I went on a date with asked me what I brought to the table. I just got up and left," Wyn said. "It was like being at a job interview."

"Where did you meet him?" Gracie asked.

"The apps." Wyn sighed. "I have no hope for the future."

"Guess you're going to have to meet someone the old-fashioned way," I said. "Mail order."

"Ah, the OG of dating apps," Wyn lamented. "Salem, you look really good."

"Thanks?" I said with a laugh.

"No, I mean it. The dressed down version of you with air-dried, wavy hair and the worn jeans. It's really working for you," Wyn said.

"She's totally right," Poet added.

The door to the bakery opened and Gracie was pulled behind the counter to serve a new batch of customers.

"Now that the shock of your surprise arrival has passed," I said. "I'm actually glad you're here so I can tell you all this in one go."

"We're listening," Poet said as she took a drink of her hot chocolate.

"I've decided to stay at the Ridge," I said, my eyes darting around the table. "For the foreseeable future."

The three of them were silent.

Wyn looked at Hadley. "Did you know about this?"

Hadley shook her head. "This is the first I'm hearing about it."

"Well, of course you're staying," Poet said, her lips quivering in sadness. "Because your dad is recovering."

"What about your job?" Wyn asked. Her blonde brows slashed together. "You can't just leave your job."

"I haven't talked to them yet," I admitted. "I only just decided . . ."

"So, tell them you'll be back," Wyn commanded. "You don't have to tell them when."

"And you expect them to hold my job for me?" I shook my head. "Even if they did, I—I have to be here. I *want* to be here. I want a relationship with my niece or nephew. I want a chance to make things right with my dad. If I go back to New York . . ."

"You hate it here," Wyn accused. "Don't you?"

"No," I said quietly. "I hated the pain that I associated with it. It's not the same now. And I need time to deal with that too."

"I don't fucking believe this," Wyn hissed. She jumped up from her chair and marched out of the bakery.

We stared after her.

I looked at Poet. "You gonna storm out of here too?"

She shook her head and wiped her eye. "It was bad enough that Hadley left. Now you're leaving too?"

Hadley pushed the plate of baked goods toward Poet.

Poet reached for an eclair. "Wyn's surprised, you know. I'm not, though."

"You're not?" I asked. "Why not?"

"Even if your dad hadn't had his accident, I always thought you'd be pulled home. Hadley's your twin. Being separated is hard on both of you."

"Is this what you wanted to tell me?" Hadley asked. "Before Wyn and Poet showed up.

I nodded.

"Are you sure you want to do this?" she asked. "There's nothing that says you can't change your mind."

"I've made up my mind."

Of course I'd left out a huge part of the story.

I'd tell them the whole truth . . .

After the wedding.

CHAPTER THIRTY-FOUR

Town

"You take Poet to the house," I said, handing Hadley the keys. "I'll find Wyn and we'll meet you there."

"You sure?" Hadley asked.

"I'm sure."

"Where do you think she went?" Poet asked.

"Not far. The town can fit on a pin head," I remarked. "If I had to guess, she went to the Copper Mule."

"They're not open yet," Hadley said. "It's just past two."

"I have a sixth sense about it," I said. "She's probably halfway into a Bloody Mary."

Poet winced. "Yeah, good luck with that."

"Maybe you should've waited to tell her," Hadley said.

"Clobber her right before she gets back on a plane to New York?" I shook my head. "This way she can be pissed at me for a few days, we'll have your bachelorette party, and then your wedding, and by the time she goes home, she'll be mellowed. Or sedated."

"Yeah, you're right," Hadley allowed. "I guess there wasn't a good time to tell her."

We waved goodbye to Gracie and headed out of Sweet Teeth which had started to get busy again.

Hadley and Poet headed for the truck on the other side of the street. "See you in a bit?" Hadley asked.

"Depends how long it takes to wrangle Wyn," I quipped.

I walked down Silver Street toward the Copper Mule. The front door was unlocked and I went inside. The main lights were on, which illuminated the scarred wooden floor.

Wyn sat at the bar, leaning over her drink and sucking on a straw.

"I knew I'd find you here." I took the stool next to her. "How'd you get Wade to serve you?"

"I told him I was best friends with you and Hadley. You *are* town royalty, after all."

"Hmm. I think it has more to do with the fact that Wade and Hadley dated in high school. That has a certain cachet."

She gestured to her drink. "Want a sip?"

"All good, thanks."

The scent of tomato juice made me queasy, so I started to breathe through my mouth.

"I've actually never been in here during the day. It loses its appeal, I think," I said as I looked around.

"What's that smell?"

"Paprika," I explained. "They make their own BBQ here."

"I think I'll like this place at night," she said.

"Hey," I said, patting her thigh. "Talk to me."

"There's something you're not telling me."

My heart tripped with nerves. "What do you mean?"

"I mean, there's something going on with you." Her eyes scanned me from the top of my head down to my boots. "I've never seen you this way."

"What way?"

"Relaxed."

"Relaxed?"

"Yeah. You're chaos wrapped in frenetic energy. You're the human equivalent of amphetamines. And here you are. Chill. That's *very* unlike you."

I laughed. "I don't know what I'm supposed to do with that."

Wade came out of the back, a box of liquor in his arms. "Hey, Salem."

"Hi Wade. Thanks for serving Wyn."

"No sweat. Get you something?"

"Nope. I'm good."

"All right, well, I've got more stock to grab. Want to be prepared for tonight." He ambled toward the back and disappeared, leaving me and Wyn alone.

"So really, what's going on with you?" Wyn demanded. She reached out and touched my tresses. "You have no product in your hair and not even a hint of lip gloss on. Hadley is distracted with her wedding, and Poet is constantly trying not to break down into tears, so that leaves me. And I *notice* things."

"You think it makes sense to wear high heels and pencil skirts when I live on a ranch?"

"I think you're deflecting."

"Did I tell you I got into a fight here a couple of weeks ago?"

"*Definitely* deflecting." She sighed. "And no. What happened?"

I breathed an internal sigh of relief that Wyn was just tipsy enough to take the bait even though she knew it was bait. I quickly explained about Amber.

"Oh man, I wish I'd been here to see that," Wyn said, laughing. But then she sobered. "It just reminds me that I won't ever get to see that."

"See what? Me getting into a bar fight?"

She nodded. "You'll be here and I'll be back in New York."

"Just a plane ride away." I took her hand and gave it a squeeze. "I'll have to come back to New York to pack up my stuff."

"Poet and I could do that for you. Like we did for Hadley."

"No, I'll take care of it," I insisted. "That reminds me that I have to talk to my boss."

"You haven't told him yet?"

I shook my head. "I've been avoiding it. Jack's been good to me. Took a chance on me—feral, insane me, even though I don't have a college degree."

She stared at me. "You really do want to stay, don't you?"

"Yeah, Wyn. I do."

"I owe Poet twenty bucks," she muttered. "She bet you'd decide to stay."

"If it makes you feel any better, I'll give you the twenty."

She wrapped an arm around my shoulder and put her head against mine. "No, it doesn't make me feel better. I'm going to miss the hell out of you."

"You could move here," I suggested.

"And do what?"

"What you do now. Be a nanny."

"I can't leave Poet in that city," Wyn said. "She needs a Viking in shining armor. Her job is chewing her up and spitting her out right now . . . I couldn't."

"She's like Hadley," I said. "She doesn't belong in that city. She's got such a good heart and she's so sensitive."

"Yeah, she's not street like us," Wyn joked. She dropped her arm from around my shoulder. "Let me suck this drink down, and then I want to see the Ridge."

"You forgive me?" I asked.

"For living your life and making the best decision for yourself?"

"Yes."

"No." She pinched my cheek. "But I'll have to get over it, won't I?"

"You know," Poet said, raising her mug of tea to her lips, "you told us about the ranch. You showed us videos and pictures, you turned the camera around on FaceTime, but nothing, and I mean *nothing,* prepared me for seeing it in person."

"Agreed, 110 percent," Wyn added.

After dinner, the four of us sat around the lit fire circle. It was like old times. If felt like when the four of us were in New York, having random moments where we were all together.

"This is nice," Hadley said. "I love having you guys here."

"Me too," I agreed. "Muddy does too. She was so happy she got to add an extra leaf to extend the dining room table. She loves a full house."

"Muddy is everyone's grandmother," Wyn said.

"And just as nosy," I warned. "So don't say anything you don't want her to pry into."

"Duly noted," Wyn said with a laugh.

"Your dad is looking better than I thought he would," Poet admitted.

"He still tires pretty easily," Hadley said. "But I'm hoping by the wedding he'll be able to at least sit through the ceremony. I doubt he'll be awake for the reception though."

"You two should do the father-daughter dance first then," I said.

Hadley smiled. "That's a good idea."

"So, Jane is nice," Poet said.

"Yeah, she's great," Hadley added.

"How are you feeling about it all?" Poet looked at me when she asked the question.

"Jane and I had lunch the other day. We're cool."

Wyn and Poet stared at me like they didn't believe me.

"It's called *growth*. I'm capable of it."

"Glad to hear it," Poet said. "Family friction is the worst."

"Heard from your parents?" Hadley asked gently.

Poet nodded but didn't elaborate.

"So how are you going to entertain us for the next few days?" Wyn asked, changing the subject.

"Well, we can do a trail ride," Hadley said. "Show you the ranch."

"But Salem won't go," Wyn said. "She hates horses."

"I don't hate horses. I love horses. Just don't like being atop them. But I will suffer a trail ride for you girls."

"You brought swimsuits, right?" Hadley asked.

"Yep," Poet said.

"Good." Hadley looked at me. "The hot spring."

I nodded. "Yes, the hot spring."

"There are hot springs nearby?" Wyn asked. "I *love* hot springs."

"The spring is on our land," Hadley explained.

"Well, that's fucking cool," Wyn said.

Hadley's face brightened. "I have a better idea than a trail ride. Why don't we do an overnight camping trip out there? We can pack the truck with sleeping bags and a tent. Food and marshmallows for a fire and such."

"Oh, that sounds really fun!" Wyn said. "Get out in nature. Wait, does that mean I have to pee behind a tree?"

"Yes," I said with a laugh. "You up to the challenge, city girl?"

"If you can do it, I can do it," Wyn said.

CHAPTER THIRTY-FIVE

THE RANCH

The next morning, I tossed another sleeping bag into the back of the red vintage farm truck and then checked it off the list on my phone.

Cas rode up on a stallion and dismounted before even coming to a stop. And I wasn't ashamed to admit it made my stomach flip.

"Hey," he greeted, a smile blooming across his face.

"Hi ya."

"Getting ready for the girls' night out, huh?"

"Yep."

"I haven't seen much of you since your friends got into town."

"Yeah."

"Or maybe you're avoiding me," he accused.

"Why would I do that?" I asked.

"Because the last thing you said to me was *enjoy your hand.*

I didn't, by the way. I mean, I did, but I thought of you the whole time."

My lips trembled with the desire to smile.

He touched the corner of my mouth and forced it up. "There ya go. How easy is that?"

"Cas," I warned.

"What?"

"Don't flirt with me."

"Why not? It's killing me, you know . . . not being able to kiss you in public."

"I know," I said, eyeing him with all the lust I felt. "Believe me, I know."

"Stop looking at me like that."

"Like what?" I asked.

"Like you're only a fan of me when I'm naked."

"I'm a fan of you when you're naked and one of my body parts is in your mouth, thus rendering you silent."

"If only you weren't going on your overnight camping trip, you could take pity on me and let me into your bed again, and I'd render *you* silent," he said.

"The idea does have appeal. But now that *I* know my grandmother knows we've been sharing a bed, it's weird. And sneaky."

He sighed. "How are you feeling?"

"Fine. Good."

"Morning sickness?"

"No. Not really. I mean, I puked when Muddy confronted me about being pregnant, but I think that had more to do with nerves."

"Okay. You haven't gone to the doctor yet, have you?"

"No, I haven't. But I don't know how I'm supposed to when my friends are in town. I wasn't planning on them coming early."

"You're happy they're here, though. Last night at dinner, you were . . ."

"What?"

"I don't know. It's like everything in your world was right."

"That's a good way to put it."

Hadley came up the driveway in her SUV and she parked next to the farm truck. She cut the engine and the driver's side door opened. Wyn climbed out of the passenger side and Poet spilled from the back.

"Hey, Bowman," Poet greeted.

"Ladies," he said. "Have fun on your camping trip."

"How's the packing going?" Hadley asked.

"Just finished," I said. "You get snacks?"

"Yep. Pregnancy-friendly snacks," Hadley said with a wry smile. "But booze and cured meats for those that can partake."

I saw Cas look at me out of the corner of my eye, but I pretended not to see him.

"I just want to say goodbye to Dad and Muddy real fast," Hadley said. "And then we can go."

"Me too," I said.

"We'll move the snacks into the truck," Wyn said.

Dad had pitched a fit being cooped up in his room and was finally enjoying time downstairs on the couch. Muddy was croqueting in her chair, the TV on low.

"We're packed and ready to go," Hadley said, leaning over the couch and kissing his cheek.

"You've got bear spray?" he asked.

"Yep," she said.

"And the revolver," I added.

"Good," Dad said. "Have fun."

Wyn and Poet were in the truck bed when we came out. Cas was nowhere in sight, and neither was the stallion. No doubt he'd taken him to the barn to give him a good rub down.

I could use a good rub down too.

Not seeing Cas for more than a few minutes at a time was making me ornery. I missed him in my bed. I missed sleeping next to him.

"Let's get the show on the road," Wyn said from the truck bed.

I climbed into the driver's side and Hadley rode shotgun. I cranked the key and the truck rumbled to life.

I rolled down the window and let the warm air enter the cab. It teased the hair at my temples and I suddenly had a vision of what life would be like in a few years. Hadley and I, taking our tots to the hot spring, Cas and Declan going with us and camping under the stars.

I'd sleep out under them tonight. No light pollution. No city noise.

New York was a living entity of entropy and constant stimulation. I loved it. And not just because I found my footing there. But because it had given me a chance to go out on my own. Discover who I was and what I wanted to be.

But it wasn't a place I wanted to raise a child.

Once I had stripped away the loss of my mother, I realized I didn't hate the Ridge or Huckleberry Hill. But sometimes it took leaving home to fall in love with it.

"Oh my God," Poet exclaimed when she saw the hot spring. "This is going to be so much fun!"

"I can't believe you never told us about this place," Wyn said.

"Did we really never tell you the story?" Hadley asked as she went to the back of the truck and pulled out the tent that slept four.

Wyn shook her head and grabbed the tent stakes.

"Our great-great grandfather built a cabin a few hundred

feet from the spring. It's why he settled here," Hadley explained.

"Oooh, story time," Poet said.

"This valley is known for its silver mines," Hadley explained. "Our great-great grandfather was an Irish prospector and struck it rich in the early 1880s. He homesteaded the first 160 acres, and he kept buying up land until the mine went dry. Salem actually still has a nail from the original cabin."

"You do?" Wyn asked. "That's really cool."

"I keep it in my jewelry box," I said. "Nails were hard to come by back then. People would literally burn down their houses or cabins and take the nails and then go settle someplace else and rebuild."

"No kidding," Poet said. "I bet the history of Huckleberry Hill is fascinating."

"No doubt," Hadley said. "You should write a book about it."

"Me?" Poet laughed. "Write a book? I have no interest in writing a book."

I helped Hadley spread out the tent. "We should tell them about the myth."

"Myth?" Poet asked. "What myth?"

"About the hot spring," Hadley said. "Supposedly it has healing powers. Eamon cut his leg so bad he thought they'd have to amputate it—but when he went to the hot spring and soaked his leg, it healed. Poof, myth created."

"Okay, yeah, Poet should definitely write a book," Wyn added.

"I'm not a writer," Poet insisted.

"But you love stories," Wyn said.

"Yeah, *other* people's stories," Poet said.

"This would be other people's stories," Wyn fired back.

"Stop pushing me," Poet snapped.

Wyn looked like she wanted to respond, but I saw the expression on Poet's face.

"Come on," I interrupted. "Let's get this tent set up so we can get into the hot spring."

"Do you believe it?" Wyn asked as she shoved one of the stakes into the tent loops.

My brow furrowed. "Believe what? About the healing powers of the hot spring?"

"Yeah," Wyn said.

"I don't know," I admitted. "It seems a little . . . out there."

"I believe it," Hadley said. "Wholeheartedly."

"Yeah?" Poet asked. "I'm struggling with this stake."

I went over to her side and took the stake from her. "It's bent. Gotta use brute force."

"Because I have so much of that," she said with a laugh. She lifted her arm up and flexed it. "I'm like Bugs Bunny when his arm sags."

"Why do you believe it?" Wyn asked, picking up the thread of the hot spring having magical healing powers.

"I don't know. Just a feeling," Hadley replied. "The two weeks before Mom died . . . Dad carried her to the truck and drove her out here. I didn't know that. Not until Muddy told me."

My throat thickened with the memories of that time. I'd known. The scent of pine and sulfur had clung to her skin.

Our friends stopped their actions to look at Hadley, waiting for what came next.

"I used to think the hot spring failed. She died anyway, you know? But now, I think the hot spring did what it was supposed to do. Because it was never going to heal Mom. Not the way we wanted her healed. But it healed something between my parents. I don't know, it sounds insane. But the two of them, those two weeks, it was about them. Under the night sky. Talking. Wishing. Saying their goodbyes."

I turned away so my friends and sister couldn't see the tears that gathered in my eyes and fell down my cheeks.

She'd died.

But that didn't mean she was forgotten. She'd never be forgotten.

"It's nice," Poet said quietly. "Having something to believe in."

"Amen," Wyn murmured.

I cleared my throat, hoping that destroyed the emotion that was threatening to choke me.

Gone. But never forgotten.

CHAPTER THIRTY-SIX

THE HOT SPRING

"I see your one M&M," Wyn said, pushing an orange-colored candy to the pile, "and raise you four black licorice whips."

"Call," Hadley said, laying down her cards.

The three of us followed.

"Son of a bitch," Wyn hissed, looking at me. "You won. Again. You promised you wouldn't cheat."

"I didn't," I said. "I swore I wouldn't and I didn't. This was luck. I swear."

I took a drink from my huckleberry soda, and then gathered my winnings, sliding them across the sleeping bag.

"Pee break," Poet announced.

Hadley handed her a flashlight.

"Wyn, will you come with me?" Poet asked. "I'm not scared of the dark. I'm scared of the critters that live in the dark."

"Sure." Wyn moved the battery-operated lantern out of

her way so she could unzip the tent flap. "We're women. We go to the bathroom in groups. Even when camping."

"*Especially* when camping," Poet said. "Because, *nature*."

The two of them climbed out of the tent and I zipped up the flap behind them. Their footsteps faded into the distance.

I popped a piece of candy into my mouth while Hadley scooped up the cards. "This is fun," she said.

"Yeah, it is."

"In fact, I don't know how my bachelorette party is going to top this. Speaking of . . . what *do* you have planned for my bachelorette party?" she asked.

"Oh, I just thought this would suffice," I teased. "So I've gone ahead and canceled the hookers and blow for your actual party."

She grinned.

I laughed. "I'm not telling you what I have planned."

"Do Wyn and Poet know?"

"Nope. It's going to be a complete and utter surprise."

Wyn and Poet returned to the tent and by tacit agreement we put the cards away and I began to divvy up my candy winnings equally between the girls.

"So, let's talk about boys," Hadley said.

"What about them?" Wyn asked.

"Any of them on the horizon?" Hadley asked.

"The only man in my life is the little boy I nanny for," Wyn said. "But I'm thinking about seeing a male therapist. Would that count?"

"You're joking. Aren't you?" I asked.

"About the therapist? Yes. But I was trying to evade the line of questioning," Wyn said. "Was it effective?"

"So, no men for Wyn," I said. "Poet?"

"None for me either," she said, her brow furrowing. She glanced around for her bottle of cider, found it, and took a long drink.

The three of us looked at each other and then waited.

"I've been lying to you guys for years," Poet said. Her eyes were wide behind her glasses. "And I think it's time I come clean."

"You can tell us," Hadley said gently.

"You'll judge me," Poet lamented.

"No," Wyn said. "We won't."

I gently pressed the bottle of cider to Poet's mouth and urged her to take another drink.

She downed another healthy swallow, took a deep breath, and blurted out, "I'm a virgin."

Finally, Wyn broke the silence. "How?"

"What do you mean *how?*" Poet glared at her.

"I mean, *how*," Wyn repeated. "You date."

Poet nodded. "Yeah."

"And you've had relationships," Hadley said.

"Not long ones," Poet muttered. "Look, I'm not trying to stay a virgin. I mean, it's not like I have some sort of attachment to my hymen."

I raised my eyebrows and my lips quivered. "Tipsy Poet is funny."

Poet glared at me.

"Sorry, continue," I said.

"I've tried losing it," Poet said. "Several times. But when it gets down to the wire and the clothes are off, I don't know, I just *can't*. What's wrong with me?"

"Nothing," Hadley said. "Nothing is wrong with you."

"Everything is wrong with me," Poet wailed. "The three of you have had sex. Lots of sex. Lots of *great* sex and I've been pretending for years that I know what that's like. But I don't and I *want* to!"

I took her free hand and gave it a squeeze.

"Have you ever considered that you just haven't met the right man yet?" I asked softly.

"I'm doomed," she mumbled.

"Why didn't you tell us sooner?" Wyn asked. "And how did you not even tell *me*? We've known each other since we met at Camp Eaglewood when we were eleven."

"Camp Eaglewood?" Hadley asked.

"It's in upstate New York," Wyn explained. "We were in the same cabin and she was the only one who'd talk to me because I was the weird, tall blonde girl who cursed in Norwegian."

"You were exotic," Poet said. "You're still exotic."

"This isn't about me," Wyn said. "Except for the fact that even *I* didn't know."

"I didn't know how to tell you," Poet said. "I'm twenty-three years old and a virgin."

"I'm twenty-three years old and got pregnant after I thought I was infertile," Hadley said.

"I'm twenty-three years old and get into bitch fights at bars," I added.

"And I'm twenty-three years old and my habitual sleeping partner is a mini dachshund that hogs the bed," Wyn said.

"The point of all that is what?" Poet asked.

Hadley grinned. "We've all got shit."

"Yeah, but your shit turned into a love story and a wedding," Poet said to Hadley.

"Alls well that ends well," I said with a grin.

"I haven't ended *well*," Poet said bluntly. "That's my entire point!"

Wyn let out a giggle, and then that got Hadley started. I couldn't help it either and burst into laughter. Finally, Poet joined in.

When we were all under control, Poet set her cider bottle down and got up again.

"Where are you going?" Wyn asked.

"The hot spring," she announced. "I'm dunking myself in hopes that the magical healing powers of the spring are real."

As the sun rose the following morning, Hadley popped out of the tent, upchucking the contents of her stomach. I lazed in my sleeping bag for a moment, but then my stomach rebelled too.

Oh no.

I slid out of my sleeping bag and quickly made it out of the tent barefoot. I found the closest spot I could and then puked behind a shrub.

Why the morning sickness had to show up now, of all mornings, was anyone's guess, but what a sense of humor the universe had.

"What's with all the puking?" Wyn asked as she popped her head out of the tent and rubbed her eyes.

"I'm pregnant," Hadley snapped.

"Yeah, that I know." Wyn looked at me. "Then why are you puking?"

"Too much sugar last night," I lied.

Her gaze narrowed. "Hmm."

"So much noise!" came Poet's voice. "It's early."

"Yeah, what time is it?" Wyn asked.

"Almost five," Hadley announced.

"*Excuse me?*" Wyn screeched. "Five? As in five a.m.?"

"We're really far north," I said, standing upright and wiping my mouth. "In the summer it gets light really early and dark really late. The sun didn't set until nearly nine o'clock last night."

"Oh crap," Poet muttered.

"What?" Wyn asked, looking behind her.

"I just got my period," Poet groaned.

"Time to pack up," Hadley said.

"This sucks!" Poet yelled.

"Early," I grumbled. "Loud."

"You're one to talk," Poet snapped.

"Nature," Wyn said. "Bringing out the best in us."

"There's good news," I said. "The Diner will be open by the time we get back. Let's pack up and get out of here."

I breathed a sigh of relief. Poet's distraction had saved me. But how much longer was I going to be able to keep my secret a secret?

CHAPTER THIRTY-SEVEN

THE RANCH

"You didn't," Hadley said, her mouth dropping open.

I grinned. "I did."

Hadley squealed and hugged me. "Thank you."

The back porch had four lounge chaises with pillows, blankets, and tables covered with snacks and candy. A movie popcorn machine was currently popping kernels and the smell of oil and butter hit me with a nostalgic smack.

I'd strung up garden lights, like the ones that used to be on the cabin porch, and a huge movie projector had been delivered earlier in the day and set up. I'd asked Wyn and Poet to keep Hadley occupied so I could unveil the surprise.

"What are we watching?" Poet asked.

"Hadley's three favorite movies," I said with a grin. "We're starting with *Seven Brides for Seven Brothers*, then we'll move on to *Meet Me in St. Louis*, and finish it off with *The Harvey Girls*."

"I have to watch them in that order, and always all together." Hadley grinned. "I don't make the rules. That's just the way it is."

"You guys are okay with crashing in the den tonight, so you don't have to drive back to The Regal Beagle?"

"Yep," Poet said. "You told us to bring our overnight bags, so we've got them."

"Good," I said. "Gracie wanted to come, but Cole is working tonight and the grandparents who would normally watch their daughter are at an antique road show in Montana."

"We're missing a few things," Wyn said.

"What?" I asked. "I've thought of everything."

"I need a dog to snuggle," Wyn said.

"We've got four Border Collie Aussie puppies," Hadley said. "But they're working dogs and don't really understand the word *chill.*"

"I'd settle for your goat," Wyn replied. "Where is she, anyway? Did you leave her with Declan?"

"Nope," she said. "She's upstairs with my dad and Jane. Declan went out about an hour ago with Bowman for his bachelor party."

"What does that entail?" Poet asked. "The town is cute, but I didn't see a lot of activities suitable for a bachelor party."

"They're going to the Copper Mule to play pool," Hadley said with a wry smile. "The Monroe brothers are joining them."

"Wild and crazy," Wyn said mockingly.

"So wild. So crazy." Hadley laughed. "Let me get the goat, and then our night can commence."

We were in the middle of our second movie when the sun finally set. Hadley conked out. As soon as Tempest saw Hadley roll over onto her side, she jumped down from snuggling Wyn and went to curl up next to Hadley.

Hadley instinctively reached out and pulled the baby goat close to her.

I took out my phone, snapped a photo, and sent it to Declan.

ME

Your fiancée is partying hard

Declan's reply was almost instant.

DECLAN

Me too. I'm two beers in and refusing shots

Smiling, I tucked my phone aside, but it buzzed with another text.

CAS

you've ruined me forever.

ME

What a nice compliment

CAS

Seriously. I'm hanging out with the guys playing pool, shooting the shit and all I want is to be at home with you. you've domesticated me.

I slid my hand beneath the blanket and let it rest on my stomach. There would be one day, not too far from now, that Cas and I would be curled up together on the couch, my belly round.

For the time being, I was suspended in a place of secrecy. Cas and I shared something private and I realized this was a true relationship. We were building something. A foundation for a life together. A foundation for a family.

It made sense now. I hadn't understood before when Hadley had no desire to stay in the city and hustle her way through life, grinding for some modicum of success. She'd found a man who loved her. She was having a child. She was home with her family.

And I wanted that now too.

I caught Poet looking at me, her expression pensive. I smiled at her, but she didn't smile back.

We all had our own paths to walk.

And if you were lucky, you'd find a few friends that would be by your side along the way.

◡

"Salem," Cas groused. "Move over."

"What are you doing in here?" I grumbled, my face smushed into the pillow.

"I miss you. I don't want to sleep alone."

He removed his jeans. His belt buckle clanged, and then denim hit the floor.

"This is bullshit, Salem," he said as he climbed into bed next to me.

I pulled the covers up over us. "What's bullshit?"

"This. You and me, sneaking around like teenagers."

"The wedding is in two days," I reminded him. "We're almost done with the sneaking around. And in a way, it's been fun. Admit it."

"Fun for about five minutes," he growled, pulling me close, his lips finding mine.

I put a hand between our mouths. "No kissing."

"Why not?"

"Because kissing leads to other things, and we've got a full house tonight. Wyn and Poet are crashing in the den. And Muddy no longer sleeps with ear plugs."

He sighed. "Great. So I'm going to wake up with your ass pressed against me and I'm not going to be able to do anything about it."

"What do you want to do to my ass?" I asked, making my voice even softer.

"You want me to tell you?"

"Yes. Tell me."

"I want to fuck it. Slow. While my fingers are inside you."

I shivered at the filthy picture he painted.

"Would you like that, Salem?" he rasped.

"Yes."

He rocked against me. "Have you ever been fucked that way before?"

"No," I whispered. "You'll be the first."

"I'll be the only."

He brushed his lips against my forehead. "I'll make it so good for you, you'll beg me to do it again and again."

"You're not playing fair."

"If I have to suffer, so do you."

"Misery loves company, huh?"

"Yes."

I raised my chin and bit his lip, causing him to curse. And then I soothed his pain with my tongue.

"Two can play that game," I stated. "I'm not having sex with you until after the wedding. If you want to torture me, then I'm going to return the favor."

"You wench."

I moved against him, brushing against his erection which caused him to hiss.

"I have no one to blame but myself, do I?" he rumbled.

"Kinda. Yeah."

I grinned and kissed his chin. "Good night, Cas. Sleep well."

And then I rolled over and wiggled my ass against him.

With a growl, he wrapped his arms around me and pulled me tight to his chest. "Go to sleep, tater tot."

CHAPTER THIRTY-EIGHT

"Get up!" I hissed at Cas.

He cracked an eye open. "Shhh. It's early."

"It's not that early," I snapped, sitting up and climbing out of bed. "Don't you hear what's going on?"

He frowned. "There are people moving around downstairs."

"People," I repeated. "As in, the house is already awake, but you are still in my room."

There was a knock on my bedroom door.

"Salem?" Wyn called.

"Hang on," I called back.

I shoved Cas out of bed. "*Bathroom*," I mouthed.

He quickly gathered his clothes and boots and made a dash for it. I appreciated his muscled backside for a moment before mentally smacking my forehead and forcing myself to remain chill.

I went to the door to open it. "Morning."

Wyn eyed me, her gaze taking me in from my messy bed head to my bare feet. "Hey."

"What's up?" I asked.

"Muddy wanted me to wake you up," Wyn said slowly. "The tent people are here."

"Oh, right," I said. "Let me just get dressed real fast and I'll —can you hang on a second?"

Before she could reply, I closed the door in her face.

My stomach rolled and I made a run for the bathroom. After my bout of morning sickness, I flushed the toilet. I brushed my teeth, and then I went back into my bedroom.

Wyn was sitting on the edge of my unmade bed, staring at me with a stoic expression on her face.

She held up one of Cas's gray socks he'd forgotten in his haste to leave my room.

"This looks like a man's sock," she said.

When I didn't reply, she went on, "And this is the second time I've seen you vomit in the morning. Don't you dare lie to me and say it's from too much sugar this time. You hardly ate anything sweet last night anyway."

I stared at one of my best friends and realized my body had betrayed my secret long before I'd wanted to admit it to anyone.

"I'm pregnant with Cas's baby," I said.

Her eyes widened. "*What?*"

"It happened the night I flew home when we had our one-night stand. But we've been sleeping together in secret for weeks. We're in love and we haven't told anyone yet. I wanted to wait until after the wedding to tell people."

Wyn suddenly spread her legs and put her head between them. I went over to her and patted her back. "You really should be comforting me."

She turned her head to look at me. "Hadley doesn't know?"

"No."

"And you didn't tell her because you want her wedding to be all about her."

"Yes."

"You're having a baby."

"Yes."

"You're in love with Bowman."

"Yes."

"I knew there had to be more to the story," she said, finally sitting up. "I knew you weren't just going to move home to be around your family."

"I'd planned on doing that before I found out about the baby. The baby was just the icing on the cake. Speaking of cake, I better get dressed and help Muddy and Hadley with the wedding preparations."

"Uh, hold on a second there," Wyn said, grasping my wrist and forcing me to stay on the bed. "You just dropped this huge bomb on me and you expect me to keep it to myself?"

"Yes. You have to."

"Okay." Her brow furrowed. "Are you guys getting married?"

"Eventually."

With her free hand, she rubbed her third eye. "Poet doesn't know, does she?"

I shook my head. "Muddy's the only one."

"You told her?"

"No, she figured it out," I said with a wry smile. "It's like she's psychic or something."

"So, your dad doesn't know."

"Not yet."

"Jane?"

"Nope."

"Why didn't you tell me?" Wyn demanded.

"Uh, maybe to avoid this conversation that we're having right now?"

She grinned. "Fair. *Wow*. You and Hadley. Having babies."

I nodded. "I hope she's not mad at me when she finds out."

"Why would she be mad at you?"

"Because I always do this."

"Do what?"

"Steal her thunder," I mumbled.

"You're not stealing her thunder. You're waiting until after her wedding to tell people. Not a moment too soon, if you ask me. Can't hide the morning sickness much longer. Maybe if you weren't living in an environment that resembles a youth hostel, it would be easier to keep a secret."

"Yeah."

"Bowman was in your bed when I knocked on your door?"

I nodded.

She sighed and smiled. "Ah, to be young and in love."

The day flew by in a flurry of deliveries and set up. After the bridal clothes had been delivered, Hadley grabbed my hand and said, "Let's go for a walk."

"You sure they can spare you?" I asked.

"Muddy's got everything under control. Between her and Declan's mom, everything is handled."

"So, a small wedding on the family ranch was the right decision," I said.

"Yes. Absolutely. This was always my dream."

The tent had been set up within walking distance of the house, so the catering staff could use the kitchen and guests would have easy access to the bathrooms. It was only going to be about fifty people attending the wedding anyway.

Hadley and I linked arms and ambled away from the cattle pens and past the barn.

"I've been thinking about Mom," Hadley said. "A lot, actually. Especially in the last few days."

"Sure," I said. "That makes sense."

"You've been thinking about her, too." She looked at me.

"Hard not to," I admitted.

"You seem different. Lighter. Almost . . . dare I say, unburdened."

I nodded slowly. "Yeah. I think you're right."

"You haven't told your job yet, have you?"

"No. Not yet."

Hadley nodded slowly. "I think you should go back to New York. Permanently."

"*What?*" I whipped my head around to look at my sister, my twin. "Why?"

"You'll get bored here." Hadley shrugged. "I love it here. I love riding, I love mucking out the stalls and feeding the chickens. But you don't like any of that."

"No, I don't," I agreed.

"So, what are you going to do here, Salem? Drive Dad to his physical therapy? Finally let Muddy teach you how to crochet?"

"I haven't thought about it."

"You *should* think about it. Look, I want you to stay. More than anyone. It would be a perfect life for me if you came home. But it won't be enough for you. At some point, you'll get restless. You'll want to move on, move away."

"Are you saying I can't want something different?" I asked.

"I'm saying that I know you. And this won't make you

happy. Not long term. And that'll kill me. Watching you wither and grow resentful."

"Mom settled here," I pointed out. "Nomad spirit and all. She found a way to be happy here."

"She had a purpose," Hadley said gently. "Outside of Dad. Outside of us. She was a vet and she had her practice. What do you have, Salem?"

"Don't worry about me."

"Don't worry about—are you kidding me? All I do is worry about you."

I took her hands in mine and forced her to face me. "That's not your job anymore. You don't need to worry about me. You need to take care of yourself and the baby. You need to be happy and in love."

"Yeah right," she muttered. "I've always worried about you. That's my job. That's who I am."

"Then do me a favor," I said. "Put it out of your mind for now. Because tomorrow is all about you and Declan and the start of your life together. That's all you need to think about."

She smiled. "I'm getting married tomorrow."

"You're getting married tomorrow."

"It's strange, you know? Being so happy, but missing Mom so much."

I swallowed. "Yeah."

"I wish she was here."

My eyes slid away from my twin sister to peer out at the family ranch behind us, the tent visible from our spot, the nicker of horses in the barn audible.

"She is, Hadley. She is."

CHAPTER THIRTY-NINE

Hadley turned to face the three of us in her childhood bedroom, donned in her gorgeous wedding dress and veil.

"Hadley," Poet whispered.

"You look incredible," Wyn added.

"You really do," I agreed. "I can't wait to see Declan's face when he gets a look at you."

"Make sure one of the cameras is pointed at him," Hadley said. "There's always a ton of photos of the bride, but there are never enough of the groom. And I want his face immortalized."

"Don't worry, we've got it all covered," Wyn said.

The four of us had gathered the morning of Hadley's wedding in our childhood rooms as our staging area while the men had gotten ready in the cabin.

Hadley's wedding dress was unique; not the traditional white of your average bride. It had a pattern of spring flowers that looked whimsical and painted. Each of our bridesmaids dresses were the color of the flowers. Wyn's was a soft yellow, Poet's a robin egg blue, and mine was sage green.

Our bouquets were wildflowers from the ranch, twined with cream ribbon.

There was a knock on the door.

"Come in," Hadley called.

The door opened and my father stood in the doorway. He was in a sport coat with no tie, the collar of his shirt open at the neck to reveal tanned skin from the years he'd spent on the ranch. His hair was combed, and for the occasion, he wore a brand-new pair of cowboy boots.

"Looking snazzy, Mr. Powell," Wyn said.

"Thanks," he said with a grin. "Ladies, do you mind if I have a private moment with my daughters?"

"Not at all," Poet said.

Poet and Wyn strode past my father who came fully into the room and closed the door.

He reached into his inner breast pocket and pulled out a long black velvet box and handed it to Hadley.

"I had this restored for you," Dad said.

Hadley opened the box and gasped. *"Dad."*

My sister flipped the box around to show me the gold heart locket that had Mom's initials engraved on it.

"She'd be so proud of you, Hadley," Dad said, his voice somber.

His eyes were suspiciously glassy.

"This is beautiful." Tears gathered in her eyes. "You should've given this to me before I did my makeup."

Dad chuckled. "Probably."

I reached into the pocket of my dress and extracted a handkerchief. "Look up."

Hadley tilted her neck back and stared up at the ceiling so I could gently blot the tears beneath her eyes.

"I think you're safe," I said.

Hadley handed me the box. "Will you put it on me?"

I smiled and nodded.

Once the necklace rested against Hadley's skin, I ensured her veil was straight and stepped back and linked my arm through my father's.

"She looks perfect now, doesn't she?" I said.

Dad nodded. He turned his head and kissed my hair. "You both do."

There was another knock on the door right before it opened. Muddy came into the room; her face wreathed in a smile. She wore a lavender dress and low heels. Her cheeks were bright and her silver hair was pleated, woven through with wildflowers.

"You mind if I have a word with the bride?" Muddy asked.

"She's all yours," Dad said.

The two of us walked into the hallway and then went downstairs. Jane had waited in the kitchen for my father, and when the two of them looked at each other, I wondered when we'd be attending their wedding.

"We should take our seats," Jane said to my father.

Dad hugged me and whispered in my ear, "I would give anything to see you as happy as Hadley."

I smiled up at him, metaphorically biting my tongue.

If only he knew.

Well, he'd know soon enough. Maybe in a few hours after all the guests were gone and it was just family.

"You look beautiful," Jane said to me.

"Thanks, Jane," I said, my tone sincere. "So do you."

And she did. Her brown hair was down and curled, her cheeks pink and her eyes bright.

The two of them headed out the back door and I waited for Muddy and Hadley. They came downstairs about five minutes later and the three of us made our way to the wedding ceremony. Chairs had been set up, and at the end of the aisle Declan stood with the minister and Cas at his side.

Jane had gotten Dad to his seat in the front and now we waited for the musicians to start. They struck up a chord and the guests who'd been talking in low voices ceased, turning their attention to the back of the aisle.

Wyn walked first, followed by Poet. When it was my turn, I looked over my shoulder at my sister, shot her a wink, and then glided down the aisle.

My eyes immediately went to Cas.

Our gazes locked on one another and my heart flipped in my chest. It was as if there was no one else here, as if this wedding wasn't my sister's, but mine.

And in our tacit communication, we promised each other forever.

I made it to the platform and took my place in front of Poet.

And then I watched my grandmother walk my sister down the aisle.

The veil didn't cover Hadley's face—it was merely an adornment. And it was perfect because it meant I could see her expression.

Her beautiful, serene expression when she saw the man she loved waiting to make her his wife.

When they arrived at the platform, Muddy squeezed Hadley's hand and kissed her cheek before letting her go.

Declan held out his hand to Hadley. She took it, and then stood on the platform, facing him.

He refused to drop her hand and instead, pulled her close and kissed her on the lips.

"I haven't gotten to that part yet," Minister Bainbridge teased.

"Well, hurry up then," Declan stated, causing everyone to laugh.

Hadley, still chuckling, turned and handed me her bouquet.

Then she faced her husband to be.

They didn't write their own vows, choosing to go the traditional route. And while they recited their pledge of *'til death do us part*, I once again found myself staring at Cas.

His lips lifted up into a smile, as if he knew exactly what I was thinking.

"You may now kiss the bride," Minister Bainbridge said. "Again."

Declan gently cradled Hadley's face and pressed his lips to hers. He then stood back, grabbed her hand and raised their clasped hands in the air.

Everyone in the audience cheered.

I handed Hadley her bouquet, and then the two of them walked down the aisle.

"Now we feast," Wyn said, drawing my attention to her and Poet.

Poet wiped a finger underneath her glasses. "That was so beautiful."

"It really was," I agreed. "Come on, waterworks. Let's get you a glass of champagne."

"Yeah, that's all we need," Wyn teased. "A weepy, sappy Poet."

"Well, we are at a wedding. If not now, then when?" Poet demanded.

"May I escort you to the tent?" Cas asked, coming to stand by my side.

I smiled up at him. "Sure thing."

He offered me his arm and I took it.

The tables under the tent were adorned with cream-colored tablecloths and vintage, mismatching cutlery and china that Muddy and Hadley had found in antique stores over the past few months. Votives of candles tied with lavender ribbons and bouquets of wildflowers graced the center of each table.

There were no assigned seats except for the table that included the wedding party along with Muddy, Dad and Jane.

"This is beautiful," Poet said. "The vision totally came together."

Wyn nodded. "And at the moment, no scent of ranch life."

"Just wait until the wind changes," I quipped. "I don't even smell it anymore."

"Well, you're used to it," Wyn said.

"Can we not talk about the smell right before we eat?" Poet asked. "I'm begging you."

Wyn mimed zipping her mouth shut.

"Can I get you ladies something to drink?" Cas asked.

"Glass of champagne for me," Wyn said.

"Same," Poet added.

Cas looked at me and raised his brows. "Will you help me carry the drinks?"

"Sure." I nodded and moved toward the Copper Mule's mobile bar—a vintage Airstream trailer with their logo on the side.

On our way, Lucy and Eloise waylaid us, forcing us to stop.

"It was such a beautiful ceremony," Eloise chirped. "Hadley looks stunning, doesn't she?"

"She does," I agreed.

"And look at you, you tall drink of water," Eloise said, batting her eyelashes up at Cas who peered down at her with an amused smile.

While Eloise engaged Cas in conversation, Lucy grasped my elbow and turned me away for a measure of privacy.

"Amber Winston is here," Lucy said.

"Amber's here?" My brows slashed together.

Lucy nodded and gestured with her chin to the other side of the tent.

Amber was standing with Harlan, her hand on his forearm while they talked.

"Why is she here?" I asked, concern bubbling up within me. It wasn't like she was friends with Hadley, or with me.

"I guess she came as that young man's plus one," Lucy said.

"But why would she *want* to come to Hadley's wedding?" I asked with a frown of confusion.

"I don't know," she admitted. "I hope she doesn't cause any trouble."

"You and me both," I murmured. "I think she's making a play for Harlan."

"Harlan? Oh, yes. Well, he's very charming. I met him and his brothers when they came into the store a while back. As for Amber, I'll keep an eye on her."

"Thanks," I said. "Why don't you and Eloise find a table? Food should be served soon."

Lucy squeezed my hand and then went to extract Eloise from her flirtation with Cas.

"I think she wanted to detach her jaw and swallow you whole," I quipped as Cas and I continued toward the mobile bar.

"There's an image," he stated, looking at me with a raise of his brows.

"Behave," I warned.

"Only for a few more hours," he said. "You think we'll be able to get away with dancing together?"

"You are the best man and I'm the maid of honor," I said. "I think we can get away with it. So . . . Amber is here. She's standing with Harlan."

"Amber?" Cas looked away from me to peer at the guests. His jaw clenched. "You think she's going to start shit?"

"I *know* she's going to start shit."

"Then we'll run interference," he said. "All day if we have to. She's not ruining their wedding."

"I should probably pull Harlan aside and give him a head's up."

"That's a good idea," he said.

We stepped up to the bar to order.

"What are you doing?" I demanded. "You're a guest today. Not a bartender."

Wade grimaced. "One of my bartenders called out, so naturally I wound up doing what I do best."

"You left Chelsea alone?" I asked.

"My parents are entertaining her," Wade said.

"I'll make sure you still get food," I said.

"Thanks, Salem. What can I get you guys to drink?"

We gave our orders as more people began to form a line behind us. Wade served the drinks quickly and efficiently.

"It's almost like he's a professional," Cas said as he took a drink of his whiskey.

"Almost," I said. "Let's get these drinks to Wyn and Poet, and then I'll see if I can extract Harlan from the harpy."

CHAPTER FORTY

As soon as we dropped off drinks, Muddy clinked her champagne flute and asked people to take their seats.

I took my chair next to Hadley and Cas sat on the other side of Declan. Declan poured the bottle of sparkling water into Hadley's glass.

Peach burrata basil salads were served.

"Do you forgive me?" Hadley asked with a look at me.

"For what?" I picked up my fork.

"For having a salad instead of poutine?" She grinned.

"Your wedding, your food. Can you eat this? Because you're pregnant?" I gestured to the cheese sitting in front of me.

Could I eat this . . .

"It's pasteurized," she said. "Hell yes, I can eat this."

"This is unbelievable," Poet said. "The peaches taste like they just dropped from the tree."

"They're local," Hadley explained. "All the food served today is local."

As I ate, I kept my eyes on Amber.

"What's with the assassinator look you've got going on?" Wyn asked me, leaning close and lowering her voice.

"Amber's here," I whispered.

"Where?"

I gestured with my chin. "She's the one with the nearly jet-black hair."

"How'd she get in here?" Wyn demanded.

"Apparently, she came as Harlan's plus one. I haven't been able to talk to him about her yet," I said. "I need to warn him."

"And Harlan is the guy she's currently draping herself over?"

"Yep."

"After the main course," Wyn said. "I'll distract her and you pull him aside."

"And after that, we should fight crime," I quipped.

"In black jumpsuits. We'd look great in black jumpsuits."

I looked at Hadley who'd devoured half of her salad already. "Hey, did you know Amber is here with Harlan?"

She kept her eyes trained on her food. "Yes. I meant to tell you . . . I invited her."

"*You* invited her?" I hissed.

"She actually called me several days ago. Amber got a job at the Huckleberry Hill Crier and offered to do a piece on the wedding."

"And you said yes?" I demanded. "*Why?*"

"Because," Hadley said, finally looking at me. "We're not in high school anymore. And I want to put all of that mess behind us. She held out an olive branch and I took it."

"You could've warned me," I murmured.

"I wasn't in the mood for one of your . . ." She paused.

"Meltdowns?" I supplied.

"Tantrums."

"Uhm, *ouch*."

She smiled and touched my arm. "Come on. Rise above with me."

Once the salad plates were cleared away by the catering staff, Declan rose from his seat. He took an empty flute and tapped his butter knife against the crystal.

"Don't worry, my speech won't be long," Declan said, a smile tugging at his lips. He looked at Hadley, and then the guests. "First, I want to thank you for coming to our wedding and celebrating this day with us. A few months ago, after I proposed to Hadley, I had an idea for a wedding gift."

Hadley raised her brows. "A gift? This is news to me."

A couple of people chuckled.

Declan placed his hand on her shoulder and gave it a squeeze. "I had this idea, but I had no skill in the execution. So, I enlisted Wade and his father, who happens to be an expert brewer."

Declan inclined his head in the direction of the mobile bar.

"They helped me brew and bottle a stout beer that would be ready to drink at our wedding," Declan said.

Wade, along with several catering staff, came to the tables and began handing out half pints of dark beer.

"I'm saving one for you," he said, looking at his wife. "And in six months, we'll toast the birth of our child. But for now, our guests will get to enjoy the fruits of my labor."

Hadley rubbed her belly. "This is a fruit of your labor, too, you know."

There was another round of laughter.

"Everyone have some beer?" Declan asked, looking at the guests. He lifted his glass. "To Hadley, and a beautiful life together."

I raised my glass of beer and brought it to my nose. It was strong and smelled of malted chocolate.

"How is it?" Hadley asked me.

"Delicious," I lied.

Poet frowned. "You didn't even drink—"

Wyn swiveled her body and thrust her elbow, *accidentally* on purpose jostling the glass in Poet's hand which caused her to drop it onto the table.

Poet and Wyn shot back from their seats to avoid the spill.

"Sorry," Wyn murmured, shooting me a look.

Thank you, I mouthed.

She grinned and grabbed her cream napkin and began to pat the spill dry. Cater waiters jumped in to help.

"Did it get you?" Wyn asked Poet.

"No, I don't think so." She glared at Wyn. "Klutz much?"

I offered her my beer. "Here."

"Thanks," Poet muttered and took a sip.

I turned to Hadley. "How's Dad doing, you think?"

Hadley leaned forward and looked down the table, past Declan and Cas to Dad. "He looks okay. But maybe we should do the father-daughter dance before the main course, just in case."

Nodding, I stood up and walked over to my father. I crouched down next to him and told him the plan. I then went to the band that had set up in the corner of the tent. I spoke to the lead singer and then stood off to the side.

The band waited for my father and Hadley to reach the dance floor before they began to play "Take me Home, Country Roads" by John Denver.

It was my mother's favorite song.

I hadn't cried at the wedding so far.

Not through the vows. Not when my father had given Hadley our mother's locket.

But I cried now.

Silent tears poured from me as I watched my sister dance with our father at her wedding.

The wind shifted, ever so slightly. But I didn't smell the strong aromas of ranch life.

Instead, I smelled the faintest trace of lavender perfume.

My mother's signature scent.

And I swore I felt her arms wrap around me.

She was here.

As she was always meant to be.

After the father-daughter dance, Dad hung around for another twenty minutes before he and Jane left the reception.

"I feel old," he grumbled as I walked with him and Jane toward the house.

"You're not old," I assured him.

"A weak old man who can't even make it through his daughter's wedding."

His mood quickly deteriorated and I shot Jane a worried look. She shook her head and mouthed *I've got it.*

The doctor had warned us about potential mood swings. When he was tired or had a headache, his personality underwent a rapid change.

"I promise to bring you a slice of wedding cake," I said as we made it up the back deck.

"Thanks." Dad looked at me and his brow unwrinkled. "I know how I sound. I can't help it, I'm sorry."

"Hey," I said, taking his strong, tanned hand that had worked a ranch for years. "You don't have to apologize. For anything. You just have to rest and take care of yourself. You're no good to us grumpy."

"Or bedridden." He nodded. "Yeah. I know."

"You'll be back on a horse before you know it," I assured him. "Remember it's in the Powell genome. We're stubborn."

"It's also a Sullivan gene," he said. "So, you and Hadley got it from both sides."

"I'm not *that* stubborn," I quipped.

"Mhhm. You refused to come home for years," Dad said. "I call that stubborn."

"No, that's just pigheaded," I teased. "And the doctor didn't say anything about bluntness being a side effect of your injury."

"I've always been blunt," he said.

"Truth."

I hugged him again, and then I let Jane take him into the house. I hadn't given her enough credit. She never lost her composure; she never lost her cool. She put up with his mood swings. She drove him to doctor's appointments. She was a true partner to him.

She'd become family.

I sighed at the thought.

Hadley had been right. She knew I'd like her.

"Stubborn," I muttered as I turned and headed back to the wedding.

The main dish had been served while I'd been helping Jane with Dad. I took my seat and put my napkin on my lap.

"Is he okay?" Hadley asked as she picked up her fork.

"Yeah, just tired," I said.

She sighed. "Good call on the father-daughter dance. Try the trout. It's amazing."

Hadley fed me a bite of trout from her fork.

"Yum," I said.

"You guys playing the airplane game?" Wyn teased.

I cut into my steak and saw red in the center.

"Barely warm," Hadley said. "I made sure they didn't over-cook it for you."

"Thanks," I said, setting my fork down.

Hadley frowned. "Something wrong?"

"No. I'm just not very hungry. The salad filled me up, you know?"

Hadley's gaze narrowed. "Right."

"Have you told Declan about the cake?" I asked.

"I heard my name," Declan said, turning his head toward us.

"No, I haven't told him," Hadley said. "It's a surprise."

"What's a surprise?" Declan asked.

"About the cake," Hadley said. "Salem shouldn't have said anything."

"What's the surprise?" Cas asked. "Is someone going to jump out of it?"

"We're at a wedding, not a bachelor party," Hadley said.

"What *did* happen at your bachelor party?" I asked. "Anything interesting?"

"We were at the Copper Mule," Declan said. "And since you weren't there, there were no bar fights."

"Uh, ouch," I said.

"Don't be offended," Declan remarked. "If I ever need back up, I'm calling you."

"What about me?" Cas asked. "I've gotten you out of a few fights over the years."

"You also got me *into* a few fights," Declan added.

"Really?" Hadley asked. "Why haven't I heard about this?"

"Youthful indiscretions," Declan said. "I've mellowed."

"I want to hear all about these youthful indiscretions," Hadley exclaimed.

"Later," Declan said.

"When later?" she demanded.

He leaned over to her and whispered something in her ear that made her blush and laugh.

"Oh, he said something dirty," I quipped.

My gaze went to Cas's. He looked at me like he wanted to get me naked.

I glanced away and reached for my glass of water.

And caught Amber Winston looking right at me.

CHAPTER FORTY-ONE

THE RANCH

Every time I tried to approach Harlan, something got in the way. Either a guest wanted to talk to me or there was a problem with wedding logistics.

Muddy was three sheets to the wind and dancing up a storm, which left me to handle any issues that arose.

"I'll have another ginger beer," I said to Wade.

"We just ran out," Wade said.

"What do you mean you just ran out?" I demanded.

"I mean I have no more ginger beer," Wade said.

"There's another case back at the house," I explained. "In the cellar."

"I'll grab it," Wade said.

I shook my head. "Don't worry about it. I'll get Cas's help."

"Cas? Who the hell is Cas?" Wade asked.

"Bowman," I clarified.

"You sure?" Wade asked.

"Yeah." I nodded. "I'm the undesignated wedding planner right now. If there are any fires, I'll put them out."

I left the mobile bar and went to find Cas. He was talking to Gracie and Cole. Their toddler was perched on Gracie's hip and she smiled and reached for me the moment I joined them.

"Oh, hello," I said, taking Bella before she launched herself out of her mother's arms.

"This is new behavior," Cole said in surprise. "She's usually pretty reserved with strangers."

Bella's hands went to my tresses.

"Oh, she's going to mess up your hair," Gracie said as she extracted her daughter from my arms.

"Worth it," I said, taking one of Bella's hands and kissing it. "She's adorable."

"She's on her best behavior," Cole said. "But a meltdown is imminent. If we're lucky, we'll make it to the cake before that happens."

"What is the cake?" Cas asked. "Hadley mentioned it, but she was mysterious about it."

"Nah, you have to wait like everyone else. It's a secret between me and Hadley. But I told Cole he'd love it," Gracie said.

"I bet Salem knows," Cole said, looking at me.

I shook my head. "Nope. I know nothing about it. I'm just here for the cheese." I looked at Cas. "Can I borrow you for a second? Wade's out of ginger beer, but there's a case in the cellar in the house."

"And you want me and my brawn to carry it, right?" Cas asked.

"Yes. Exactly." I grinned and then turned back to Cole and Gracie. "See you guys in a few."

"Cake," Cole urged. "Send out the cake."

Gracie dumped their daughter into his arms. "You had your wedding with your very own cake. Patience."

Cas and I walked toward the house. I caught Gideon's eye. I waved and he waved back before continuing his conversation with his father.

We ducked into the house and found the catering staff on a break, enjoying lemonade and iced tea.

"We're just here to get a case of ginger beer," I said when a few of them shot up from their seats. "At ease."

"I guess we'll tell them to get the cake ready when we head back up," Cas said as he followed me down the cellar steps.

I hit the light and an Edison bulb flickered, illuminating the brick-and-mortar room.

The temperature immediately cooled. We passed the stored onions and potatoes, along with several other root vegetables. There were shelves and shelves of canned and pickled foods.

"Ah, here's the case of ginger beer," I said.

"That's not a case, that's a crate." Cas bent down and lifted one of the bottles. "Ginger beer. You mean, homemade ginger beer? That's what Wade's been serving the guests?"

I grinned. "Why do you think we went through a batch already? He's using it for Moscow Mules and Dark and Stormy's. Hadley and I are also drinking it straight."

Cas set the glass bottle down and stood.

"Cas?" I asked as he stalked toward me.

"I've been fantasizing about getting you alone, but I didn't have a good excuse," he growled.

His tone sent shivers up and down my spine.

"*Cas,*" I warned.

"I can't wait, Salem. I can't wait to have you again."

His hands hiked up the skirt of my dress, bunching it

around my waist, and his fingers plowed into my lace panties.

I held on to his shoulders and lifted my leg to wrap around his hip, giving him better access. He slid his fingers inside me and curled them, causing me to shudder. His thumb grazed my clit and I gasped.

"I can't wait to see you in a few months, round and swollen with my baby. So everyone knows you're mine. Everyone will know what we created together."

"Cas," I whispered.

"Come on my fingers, Salem. Make a mess."

His words pummeled through me and I erupted around him. I rode his hand, taking my pleasure, mindless of everything else.

Cas slid his fingers out of me and I lowered my leg from his hip.

He stuck his fingers into his mouth and cleaned them, his gaze heated.

All I wanted was for him to unbuckle his belt and fuck me against the cellar wall, but we were already playing with fire.

He pressed a kiss to my brow, and then helped me with my dress, making sure my skirt was straight and free of wrinkles.

"Did I tell you that you look beautiful?" His voice was raspy.

"I don't remember. Tell me again."

"You look beautiful. Even more beautiful with your cheeks flushed and your eyes bright."

"Come on, Caspian, let's get the ginger beer back to Wade. We've been gone long enough already."

Cas picked up the crate and followed me up the stairs. I turned off the light and closed the door behind me.

"Where's the catering staff?" I asked, looking around at the empty kitchen.

"No clue," Cas said. "Maybe someone came to tell them to get the cake ready."

"Probably right." I opened the sliding glass door for him and then followed him to the mobile bar.

"What took you guys so long?" Wade asked when we finally delivered the crate.

I didn't think we were gone that long, but apparently long enough for Wade to notice.

"Had to hunt for the ginger beer," Cas lied easily. "It wasn't where Salem thought it was."

"Yes. It's all my fault," I agreed.

When Wade wasn't looking, Cas shot me a sexy wink.

"There you are!" Poet said, running up to the both of us. "They're bringing out the cake in the next few minutes. I thought you guys were going to miss it."

"We'd never miss cake," Cas quipped.

"Especially because there's all this air of mystery surrounding it," I added.

"Well, I did get a little bit out of Hadley. It has chocolate in it," Poet whispered. "But that's all I know."

People congregated on the dance floor, holding their drinks and talking to one another while we waited for the cake to be unveiled.

Gracie pushed a barrel on a wheeled carrier onto the dance floor, flanked by two cater waiters, ready to lend a hand if there was trouble. But Gracie got it onto the dance floor and pressed the brakes on the wheels to keep it in place.

"Hadley, you want to do the honors?" Gracie asked.

Hadley stepped forward toward the barrel and lifted the top. It swung back like a hatch to reveal a three-tiered chocolate cake with edible chocolate horse imprints around the sides. On top were two chocolate molds. A cowgirl lassoing a cowboy.

"I can see why you wanted to keep this a surprise," Declan stated. "This is incredible! Gracie, you did this?"

"I did," Gracie preened.

"That's not the only surprise," Hadley said, taking Declan's hand and looking directly at him. "It's a cherry mash cake."

"No," Declan said.

"I'm serious," Hadley said with a laugh.

"What's a cherry mash cake?" someone asked.

Hadley turned to address the party-goers. "A cherry mash is Declan's favorite candy. It's cherry fondant on the inside with a chocolate peanut coating on the outside. There are no peanuts in this cake, because I don't want to kill anyone who might have an allergy."

There was another chorus of laughter.

"You had Gracie make a cherry mash wedding cake," Declan said.

"Yes." Hadley nodded.

He cradled her cheeks and kissed her.

The two cater waiters set up a table near the barrel and one of them handed Gracie a knife.

"Did we get pictures of this masterpiece?" I asked. "To go down in history as the most incredible wedding cake of all time?"

"We got photos," Hadley assured me.

Gracie stepped up to the cake. "Should I start slicing?"

"Yep, I'm ready," Hadley said.

"Surely not the most incredible wedding cake to go down in history," Amber said as she stepped forward out of the crowd.

Wyn frowned at her.

Hadley turned to look at Amber. "What do you mean by that?"

"Salem's wedding cake will be even better, don't you

think?" She lifted her Tom Collins in mock cheers. "After all, she can't help but always one-up you, Hadley."

I took a step toward Amber with the intent to silence her but stopped when Harlan grasped her arm. He gently tugged on it, but she wrenched her arm from his clasp.

"I've heard about you," Wyn said. "Why are you even here? We don't even *like* you."

Poet cleared her throat and threw me a nervous look.

"I invited her," Hadley said. "As a gesture of good will. She's writing a wedding piece for the town paper."

"Well, that was a mistake, clearly," Wyn stated.

"Amber, let's go talk somewhere," I said, keeping my voice calm even though I was raging inside. Raging and nervous, because Amber was running her mouth and Wyn had clearly been imbibing. Which meant she had no filter . . .

"Oh, I don't think that's necessary." Amber flashed a red-lipped grin. "But Salem, aren't you going to tell everyone your good news?"

"What news?" Hadley asked, her attention turning to me.

Even Gracie, who'd cut a few slices of cake, had stopped to peer at me.

Amber's eyes lit with excitement. "Oh, to hell with it, I'll tell them for you."

"Harlan," Cas snapped. "Get her the fuck out of here. Carry her if you have to."

I marched across the dance floor toward Amber, ready to take matters into my own hands, praying I got there in time.

But my weak ankle gave out and pain shot through my leg, momentarily distracting me.

"It's truly a time for celebration!" Amber crowed, looking at Hadley. "Not only did you just get married, but Salem and Bowman are having a baby!"

CHAPTER FORTY-TWO

THE RANCH

It was so quiet you could hear the horses nicker in the barn. Everyone seemed frozen for a moment, and then it was like a director yelled cut and all the actors started moving again.

"That's it," Wyn snapped. "I've had enough out of you and your trouble-making ass." Wyn set down her half-drunk cocktail on the edge of the cake table and stalked in Amber's direction.

Amber must've seen the look of determination in Wyn's eyes because she backed up a few steps.

Unfortunately, she plowed into Eloise and Lucy, who'd been going drink for drink with Muddy, and they were in no mood. Each of them grasped one of Amber's arms.

"We'll hold her for you," Eloise offered.

"Let her go," Wyn said, and cracked her knuckles. "I want to see her run."

Amber let out a squeak and attempted to burrow herself deeper into Eloise and Lucy's grip, but they flung her away.

"I'll give you a five second head start," Wyn murmured. "But fair warning, I was on the track and field team in high school, so choose your direction wisely."

Amber dashed from the party, heading for the hills.

Literally.

"One, two . . ." Wyn counted to five. "I'm coming for you!"

Wyn ran after Amber.

Declan glared at Cas. "Are you fucking kidding me?"

"What?" Cas demanded.

"You got Salem pregnant?"

I moaned. "Can we not do this now? It's your wedding day."

"Oh, we're doing this now," Declan said, grabbing the remainder of Wyn's drink and downing it in one swig. "I told you to stay away from her."

"Yeah, you did. And you also told Salem I wasn't a family man." Cas's cheeks heated with anger and alcohol. "What the fuck was that about?"

"Keep cutting the cake," Poet said to Gracie as she picked up a few slices and began to hand them out to guests.

"Got it," Gracie said, but her gaze strayed to me.

I noticed, but my attention bounced to Hadley who hadn't shown an ounce of emotion yet, and then to Cas and Declan.

Liquor and emotions were running high.

"You knocked up my wife's sister!" Declan yelled as he stepped toward Cas.

"Aww, he called you his wife," Poet said to Hadley, a dopey, boozy grin on her face.

"So what?" Cas yelled back. "I'm not sorry it happened! I love her."

The guests collectively gasped.

Declan pulled back his arm and made a fist, clearly preparing to punch Cas.

And Cas did nothing except stand there, ready to take whatever Declan doled out.

The two of them stared at each other.

"Declan," Hadley said softly.

Her words penetrated Declan's haze of anger and he slowly lowered his arm. She went to him and cradled his cheeks in her hands. He stared down at her as she whispered something no one else could hear. Declan turned his head and kissed her palm before extracting himself from her and stalking out of the wedding tent.

She turned and pointed at me. "You. With me. *Now.*"

Without waiting to see if I would follow, Hadley hiked up her wedding dress and headed toward the barn.

"Did she just leave her own wedding?" Poet asked.

"Yes," I said, hiding my head in shame.

Muddy shoved a slice of wedding cake into my hands, along with a fork. "Bring her this. She might be in a better mood with some sugar."

I gestured to the wedding guests. "What about them?"

"I've got it," Muddy said. "Go."

I looked at Cas, our eyes meeting for a moment, and then I ran after Hadley to the barn. She was stroking Goldie's nose when I arrived.

"You're not thinking of going for a ride, are you?" I asked.

"No. I just need a minute. Or ten. Is that for me?" She dipped her head at the piece of wedding cake I was holding.

Wincing, I handed it to her. "Hadley, I'm so sorry. I didn't mean to ruin your wedding."

She sliced a bite of cake with her fork but didn't eat it. "You didn't ruin my wedding. Amber did. I should've known she couldn't bury the hatchet."

"Except in my back." I sighed. "Cas was right. I should've told you I was pregnant. Then none of this mess would've ever happened."

Hadley sighed. "Salem, I already knew you were pregnant."

My jaw dropped open. *"What?"*

She nodded. "You think I didn't know? Of course I knew. Not drinking, not eating the cured meats while we were at the hot spring. And lying about having too much sugar as the reason you puked? Come on. Thin arguments. I saw right through them."

"But—why didn't you say anything?" I demanded.

"Why didn't you?" she asked. "We're twins. We tell each other everything."

"I didn't want *this* to happen. And by *this*, I mean the drama that I always seem to cause. And I didn't want it to happen at your wedding."

Hadley's lips quivered. "A little late for that, don't you think?"

I let out a loose chuckle. "I made Cas promise not to say anything until after your wedding. I wanted this day to be all about you and Declan."

"Oh, Salem." She sighed and shook her head. "I wish you'd have told me. So then we could've had double the reason to celebrate."

"You're really not mad at me, are you?" I asked in confusion.

"Mad?" Her eyes brightened and her smile widened. "How the hell could I be mad? You're moving home! We're having babies together. They're going to be best friends. This is all I've ever wanted."

"Hadley," I whispered, tears gathering in my eyes.

"But it's not all *you've* ever wanted," she said, her tone gentling.

"Oh, so that's what yesterday's talk was really about?"

She nodded. "I was hoping you were going to admit it to me then . . . that you were pregnant. But nothing I seemed to do would get you to spill the beans."

I narrowed my gaze at her. "You did the rare steak thing on purpose, didn't you?"

She bit her lip to stifle a grin. "I can be evil, too, if I'm trying to get you to admit something."

I laughed again but then sobered. "For what it's worth, I decided to stay before I even found out I was pregnant."

"You did?"

I nodded. "It's what I wanted."

"You sure?"

"I'm sure. The baby just . . ." I put my hand to my belly. "Was just the icing on the cake. Can you imagine me bunking with Poet and Wyn in a shared apartment? With one bathroom and a screaming newborn?"

"Well, you'd have built-in help. Wyn being a nanny and all. But then, what about Bowman? Would he go with you to New York? How could he, really? So, what's happening with all that? He said he loved you. In front of God and guests," she quipped.

"Yeah, that was a pretty public declaration, wasn't it?" I shook my head in surprise. "We're together, Hadley. And we're going to be a family."

She was quiet for a moment, and then asked, "What does that mean for his career? And yours?"

"I'm not sure about what he plans to do," I said with a frown. "We haven't talked about it, actually. As for my career, I don't really have one. I mean, I had the start of one. But I wasn't established. Not yet."

"But you love your job," she said. "How can you give up that potential?"

I smiled and shook my head.

"What?"

"You of all people are asking about a job over a family?"

"I'm me and you're you," she said. "Life here is simple. You never wanted a simple life."

"Meaningful," I said quietly. "And if, at some point, I want something more, then I'll start my own firm. I have the contacts. And my future husband is a legendary rodeo star. You don't think he has connections too?"

"Future husband. Does that mean a wedding is imminent?"

"Not *imminent*. But maybe in the distant, near future."

"That's an oxymoron. And Dad won't stand for it, you know. He'll want you to get married ASAP."

"Cas will be glad to hear that," I muttered. "But this is my choice, and I won't be roped into it before I'm ready."

"Hmm. Just to make sure, we'd better ask Muddy to hide Dad's shotgun."

"You're really not mad at me?" I asked.

"I'm really not mad at you." She took my hands in hers. "And I love you so much for not wanting to steal my thunder on my wedding day."

"Even though I did it anyway . . ."

"Hmm. No, Amber did that. When she dropped the secret baby bomb." She frowned.

"What?"

"How did she know? About you and Cas?"

"I have no idea," I admitted.

"We should probably get back to my wedding and face the music."

"Or at least see how bad Wyn kicked Amber's ass."

Hadley laughed. "And they say nothing happens in small towns."

CHAPTER FORTY-THREE

Hadley looked around the wedding tent. "I don't see Declan or Bowman."

"Or Muddy," I added.

"The three of them are at the house," Poet said.

Wyn sat in a folding chair as Poet attempted to tidy Wyn's hair. "It's no use, girl. I can't fix this without hairspray and prayer."

"Leave it," Wyn said, batting Poet's hand away from her head.

"At least let me get the leaves out," Poet muttered.

Wyn ate her slice of cake as Poet tended to her. "God, this is good."

"You didn't kill her, did you?" I demanded.

"I didn't even get my hands on her," Wyn stated. "I tripped and went down. By the time I got up, she was nowhere in sight."

"Probably for the best," Hadley said. She looked at the

mobile bar and yelled, "Wade!"

"Yeah, Hads?" he called back.

"I don't want any liquor left when the day is done, understand?"

"Yes, ma'am," he called back.

Lucy came up to me and gave me a hug. "Congratulations, by the way."

"Yeah, congratulations," Gideon added as he approached.

Wedding guests continued to offer me their felicitations and well wishes. But then the questions started.

"Does this mean you're moving home for good?"

"Are you and Bowman getting married?"

"Does your father know?"

On and on they went.

Poet wormed herself between me and a few guests. She placed her hands on her hips, peered up at me, and glowered.

I waved at her. "Hi."

She pointed her finger at me. "Don't *hi* me. Wyn said you told her you were pregnant."

"She caught me puking a few days ago," I said lamely.

"And Muddy said she knew too," Poet added. "I'm guessing you told Hadley as well?"

"No," Hadley interjected. "Salem didn't tell me. I already knew, though. Because Salem was acting weird and not eating certain things and she threw up when we camped out."

"The beer . . . that spill was on purpose," Poet said in real-ization.

"Yep," I said.

She frowned. "I was the last to know. *Again.*"

"My father doesn't know yet," I said, patting her hand. "So technically, he's the last to know."

"He knows," Muddy said from behind me.

I whirled. "Don't sneak up on me!"

She shrugged.

"And what do you mean Dad knows? Who told him?" I demanded.

"Your fiancé," she said. "He just asked your father for your hand in marriage."

"Oh no," I murmured.

"He wants to see you," Muddy said, giving me a little push toward the house.

"But I'm at a wedding," I said lamely.

"I'll go with you if you want," Hadley said.

"No, I'm no chicken. I can handle Dad." I grimaced. "You think he'll lecture me?"

"About what?" Hadley asked with a wry grin. "Getting pregnant? He'd have to lecture me, too."

"I meant, do you think he'll lecture me about falling in love with a bull rider?" I corrected.

Wyn turned to Poet. "We've got to get the fuck out of here. Like, immediately."

"Why?" Poet demanded.

"Because there's some sort of fertility juice in Huckleberry Hill. And I have no interest in getting pregnant," Wyn said.

"It's not so much Huckleberry Hill," Poet said. "Just steer clear of hot cowboy bikers and you should be good."

"Like cowboy sperm isn't already potent enough? You gotta add the biker aspect to it?" Wyn asked. "It's like a double whammy."

"No pun intended," Poet said gesturing to both me and Hadley.

CHAPTER FORTY-FOUR

THE RANCH

I knocked gently on my father's bedroom door.

"Come in," he called.

I opened the door and stepped inside.

"*Salem,*" Dad said.

"I know that tone," I groaned.

"Tone? There's no tone."

"There was definitely a tone." I closed the door and moved into the room. "That was the *I'm very disappointed in you, young lady* tone."

Dad's lips flickered like he wanted to smile. "Even if that were true, when has that tone ever worked on you?"

He patted his bedside.

"Cas came to talk to me," he said.

"Yeah, I heard," I muttered. With heavy feet, I trudged to the vacant side and curled up at the foot of the bed.

"Come closer."

I inched up the bed coverlet.

Dad reached his hand out, searching for mine.

I gave it to him.

"You and your sister are determined to turn my hair gray," he said.

"You're blaming Hadley too?" I beamed. "That's a first."

Dad chuckled. "It's true you've caused more turmoil over the years, but lately, Hadley's held her own."

"You're disappointed, aren't you? In me?"

"I've never been disappointed in you."

"That's not true."

"It's very true." He squeezed my hand. "You're making me a grandfather. How the hell am I supposed to be disappointed with that news?"

"But the timing," I said.

"Timing's a bitch. And babies work on their own time. Ask me how I know."

I cleared my throat. "So, Cas talked to you?"

"He did."

"About what?"

"Many things," Dad said with a smile. "Important things."

"Things like weddings and such?"

"Hmm. Yeah. There was talk of a wedding."

"I'm not getting married because I'm having a baby. That's antiquated," I said.

Dad shrugged.

"What, no fight?"

"I think I'll let Cas field this one," Dad said. "He's stubborn and determined."

"What happened to you?" I demanded. "You were such a beast when it came to Hadley and Declan."

"Declan worked for me and Hadley had come home heartbroken. It was different. You're different."

"You mean I'm not worth the effort of finding your shotgun and threatening Cas to marry me?" I snapped.

"Who has to threaten?" Dad asked. "As for the shotgun, Muddy hid it again. Not from me this time—from Declan. Declan's pissed as hell. And I'm not supposed to get upset or stressed."

"Then I'd better leave," I muttered, dropping his hand and attempting to get off the bed.

"You're a black sheep, Salem. Always have been, always will be. I learned my lesson. I won't put you in a box or try to make you anything other than what you are. I love you *exactly* as you are. And so does Cas. Which is why I gave him my blessing. Not that it would matter anyway. Because you'll do exactly what you want to do, when you want to do it. So, as it turns out, the person who needs to say yes is *you*."

"Oh, Dad." I launched myself at him and embraced him a bit too hard.

He kissed the top of my head. "I just want you to be happy. Are you happy?"

I pulled back to look at him and nodded.

"Then that's all a father can ask for. Now go see Cas. And try not to give him too much shit."

"Then I wouldn't be me, would I?" I asked with a laugh.

I climbed off the bed and headed for the door.

"Same goes for you, you know," I said with my hand on the knob.

"What's that?" he asked.

"I want you to be happy."

"I am."

"With Jane?"

"Yes."

"Good. She's young. She'll keep you young. Can't have you getting too old to take your grandkids on trail rides."

He smiled, his eyes bright with the idea. "Ah, just another reason to heal."

"Rest up, Dad. We're not going anywhere."

◡

Cas was sitting in a camp chair at the fire circle, his expression sullen. He picked up a bottle of beer and took a sip.

I approached, crossing my arms over my chest and glaring at him.

"Not in the mood, woman."

"Don't *woman* me, you scoundrel. You told my dad I was pregnant before I got a chance to do it."

"I—"

"No, *I'm talking*," I snapped. "You told my father I was pregnant."

"We're not speaking."

"You and I? Oh, we're speaking. We're going to be doing *a lot* of speaking."

"Not you and I. Declan and I. Declan and me? Whatever. We're not talking." He sighed. "I feel like an ass."

His shoulders slumped and my anger vanished. I went to sit in the chair next to him and scooted it closer.

I put my hand on his knee. "This is a fucking mess, you get that, right?"

"Yeah." His hand covered mine. "My best friend isn't talking to me."

"And you're not talking to him," I pointed out. "Mutual anger, it would seem."

"What about you and Hadley?"

"We're fine. Turns out, she knew I was pregnant all along."

"Did she? Nice of her to say something," he muttered.

"She was trying to trick it out of me. Raw steak, Declan's wedding brew . . ." I shook my head.

"And how did everyone else react to the baby?"

"Once everything died down, they were all really happy

for us. My dad was a big surprise, actually. I expected a lecture."

"No lecture?"

"None. He just wants me to be happy. And," I added, looking at Cas, "he said, his blessing didn't matter because it was my blessing you needed in order to marry me."

"Well, sure." Cas nodded. "I know that. But there are societal norms, traditions, that are expected. If our daughter's future husband doesn't ask for my blessing, I'll be very unhappy."

"What if we have a son and he comes home married from an elopement?"

Cas's eyes widened. "Are you trying to kill me already?"

"No, darling," I teased. "Our child will be the source of all your gray hair. I promise you." I raked my fingers through his locks. "You'll look good gray. Sexy."

"I have a few more years before that happens . . . hopefully," he murmured.

"Declan was ready to punch you. And you were going to let him."

"Seemed only right. I did fuck his wife's sister."

"And get her pregnant," I added.

"No apologies for that, tater tot."

I fell silent for a moment.

"What is it?" he asked.

"Why does Declan think you're not a family man?"

"Because I'm not. I don't have a family. I don't know what a healthy marriage looks like. I don't have a shining example of what a normal family is. He doesn't think I'm good enough for you," Cas said, his tone soft, somber. "And so even though he considers me his best friend, he doesn't think I deserve someone like you. He thinks I'm no good for you."

I kissed his hand and rose.

"Where are you going?" he asked.

"To have some of my own words with Declan."

"Salem, don't. He's not wrong."

"Not wrong? Of course he's wrong. He's so fucking wrong I can't even believe he'd—look, I know he warned me away from you when we first got here. But to say you're not a family man? That's bullshit. You were the one that decided to stick around when Muddy needed help, when we needed help. Don't you get it, Cas? You're a family man who never got a chance to have a family. And we're your family. You're *my* family."

Cas grinned. "Okay, tater tot. I'll marry you."

"What?"

"That was a proposal, wasn't it?"

"No." I scoffed. "That wasn't a proposal."

"Felt like a proposal."

"You're an ass."

"But I'm your ass." He chuckled. "Now come back here and kiss me."

CHAPTER FORTY-FIVE

"You've got sex hair," Wyn said the next morning when I opened the door to my bedroom.

I stepped into the hallway and closed the door behind me, and then hastily ran my hand through my locks.

"Not gonna help," Poet said with a cheeky grin. "You must've had a good night. You never did make it back to the reception."

"I don't kiss and tell," I said. "But if I did, I'd tell you Cas and I spent the night in the barn loft and snuck in around four in the morning."

Wyn smirked. "So proud of you, girl."

"Why are you guys here so early?" I asked, running a hand down my face.

"It's nine a.m.," Poet said.

"Is it?" I asked. "Wow."

"We called Hadley, but she's not answering her phone. We were going to knock on the cabin door, but last night was her wedding night. So it feels kind of weird to be interrupting their honeymoon," Wyn said.

"Can you call it a honeymoon if they don't go anywhere?" Poet asked. "Not even to The Regal Beagle for sparkling water and strawberries?"

"I kind of understand why they didn't go on an actual honeymoon," Wyn said.

"You guys have been up for hours," I said. "I'm a little slow today. So give me a minute."

"Oh, a minute to puke up your guts?" Poet asked, crossing her arms over her chest. "I'm still mad at you for not telling me."

"Meet us at the fire circle," Wyn said. "We're going to get Hadley."

Nodding, I went back into my room and closed the door.

"Come back to bed," Cas commanded.

"I didn't know you were awake. My friends are demanding a meeting at the fire circle."

I slipped into the bathroom to brush my teeth. While I was slathering my brush with toothpaste, Cas appeared and hovered in the doorway.

I met his gaze in the mirror.

"Yes?" I asked.

He came up behind me and slid his hand into my pajama pants. I wasn't wearing panties.

"Salem," he growled.

"Didn't you get enough last night?" I asked. "And early this morning?"

"No."

He brushed his lips along my neck, and I dropped my toothbrush into the sink.

I leaned back into him. "We can't, Cas. Not here."

"Yes, here. It's not the middle of the night. The house is probably empty."

He removed his hand from my underwear, and then turned on the shower.

"That should mute the sounds you make. But for all that is holy, try to be quiet."

His tone was husky as he went back to stroking me until I was wet and ready for him.

He shoved the sweats down my legs and did the same with his boxers. Cas gently pressed his hand to my lower back, silently urging me to bend over.

I spread my legs.

"God, I'll never get tired of this view."

His crown teased my entrance.

"I'll never get tired of watching you take my cock," he said, his voice pitched low.

He fed me inch by inch until he filled me completely. I hissed at the soreness between my legs, but that didn't stop him.

With one hand, he held my hip. With the other, he slid his fingers between my thighs.

"So fucking wet. So fucking greedy."

I stifled my cry of pleasure as I gripped the old counter.

My body was so sensitive, so primed. It took only a few deep thrusts and the stroking of his fingers before I clenched around him.

He bit my shoulder and growled out his release.

"Shower," he said as he pulled out.

"Not with you," I said, recovering my breath. "If I get in there with you, you'll never let me leave."

"Now you're getting it." He wrapped his arms around me and held me to him. All I wanted to do was curl up with him and go back to sleep. Which was the danger of Cas.

I forced myself out of his arms.

He adjusted the temperature. "Fine. I'll let you shower alone. But don't make a habit out of it, yeah?"

"I won't." I kissed his lips and then stepped into the shower. I closed the shower curtain and immediately grabbed the bar of soap. "You're still in here."

"Yeah."

"Why?"

"Fantasizing about you wet and naked, and hoping you'll change your mind."

"If you can promise me you'll keep your hands to yourself, you can come in."

"Can't promise that, so I'll stay out here."

When he still didn't leave, I sighed. "What's on your mind?"

"How did Amber find out about us?"

"I don't know. Does it really matter at this point? The cat's out of the bag."

"And the bun is in the oven."

"Clever." I snorted. "You gonna talk to Declan today?"

"No."

"Oh good. We're taking the mature route."

I turned off the water and stuck my hand out of the shower. A moment later, my fingers grasped a clean towel.

"You're fast," he said when I pulled back the shower curtain.

I smirked. "In more ways than one."

He kissed me and wrapped his arms around me, towel and all.

"Get out of here, woman. Stop tempting me."

Ten minutes later, phone in hand, I headed downstairs. The den was quiet. I put on a fresh pot of coffee and had just poured a cup when my sister and friends arrived.

"Gimme," Hadley said, reaching for my cup.

"Long night of honeymooning?" I teased.

"Hmm." She took a sip of coffee and closed her eyes for a moment. "Yep."

I handed Wyn and Poet two coffee mugs and then grabbed another for myself.

"By the looks of it," Hadley said, raking me from head to toe, "my wedding night was lucky for you, too."

"Am I wearing it like a badge?" I demanded.

"A scarlet badge of honor," Wyn said.

The four of us took our coffee mugs out to the fire circle.

"So, I call this meeting to order," Poet said as she sat down.

"And normally, we would've let you both sleep, but there's something that needs attention," Wyn said.

"What's that?" I asked.

Wyn looked at Poet. "You tell them. You're gentle."

Poet nodded. "Wyn and I went into town this morning for breakfast."

"Oh no," I murmured.

"Yeah, everyone was talking about the wedding," Wyn said.

The two of them fell silent.

"And?" I prodded. "Go on. There's more. There's always more."

"And the news of both Powell sisters being pregnant," Wynn added. "And the drama of how it all came out."

They went silent again.

"The rest of it," Hadley demanded.

Poet cleared her throat. "It's on the front page of the Huckleberry Hill Crier."

"With photos," Wyn added. "Of Declan's hand pulled back ready to hit Bowman, Hadley's stricken look, and Salem's gobsmacked expression."

"That's not that bad," Hadley said, her gaze darting to mine. "Not nearly as bad as Salem being on the front page for the bar fight with Amber."

"Thank you for that." I wrinkled my nose in distaste.

"How is that possible, though? Amber left the party. It's not like she was able to take candid photos of the drama going down. Not when she was involved in it."

"The wedding photographer from the paper," Hadley murmured. "Who came with Amber."

"No. It can't be. They signed an NDA, right?" I asked Hadley. "You had them sign an NDA so they couldn't share their photos without your approval, right?"

Hadley shook her head. "No. Why would I have done that? They literally came to do a story on the wedding and us. I didn't intend for it to turn into a saga."

Poet sighed. "There's more."

"More?" Hadley demanded. "How much more?"

Poet winced at Hadley's tone. "It's all over social media. The town paper's social media account posted a video of the —er—baby daddy reveal. And then they tagged Sweet Teeth because Gracie made the cake. And because Sweet Teeth went viral not that long ago, they had a bunch of new eyeballs on their page . . ."

Hadley pulled out her phone, her fingers flying across the screen. I watched her face fall.

"What?" I asked, dread curling inside me.

"Our family's dirty laundry is all over the front lawn and being set on fire," she intoned, holding the phone out to show me.

I grimaced.

"How bad is it?" Wyn demanded. "It was at two hundred and fifty thousand views when we knocked on the cabin door."

"It's at a million views now," Hadley said, swallowing. "And in the comments, people are tagging Bowman's sponsors' accounts."

The back door to the house opened and Cas stepped out onto the deck. "Sorry to interrupt girl time. But I need to talk to Salem."

Nodding, I hurried toward him.

We went inside the house and closed the door to give us privacy. He raked a hand through his hair. "My manager just called me."

"Oh." I nibbled my lip. "What about?"

"Seems you and I are both kind of famous now," he said.

I winced. "That's what Poet and Wyn wanted to talk to us about. The news is all over town, and in the town paper, and on social media."

He nodded slowly. "Yeah. I know. I've been tagged I don't even know how many times."

His phone rang and he fished it out of his jeans pocket. "It's my manager. I've got to take this."

Nodding, I turned to leave and give him privacy, but his fingers clasped around my wrist to stop me from leaving.

"Hey, Danny," he said into the phone. "What's up?" He listened, his expression braced for bad news. "Oh? Oh, really? You're shitting me. Okay, yeah. Thanks."

He hung up and lowered his hand, still clutching his cell phone.

"Bad?" I whispered.

"The owner of Cowboy Coffee saw the video."

"Cas," I whispered. "I'm so sorry."

He frowned in confusion, and then he cracked a smile. And then he began to laugh.

"What?" I demanded. "The implosion of your life because I have an archnemesis is funny?"

"No," he said, his laughter quieting. He cradled my cheek in one hand. "He saw the video and he loves the fact that I'm now a family man with a woman and a baby on the way."

I blinked. "You're kidding."

He shook his head. "Nope."

I let out a deep breath. "So, you're not in trouble?"

"I'm not in trouble," he said.

My phone rang and I glanced down at the screen at my boss's name.

"Yikes," I murmured.

"What?" Cas asked.

"*I* might be in trouble."

"Won't know until you answer."

With a deep breath, I pressed the screen and put the phone to my ear. "Jack. Hi."

"Salem Powell," my boss greeted with a chuckle. "I've been talking about you all morning."

"Oh?" I asked, my eyes shooting worry at Cas.

He took my other hand and linked his fingers through mine, lending me his support.

"Rudolph Lancaster demanded a meeting. They just left the office."

My heart beat in my ears as I waited for Jack to deliver the final blow to my career.

"Why the hell didn't you tell me you were dating a professional bull rider?" Jack demanded. "I had to find out from them."

"Oh, well," I stammered. "It's new."

"They want you both in their campaign."

"What's that now?"

"They want you and your bull rider as the faces of their campaign. A rancher's daughter and a professional bull rider fall in love? What could possibly be more authentic than that?"

The blood rushed from my head, leaving me dizzy. Cas immediately guided me to a kitchen chair and then knelt in front of me.

"They're offering you both a decent paycheck. I mean, it'll probably seem like chump change compared to what

Bowman makes on the circuit. But there you have it. Oh, and congrats on the baby."

When I didn't reply, Jack pressed, "Salem? You still there?"

"Still here," I croaked. "And trying not to pass out from shock. You mean I'm not fired?"

Jack laughed. "Fired? Kiddo, you may have just jump-started a whole new direction in your career."

CHAPTER FORTY-SIX

THE RANCH

Three days later, Wynn hugged me. "I don't want to leave."

I bear-hugged the shit out of her. "You have a job and a life to get back to."

"I don't have a life," Wyn protested. "I work all the time."

"And I hate my job," Poet blurted out from beneath Hadley's arm.

"Finally admitting it," I said, dropping my arms from around Wyn. "Just when you're leaving and we can't hash it out and figure out what to do."

"There's nothing to do," Poet said. "Either I suck it up or I quit."

Wyn and Poet swapped places and it was my turn to hug Poet.

"I'd love for you guys to stay. In fact, move here," Hadley commanded.

"Don't tempt me," Poet muttered.

"I'm not moving here," Wyn stated. "Never gonna happen."

"Afraid that pregnancy is catching?" I asked with a laugh.

"That," Wyn said. "And there's very little in the way of hobbies."

"What do you mean?" Hadley demanded. "There's tons to do here."

"Yeah, Grandma and Grandpa hobbies," Wyn said. "Like crocheting, bird watching, you know. Sedate, might-as-well-take-a nap kind of hobbies."

"Nesting hobbies," Hadley quipped.

Poet rolled her eyes and changed the subject. "Have Declan and Bowman talked at all?"

Hadley shook her head. "They're both being elk headed."

Wyn blinked. "Don't you mean pigheaded?"

"Elk Ridge, elk headed," Hadley said with a shrug.

"Only time will sort this out," I said.

"Might want to do something about it sooner rather than later, or they might never talk again," Wyn advised.

"Yeah, we'll have to noodle on that," I said with a nod.

"You're queen of the shenanigans," Poet said. "I'm sure you'll think of something."

"Oh, and by the way," Hadley said, "I know how Amber found out about Salem and Bowman."

"This is news to me," I said.

"Lucy did some sleuthing." Hadley grinned. "While you and Bowman had your interlude in the cellar, Amber came into the house to use the restroom. Apparently, someone forgot to close the cellar door."

Wyn raised her brows. "Salem, I'm ashamed of you."

"You are?" I demanded.

"Yes. Everyone knows you ensure the door is closed before you engage in carnal activities."

"Before she starts to lecture, we'd better get out of here," Poet said.

"Text the minute you land in New York," Hadley said to them.

"We will," Poet promised. "And we'll be back for the baby showers before you know it."

"Just one shower," Hadley corrected. "Salem and I are having a joint baby shower. Doesn't make sense to have two with the babies so close in age, does it?" She looked at me as she said it.

I smiled. "No. Not really."

"And you'll keep us posted?" Wyn asked. "About Declan and Bowman?"

"I will," I said with a sigh.

Wyn finally climbed into the driver's seat of the rental and Poet, ever the passenger princess, got in too.

"Safe travels," I said, and then shut Poet's door.

Hadley and I stood by, waving to them as they backed out of the driveway and left the ranch.

"And then there were two," she said, linking her arm through mine.

"I'm already lonely," I lamented. "Is it wrong that I hoped they'd stay forever?"

"Nope. It's what I wished for the night all four of us were at the hot spring," Hadley said. "I know I'm not supposed to tell anyone my wish, but there you have it."

"I wished for it too," I admitted.

"Well, maybe we've got twin hot spring power on our side."

We went back into the house and Hadley beelined to the fridge and pulled out a plate of fried chicken. "I'm eating it cold. Don't judge."

"Hand me a drumstick," I stated. "I'll join you."

I opened the cabinet and grabbed two plates and several paper napkins before returning to the kitchen table.

"Have you guys decided what you're going to do?" she asked.

"About the Rudolph Lancaster campaign? No. About Cas's career? Also no. I wish he and Declan were talking, so he could have someone else's perspective."

"You've brought it up, though, right? Talking to Declan."

"Well, sure. But every time I broach the subject, he distracts me."

"With?"

"His tongue," I admitted.

She chuckled. "Declan does the same."

"This is so stupid," I said. "They're best friends. They can't throw away years of friendship over this."

"I thought for sure Declan's mom would be able to talk some sense into him, but it was no use. Should we lock them in a room together and force them to speak?" Hadley asked. "Use trickery like Wyn suggested to get them back to being buddies?"

"Maybe." I sat down.

She dropped a drumstick onto my plate. "Declan thought he had to protect you from Bowman, what with you being his future sister-in-law, but you're already pregnant and Bowman loves you, so . . ."

"And Cas was mad that Declan said he wasn't a family man, implying he wasn't good enough for me."

"Boys are dumb." She bit into her chicken thigh.

"If they weren't so damn hot—"

"Or good in bed—"

"We'd have nothing to do with them." I raised my drumstick, and she tapped it with her chicken thigh.

The front door opened, and I heard a set of keys clank on

the foyer table. Muddy appeared in the kitchen, holding a plastic bag.

"What do you have there?" Hadley asked her.

"Alpaca yarn," she said. "I'm starting a new crocheting project."

"Are you going to tell us what it is?" I asked.

"It's a surprise." She set the bag of yarn down and patted my head. "You gonna save any of that chicken for me?"

"Get it while you can," Hadley quipped. "It's a hormonal feeding frenzy."

Muddy went to the cabinet and pulled out a plate. "The girls left?"

"Yeah. Not too long ago," I replied.

"I said my goodbyes to them this morning, before either of you were awake. I hope they come back soon," Muddy said. "The house feels empty without them."

"Empty?" Hadley repeated. "How can this house feel empty? Every room is occupied."

"I don't know. It just does. They're family," Muddy explained as she took a seat at the table.

I pushed the plate of chicken toward her.

"And not every room is occupied," Muddy said. "What with Cas basically moving into Salem's room."

I stilled. "Does Dad know?"

Muddy shrugged.

I sighed. "Cas. You're calling him Cas now?"

"Bowman feels too . . ." Muddy searched for the word.

"Male athlete that smacks other male athletes on the behind," Hadley supplied.

"That." Muddy plunked a piece of chicken onto her plate. "Family meeting tonight."

"When you say *family*," I began.

"You, Hadley, both boys, and your father," Muddy said. She took a bite of chicken. "Damn, I'm a good cook."

I sniggered.

"What about Jane?" Hadley asked.

"No Jane," Muddy said. "Not until your father puts a ring on it."

I frowned. "Cas hasn't put a ring on it yet."

"But he will. When you let him." She winked. "Besides, I've already spoken to Jane and she understands about the family meeting tonight. She's not offended."

"Why do I get the feeling you're trying to back Dad into a corner so he'll propose to Jane," Hadley drawled.

"Because that's exactly what I'm doing," she said. "He wants to marry her. She wants to marry him. I don't see the issue."

"Uh, how about the fact that he's recovering from brain surgery?" I said.

Muddy shrugged. "We're all recovering from something, aren't we?"

"Touché," Hadley murmured.

"What's the family meeting about?" I asked.

"We'll talk tonight," Muddy said. "Now eat your chicken before I do."

CHAPTER FORTY-SEVEN

"Enough," Dad said. "I've had enough of this bullshit."

Declan opened his mouth to speak but Dad shook his head. "No. You've had your say. You've had plenty to say. Now it's my turn to talk."

Dad sat on the couch, with Hadley and I flanking him. Muddy was in her patchwork chair. As for Declan and Cas . . . they were the farthest away from each other they could get while still being in the same room.

"You two need to make amends," Dad said. "Declan, I know you feel protective of Salem, but Cas is your best friend. And like it or not, he's with Salem now and that's not changing. You were best friends before you each fell in love with a Powell sister. And when Cas marries Salem, you'll be brothers."

The two men looked at each other. Declan stepped forward and muttered, "Sorry."

"Yeah, sorry," Cas parroted.

"You've got to be kidding me," Muddy said. "You think we bought that? No one bought that."

"I'm not ready to forgive him," Declan seethed.

"Neither am I," Cas announced.

"Stubborn fuckers," I snapped. "We're not doing this."

"Damn right we're not," Hadley said, crossing her arms over her chest and glaring at her new husband. "You've been friends for over a decade. Don't let pride end your friendship."

"This isn't about pride," Declan stated.

"Then what is it about?" Hadley asked.

"I'm good enough for Salem," Cas said. "Even if you don't think I am."

"What the hell are you talking about?" Declan demanded.

"You don't think I'm good enough for her," Cas said, his face marred with anger. "That's why you told her I wasn't a family man."

Declan held his head and sighed before looking at his best friend. "You dumb fuck."

"Oh no," I murmured.

"Wait," Hadley said to me.

"Because you're *not* a family man. You've been on the circuit for years and"—his eyes darted to me before returning to Cas—"never showed any signs you wanted to settle down."

"Did you want to settle down until you met Hadley?" Cas asked bluntly.

Declan paused. "Fair point."

"I didn't plan this," Cas said. "You of all people know how that shit goes."

Declan straightened his spine. "So, what are you going to do? You're at the top of your career. And you've got spon-sorships . . ."

"I've also been offered the chance to be the face of Rudolph Lancaster's new western line," Cas said.

"You're kidding!" Muddy gasped.

Cas looked at her and shook his head.

I cleared my throat. "They, ah, found out Cas and I were together and having a baby, and now they want us both to model in the campaign."

The room was silent.

"Nothing's been decided," Cas finally said.

"What do you mean *nothing's been decided?*" Declan asked.

"I mean, there's a lot of moving parts," Cas stated. "My career. Her career. That'll get sorted. But I don't want to be at odds with you."

"We're not at odds." Declan cleared his throat. "I overstepped, brother. I won't interfere in your relationship again."

I held my breath as the two old friends stared at one another.

Cas held out his hand and Declan clasped it.

"Thanks, man," Cas said, shaking Declan's palm.

"I never did say congratulations," Declan replied.

"No, you didn't," Cas agreed. "I'm sorry we weren't upfront about our relationship."

"That's my fault," I said. "I asked Cas to keep it quiet until after the wedding. I had no idea Amber would—anyway, I'm sorry too."

Declan shook his head. "Don't apologize, Salem. Hadley told me why you kept the news a secret. Still, it would've been nice to be clued in. Then we could've had double the celebration."

I looked at Hadley.

She smiled. "Told ya. We would've been fine with an extra dose of happiness."

I glanced at Muddy, and then at Dad. "So I guess that's it then. We're all good?"

"No, there's more," Dad said. "Your grandmother and I gave Hadley and Declan acreage on the ranch to build their house. When you officially get engaged, we'll do the same for you. But not until I see a ring on that finger. You understand?"

I raised my brows. "Yes, oh traditional one, I understand."

"Don't worry, sir. I'll wear her down." Cas shot me a wink.

"Speaking of engagements, why don't you till your own soil?" I said to Dad.

"What do you mean?" Dad asked.

"Seriously? Jane, Dad. It's not right that you've had the woman move in without the promise of marriage and a future. In fact, living under the same roof without the same last name is a little hypocritical, don't you think?"

Muddy cackled. "She's got you there, Connor."

"We're not talking about me," Dad said.

"Let's talk about you," Hadley said with a grin. "I think next spring would be a great time for you and Jane to tie the knot."

"It'll give him time to recover so he can stand at the altar," I agreed.

"Wait a second—" Dad interjected.

"What do you think, Muddy?" I asked. "You good with a spring wedding?"

"Perfect. We might have to do it inside though. Rainy season and whatnot," she said.

Dad rubbed his head. "Are you all finished?"

"For now," I said with a laugh.

Hadley took Dad's free hand and gave it a squeeze. "This is our way of giving you our blessing."

Dad looked at Hadley, and then at me.

I nodded. "She's right."

"Well, shit," Dad stated. "I better shop for a ring."

◡

"You're still awake," Cas said from the doorway of the connecting bathroom.

I looked at him and lowered the book I was reading to my lap and smiled up at him. "It's nine o'clock."

He padded over to the bed, and then all but flopped down next to me. "I like coming home to you after a wild night out."

"And by wild, you mean . . ."

Cas laughed. "One beer with Declan at the Copper Mule."

I raked my hand through his tousled hair. "And how did that go?"

"Good. We're good." He briefly closed his eyes and sank into my touch for a minute. "He helped me hash some things out."

"I knew he would. It's good you guys are buddies again."

He opened his eyes and sat up to face me. "I'm going to retire, Salem."

"What? No, you don't have to do that," I said.

"I don't?"

I shook my head. "We can figure something out. You can fly home in between events. I'll go with you to some of them. It doesn't have to be all or nothing. Besides, you've got spon-sorships. You can't just give up everything you've ever—"

"Hey, hang on. My turn."

"But—"

"Nope. You get to listen now." He grinned when I glared at him. "And I know how much you love listening."

He took the book from my lap and set it aside, and then

he grasped my hands. "I'm going to finish out this season. We'll schedule the Rudolph Lancaster photoshoot in between events. I'll fulfill all my sponsorship requirements I have left on contract, but after that, I'm done."

"What are you going to do then?" I demanded. "Work under Declan for the next many years on my father's ranch? A ranch can't have two foremen."

"That's part of what Declan and I were talking about." He took a deep breath. "We're going to open a rodeo club and be partners."

"Where are you going to do that?" I asked in confusion.

"Here. On this land."

"A rodeo club," I murmured. "You're going to teach bull riding and calf roping?"

"Yeah, and we've already got a plan for how it's going to pan out. Between the two of us, we can get sponsored riders to come here on the company dime to learn how to be better riders and ropers. The better they get, the more they make. And the companies who sponsor them will make even more sales off the promotions. It's a win for everyone involved and we'll still get to rope and ride, just not on the circuit anymore. So, what do you think?"

"I think you have it all figured out," I said.

"We're going to need someone in charge of marketing and social media. You know anyone good?"

I smirked. "I have a few names I could pass your way."

"What about your name and my name? I mean, your first name with my last name? Salem Bowman has a nice ring to it, don't you think?"

"It sounds pretty good, Caspian Bowman."

"Casimir," he said softly. "Casimir William Bowman."

I traced his lips with my finger. "Casimir William Bowman, legendary bull rider."

"Casimir William Bowman, the man who's not doing a good enough job convincing you to marry him."

My fingers trailed down his chin to his neck and then lower . . .

"Maybe you should get creative."

His grin was wicked. "Thought you'd never ask."

CHAPTER FORTY-EIGHT

The next morning, I took the side-by-side and went for a drive. I wasn't sure where I was going. But I drove to clear my head. After a night of pleasure in Cas's arms, I still hadn't said yes to his marriage proposal.

I loved him. I was having a baby with him. But I just wasn't ready. I needed more time. My life had changed at a breakneck pace. I wanted a moment to catch my breath.

So I let the sun warm my skin and the air blow through the cab of the vehicle.

Before I knew it, I was at the hill. I got out of the side-by-side and walked to the tree where my mother had carved our initials. I leaned my cheek against the dead bark.

I traced her initials with my finger.

I'd never have a moment with her before my wedding. Where it was just the two of us and she imparted words of wisdom and then cracked a joke to lighten the mood.

She wouldn't be there to hold Hadley's baby. Or mine.

She'd never get to meet Declan or Cas.

But a part of me believed she sent them. She gave Hadley a baby and a man who loved her unconditionally. She gave me a man who was strong enough to handle my obstinance. And she'd given me a baby of my own to ground me. To force me to think about someone other than my own free spirt.

I even believed she sent Jane, so Dad could love again. Laugh again.

Muddy was right.

Everything seemed to work out how it was supposed to. Even when you were in a dark tunnel and there wasn't even a pin light of hope that you were going in the right direction.

Maybe there were no right directions. Maybe all of life was a series of twists and turns and it was how you handled them that mattered.

I needed to show Hadley the tree. I was ready to share it with her.

A flock of birds flew from the treetops up into the sky. I watched them soar away, but the bright sun marred my vision.

My gaze strayed back to the forest. The brush moved. Rabbits, squirrels, and other rodents began dashing across the ground. One by one beneath the thick forest floor they scrambled in the same direction.

My eyes widened and I looked at the sky again and saw the curtain of white and gray floating up into the clouds.

Smoke.

"*Oh, fuck,*" I gasped.

Rustling leaves and twigs snapped as I hastily backed away from the tree line. A small herd of deer burst from the forest too fast for me to even jump out of the way, but they missed me as they sprinted away from the smoke.

I turned and ran for the side-by-side, but I wasn't paying attention. My left foot sank into a hole and I fell over. I braced myself for the fall with my hands and my wrists took the brunt of the impact.

A scream of pain echoed through the air as my right wrist snapped. Tears blurred my vision as I cradled my hand to my chest. I lifted my foot, gasping again when a tremor of pain shot up my leg. My foot was trapped.

I bit down on my lip.

One. Two. Three.

With all my force, I yanked my foot and freed it from the hole. I limped toward the side-by-side but stopped when I heard a yelp.

It sounded like a wounded dog, crying in fright. I turned, attempting to locate the source of the noise. I followed the whimper toward the tree line. I brushed aside leaves and branches and found a lone red fox kit lying beneath a bush. One of its back legs was twisted and I could see that it was broken. I looked around but saw no others of its kind.

"Come on, baby, we can't stay here." I reached down to pick it up. It bared its teeth at me and swatted one of its paws in my direction.

"Hey, I won't hurt you," I crooned.

Despite my throbbing wrist and bum ankle, I crouched down to get closer to the wounded animal.

"You won't survive without me. Please, let me help you."

Something about my tone must've eased the kit's nerves because it wiggled onto its belly and crawled toward me.

I removed my button-down shirt, grimacing as my wrist protested. I wrapped the kit and cradled it against my chest. It snuggled against my tank top, seeking comfort.

"We got this," I said, more so for my benefit than for the fox's.

The scent of smoke teased my nostrils and I prayed the wind wouldn't shift, bringing the fire closer to our land and the ranch.

I limped my way back to the side-by-side and got the door open. I settled the fox wrapped in my shirt onto my lap and reached for my cell phone resting on the passenger side seat.

But there was no cell service out here and I hadn't brought a radio.

"Fuck."

The kit whined.

"Sorry," I said absently. I lifted my phone in the air and moved it around, but it was no use. Tucked between mountains, there was no chance of service.

I tossed my phone aside and then cranked the key.

The engine turned over.

And over, and over.

I waited for the roar of the engine to come to life.

The side-by-side made a gurgling noise and then sputtered to a silent death.

"You've got to be shitting me."

My heart drummed in a heavy staccato as I hit the dashboard. I tried the engine again, but it refused to start.

"Okay, time for plan B." I wrenched the door open, grabbed my phone and the kit, and climbed out.

I'd have to walk. Injured and without cell service, carrying a wild animal, with an impending forest fire that could move swiftly through the brush.

As long as the wind doesn't change.

As long as the wind didn't change, I would be fine.

I hadn't taken two steps when the scent of fire grew stronger and thick and nearly blinding smoke engulfed me.

"I'm glad you're with me," I said, looking down at the fox wrapped in my shirt.

I put one foot in front of the other, but it was slow going. My wrist throbbed, my ankle twinged, and I could feel a deep, painful bruise forming on my knee.

The wind carried not just smoke, but a drastic shift in temperature, too. I felt the change from fresh air to warmth on my back as the smoke licked against my skin. It was a tease of what horror would ensue if I didn't get clear of the forest soon. The wind had changed course and I was now in the direct path of the fire.

I looked at my phone again, hoping for a pocket of cell service. But no luck. And my battery was nearly dead because it kept searching for a cell tower.

My throat was dry and my lungs were beginning to sting from smoke inhalation. My energy waned and my pace slowed with every passing minute. My heart thundered in my chest as I was able to see less and less, and the smoke grew thicker and thicker.

I started to cry as fear overtook me. I held the fox kit in my arms and sobbed as I imagined me and my baby not making it out alive.

It all seemed so trivial. My reasons for not accepting Cas's proposal. What was I afraid of?

A life with Cas was a blessing—and at the moment, not even a given. Because what if I didn't make it out of this? What if this was the end of my story?

I can't breathe.

There was a tree on the path and I sat down underneath it to get away from the smoke. A breath of fresh air on the forest floor cleared my head, but I knew I had to move again —or die.

Then I heard the sound of a horse in the distance.

Louder.

Branches began to crack and the thundering of hooves drew closer.

I squinted and saw a figure on a horse through the haze of smoke.

"Hey!" I yelled.

The mount burst through the smoke and relief swirled through me as Cas came into view.

He rode nearly right next to me and slid off the horse with the reins still in his hand. "Salem!"

I scrambled up from my seat, limped toward him, and fell into his arms.

"You're hurt."

I nodded. "My right wrist. And my left ankle."

Cas embraced me and a hissing noise came from the fur ball pressed against me.

"What the hell is that?" Cas asked.

"A fox kit," I said. "He's hurt. I couldn't leave him. How did you know I was out here?"

"Gut feeling." He swept me into his arms. "I'm here now. I've got you."

CHAPTER FORTY-NINE

"Yeah, you broke your wrist," the doctor said without preamble when he came into the exam room. "The X-ray showed a clear break. You'll be in a cast for six to eight weeks."

"What about her ankle?" Cas asked.

"Just a sprain," he replied. "The knee, though. You bashed it good when you fell. It's going to swell and there's a pocket of fluid behind the kneecap. It's going to be gruesome looking but icing it and keeping it elevated will help and it should heal just fine."

"What about her pain?" Cas demanded. "What are you going to do about that?"

I reached up to him with my good hand. "Easy, Cas."

Cas looked down at me. "You're in pain and you're pregnant with my baby. There is no *easy*. Not right now."

"I'm not taking anything," I said. "I'll suffer through the pain."

"Salem—"

"I'll be fine, Cas." I looked at him. "I got this, okay?"

"I don't like seeing you hurt," he said, his voice low.

My smile wobbled. "I know."

The doctor cleared his throat. "We'll get your wrist in a cast, and then you can go home."

"Thanks, Doc," I said.

The doctor left us for a moment.

"You're so brave," Cas said, cradling my cheek.

"Me?" I turned my head and kissed his palm. "You were the one who came charging in on a horse."

"I've never been more terrified in my life, Salem. Not even when I was on the back of a bull named Diavolo."

"I'm sorry," I murmured. "I was scared too."

He stared at me. "You admitted you were afraid."

"Of course I was afraid," I said in exasperation. "Only an idiot would lie about it."

"I just meant, you're not known for admitting fear."

"Yeah, well. Try not to hold it against me, okay?"

He skimmed my cheek with his thumb and then dropped his hand. "Never."

"Any word from Muddy about the fire?"

He shook his head. "Last I heard, Cole and the other smokejumpers were having trouble containing it. No idea about the damage or what caused it."

"Do we have to evacuate?"

"Not at the moment. No."

My phone pinged with an incoming text. I opened my cell and smiled at the message from Jane. I turned my cell to Cas who grinned at the photo of the male fox kit with a cast on his back right leg.

"Damn cute thing," Cas said. "You'll have matching casts. You took a huge risk, you know. He could've had rabies."

"I grew up on a ranch. I'm familiar with rabies. I knew he was fine. Cas, I want to keep him," I said.

"You can't keep him."

"If not pet, then why pet shaped?"

"He's a wild fox."

"Without a mom," I pointed out. "And by the time he's done recovering, he'll be domesticated. He'll never find his mother, and even if he did, she might not take him back."

He sighed. "I'm not going to have a say in this, am I?"

"Did Declan have a say in the baby goat Hadley got?"

"Good point. We're here to serve the Powell sisters. Whatever you want, you get."

"You never really did tell me how you found out where I was," I said.

"Next time you get up while I'm still sleeping, maybe you could leave a note or text about where you are," he said. "Hadley texted me and said you weren't answering her calls. And about ten minutes after that, Muddy sent out a family text about the fire in the area near your mom's tree. I just knew. I *knew* you were out there. Had to talk to your mom about my proposal, huh?"

"Damn, I've already become predictable," I muttered.

"No, I just know you really well." He smiled. "While they were all planning for a potential evacuation, I got on Merlin and rode out to find you."

"Cas . . ."

"I'll always come for you, Salem. Always."

I hobbled into the house. My body was a mess of pain and bruises, but I was safe and healthy overall, and so was the baby. I'd been lucky.

"Right into the den, sugar," Muddy said as she closed the door behind me and Cas.

I sat down onto the couch and Muddy placed a pillow on the coffee table and then helped me lift my leg.

"How did you know about my knee?" I asked.

"Cas sent a text. I've had time to prepare."

"Uh oh," I muttered.

"Uh oh? What, uh oh?" Cas asked.

"She's got salves and compresses," I explained. "Muddy is kind of a witchy woman."

Muddy touched Cas's arm. "Nothing I use will harm the baby. You have my word."

He let out a breath and nodded. "She refused painkillers."

"Of course she did." Muddy grinned. "Because she knew I would take care of her."

"Where is everyone?" I asked.

"Jane is at the clinic with your fox. Your father, damn his hide, is with Clint, in town. Hadley and Declan went with him," Muddy explained.

"Can't keep Dad bedridden for long," I said.

"He's gotta feel useful," Muddy said. "I don't blame him. Cas, why don't you head into town. Things are kind of a mess. They had to evacuate the animals at Mountain Mutt Rescue."

"Has anyone been hurt in the fire?" I asked.

"No," Muddy said. "Thank God. And it's finally been contained and should be out by morning. Give my love to Gracie, will you? As the wife of a smokejumper, she's bound to be a bundle of nerves."

"I'll tell her," Cas said. He looked at me. "You're good?"

"I'm good."

He kissed me on the lips, squeezed my shoulder, and then left Muddy to tend to me.

"He's a good man, Salem," she said. "Good in a crisis, too."

"Thank God, because I don't know what I would've done if he hadn't found me." I handed her my phone. "Will you charge this for me?"

"Sure." She took my phone and plugged it into the charger. "I'm getting you ice and a salve, and then you're going to tell me where you were and why you were out of cell range."

"Yes, ma'am." I sighed.

A few minutes later, Muddy returned with a hoard of supplies and a dark beer bottle.

"The last ginger beer," she said, handing it to me. "How's your pain?"

"Knee's about a five. Ankle is a two. The wrist is an elevendy-squillion."

"Sounds about right." She inched up the pajama pants to reveal my leg. "Hot diggity dog. That's brutal."

My knee was angry, swollen and red. "It would be nice if this family could stop getting injuries that cause us to be bedridden for days on end."

"Agreed. So, where were you?"

"North side of the property. Where the acreage butts up to national forest."

"What were you doing all the way up there?" she asked.

"Mom never told you about our tree, did she?"

"What tree?"

Muddy's hands were gentle as she dowsed my knee in salve. I hissed.

"Sorry, sugar. Almost done."

"It's fine," I lied, my vision going spotty. "There's this huge red cedar. It was already dead when we found it, and Mom and I carved our initials into it. It's always been our secret place. Not even Hadley knows about it."

"No?"

I shook my head. "I hope the fire didn't destroy it."

She didn't say anything, she just moved on to my ankle. The salve made my knee warm, and it began to tingle.

"Have you decided to put Cas out of his misery and accept his proposal?" she asked.

I looked at her.

"What? That's why you went to visit the tree, right? To get your mind and heart right?"

"I forgot how well you know me," I joked. "As for the proposal . . . I didn't know why I kept saying no. My reasons sounded stupid."

"Life-and-death experiences seem to bring about a sort of clarity, don't they?"

I nodded.

"You've got a guardian angel, sugar."

"Yeah. It's Mom," I said quietly. "She protected me when I was a kid. And now she protects me from . . . wherever she is. Pretty sure she sent me Cas."

Muddy smiled. "I have no doubt about that."

She finished doctoring my ankle and placed the ice pack on my knee. Then she handed me the remote. "You rest. I'll fix you something to eat."

"You take such good care of us," I said, meeting her gaze. "I don't know if I ever thanked you for that."

Muddy leaned over and pressed her forehead to mine. "It's an honor, Salem. Truly an honor."

After I was fed and sleepy, Muddy moved to her crochet chair and worked on her project. She still wouldn't tell me what it was, no matter how many times I asked.

My eyes were just starting to close when the front door opened. The sound of paws scrambling across the wooden floor had me sitting up and looking around.

"Who is this?" Muddy asked as a snout appeared from around the back of the couch. At the timbre of Muddy's voice, the dog rushed over to her and placed its head in her lap. Its black tail with a white tip wagged like a car antenna.

"This is Fig," Cas said as he came into the room and set a leash down onto the end table. "She's a three-year-old beagle mix and she was one of the dogs at Mountain Mutt Rescue."

Fig lifted her head, complete with floppy beagle ears, and looked at me with golden brown eyes. Then she came over to greet me.

"Beagle mix, huh?" Muddy said. "Does she bay?"

"Not yet," Cas said.

Fig jumped up onto the couch without invitation and curled into my side. My hand went to her neck and I began to stroke her. She made a little whoof of contentment.

"I thought you could use a buddy while you're laid up," Cas said. "According to one of the volunteers, Fig has couch potato like tendencies, but she also has an affinity for mischief."

"You got me a dog?" I asked him, tears gathering in my eyes.

"Dogs are closer to foxes than goats," he said, leaning down and pressing a kiss to my head. "And when the fox is ready to be released back into the wild, we'll do it here. So maybe he'll be a bit domesticated and come for a visit from time to time."

I was going to have so many of this man's babies, it wasn't even funny.

"We'll have a fox and a hound," I said with a grin.

"Almost like it was meant to be," he joked. "Fig's not sleeping in the bed though."

"That's what Declan said about Tempest," Muddy announced.

"I have more willpower than Declan," Cas boasted.

Fig lifted her head and stared at Cas, and then her tail began to thump against the couch.

Cas sighed. "Fuck."

CHAPTER FIFTY

"Your mouth is stained with huckleberry juice," I said to Hadley.

She looked at me from behind her sunglasses. "Just lording my pie-eating win over you."

Hadley placed a hand on her belly, which had finally popped.

"Today is glorious," I said as I looked out over Silver Street.

"The Huckleberry Festival all weekend and fireworks over the lake tonight," she said. "What could be more perfect?"

I peered at her. "You know something."

"I know nothing," she said with a teasing grin. "When is the crew due to arrive?"

I lifted my wrist, complete with cast, and pointed at her. "You *do* know something, otherwise you wouldn't be changing the subject."

"Even if I knew something, which I don't, I want to talk about your job."

I shook my head and shot her a grin. "Fine, we can play that game. The crew is arriving in three days and all the rooms at The Regal Beagle are booked for the week."

A month ago, I'd pitched the idea to use our family ranch for the Rudolph Lancaster photo shoot. They not only loved the idea, but they were happy to work around Cas's event schedule.

"I still can't believe you and Cas are going to be the faces for Rudolph Lancaster's western line," Hadley said with a laugh. "That's so wild."

"It is," I agreed. "But hey, you gotta go where life takes you, huh?"

I placed a hand on my stomach. I wasn't showing yet, but I no longer fit into my pants. My due date was nearly two months after Hadley's and I still had trouble believing that our babies would be so close in age and that we'd get to raise them together.

"Cas hasn't brought up marriage in a while," I said.

"What's a while?"

"Two weeks." I frowned.

"Yeah, that is weird," she admitted. "But maybe he's just tired of you saying no."

"I won't say no," I mumbled.

"What was that?" she pressed.

"I said, I won't say no this time," I admitted. "I'm ready. I was ready after the fire, and told him so, but he just shrugged and hasn't brought it up again."

"He's not gonna want to wait," Hadley said. "The minute you say yes to his proposal, he's gonna get your ass down to the courthouse."

"Fine by me. I've never wanted a wedding."

"True, you haven't," she agreed. "Still, I think you'd make a beautiful bride."

"Hmm. *You* made a beautiful bride, Hadley."

"I did, didn't I?" She grinned. "Sweet Teeth?"

I nodded and looked at my watch. "We've still got about twenty minutes until the lumberjack competition."

"We need to get there early and grab front row seats. Then we have to call Wyn and Poet so they can enjoy the view," Hadley said.

We headed in the direction of the bakery which had had a line out the door all day since they opened. "They should expand. The building next door is vacant."

"They don't want to expand," Hadley explained. "Cole and Gracie are talking about having another baby. That's a lot to add to life on top of an expansion, you know?"

"Another baby, really?" I asked in surprise. "Bella's only a little over a year."

"Well, they want them close in age." She shot me a pointed look. "Almost like something we did on accident."

I grinned. "Does this mean family planning will always include each other?"

She laughed. "I wouldn't say no to that."

"How many do you guys want?" I asked.

"Two is a good number, I think. Subject to change, of course."

"Two is good," I agreed.

We got up to the counter and ordered what was left of the pastries.

"Sorry," Gracie said. "You caught us in between batches."

"No worries," I said. "Are we saving you a seat at the lumberjack event?"

"Hell yeah." Gracie laughed. "Cole entered this year; I've got to see him swing an axe."

"Pretty sure there's about to be a population explosion in Huckleberry Hill," I said.

"Remember a few years ago when there was a snowstorm?" Gracie asked. "The power was out for three days. How many babies were born nine months later?"

"Muddy said at least fifteen," Hadley remarked.

"Well, what else are you going to do in the dark while you're trying to keep warm?" Gracie asked.

"Yeah, and you're definitely not running out for condoms in the middle of a snowstorm," Hadley said with a laugh.

Hadley and I took our bakery bag and headed out onto the street. The lumberjack event was held in the town's park at the edge of downtown, which meant the walk was only a few blocks.

Folding chairs had been set up in several rows and people had already begun to arrive. Hadley and I snagged two seats in the front row and we set our purses down onto the chair next to us for Gracie.

Hadley's phone buzzed in her lap, but she had a mouthful of pastry so I answered it for her. Wyn and Poet appeared on the screen.

"Did we miss it?" Wyn asked. "Please tell me we didn't miss it."

"You didn't miss it," I said. "We got here early and found prime seats. Don't worry, we're close enough to see sweat and chest hair."

"Yay." Wyn grinned. "I'm a sucker for chest hair."

"So am I," Hadley said.

The three of us chanted at the same time, "We know."

Hadley giggled. "Declan's chest hair was my downfall."

"Literally. You literally fell on him," Poet said.

"You guys are still planning on making it out here in a few months, right?" Hadley asked.

"Yeah," Poet said. "I've got Labor Day Weekend off."

"You won't have to stay at The Regal Beagle," Hadley said. "Cas moved into Salem's room."

"Hmm, thanks, but we'll stay at The Regal Beagle," Wyn said.

I frowned. "Why?"

Poet and Wyn exchanged a look.

"What?" Hadley demanded.

"We don't want to hear your dad and Jane going at it," Wyn finally said.

"What?" Hadley and I exclaimed at the same time.

"Oh please." Wyn rolled her eyes. "That kick to your dad's head did something to him. I swear, he's like a new man."

"A new man, how?" I asked.

"He's rocking a mustache," Poet said.

"Okay?" Hadley frowned. "I don't get it."

"Some women have a thing for chest hair. Other women have things for facial hair," Wyn pointed out. "And your dad looks like he knows how to—"

"Stop. Right. Now," I commanded. "We're in a public place and we know people here. We don't need to talk about our father's mustache."

"Save a horse, ride a mustache. That's all I'm saying," Wyn said.

Someone tapped me on the shoulder. I turned and smiled. "Hey, Lucy."

"Hi," Lucy said. "Who are you two talking to?"

"Wyn and Poet." I angled the phone toward her so she could see our friends.

"When are you girls coming back to town?" Lucy asked. "Things have been boring since you left."

"Boring? With Salem there? I find that hard to believe," Wyn teased.

"She's been domesticated," Lucy said with a wink. "Plus,

with Amber moving to Coeur d'Alene, there's nothing going on. We need some more spice around here."

"Lucy, how do you feel about mustaches?" Poet asked.

"I think they're delightful," Lucy said.

"I couldn't agree more," Wyn said with a raised brow.

"Fine," I sighed. "You'll stay at The Regal Beagle when you guys come."

"You're coming to town!" Lucy exclaimed.

"Labor Day," Hadley said.

"Oh good. I'll make sure to order those special candies you like so much, Poet. And you'll text me the soda you like, Wyn?" Lucy asked.

"Will do," Wyn said.

"Thanks, Lucy," Poet said.

"Wait, you guys text?" I asked in surprise.

"Of course!" Lucy said. "You two are so busy now, I gotta make sure they're not out of the loop."

Hadley and I exchanged a dumbfounded look.

"Oh, the boys are showing up," Lucy said, her attention moving to the front of the show.

I gave Hadley back her phone and she turned her cell so Wyn and Poet could watch. Declan and Cas sauntered up first and took their places next to one another at two wood piles. Cole and Gideon followed.

Chelsea, Wade's girlfriend, saw me and waved. There was still a free chair next to Hadley and she immediately sat down.

"Wade's not doing the competition?" Lucy asked her.

Chelsea shook her head. "He and his dad are crazy busy at the mobile bar right now. Their summer mocktails are flying off the proverbial shelves." She looked at me. "No Muddy? Or your dad?"

"This isn't really our dad's type of event," I said. "And I

have no idea where Muddy is actually. Do you know where she is, Hadley?"

"Nope." Her eyes flitted away from mine and my gaze narrowed at her.

"When he was younger, this was definitely your father's event," Lucy said. "He won several times. Impressed the hell out of your mother, if I recall."

Gracie joined us, cheeks flushed and hair askew. I touched her face. "Bakery oven, you ran here, or something else?"

Her hands went to her face. "All of the above. Plus, Cole texted me something naughty . . ."

She flashed her husband a grin and waved to him. He waved back.

"Oooh, we've got some new blood this year," Eloise said as she took the seat next to Lucy. "Are those the Monroe boys? Where's the other one?"

"Chase went to Waco to visit his girlfriend," Hadley explained.

"All right, ladies," Eloise said. "Let's start the betting."

Cas unbuttoned his shirt and took it off to reveal muscles and ink and a chest I wanted to run my tongue all over.

The other contenders removed their shirts and tossed them aside.

"Oh my," Lucy said. "This just got interesting."

I looked at Hadley and grinned. Her eyes were glazed and she couldn't look away from Declan.

"So, I'm starting to think two isn't enough," I teased.

Hadley chuckled and glanced at me. "I think you're right. Five sounds good to me."

I turned my attention back to Cas just as he grabbed an axe that had been sunk into a log and pulled it out. His arms bulged and flexed, making the ink on his skin dance.

He looked down at me and winked.

I snorted. "Five? I'm going for six."

Mr. Bixby stepped up to the podium and said, "Lumberjacks, take your spots. Everyone else, place your bets."

"Twenty bucks on Harlan!" Wyn screamed from the phone.

"Who said that?" Mr. Bixby asked.

Hadley raised her hand. "We've got a long-distance bidder."

"The first lumberjack who chops their entire pile of wood wins the grand prize," Mr. Bixby announced.

"What's the grand prize?" Poet asked.

"A gift certificate to Sweet Teeth, a free haircut from Pouffant, and a trophy," Gracie said.

"Gentlemen, assume your positions," Mr. Bixby said.

I took out my phone and began to record. "For posterity. And spank bank material."

"Lower your voice, we're in public," Hadley stated. "But also make sure you get some shots of Declan for me."

"Don't worry, honey," Lucy said, raising her cell phone. "I've got you covered."

CHAPTER FIFTY-ONE

The Lake

"It was nice that you let Declan win," I said to Cas.

He offered me his hand and helped me into the waiting rowboat that bobbed on the bank of Lavender Lake.

"I didn't let Declan win," he said. "I lost because of *you*."

"What do you mean because of me?" I demanded.

He handed me a picnic basket, and I set it down in the back of the rowboat before lowering myself down onto one of the soft pillows.

Cas got into the boat and took the spot across from me on the other end so that we were facing one another. "I could see your nipples through your dress. You're lucky I didn't cut off my own hand."

I looked down at my chest. "Really? You could see them?"

"Okay, maybe I couldn't see them," he amended. "But I was fantasizing about them. About how they'd taste. How they'd feel in my mouth. Have you ever swung an axe with an erection?"

"Can't say that I have." I laughed.

He grabbed an oar and pushed us away from the bank. The oar slid into the water, and he began to paddle us toward the center of the lake. It was dusk and when the sun set in an hour, the fireworks would start.

"What treats did you pack us?" I asked, reaching for the picnic basket.

"No peeking," he warned.

I dropped my hand from the picnic basket. "I got a good video of you chopping wood, though. I think it would be perfect to post on your social media."

"Do it," he said. "You're in charge of my page now. Rudolph Lancaster loves everything you're doing for buzz."

"I post from the female gaze. Ergo, more women are drooling over you each day. Ergo, more women telling their boyfriends that they should dress like you. Ergo, men running out to buy whatever clothes you put on your body to please their women. It's a win for all of us."

"I never thought I'd be a model," he quipped.

"How do you feel about billboards?"

"Obnoxious. Annoying. Huge."

"Like your ego?" I grinned.

"You like my huge ego. Just like you like my huge—"

"Billboards," I interrupted. "As in, how would you feel about being on one? In Times Square?"

"Holy hell, are you serious?"

I nodded.

"I have to be wearing clothes," he warned. "I'm not going to be a naked sex symbol. I've got my pride, you know?"

"You've also got a very jealous, hormonal girlfriend," I said with a chuckle. "I already told them you have to be in clothes. Maybe you can have one button undone. Two at the most. But that part of you is so damn lickable, so I don't know if I want everyone else to see it."

"Lickable, huh? Come here." He rested the paddle in its holder and held out his hands to me. I inched toward him on my haunches, my dress riding up my thighs.

"You're so beautiful," he said when I was close enough to touch. He cradled my cheeks in his hands and kissed my lips, and then he pulled back. "Hand me the picnic basket."

I leaned over to grab it and nearly lost my balance, but I knew if I fell Cas would be there to catch me.

He took the basket from my hands and opened the flap. "I had Muddy help prepare all of this."

"All of what?" I asked. "The food?"

"The food, the rowboat, everything." He peered at me for a long moment, the sunlight streaking through the clouds behind him.

I closed my eyes.

"What's wrong?" he asked.

"Nothing," I whispered. "I'm just—taking a mental photograph of you. In this moment, looking the way you do. So I can always remember it. Or at least the feeling of it."

I took a few deep breaths, breathing in the scent of the water, the dying heat of the air from a hot summer day.

And when I finally opened my eyes, Cas was sitting in front of me, holding out a ring box. It was open and presented toward me.

It was an emerald cut sapphire nestled among diamonds in a gold setting. It was beautiful and unique, and I knew just by looking at it that the moment I slid it onto my finger, I'd never want to take it off.

I looked at him and met his solemn gaze.

And then I held out my left hand to him.

He took the ring from the box and slid it onto my finger. Then he brought my knuckles to his lips.

"A perfect fit," he rasped.

"Yes, we are." I leaned forward and kissed him.

His tongue slid into my mouth and my body hummed with pleasure.

"Wait," he said, pulling back. "There's more."

"I don't need more," I protested. "Kiss me again."

He let out a low chuckle. "You'll like this, I promise."

Cas riffled through the picnic basket and pulled out a piece of wood encased in resin. It was smooth to the touch and there, through the crystal clear resin, I saw my carved initials, along with my mother's in the bark of the red cedar from the forest.

"The fire burned most of the tree, Salem." His tone was sad. "I didn't want you to lose your special place, so I took a chainsaw and cut out the initials and had it put in resin. Turn it over."

I flipped over the resin encased wood. The back was flat and numbers had been burned into it.

"I don't understand." I looked at him for an explanation.

"Those are the coordinates of where the tree was. I was thinking it would be a unique tattoo. After the baby's born, of course."

I pressed the piece of wood to my chest as tears gathered in my eyes. "No one has ever—God, Cas. Thank you. Thank you so much."

We reached for each other at the same time, our lips meeting. Not in desire, but in fortitude. In vows. In promises.

He gathered me into his arms and held me for a long moment, but then my stomach rumbled.

With a laugh, he let me go. "Let's feed you."

He opened the picnic basket and pulled out homemade ginger beer, watermelon salad, and brisket from the Copper Mule.

As the sun sank behind the mountains, we ate dinner underneath the night sky. And when the fireworks started, he laid me down in the bed of the rowboat and made me see my own fireworks.

After I came undone, he sat behind me and wrapped his arms around me. His hands went to my belly. He lovingly stroked his thumbs up and down my stomach and I covered his hands with mine, the light of the fireworks winking off my sapphire engagement ring.

"Casimir William Bowman, you sure do know how to propose to a girl." I looked up at him and smiled.

He pressed a kiss to the end of my nose. "Salem Kathleen Powell, you sure do know how to drive me insane."

"You'll never be bored."

"Nope."

"Me and our six children will keep you on your toes."

"Six? Good God, woman, are you determined to drain me of seed?"

"You don't want six?"

"I want as many as you want," he said. "But holy hell, Salem. That changes things."

"Changes what?" I asked with a furrowed brow.

"Well, the plans for the house, first of all. I better talk to Grady before we finalize the blueprint."

"Is that all?" I asked in amusement.

"No, that's not all."

He moved one of his hands up from my belly to slide into the top of my dress and cupped a breast. His thumb grazed my nipple and it pebbled instantly.

"It's going to be a full-time job," he whispered huskily. "Keeping you satisfied. I heard pregnant women are insatiable."

I wiggled back against him. "Are you up to the challenge?"

He hiked up my dress with his other hand and I immediately let my legs fall apart.

"I ride bulls for a living. I can handle you."

I let out a throaty chuckle. "I'm more unpredictable than a bull."

He slipped his fingers into my panties and then slid two of them inside me. "I know how to keep you in line, you brat."

His thumb grazed my clit.

"My new job description: full time brat tamer."

"It'll be the hardest job you've ever done." I gasped when he bit my ear lobe.

"Hmm. I like a challenge. You still owe me, you know."

"Owe you what?" I asked.

It was hard to focus on the conversation because Cas's hands were magic.

"A night of doing anything I want to you."

His fingers thrust harder inside me as his other hand teased my nipple.

"Just remember, turnabout is fair play," I hissed. "You might wake up one morning, handcuffed to the headboard."

He paused his ministrations and I whined in despair.

Cas removed his fingers from my body and stopped playing with my nipple.

"You fucking bastard," I seethed. "I was close."

He didn't say anything, he just urged me to sit up.

"What are you doing?" I demanded as he grabbed the oar.

"Getting back to dry land." His eyes met mine. "You think we can find a pair of handcuffs at this hour?"

I let out a laugh. "You *are* crazy."

"Crazy for you." He leaned over and kissed my lips. "Now grab the other paddle and help me, will ya? I've got to see a man about a pair of handcuffs."

EPILOGUE

Six weeks later

POET

"Hold on, I'm sending some photos through," Salem said.

I sat at my desk and glanced at the clock. I still had ten more minutes on my lunch break. Dread curled through me. I had a meeting with my boss at one and I wasn't looking forward to it in the least.

"Did they go through?" Salem asked. "My service is shit out here."

"Let me look." I lowered my phone. A moment later, it buzzed with a text from Salem. I clicked over to it and scrolled through the photos from the Rudolph Lancaster photoshoot many weeks ago.

Most were of Cas, of course, but there were several with Salem and Cas together. They'd also gotten Declan to model. But unlike most model shots that looked like they were in the studio, these were rustic, authentic, with Idaho mountains and a real working ranch.

I put the phone back to my ear. "Are they selling clothes or a way of life?"

"I know, right?" Salem asked.

"You look gorgeous, by the way."

"Airbrushed," she said.

"Huh, right. They airbrushed the hell out of you with pregnancy glow. Seriously, Salem."

"Thanks, girl," she said. "It was so fun and everyone is ecstatic with how the shoot turned out."

My phone buzzed with another text from her.

"What was that text?" I asked.

"More photos. Not of Declan and Cas, but our two new ranch hands. The photographer got a little carried away and accidentally on purpose took a lot of photos of them. Look."

I once again lowered my phone, clicked over to the messages, and blew up the photos. There were two men, shirtless by a fence, but the sun was directly behind them so I could only see the face of one of them clearly. He had a smile on his face and a dark mustache.

My eyes immediately went to the other man, the faceless man. His back was sculpted and ink splayed across the breadth of his broad shoulders.

"Poet?"

"Sorry, yeah, I'm here."

"They're nice to look at, aren't they?" she asked knowingly.

"Very nice," I agreed, wondering why my belly was warm and I suddenly felt like I had a fever. "Which one is the ex-con?"

"The one without the mustache."

"I can't believe Muddy was okay with an ex-con working the ranch."

"You'd never know it by talking to Brooks. He's quiet, keeps to himself, but is respectful. I've never seen him smile, though."

"What was he in for?" I asked.

My phone chimed with my alarm.

"Crap, sorry, Salem, I gotta go," I said. "My meeting is in five minutes and I'd like to hit the restroom real fast."

"Call me after. I want to know how it went," she said. "I worry about you."

"That's sweet, but you don't have to," I lied.

"Kind, gentle Poet, of course I worry about you because of that snake you work with. Okay, bye."

I hung up with Salem and then rose from my office chair. The bathroom was empty and I quickly did my business. As I washed my hands, I stared in the mirror and gave myself a pep talk.

Wyn had called earlier that morning to give me one of her cheerleader speeches, but it was more of *I'll kick anyone's ass who makes you cry* speech. Hadley was much calmer and listened when I talked. I needed my friends to have those protective attitudes. I hadn't been born with one at all.

I was one step below people pleaser. I just let them walk all over me.

Bracing my shoulders, I pointed at my reflection. My new glasses gave me confidence, and I was determined to hold my own in this meeting.

I walked back to my desk and saw my boss's door cracked open. Frowning, I went over and knocked.

"Come in," Candace called.

I pushed the door open and stopped. Alma, my work nemesis, sat in one of the chairs in front of the desk.

"Oh, sorry, I didn't know you were already in a meeting," I said, attempting to back away.

"I called this meeting to talk to you both," Candace said. She waved at the vacant chair.

I paused, and then came inside, closing the door behind me. I lowered myself into the chair and then sat on my hands so I wouldn't fidget with nerves.

Alma looked at me, cool and composed. She was the kind of woman who belonged in the corporate world. She was a machine that never tired. Her clothes were never wrinkled. And her bob was just the right mix of angry and chic.

She looked like a mini version of Candace.

Candace 2.0.

I still didn't know why Candace had hired me.

"I'll get right to the point," Candace said. "We've been bought out. We're merging with Hawthorne Whitaker."

"Are we fired?" Alma asked.

Candace shook her head. "No. There will be layoffs, but we're not there yet. However, for the next six weeks, we will have a consultant in the department. Let me be blunt with you both; their job is to find the fat and cut it. Corporate restructuring or whatever. One of you was going to get a promotion, but unfortunately, there's only one job after the merger. So, my advice to you both is this: eat, sleep and breathe your work for the next six weeks. At the end of that time, one of you won't work here anymore."

"I won't even go home to shower," Alma promised without delay. "My gym is just down the street. I can shower there."

Candace beamed at her.

Kiss ass.

Candace grabbed her pen and went back to the papers on her desk, effectively dismissing us. Alma got the hint and stood, leaving Candace's office, but I sat there like a perplexed idiot.

I already worked like a dog. I spent far too many lunch breaks crying in the bathroom stalls. Now I had to work even *harder* to prove to someone who didn't even know me that I was worthy of keeping my job on top of fighting for a promotion.

I looked around Candace's office. The Montblanc pen, the crystal St. Louis paper weight on the ornate, old world antique desk, the dozens of framed book covers on the walls that had hit the top of the bestseller lists.

These were Candace's crowning achievements. Achievements I had wanted to accomplish at almost any cost. But at the moment, they seemed superficial and hollow.

What was the point? I would never be a Candace. I'd never be an Alma. Clawing my way up the corporate ladder. For what? Hoping someone didn't shove me off when I finally reached the top?

My brain flashed forward twenty years.

Me. Late at night. In an office. Surrounded by things instead of people.

Tired.

Single.

Lonely.

No. Absolutely not.

"You can go now, Poet," Candace said pointedly.

When I didn't reply, she looked up from her papers.

The spine I usually lacked snapped straight.

And a voice that had never come out of my mouth said, "No."

Her Botoxed forehead didn't move, but her tone implied a furrow. "No? What do you mean *no?*"

"This—this whole situation. The merger. The six weeks .. . I'm not doing this. I'm not doing any of it."

"You don't have a choice," she said. "If you want to keep your job, this is what you have to do."

"There's no guarantee I'll even have a job at the end of six weeks anyway."

"So, you're giving up before you even start." She shook her head. "Accepting failure without even trying for success. I knew it was a mistake to hire you. You don't have what it takes to succeed. You're not cutthroat. You never were."

I suddenly smiled.

She stared at me, uncomprehending.

I rose from my chair. "You're right. Thank God, you're right." I turned to leave, and just as I crossed the threshold of Candace's office, I pivoted slightly and looked back at her over my shoulder. "So I quit."

She scoffed. "You can't quit. People don't just *quit*. What are you going to do?"

"Well, like every main character, I'll figure it out."

And then I walked out on my old life.

Oh, God. What have I done?

ADDITIONAL WORKS

Saddles & Spurs Series:

Huckleberry Hill

Lavender Lake

Prospector's Peak

Maple Mountain

Tarnished Angels Motorcycle Club® Series:

Wreck & Ruin

Crash & Carnage

Madness & Mayhem

Thrust & Throttle

Venom & Vengeance

Fire & Frenzy

Leather & Lies

Heartbeats & Highways

SINS Series:

Sins of a King

Birth of a Queen

Rise of a Dynasty

Dawn of an Empire

Ember

Burn

Ashes

Fall of a Kingdom

Standalones:

Peasants and Kings

<u>**Writing as E. Slate**</u>

The Sibby Series

Queen of Klutz
Sibby Slicker
Mother Shucker
Sibby's Spawn
Hot Mess Express

Standalones:

From Stardust to Stardust

ABOUT THE AUTHOR

Wall Street Journal & USA Today bestselling author Emma Slate writes romance with heart and heat.

Called "the dialogue queen" by her college playwriting professor, Emma writes love stories that range from romance-for-your-pants to action-flicks-for-chicks.

When she isn't writing, she's usually curled up under a heating blanket with a steamy romance novel and her two beagles—unless her outdoorsy husband can convince her to go on a hike.

Emma also writes rom-com and contemporary romance as E. Slate.

9 781955 098762